"*I* must look a mess. What must they think of me?"

Chuckling, Ian wound his arm around her waist and started them toward the carriage. "They're thinking you're a lovely bride and that I'm a lucky man to have won you, especially if we give them a little demonstration of what a happy bride and groom we are."

The glint in his eyes and the devilish grin on his face made his intent obvious. Ana gasped. "We will do no such thing," she declared *sotto voce*. "Kissing in public would be most improper."

Before she could rush away, he caught her up against him again and murmured against her brow, "Afraid you might change your mind about this in name only business, Mrs. Patterson?"

Stiffening, she reminded, "You agreed to the arrangement."

"Yes, but there's nothing in our agreement about trying to change your mind," he said and promptly kissed her. And not just a brushing of the lips like he'd done at the end of the wedding ceremony, but a full possession that left her gasping for air when he finally relinquished her mouth. "Not a thing improper about a man kissing his bride in public on their wedding day."

By Janet Bieber
Published by The Ballantine Publishing Group:

HIGHLAND BRIDE
IN NAME ONLY

Books published by The Ballantine Publishing Group
are available at quantity discounts on bulk purchases
for premium, educational, fund-raising, and special
sales use. For details, please call 1-800-733-3000.

IN NAME ONLY

Janet Bieber

IVY BOOKS • NEW YORK

An Ivy Book
Published by The Ballantine Publishing Group
Copyright © 2000 by Janet Bieber

www.randomhouse.com/BB/

Library of Congress Catalog Card Number: 00-103274

ISBN 0-449-00285-3

Manufactured in the United States of America

First Edition: July 2000

10   9   8   7   6   5   4   3   2   1

For Margaret and Emil Parker, my parents, who gave me a wonderful childhood along Lake Erie's shore where I could see the shadowy shapes of the chain of islands scattered across the western basin. I'm still making up stories about those islands—finally one in print.

And thank you, too, Mom and Dad, for my Scotch-Irish heritage, passing on to me your appreciation of history and books, and most of all for your loving support in all my endeavors.

Prologue

"The bondage of corruption break, for this our spirits groan . . ."

The singing of the opening hymn progressively faltered as the Ian Patterson family moved down the aisle of Grace Church. They were a handsome family. Four children—two boys and two girls—walked hand in hand behind their parents. The two youngest, a girl of five and a boy of only three, favored their mother with their fine-boned frames and dark hair. The older pair, an eight-year-old girl and a seven-year-old boy, favored their father with copper hair and features that promised tall, sturdy frames.

Seemingly heedless of the preacher's censorious glare for their late arrival, Patterson greeted his neighbors nearest the aisle with smiles and nods. He was conservatively attired, and his ruddy complexion, tall, brawny frame, and rugged features were the perfect foils to his delicate wife.

The top of her lavishly ornamented bonnet barely reaching her husband's shoulder, Lileas MacPherson Patterson drew attention from men and women alike. Her ivory skin, raven curls, and beautiful face were enough

1

to tweak the envy many a man already felt toward the successful young shipper. And any public appearance of the fair Lily always evoked envy and a great deal of curiosity in much of Cleveland's female population.

As always, her attire reflected her husband's wealth and the skill of Cleveland's newest modiste in re-creating the latest fashions from templates imported straight from New York. Some said they came all the way from Paris. Not since her marriage to Cleveland's most eligible bachelor had the preacher's second daughter plied her needle to anything beyond the occasional piece of decorative needlework.

From top to toe, she was arrayed in periwinkle blue wool liberally trimmed with silk ruching, braid, and cabbage roses. Worn by any other young matron, the color would have been judged overbright and the ornamentation far too overblown for Sunday-morning services. But being as how it was sweet and "oh so pretty" Lily Patterson, the ensemble was greeted with the same gladness as the early spring flowers just beginning to poke through the winter-grayed landscape.

Graciously, Rose, Valeriana, Laurel, and Primula MacPherson—the preacher's wife and other daughters— shifted to make room for the latecomers in the foremost pew. With a great deal of shuffling and rustling that even the final lines of the hymn couldn't smother, the young family took their places.

The Reverend John MacPherson tolerated no breach in pious decorum during Sunday-morning services from any quarter, least of all from a member of his family. Hence, the two young Pattersons who dared whisper and giggle as they awaited the opening lines of the sermon were subjected to a quelling glare from the pulpit. However, that glare paled in comparison to the one aimed at their father as MacPherson launched his sermon.

"Revelers. Drunkards. Fornicators. The Lord our God doth know who you are!"

The altar candles fluttered and the windowpanes shuddered as the reverend began a fiery denouncement of every form of debauchery. "Brothers and sisters, the furnace is hot and ready to receive them who part with the Lord for the pleasures of the flesh."

Leaning over the lectern, MacPherson shifted his gaze from his son-in-law to first one then another and another of his flock. Some faces blanched. Others blushed. Still others took intense interest in the magnificent stained-glass window behind the chancel—Ian and Lily Patterson's latest gift to her father's church.

Most craned their heads for a better view of the family pew. The ongoing battle between MacPherson and his son-in-law over the latter's continued refusal to sign "the pledge" was why Grace Church was overflowing this Sunday.

Everyone knew the *Ulsterman*, the flagship of the Patterson Shipping Line, had slipped into its home berth Thursday afternoon. And if the *Ulsterman* was docked in Cleveland, then so was Ian Patterson—patronizing the waterfront taverns each and every evening. And, as per usual on those Sundays when he was in town, he dutifully accompanied his wife and children to church. It was a fine show.

MacPherson's graying side whiskers fairly bristled as he warned, "You live only at God's whim, and He may take your life at any time. Swear off strong drink and all forms of debauchery, for they will lead to your destruction and the destruction of your family."

When he paused, the preacher's hawkish features softened noticeably as he rested his gaze upon Lily and then one by one upon her children. But when his gaze moved to the end of the pew, he visibly recoiled as if confronted by the devil himself. His eyes widened. His nostrils flared. There was no mistaking upon whom he was gazing or to whom his next volley was directed.

"Sinners! Repent thy selfish and vile ways while there is still time for your soul to be welcomed into God's kingdom. If you care not for your own soul's ultimate destination, think on the loved ones you will leave behind. Would you have them suffer the anguish of knowing that you burn for all eternity in the fires of hell?"

Unwavering, Patterson met MacPherson's gaze. By not so much as a twitch of a muscle or a blink of his eye did he grant the older man victory. His large hands crossed loosely in his lap, his expression was bland as he faced the pulpit. Finally, a vein throbbing at his temple, MacPherson shifted his gaze to the congregation in general.

"Turn away from heathenish darkness! Abstain from the filthy sins of strong drink and fornication! Live soberly as thou ought or surely God will allow the devil to take you."

The wooden pews creaked as men settled back and folded their arms across their chests. The ladies adjusted themselves upon the hard pews as comfortably as they could, ready to do whatever was necessary to keep their children quiet. If there was anything for which the gathered was more certain, they surely could not think of it: They were in for a lengthy sermon.

MacPherson had his wind up and was ready and raring to preach hellfire, and brimstone the likes of which they had not heard since the last time the *Ulsterman* had slipped into its berth. But MacPherson could threaten hell and damnation from now to kingdom come and it wasn't likely his son-in-law was going to pitch to his knees and beg forgiveness for downing the occasional glass of whiskey with his fellows or anything else the preacher imagined he'd done.

Chapter One

April 10, 1834

Lily Patterson was dead.

The day she and her tiny stillborn child were laid to rest dawned as bleak as the hearts of those who mourned her. A flurry of snow the night before had dusted the ground in patches. As cold and dismal as the morning was, most of Cleveland turned out for her funeral.

They patted the survivors, mumbled their condolences, and wiped their eyes as "dear Lily's" parents, sisters, husband, and children said their final good-byes. Though the family had gone home long ago and the sky threatened rain, the crowd was reluctant to leave the cemetery. Huddled in little groups against the bitter wind blowing in from Lake Erie, they talked in hushed tones.

Everyone thought Lily's pa had preached a fine service for her. MacPherson's voice had faltered now and then, but that was to be expected. The preacher had been mighty fond of his second eldest daughter.

Her husband and children had borne up well—all things considered. The four little mites looked so lost standing there with their pa, grandma, and aunts. In shock, most likely.

It was not surprising because everyone was shocked.

"I saw her Tuesday. Pretty as ever, she was, and the

very picture of health. I surely did not think to be attending her funeral by Friday. So sad. So very, very sad."

"Didn't even know she was carrying again, did you?"

"She weren't so far along she showed."

"The Lord giveth and the Lord taketh away."

These and similar remarks were met with sighs, slow shaking of heads, and muttered, "tsk, tsk, tsks."

As tragic as Lily's sudden passing had been, the cause was not so unusual as to merit much discussion. Women sometimes died in childbirth. It was a fact of life.

What was really keeping everyone gathered at the cemetery was what had happened immediately after the funeral.

The reverend had cast the first handful of dirt upon the smooth cedar casket holding Lily and her tiny infant's remains. "Earth to earth, ashes to ashes, dust to dust; in sure and certain hope of the resurrection unto eternal life. Amen."

The family had followed his lead, first Ian, then Rose and the children. Instead of a handful of dirt, Rose and the children had tossed sprays of forsythia, the only blossoms blooming this early in Rose's vast garden behind the parsonage. Valeriana, Laurel, and Primula had stepped up then and added more of the fragile yellow blossoms. Then the family had slowly begun to wend their way through the crowd toward the carriages waiting at the edge of the cemetery.

The crowd was quiet and solemn as, one by one, each gathered up a handful of the soil and cast it into the grave.

Suddenly the silence was broken. Crying, "Beauty is gone from this world! I cannot bear it. I must leave it, too." Anson Phillips threw himself into the grave.

The grave diggers had a devil of a time getting the man out so they could finish their work.

"Always thought that painter man was a bit odd," someone finally had the courage to say. Thus the silence that had been weighing so heavily ever since Phillips had been led away was broken.

"Heard he painted Lily's portrait more 'n once and was teaching her to paint. Said she was the most beautiful woman he ever painted and a promising pupil, too," one of the men remarked.

"Still no cause to make such a spectacle of himself," his wife stated with an appropriate huff.

"Well, artists are a sensitive bunch, I'm told," someone else offered.

"Best he move on. Won't be many folks in these parts wanting him to paint their pictures or teach their children after this."

"Shoulda left the fool in there and thrown the dirt on him. Never did think he was much of a painter, or much of a man, neither."

"God be thanked the family wasn't here to witness such a thing."

Finally, the heavens opened, and the rain effectively put an end to the discussions . . . at the cemetery.

As certain as the sun would come up the next day, and the day after and the day after that, Lily Patterson's funeral would be discussed for weeks, perhaps months. At least until something more interesting occurred.

At the Patterson house on Euclid Street, a pair of black-ribboned mourning wreaths hung on the wide double doors. Having deposited the family safely at the door, two carriages were just pulling away from the wide portico that sheltered the main entrance of the house. The family had arrived just as the rain began.

Inside, "the Marys"—as the family called the two

maids, Mary Flick and Mary Cunningham—had just finished lighting the lamps and stoking the fires in the hearths. It was not yet midday, but the lighted lamps and crackling fires chased away some of the gloom and damp, as did the scent of cinnamon and other spices that wafted from the kitchen.

The cook and housekeeper, Gerta Hosapfel, had been baking almost nonstop since the night her mistress had died. What she hadn't prepared, others had. A steady stream of visitors had been arriving bearing linen-covered baskets since the word had spread of Lily Patterson's passing.

Helpless in the face of death, women found their own comfort in the preparation of nourishment for the living. And so they had come, bearing the fruits of their labors until the larder was full and both the sideboard and the long table in the dining room were fairly groaning with every manner of food. During the wake, a sizable dent had been made in the potages, cakes, pies, and heaping platters, but several more crowds of visitors could have been sustained by what still remained.

Having been in an understandable daze until now, Ian looked upon the largesse as if seeing it for the first time. Running a hand through his hair, his deep voice cut through the awful silence that shrouded the house. "Rose, please take some of this food home with you today. I know there are people in and out of the parsonage all the time. And if you could draw up a list of those who could use some of this, I'll have it packed up and distributed."

"I'll see to it, Ian, dear. Here, now, you must keep up your strength." Rose thrust a heaping plate of food in his hands.

"Where are the children? They must be hungry." He

took the plate but didn't look at it. Eating was the last thing on his mind.

"Ana has taken them upstairs to the nursery. Laurel and Primmy are with them, too. I've already sent the Marys up with trays for them."

"I must go to them."

Rose slipped her plump arm around Ian and guided him to a chair at the table. "You will eat something first, dear boy. John? You, too." Having settled her son-in-law, Rose pushed her husband down in a chair on the opposite side of the table.

Needing to keep herself busy, Rose fluttered about the dining room preparing a plate of food for her husband. After serving him, she pushed through to the kitchen, ostensibly to order pots of tea and coffee. In reality, she could not bring herself to sit down. She knew once she stopped moving about and seeing to the needs of others, the depth of her sorrow would overwhelm her. When she did sit down, she remained busy, preparing the list she'd promised Ian. She did it at the kitchen worktable, a place she found infinitely more comfortable than the lavish ostentation of her daughter's dining room.

In the dining room, but for the occasional clink of a fork against china, silence prevailed. Ian didn't know or care what was going on in his father-in-law's mind. All he hoped was that the man would leave soon and take all his family with him.

He was genuinely fond of Rose and her two younger girls, Laurel and Primmy. If they shared John's narrow piety and philosophies, they didn't go around advertising it. However, Valeriana, or Ana as the family called her, was her father's daughter through and through. If she'd been born male, MacPherson would most likely have sent her to Princeton and the seminary so she would follow in his footsteps. As it was, he'd tutored her himself, and she'd acquired the equivalent of a university education. Unfortunately, her education was heavily colored by MacPherson's own philosophy and ethics. As far as Ian could tell, if Ana wasn't evangelizing, she was censuring the lesser beings of the world—namely anyone who didn't follow the strict teachings of Calvin. The less time he had to endure in that woman's company, the better.

Mainly, he just wanted the house to get back to some sort of normalcy. It was a relief to get the funeral over with. Having their mother lying in a coffin in the parlor and all the people trooping in and out for her wake had been an ordeal for the children. He wasn't sure Maara or Rob quite understood the finality of death. He knew the little ones, Jessie and Joseph, didn't.

He ought to say something to John. Normally MacPherson was so voluble. It was odd to experience such a length of silence while in his company. But then the man had just buried one of his daughters.

Lily had been Ian's wife, and despite all he was sincerely sorrowed by her death. However, it was one thing to bury a wife, quite another to bury one's child. Ian grieved for the little one who'd died before it could take its first breath, but knew it to be but a small fraction of the grief he would suffer if fate should be so cruel that he should ever have to bury one of the others.

Unable to think of anything else, he broke the silence by saying, "That was a fine service you gave for Lily, John. I know it was difficult for you. I admire your strength. Mine would have surely failed me under similar circumstances."

"The Lord God grants strength when His children are in need of it," MacPherson said, though his voice lacked its usual power. With a shaking hand, he reached for the cup of tea Rose had set before him, started to lift it to his lips, then changed his mind. The cup tilted dangerously before it clattered back onto its saucer.

"Couldn't have borne it if anyone else had done my Lily's funeral. I baptized her, welcomed her into the church, married her, and baptized her babies. Had to do her funeral. Had to. No one else."

MacPherson's pallor grew more ashen as he spoke, and his eyes appeared unfocused. "Had to do it. So beautiful. Gone ... gone ... my precious, innocent angel, gone." His voice hoarsened and his speech rambled until he was muttering unintelligibly.

Alarmed, Ian rounded the table and grasped his father-in-law's shoulder. "John?"

MacPherson seemed not to hear him and continued his disjointed muttering. Gently, Ian shook him again, but MacPherson was in a world of his own.

Hating that the woman should have to be further burdened, Ian went in search of Rose. He found her washing dishes in the kitchen. She'd made Gerta sit down to rest. He wasn't surprised.

"I'm afraid John is not himself, Rose," he said, then marveled at her calm as she took over the care of her distraught husband. But then, that was Rose. Always calm no matter how grim or shocking the event. She'd been that way throughout the long night of Lily's suffering, delirious ravings, and eventual death.

"I'll come with you and help get him into the parsonage," Ian said a short time later as he helped Rose load her husband into the carriage.

"Thank you, dear, but your place is here. I appreciate the use of the carriage and your Mr. Ferguson to drive us. Laurel and Primmy will be help enough."

Ian took in the anxious faces of his two young sisters-in-law seated on either side of their father. He smiled gently, hoping to reassure them. "With the inestimable MacPherson ladies attending him, John is a fortunate man," he remarked, and meant it.

Laurel and Primmy were young, but each was quite remarkable in her own way. Laurel was only seventeen, or perhaps eighteen, he really couldn't remember right then, only that it was Laurel who called upon the sick and often stayed to nurse and comfort them.

Primula was as bright and sunny as the flower for which she'd been named. She was a delight to the family and everyone she met. A year or two younger than Laurel, she was usually bubbling with joy and chatter. Except for the past few days, he'd rarely seen her serious.

And Valeriana was . . . Ian frowned. Where was Valeriana?

He turned and saw his eldest sister-in-law, sans cloak and bonnet, embracing her mother in the open doorway . . . as if saying good-bye.

"I'll send someone around for James Cooke," Ian offered, watching with growing dismay as Rose patted her eldest daughter's cheek and started toward the waiting carriage.

"Oh, don't bother the doctor, Ian, dear. I'm sure all John needs is rest. He'll be better tomorrow."

The way MacPherson was hunched down and continuing to mutter to himself, Ian was unconvinced. "I'd still feel better if a physician were to look at him."

"If you feel you must." Rising up on her toes, she pressed a kiss to Ian's cheek. "You're a good man, Ian Patterson. You have suffered and done more than any man should be expected under such—"

Closing her eyes, she sighed heavily. "Oh, it is over now and best left in the past. God bless you, Ian, and forgive me." She patted his cheek lightly and forced a smile before climbing into the carriage.

Ian closed the door. Uncomfortable with Rose's comment and more so with what she'd refrained from saying, he concentrated on the present. "I'm sure it'll be a comfort to you to have all your daughters at home, Rose. Once the children are settled for the night, I'll see that Valeriana gets home safely. She's been a great help these past days, but I know her place is with you and John."

"No, no. All her things are already moved, and John wants her to stay here."

All her things? Here? A sinking feeling settled into Ian's stomach, sending disturbing memories scurrying. Desperation prompted him to say, "That's very . . . uh . . . thoughtful, but she's done so much already. I know how much John relies on her to help him with his sermons and other church business. And of course the classes she teaches at Mrs. Parker's. I couldn't impose any longer."

"Doing for family is never an imposition, dear. Now, we really must be getting John home."

Speechless, Ian watched the carriage move down his driveway. Just how long was Valeriana to stay?

When she'd arrived the morning after Lily's death, portmanteau in hand, he'd assumed her stay would be but a few days. If there had been a trunk or any other baggage accompanying her, he hadn't noticed, but then his greatest concern that morning had been how to tell his children that their mother was dead.

To think he'd actually been glad to see her. With all the arrangements to be made and the stream of people in and out of the house, he'd had little time to spend with his children. It was a comfort to know that someone who loved them was there to care for them and stay with them constantly. They needed a familiar face, and their aunt was that. Since their very births, she, and Laurel and Primmy, too, had been in and out of the house almost daily, taking responsibility for the children when Lily was away or busy.

Turning at last, he took in the drawn look on Valeriana's face and the way she was worrying the handkerchief in her hands. "Sister, I know you're worried about your father," he began, hoping he could appeal to her good sense. Rose had clearly been more addled than he'd supposed.

"I simply cannot impose upon your kindness any longer," he said, deciding to appeal directly to the source. "Please, gather up what you might need for tonight and allow me to see you home. I can have the rest of your things sent over tomorrow. It wouldn't be fair of me to keep you here when you are clearly needed at the parsonage."

Ana shook her head, the movement sending the black ribbons of her cap swinging and his hopes plummeting. "No, Brother Ian. Thank you for your concern, but Mama is right. It would be best if I remained here. It would only upset Papa further if I were to return home."

"But what of your classes at the girls' seminary?" Raking a hand through his hair, Ian grabbed desperately at what he knew was his last hope. "Educated women like yourself are scarce. Mrs. Parker surely cannot do without you for long."

"I appreciate your concern, Brother Ian," she replied with uncharacteristic airiness. "But I taught only one class this term. Mrs. Parker understands I'm needed far more here and has volunteered to take over my students herself."

With a rustle of bombazine sliding over starched petticoats, Ana moved briskly into the vestibule and headed for the stairway. "I left one of the Marys with the children, but I must get back to them. Do come inside,

Brother Ian; you're letting all that cold and damp into the house."

Her peremptory tone grated, and briefly Ian considered standing out in the rain with the door wide open just to spite her. Lord, help me, he beseeched as he followed in her wake.

She's a good woman, and she means well, he chanted inside his head as he closed the door with more force than was necessary. The heavy door shuddered as it came to rest, and the sound of the latch clicking into place echoed through the large vestibule.

It was a childish thing to do, akin to stamping his foot in a show of pique, but it had felt good to slam that door. He felt even better when he saw Valeriana pause at the sound. Perhaps a few more slamming doors would distress her enough that she'd pack up and leave. He dismissed that thought as soon as it formed. It would take more than a few banging doors to exorcise Valeriana MacPherson from his house.

"I'll . . . uh . . . be up to see the children in a little while," he said, and headed for his study at the back of the house. He didn't hear an answer and assumed she'd continued on up the stairs. Good, he could use a little time alone.

In the simply furnished room that was his private sanctuary, he opened a cabinet, pulled out a bottle of brandy, and splashed a small portion into a glass. Swirling the rich amber liquid in the snifter with one hand, he picked up the poker and stirred the coals in the hearth. He took a sip of his drink and savored the taste on his tongue. Warmth spread down his throat as he watched the flames come to life in the grate and begin to lick along the logs stacked there.

Images of Lily flitted in his mind. It was too soon for any of them to be pleasant memories. Her last hours had been torturous for her and all who witnessed her suffering. He took another sip of the brandy and rubbed at the ache in his forehead. If only memories of that night and too many other times were as simple to ease.

He lifted the glass to his lips again, draining the remains in one swallow. Lily had left him four beautiful children. The joy they brought canceled all else. They gave his life meaning and purpose. Anything he'd done in the past nine years or all the years ahead of him would be for them.

Above the mantel hung a large map of Lake Erie. At the western end of the lake was a group of twenty or so islands. Involuntarily, he lifted his hand to them, his index finger falling unerringly on one in particular. "No. 8" was written next to it and a circle drawn around the island and its label. The circle was his own addition, drawn years ago when he'd first set his sights on owning the twenty-five hundred acres of rock, hardwood forests, and sunny meadows.

"High time that island had a name," he muttered to himself as he lifted the map from the wall. After carefully scraping away the notation and circle, he pulled a quill from the well. He'd written the first two letters and paused. Giving it his own surname seemed wrong. He didn't mean for it to be his own private kingdom but a place that welcomed any who wished to live there.

When the map was back on the wall, he stood back to admire his work. Its new name was now emblazoned boldly where the modest No. 8 had been. It was too late to save Lily, but it wasn't too late for the children. Their future lay on that island. And it would be a bright one, free from any hint of scandal or gossip. He knew it couldn't be perfect, but he'd make it as perfect as was humanly possible. And so he'd named it Parras, the Gaelic word for paradise.

Innocents would not suffer for the deeds of others as long as there was a breath in his body. He poured himself another swallow of brandy to seal that vow.

"Brother Ian! Would you stumble up the stairs to your children with that evil on your breath?"

Startled, Ian nearly dropped his glass.

Valeriana glared at him from the doorway. If her hair weren't secured so tightly beneath that silly little cap she wore, he was sure it would be standing on end. The full-blown censure of the diehard temperance advocate was written all over her. The nearness of a bottle of brandy was apparently a horror to her righteous soul.

He let out a loud sigh of exasperation. "Sister, a few sips of brandy never hurt anyone. I promise I shall not stumble up the stairs nor shall my children be tainted in any way by my presence."

He set his glass upon his desk. Leaning against the desk, he crossed his arms over his chest and asked, "What brings you to my study? Have you changed your mind about returning to the parsonage?"

"Certainly not!"

Her answer came quickly and vehemently. By the way she was eyeing his nearly empty snifter and the bottle still out on his desk, he could almost read her thoughts. *Leave those precious ones in the care of a drunkard?* Why, it was not to be considered while there was a breath in her pious body. He almost laughed.

"Well, if it isn't an announcement of your imminent departure, just what is it that has made you so courageous as to beard this lion in his private den?"

Ana tightened her lips and seemed to shrink within herself. Ian was immediately sorry for his sarcasm. He was feeling surly but had no right to take it out on her. She'd lost a sister and was surely grieving deeply for the woman she thought she knew. He would not disabuse her of that memory. An apology sprang to his lips, but she spoke first.

"I regret that my presence here causes you such discomfort, but Mama and Papa believe the children need a relative, not servants, to watch over them, and I agree. I shall endeavor to stay out of your way as much as possible."

Sure that she must be choking on voicing regret for causing him discomfort, Ian managed to stem another sarcastic comment. He didn't like himself very much for descending to such tactics. It wasn't usually his way. "Please accept my apologies. I'm afraid I'm not quite myself today. Now what pressing matter has brought you here?"

"Joseph and Jessica are down for a nap. The rain has stopped, and I thought Maara and Robert could do with some activity. Perhaps you'd like to take them for a walk or a ride in the carriage?"

Her gaze strayed to the bottle again. Her brow lifted as she gauged the level in it. "That is, if you're able?"

Checking the anger that her mere presence seemed always to elicit, he informed her, "Sister, I am more than able to walk or control a team of horses."

He observed the tightness of her features and the rigid way she held herself. "You seem inordinately tense today. Perhaps you'd like me to pour you a glass of brandy. I'm sure it would do you a world of good."

Her look of horror and loud gasp were the last he saw or heard from her for the rest of that day.

Chapter Two

May

Rose MacPherson dug down beside a line of fresh shoots until she'd exposed their common root. With a small hatchet, she chopped at it, then grasped the exposed end and began to pull.

"The burning bush, hmmph," she muttered under her breath as she lifted more and more of the long root running horizontally a few inches beneath the soil. "The invading bush, more's the like." When she'd pulled out as much as she could budge, she hacked it free, tossed the length of root with the others she'd removed already, and started the process all over again.

"You have to admire the sumac's tenacity."

Resting back on her heels, Rose looked up with one of her rare frowns. "It is that, Primmy, dear. Sometimes I think it has been sent by God to test my patience and strength." She sighed, shaking her head as she looked around her garden. In every one of the flower beds fresh shoots of sumac meandered through the orderly plantings. "Every year it reminds me that it had sole possession of this space long before I came, and wants nothing so much as to take it back."

Primmy laughed lightly before picking up her mother's garden trowel and digging out a pesky shoot that was threatening the brick walkway. "Remember our first day in Cleveland when Papa spied the sumac growing on this little rise? The leaves had already turned bright red, and Papa likened it to the burning bush on Mount Sinai."

Mimicking her father's deep voice, she stretched her arm dramatically and pointed toward the church just beyond the garden wall. *"There. We shall build our church there. God has given us a sign!"* Giggling, she went back to digging out sumac shoots and roots.

Grateful for the respite her daughter's help afforded her, Rose stood and rubbed a hand across the small of her back before walking to one of the benches scattered about the garden. Resting her head against the rough bark of the pin oak behind the bench, she closed her eyes and thought back to that fateful day a little more than a decade ago.

After weeks of travel, she and the girls had been exhausted when they'd arrived in Cleveland. Not so John. His enthusiasm for the venture had never wavered. From the time they'd waved good-bye in Brookfield, Connecticut, until they alighted from the coach in front of the Erie Tavern here in Cleveland, John had been filled with such joy and excitement for finally having his own church. That there was neither church nor parsonage awaiting them and that he'd have to obtain the land and somehow find building funds locally had not daunted him a bit.

Oh, how she had worried and prayed throughout that journey and the weeks before. "Have faith, Mother," John had told her over and over again. "God will provide."

Opening her eyes, Rose looked over to where her youngest, now a budding young woman of sixteen years, rooted around in the beds. Such a nice garden it was— except for the constant battle with the sumac. The precious seeds and root stocks that had been sent to her from friends and family back home were thriving in the rich Ohio soil. The two-story house was the finest she and John had lived in during all the years of their marriage. Built of brick with a slate roof and pristine white doors and window trim, it was a companion to the larger building beside it: Grace Church.

Yes, God had provided for them—in the person of Ian Patterson. If not for his donating the land for the church and contributing so heavily to the building fund and continuing to contribute so heavily to the church, she and her family would surely not be living even half so well.

Dear Ian. How shamelessly John had thrown Lily at that young man. With discomfort, she admitted she'd not been innocent of promoting the match either. Such a fine young man, handsome, polite, and already well set up at only twenty and four. He was quite simply the answer to the prayers of a mother of four daughters, two of whom had already reached marriageable age.

Oh, she'd known in her heart of hearts that Lily could never be the kind of helpmate that a man like Ian needed and deserved. But he'd seemed so smitten by her, and so she'd hoped it would be all right. And it had been for a while.

Rose squeezed her eyes shut and sent another prayer heavenward for her daughter's soul. Her heart ached every time she thought of her. She missed her, of course, and would always feel the wound of losing her secondborn.

How blessed she and John had felt when their second child was another beautiful and healthy daughter. And then she'd taken sick and hovered so close to death for days. When she'd recovered, they'd not been able to set aside their fears and treat her normally. Having feared so for her life, they'd spoiled her and been blind to her faults and failings. John still was, and she prayed he would remain so. Her death had devastated him; the truth about her would surely kill him. That it had been Ian who had begged her not to tell John did not assuage Rose's guilt.

Clasping her hands together, she prayed the same prayer she had been praying since the night her daughter had died: *God forgive me for my selfishness. And Lily, for her weaknesses. Heal my husband's troubled mind and forgive him for his bouts of zealousness and the wrath and condemnations he heaps upon Ian. I do beseech you on Ian's behalf that he may one day be granted the happiness, peace, and love he deserves. And, Lord, guide our Ana so that she is a help and comfort to him and the children as they adjust their lives. Amen.*

"Scandalous, that's what it is. Scandalous," Ana muttered as she confiscated another bottle and dropped it in the crate.

"Ahh . . . begging your pardon, Miss Ana, but I don't think the boss is going to be too happy when he finds all his liquor gone from the house."

Ana didn't relish Ian's stable man or anyone else reminding her that she was overstepping the bounds of propriety. Her conscience was doing a very fine job of it as it was. But the strength of her belief that a much higher authority guided her actions overrode all. All, that is, but invading the man's private study. At that door, her courage had deserted her, and she'd confined her expropriatory tour to the parlor and dining room.

Eyeing the surprisingly meager collection of bottles she'd collected, she announced, "Mr. Ferguson, I have a God-given duty to raise my sister's children properly, and that does not include allowing spirits in the house where they must live."

Gingerly, she placed her brother-in-law's humidor and pipes atop the box of cigars she'd confiscated from the dining room. "Nor tobacco." Gathering up her booty, she ordered, "Come along, Mr. Ferguson. The sooner all this evil is out of this house, the better."

Hefting the crate with obvious reluctance, Ferguson remarked, "I know you're powerful strong about temperance like your pa, but the little missus, she was the preacher's daughter, too, and she never did throw out the mister's whiskey and brandy. She never said nothin' about his smoking, neither."

At the mention of her sister, a wave of grief washed over her. Struggling over the lump in her throat, she managed, "My sister was a sweet, gentle soul, Mr. Ferguson. Given her upbringing, it surely grieved her to have spirits and evil-smelling tobacco in her house. But she was not strong in will or body."

Dipping her head to her shoulder, she awkwardly brushed a tear from her cheek. "We shall do honor to my dear sister's memory by ridding her house of such wickedness. Now come, Mr. Ferguson. I trust you will dispose of the contents of that box in an appropriate manner."

Ned shook his head as he trod along behind her. Stashing the box in one of the feed bins in the carriage house seemed a fine way to "dispose of the contents in an appropriate manner," he decided. Ian Patterson was not a hard-drinking man. In all the years he'd known him, he'd never once seen him overimbibe. The boss merely enjoyed a small glass of fine whiskey or brandy after supper and a good smoke to go along with it.

The poor man had already suffered more than any one man ought. Didn't seem right to snatch away his liquor and tobacco on top of it all. He'd let the boss know where he'd stashed it all. Probably was only temporary anyway, having Miss Ana living here in the house and running things. Soon's he got around to it, the boss would be hiring somebody to take care of the children for him. Miss Ana could go back to living with her ma, pa, and sisters up the way in the parsonage where she belonged. And this house could go back to being the way it used to be. Or as close as it might with the little missus being gone.

The aroma rising from the items Ana cradled in her arms taunted her as she proceeded down the hallway to the back door. Tobacco was one of the scents that clung to Ian Patterson. It wasn't really a disagreeable scent, but like everything else about *that man*, it made her uncomfortable.

Ian Patterson had always made her feel on edge and angry. He was so big and so . . . so . . . Well, she didn't know what else exactly it was about his person that always made her feel so out of sorts, but his mere presence in a room always had.

As far back as her family's first day in Cleveland when Papa had brought him to the inn where they were staying, she'd felt uneasy around the man. That he owned not only several ships but a goodly portion of Cleveland, including the very land Papa wanted for his church, didn't make him a proper Christian gentleman. If she lived to be a hundred, she'd never understand why Papa and Mama had been so eager for sweet, gentle Lily to marry the man.

He was handsome enough, she supposed. That is if one were susceptible to the way a shock of his auburn hair tended to fall in a wave over his broad forehead. Or the way his hazel eyes so often glittered with laughter. Or the way his speech lilted with a faint Irish charm.

Of course, none of those things swayed the opinion she'd formed of him all those years ago. He was a libertine if she'd ever met one, and not even that fine baritone voice raised to the glory of the Lord on a Sunday morning or softly crooning a cradle song to the children could make her think otherwise.

A shudder snaked down her back. Even thinking of him made her feel alternately chilled and overheated. Dear Lord, how ever was she going to survive living under that devil's roof?

With God's help, she'd find the strength somewhere. Lily's children needed her. She'd already endured a month; she could persevere for the children's sakes. And if it pleased God that she achieve His design for her by rearing her sister's children to adulthood, she prayed that she would be able to do it with as little contact with their father as possible.

By the time she reached the kitchen, her strength of conviction regarding the rightness of her actions began to waver. Her faith that all the bottles of liquor must go wasn't shaken. *Never that.* Spirits of any kind were an evil that must be eradicated from God's earth.

How many times had she seen the suffering alcohol could cause? Dozens. Back in Connecticut and here. As soon as she'd been old enough to accompany her mother on her rounds, she'd seen what happened to wives and children when husbands spent all their wages on drink. Her heart had nearly broken when she'd seen the hunger and poverty. Even when she'd been no older than six, she'd realized that the baskets of food and clothing she and Mama brought to the families was not nearly enough.

At least Brother Ian hadn't drunk his family to ruination. Not yet anyway. Nor had he ever stumbled home from a round of the saloons and abused Lily or the children. Still, he ought to set a better example for his children and the men he employed.

In fairness, to the best of her knowledge, none of his employees' families was in abject straits. She supposed, also, that it was possible Brother Ian was moderate in his indulgences. That still didn't make his imbibing any form of alcohol acceptable . . . but perhaps she could relent on his smoking.

The church frowned on the use of tobacco, though not as severely as it frowned on spirits. Not that she was about to put the humidor and pipes back in the parlor or that cigar box back in the dining room. If Brother Ian must persist in this vile practice, then he could do it outside. There was no reason to let him stink up the house whenever he wished to indulge.

"Gerta? Have you a spare cupboard near the door where I might store Mr. Patterson's smoking paraphernalia?"

The cook's eyes widened at the sight of the items in Ana's arms and widened further when she saw Ned trailing behind her carrying a wooden crate filled with bottles. Wringing her flour-covered hands, she muttered something indecipherable under her breath, though a word here and there sounded like she might be sending up a plea to God. Recovering herself, the German woman crossed to a cupboard by the back door, carefully opened it, and indicated a vacant shelf.

The matter of the liquor and tobacco effectively solved, Ana turned her attention to the other changes she wanted to make. Looking around the kitchen, she smiled with approval. Spotless, well organized, and with mouthwatering aromas filling it as per usual. Gerta Hosapfel was a treasure, to be sure.

But, as good a cook as the woman was, she was the opposite as a housekeeper for any space beyond the kitchen door. Why Lily hadn't gotten someone else to oversee the other aspects of running such a large house was beyond her. But then, Lily had always been flitting about to one place or another, and her health had been so delicate, Ana supposed she'd not noticed the dust and disorder. Or perhaps she'd just not had the heart to relieve the woman of the duty. Lily never could bear to cause anyone a moment's unhappiness.

"Gerta, might I have a word with you?"

"Oh, *ja*, Miss Ana. Sit. Please." She indicated the chair at the end of her worktable and waited until Ana had settled herself there before asking, "How is your papa?"

"He is a bit better each day, thank you. Now about—"

"Thanking *Gott*. Such a sadness, the little missus dying the way she did and your papa grieving so deeply."

"Yes. We will all miss her, but as Mama says, we must accept God's will and get on with the business of living."

With a heavy sigh, the woman nodded. "*Ja*, that we must do."

"Now about—"

"Such a good woman is your mama. And such beautiful flowers she grows."

"Yes, Mama has always gardened," Ana said, inwardly groaning. If this was how communication with the woman went, no wonder Lily hadn't relieved her of overseeing the rest of the house. Lily, bless her sweet soul, had been so easily distracted, she would never have stood a chance trying to control a conversation with the woman.

Girding her loins with equal measures of backbone and whatever charm she hoped she'd inherited from her mother, Ana launched into her proposals. An hour later, she left the kitchen well satisfied with what she'd accomplished.

She was even more satisfied later that evening as she paused in the foyer to admire the changes achieved in only one day. The rugs, beaten free of dust, glowed

warmly against the freshly waxed floor, and the chande-
lier overhead sparkled. Needing only clear directions,
the Marys had done a superb job.

The tall cabinet clock chimed the half hour, reminding
her that she hadn't meant to tarry. Clutching the book
she'd come down to retrieve, she hurried toward the
stairs.

"They've already eaten supper."

It was not a question but a statement and delivered so
unexpectedly and so loudly, Ana nearly dropped Maara's
primer. "Oh!" With her hand pressed to her breast to
still her heart, it was a moment before Ana could speak.
"Bro ... Brother Ian, I ... did not realize you were
home."

"And where else would I be?" he drawled. "It's half-
past six, the usual time I sit down at the dinner table with
my children."

Her heart still thumping madly, she swallowed hard.
"But sometimes you're not home until seven, even later.
Such an hour is far too late for young children to partake
of their evening meal."

"That might be so, but it's not seven o'clock. It's half-
past six, and I am here. But I'm told you ordered supper
to be served at five-thirty. Might I ask why?"

Chilled by the barely checked anger in his eyes, voice,
even posture, she struggled to maintain her poise. She
had to give herself a stern reminder that God in His infi-
nite wisdom had given her a task to do—care for her
sister's children—and that she had set a meal schedule
that was best for their well-being.

"These past weeks," she began with a forced conge-
nial tone she prayed would defuse his temper, "it's understandable that the entire household's schedule has
been all topsy-turvy. However, I'm sure you would agree

that it is time everyone, especially the children, returned to a normal daily routine."

"Of course. But part of that *normal* routine is that I always take supper with them when I'm in town."

Clutching the primer tightly, Ana told him, "There is no reason why you cannot continue to do so, Brother Ian. Supper will be served promptly at half-past five every day. That should give you plenty of time to get home after the close of office hours."

Ian's brows rose, and his eyes widened. He opened his mouth, closed it, then took a step back. "Let me make sure I understand you correctly, Sister. Is it your belief that all business ceases at five o'clock each and every day?"

"Why, of course." Now it was her turn to be incredulous. Did the man think she never took note of the business hours posted on the various shops in town? Grocers, tailors, cobblers, the dry-goods store. All of them, including the Patterson Shipping office, locked their doors, pulled the shade, and hung a CLOSED sign in the window promptly at five o'clock. And Papa had always expected his supper at half-past five . . . unless he was called away to console the bereaved.

"And further, it is my understanding that the *good* fathers of this town hurry straight home to take supper with their families." She was immediately sorry for her choice of words. Mama would surely deem such as small and totally unworthy of her.

She would have apologized if she'd not detected the unmistakable scent of stale smoke and whiskey that had entered the house with him. Clearly, he'd been whiling away the last hour or more in one of the waterfront saloons guzzling whiskey with every sort of ne'er-do-well, expecting his children to wait for their supper until he appeared.

Was it not enough that every single night for the past three weeks he'd taken himself off immediately after the children were tucked in their beds? Back to the taverns, she was sure, to guzzle more whiskey and do God only knew what else until the wee hours of the morning. Any shred of guilt she might have had regarding disposing of the liquor he kept in his house fled.

"Sister," Ian began, a muscle ticking in his jaw and an uncharacteristic cold light shining in his eyes that increased her discomfort, "you have some very peculiar ideas as to how and when a day's business is concluded."

Pursing her lips, she raised one brow. "Humph." Oh, why didn't he take himself off on one of his ships and leave her in peace for a week or two?

The household's schedule was not the only thing that had been topsy-turvy during the past few weeks. Her stomach was doing somersaults, and she couldn't seem to keep her hands or voice steady.

For all her twenty-eight years, she'd prided herself on her calm composure. Well, perhaps not all of those years. But at least since she'd achieved adulthood. And yet, one minute in Ian Patterson's presence and she was anything but composed. To make matters even worse, she thought she saw the corners of his mouth twitch with contained laughter, as if he knew how much he disturbed her and took delight in it.

But the hint died as quickly as it had been born. There was only contempt in his expression and voice when he spoke again. "I suppose there's no changing the mind of a woman such as yourself, Sister, so I shall not even attempt to disabuse you of the notion that all business ceases in Cleveland at the stroke of five. Or that all business is conducted in offices. However, might I inquire as to why you chose not to warn me of this new schedule you've set?"

"I . . . I—"

"I assure you that had I known, I would have certainly tried to be here."

Ana had seen Ian with his children enough of late that she didn't question the sincerity of this pledge. That he thoroughly delighted in the children's company had been a revelation, to say the least. "I did not realize that was your habit, Brother Ian. Please accept my apology. I was thinking only of the children and how very hungry they are by half-past five."

Clearly taken aback by her statement, he said, "I was not aware that my children have been suffering in any way by delaying their supper hour until six-thirty or even seven."

"That is because Gerta staves them off with cookies and other pastries. By the time you finally get home and supper is served, they're so full of sweets they merely pick at the good, nourishing food placed before them. It's a wonder they're not as fat as pigs or sickly."

"I see. Then it is my turn to apologize. I had no idea. Lily never—" He sighed heavily and ran his fingers through his hair. "I was not aware of this. You are right in pushing up the supper hour. I shall endeavor to be here at half-past five."

Ana gathered her skirts and prepared to return to the children. "I believe Gerta has kept your supper warm for you. Perhaps you'd care to join the children when you've finished. There should be time, as I shall not begin readying them for bed for another hour."

"Then I had best hurry through my meal and try to make the most of what little time I'll be able to share with them this evening. I'm afraid I didn't complete my business today and must go out again tonight." With a respectful nod, he disappeared into the dining room.

Ana felt another shudder down her back and a flush rise on her cheeks as she hurried up the steps. She didn't even want to think about what kind of "business" was conducted after the sun went down.

Chapter Three

Pausing at the doorway, Ian scanned the tavern. It was a small place and located a bit up the shoreline from his usual haunts. He'd not patronized it in years.

As his eyes adjusted to the gloom, he thought he recognized the barmaid rushing to a table with a pitcher of beer. A bit plumper and understandably older than he remembered, she was still quite pretty in her own way. She looked a bit tired tonight, but still flashed that dimpled smile of hers that made a man feel welcome and important.

Susan. Susan Donavan. That was her name. A kinder, more understanding woman God had never created. Nor one more patient.

For a moment he felt like the lonely, green youth he'd been the first time he'd crossed the Seagull's threshold. He sure as hell wasn't as green as he'd been back then, but God knew he was still lonely. It had been a long time since he'd indulged himself with someone like Susan. Not since before he'd married Lily. A good, long romp with a woman who'd not only be discreet but expect nothing more than the pleasure they gave each other was tempting. But that wasn't what he was looking for tonight.

Moving farther into the tavern, he scanned the tables, hoping to God the man was here. He was heartily sick of

33

haunting the taverns and inns of Cleveland every day and night. From all he'd gathered about the bastard, he hadn't left the area nor done or said anything to indicate he had such plans. For a fella who'd been hard to escape for the last few years, he'd been damned invisible since Lily's funeral. Perhaps he'd been out in the countryside painting some farm family's portraits. He'd have to take on each and every commission offered to keep himself fed and garbed as nattily as was his trademark. The salary he earned teaching art at Mrs. Parker's Seminary for Young Ladies was certainly not enough to support him.

"Why, it's my grand, lovely boyo, all grown up and looking so fine. By the saints, it's been a long time. Give us a hug for old times' sake."

Susan Donavan had left Ireland years before he had, but her voice still held the music of its people and reminded him of mist-draped emerald hills and warm peat fires. Hearing it again tugged at a place in his heart he'd thought he left on the dock in Belfast. For a moment he welcomed the plump arms wrapped around his neck.

"Susan," he said with genuine pleasure. Over her head, he spotted his quarry seated alone at a far corner table, his back to the other customers. If luck was with him, Susan's enthusiastic greeting wouldn't have drawn the man's attention. Loosening the woman's hold, he took his eyes off his quarry only briefly. "You're looking as young and lovely as ever."

"Aww, you was never a good liar, Ia—"

Ian silenced her with the press of a finger against her lips. Bending down as if to nuzzle her ear, he kept a steady eye on his quarry as he whispered, "I've got business with a man over there, and I'll be beholden to you if you don't give him prior warning I'm here."

Susan raised her brows, then winked and whispered,

"Just see that you spend a little time with me before you take your leave. I lost my sweet Kevin a couple years back, and I hear you've lost your wife. I'm thinkin' we could use some time together, you and I."

"We might at that," Ian muttered, but his gaze was on the man at the table. He didn't hear the sigh Susan gave as he set her aside, nor did he see her wistful look. With single-minded determination, he steadily wended his way toward the back table.

"Phillips," Ian said, his deep, rustling voice just loud enough for the other man to hear. "I believe we have some business to complete."

Startled, Anson Phillips began to stand, clearly prepared to bolt. Ian dropped a heavy hand on the smaller man's shoulder, effectively keeping him seated. To the casual observer, Ian's action might appear a friendly gesture. It was not. But the last thing Ian wanted was to create a scene. This place was out of the way, and, except for Susan, he hadn't recognized anyone. But gossip had a way of spreading, and he'd rather his business here not be trumpeted around the coast.

"No reason to rise on my account," Ian said as he lifted his hand from the man's shoulder. Forcing a pleasant expression, Ian casually rounded the table and seated himself. Keeping to the appearance of a cordial meeting between himself and the painter, he caught Susan's attention and ordered a glass of whiskey for himself and a refill for Phillips.

Sweat beaded on Phillips's pale forehead and glistened in the dark hair at the edges of his narrow face. His rather prominent Adam's apple rose and fell almost convulsively. Under the best of times the man's face had little color. Right then, Ian ventured most corpses could best him.

Ian took no small amount of satisfaction from watching Phillips's panic. Just the family's painful embarrassment from the bastard's actions after Lily's funeral was reason aplenty to let the man suffer.

"Relax, Phillips. I'm not going to pound you, though I understand I've more than enough reason to do so. I've merely come to settle a debt."

"A . . . uh . . . debt?" More convulsive swallowing. "I . . . uh . . . don't understand."

Keeping his gaze steady on the man across the scarred table, Ian took a thick envelope from his waistcoat pocket and laid it on the table before him. Casually, he rested his crossed hands on the table, not touching the envelope but making it clear he wasn't yet ready to relinquish it. "I believe this should cover your fee for the many portraits you painted of my wife as well as monetary reimbursement still owed for the lessons you gave her."

In the blink of an eye, Phillips's panic was replaced with obvious relief. In another blink, greed dominated all. His fingers twitched. The beads of sweat on his brow formed together into rivulets that began running down his jaw. He was all but smacking his lips in anticipation.

Ian nearly smiled. He'd figured the effete little man for an opportunist. Counted on it. "I understand you'll soon be leaving these parts and not returning," he stated calmly, counting on two more things—that the man was not without some intelligence and had absolutely no backbone. "Ever."

Phillips's eyes shifted from the envelope to Ian. Unable to hold his gaze steady for long, he looked away, grabbed up his glass of whiskey, and gulped it down. "But I have—"

"Nothing," Ian finished for him. Leaning forward he

fixed the smaller man with a baleful glare. "Nothing and no one to keep you here."

Phillips's eyes were riveted on Ian's hands and how they curled into fists, relaxed, and tightened again. "Uh . . . yes, sir. Nothing and no one."

Ian studied the man for a long moment, then eased against the back of his chair. "Then we understand each other." Ian lifted his own glass toward the other man to seal the agreement. He took but a small sip. Pulling his watch from his pocket, he flipped it open and noted the time. Not raising his gaze from the handsome gold time-piece, he said, "The hour grows late. It'll take you a little while to get back to that boardinghouse you've been living in on Second Street. So best you get a move on, as I suspect you have some packing to do if you're to catch the stage heading east. It leaves from the Superior Street Inn around daybreak."

"But, sir, that's terribly sudden. I do have some affairs to settle before I take my leave of Cleveland," Phillips was foolish enough to argue.

Ian closed his watch with a snap, tucked it back in his waistcoat pocket, and stood. "Given what a close friend you were to my wife, I'll be happy to say your good-byes for you. It would be a shame to delay your trip, given the fearsome news you received only today."

"Fearsome news?"

"Surely the news that the life you hold most dear in all the world is but hanging by a thread is fearsome indeed." He pulled Phillips to his feet, pumped his hand, and clapped him on the shoulder, nearly knocking him to the floor with the force of each blow. "I wish you Godspeed, sir," he said loudly enough for those around them to hear. "Your leaving here tomorrow morning will not go unnoted." Leaning closer to the man's ear, he added, "Nor would your return."

Phillips alternately flushed and blanched. Jerking out of Ian's grasp, he rapidly put several paces between them. From somewhere within his scrawny body and even scrawnier character, he evidently found an ounce of bravado, for he declared, "You're rich, Patterson, but that doesn't give you the right to order people's lives. This is a country of free men."

A glance beyond Phillips's shoulder assured Ian that no one, save perhaps Susan, was paying any attention to their exchange. Shrugging nonchalantly, he stepped in front of Phillips so that the man was effectively blocked from view. Clapping one hand on the smaller man's shoulder, he held him in place.

"If you'd like to remain a free man, Phillips, I suggest you get out of town and never come back," Ian said in a low tone. "There is, of course, another alternative. I'm told it's only a matter of a few more months before the new penitentiary in Columbus will be ready for occupancy. Of course, murderers don't usually reside in prisons very long before they're hung."

"I'm not a murderer. Lily's death was . . . was . . . an accident."

"I doubt a jury would see it that way if they were apprised of the fact that it was you who mixed up that concoction Lily drank hours before her death."

"But . . . but . . . it . . . I didn't mean . . ."

As much as he'd have liked to let the quivering man drop to the floor, Ian tightened his grip to hold him up. His patience at an end with the man, he gave him a shake, then asked, "Which is it to be, Phillips? The eastbound stage tomorrow morning, or we pay a visit to the constable tonight?"

"You . . . you can't prove anything."

Transferring his grip to the man's cravat, Ian asked, "Are you willing to chance that?" Lest Phillips need a taste of the hangman's noose, Ian tugged the man to his toes by his cravat.

Red-faced, Phillips gasped, "The . . . stage. I . . . I'll be on it."

The tall cabinet clock in the front foyer was chiming midnight by the time Ian slipped quietly through the back door. All was dark and quiet. Even Gerta, who often labored long after the supper hour, had taken herself off to her room above the kitchen.

Just as well, he thought, as he shrugged out of his greatcoat. He wasn't fit company for anyone. This evening's business had been distasteful, to say the least. There had been some degree of satisfaction in it, but there'd have been a helluva lot more if he'd buried his fist in Phillips's face.

He'd have to stop by the Seagull again—and soon—to make amends to Susan. He'd been unnecessarily abrupt when he'd turned down her invitation to "relive old times." He'd felt more like punching someone than seeking pleasure in an old friend's company, let alone her body.

He struck a lucifer to the heel of his boot and lit one of the carrying candles Gerta left by the door. Cupping his hand before the flickering light, he started through the house. In the dining room, he opened a cabinet and reached for the bottle of brandy he stored there. His fingers encountered nothing but a set of crystal glasses. Not for even one second did he bother to speculate about the disappearance of his brandy.

She'd taken it. *Hell!* No use checking anyplace else; she'd probably taken every bottle in the house.

"*Damnation!*" He uttered the expletive barely louder than a whisper, but the sound seemed to echo through the stillness of the room and beyond. Unconsciously, he

glanced about, half expecting the Bible-thumping terma-
gant who'd taken over his household to suddenly appear.

Hell, that woman had not only dumped out all his
liquor, she had him afraid to swear in his own house in
the middle of the night with nobody but himself for company. The sooner he found somebody to replace her the
better. She had him on edge every time they were forced
to be in the same room. Always had.

Well, maybe not always, he remembered as he trudged
up the stairs toward his bedroom. Nine years ago when
the new preacher had introduced him to his family, there
had been a moment or two when he'd felt differently
about the eldest MacPherson daughter.

Tall and gently curved, a wealth of curling hair falling
down her back, she'd been quite a pretty young woman.
But it had been the intelligence sparkling from her eyes
and the air of confidence and strength around her that
had most piqued his interest. Those qualities had put him
in mind of his grandmother, a grand lady of whom he'd
been most fond. Briefly, he'd considered courting Ana.

Her—Valeriana. The woman who'd commandeered
all his liquor and probably emptied it on the ground
somewhere. More proof that he'd been riper for the marriage mart than he'd realized at the time. He'd certainly
been an easy mark for a matchmaking father.

When MacPherson had paraded his second daughter,
Lileas Chastity, before him, he'd thought she was
just about the loveliest thing he'd ever laid eyes on. When
she'd turned those innocent eyes and her winsome
smile on him, she'd literally taken his breath away. He'd
been in that pathetic awestruck state throughout their
courtship—a blessedly brief one to his way of thinking at
the time. Given the easy way she melted into his arms
and the liberties she allowed those rare times they were

left alone, it was a miracle Maara had been born a respectable nine months after their wedding.

Remembering how easily he'd been manipulated, he grimaced. *Thinkin' with your cock and not your head, boy.* That's what the man who'd raised him would have bluntly told him, and more. Grandmama Maara would have been far more genteel in her choice of words, but the set-down would have been more effective than anything the Squire of Fiegel could have said or done to him. Grandmama would have seen through MacPherson's scheme in a minute. If only he'd inherited more of that dear lady's good sense.

He shrugged off his regrets. Thinking of the past and the "if onlys" served no purpose. He could do nothing but learn from the mistakes and be thankful for the blessings. And there were blessings. Four very special ones.

Stealing quietly into the nursery, he paused at each bed, bent and pressed his lips to either the forehead or cheek of each of his children. Maara, Rob, Jessie, and Joe. Each as precious as the others. They had made every minute of the past nine years worthwhile. Anything he'd done or would do in the future would be worth whatever the cost.

Thinking to sit a spell for the joy and peace that always settled over him by just watching his children sleep, he'd just reached for a chair when a sharp gasp sounded behind him. Ian spun around. His own breath caught, and he nearly dropped the chair. He could've sworn his heart skipped a beat before he realized the figure with yards and yards of white muslin billowing about her was not a ghost.

Hell. He should have known *she'd* be hovering about.

"Sister," he whispered. Picking up his candle, Ian stood and motioned toward the hallway. There was plenty he wanted to say to her, that was certain, but he'd not figured on a rendezvous in the middle of the night as the best time to let her know what he thought about her high-handed takeover of his household. He was relieved when she disappeared into her room. It had been far too long a day to get into all of that at this wee hour.

That relief was short-lived, for she reappeared almost immediately. Tightening the sash of a wrapper she'd hastily donned, his nemesis led the way to the hall. Resigning himself that now was as good a time as any, given that the woman did her best to avoid him throughout the day, he closed the door behind him and asked, "Sister, is it a guilty conscience or something else that has you up wandering about in the middle of the night?"

"I . . . I heard sounds and . . . and thought one of the children—"

"As you can see, it's only me. Just wanted to check on the children before I took myself off to bed. Do you always sleep so lightly?"

"No . . . I mean yes. I . . . I suppose I do . . . now."

Great stars, what was the matter with her? She was stammering like a nervous schoolgirl who'd never talked to a man before. Of course, she'd never before talked to a man while wearing nothing but her nightgown and wrapper. And in the middle of the night with no one around. But still, there was no reason to get all stammery and jittery. Nothing untoward was going to happen. For all his dissolute proclivities, she seriously doubted Ian Patterson even thought of her as a woman.

"What I meant to . . . to say was that sleeping so lightly has not been my life habit," she said, trying to ignore the amusement he was clearly deriving from her stammering. Impatiently, she yanked on her wrapper's sash again. "Only since I've been staying here."

He raised one of his brows and drawled in a deep,

husky tone that sent shivers down her spine, "Really? Something about living here bothers you, does it?"

And then he grinned, a salacious grin if she'd ever seen one. Involuntarily, Ana took a step backward and crossed her arms over her bosom.

Everything and anything about Ian Patterson bothered her, but she wouldn't give him the satisfaction of admitting it. He'd probably delight in the knowledge and do all he could to make her so miserable she'd pack up and leave. That she'd never do. No matter what he did or how he acted, she was not going to forsake the children. But she surely wished he'd quit staring at her.

Fighting the urge to run a hand over her hair to determine what there was about it that so held his attention, she said, "I sleep lightly so that I can hear the children." When he continued to stare at her hair with no outward sign that he'd heard the statement, she repeated it. Louder than the first time.

He blinked and shifted his gaze to some spot beyond her, the way he usually did when they were forced to speak to each other. Ana almost sagged in relief. "They seemed well when I saw them earlier. They've not taken ill since then, have they?"

"Their health is perfectly fine, Brother Ian. Perhaps I'm being overcautious, but I've put myself on alert, so to speak, in case they should have a bad dream or need comforting in the middle of the night."

"Have you had to do much of that?" Before she could answer, he rushed on. "I had no idea. I mean, I know it's only natural that they'd miss their mother, and even Maara and Rob must have trouble understanding that she's gone forever, but to be crying in their sleep. I had no idea they would be grieving so deeply."

"Oh, but they're not," she rushed to assure him.

"Crying in their sleep, that is." He looked positively anguished, so in need of comfort himself that she was shocked at how difficult it was to keep herself from comforting him the way she would one of the children. With her arms wrapped around him. His head pillowed against her heart. Her hand smoothing soft circles on his back. Involuntarily, she swayed toward him.

She nearly jumped when her good sense practically screamed: *Ana MacPherson! What are you thinking?* Ian Patterson was a grown man. Words would suffice. Anything else would be unseemly and an embarrassment to them both.

"I just thought that perhaps they *might* cry in the night," she clarified. "They've all put on such a brave front each day, I . . . worried that perhaps in their sleep . . ."

Unable to withstand the pain she saw in his eyes, she dropped her gaze to the floor. "But as I said, you need not worry on that score. They are sometimes less boisterous than is normal for them, but crying? No. Except for the first few nights after . . . after . . ."

She could not bring herself to say the words *Lily's death*. In truth, it was she who sometimes awoke in the middle of the night to the grim knowledge that she would never see her sister again in this life. But it was other things that plagued her sleep far more. Dreams that reflected such covetousness on her part, she couldn't bear to examine them in the light of day.

"Sister? Are you all right?" The feel of a large warm hand upon her shoulder pulled her out of the quagmire of guilt she flailed in whenever she allowed herself to think about those dreams.

She shuddered and quickly stepped away from his reach. "Yes, I'm fine." For a moment his hand hung awkwardly in the space where she'd been. "I'm just tired."

As if it were of the utmost importance that the fringed

ends be straight and untangled, she busied herself with the sash she had knotted at her waist. Anything to occupy her mind so it would not stray to the disturbing thoughts and feelings that plagued her dreams.

"Of course you're tired. Forgive me for disturbing you and for calling you out here in the middle of the night. I should imagine you put in quite a day with those four in there." He tipped his head toward the closed door behind him. "You need your rest. I regret that I've been unable to remain at home in the evenings these past weeks, but I had some rather urgent business that needed to be taken care of before I leave tomorrow."

Relieved that he'd be resuming his normal traveling schedule, she nearly hooted for joy. Instead, she kept an even tone and asked, "How long will you be gone this trip?"

"Two weeks, I think. I wish it weren't necessary, but if all works out as I hope, my traveling will be at a minimum in the future, if at all."

At a minimum? Oh, my stars, what will I do? "The children will be happy to have you at home more," she managed through her despair.

"Home. This place?" He made a derisive sound and swept his gaze down the hallway covered with hand-stenciled wallpaper and heavily carved woodwork. "Well, Lily loved it." Shaking his head, he said, "It'll be a big change for them, but I think— No, I know we'll all be happier and the better for it."

Before Ana could form any comment on his last statements, he pushed away from the door and said, "Ah, but I'm keeping you up unnecessarily. What I have to discuss can wait until another time, perhaps after I'm back from this trip. I'll bid you good night and hope the rest of your night is peaceful."

"Thank you. And . . . and I hope the same for you."

She would have started back through the nursery door, but he was still blocking her way. "Was there something else, Brother Ian?"

He sent her one long, measuring gaze, then shook his head. Frowning, he ran a hand over his face, cleared his throat, and tugged at his collar. "Forgive me, I . . . uh . . . must be more tired than I thought," he said, and started down the hall, muttering as he went.

Ana shook her head in disgust as she let herself into the nursery and made her way to her room.

Spirits. They were an evil that turned even good men into babbling fools. God only knew what was going on in Brother Ian's whiskey-soaked mind.

Chapter Four

As was her habit, Ana was awake at dawn but feeling decidedly out of sorts. She'd been a long time getting back to sleep after the midnight conference with her brother-in-law. The way he'd stared at her hair did not set off any sort of fear but ignited an uncomfortable restlessness deep within her.

An image of Ian's face had floated through her mind most of the night. It haunted her now as she went about her morning's ablutions. Not that salacious grin, disturbing as it had been. Rather, it was the look of tenderness he'd had while gazing upon his sleeping children that she found so disconcerting. And later, the gentle smile when he'd bidden her good night.

And his voice. The sound of each hushed word he'd spoken to her had rippled over her flesh and sent a tingling sensation down her spine and the backs of her legs. Even his scent, that unique mixture of tobacco, fresh air, and bayberry soap, had stimulated her senses. Had it not been for that faint touch of whiskey on his breath, Lord only knew what she might have stammered as they stood together in the candlelit hallway.

Too little sleep and none of it restful made it difficult for her to hold on to her patience as she progressed through the first part of her morning.

First, she had a devilish time getting her thick, curling

mass of hair smoothed back from her face, secured at her nape, and attached securely to her lace cap. Then Jessica's and Maara's hair slipped and slid through her fingers until she gave up trying to force their long locks into plaits and just secured the sides away from their faces with ribbons. The laces snapped on both boys' shoes and had to be knotted together, as no replacements could be found. Buttons had come loose, and she'd stabbed her fingers with the needle several times while stitching them back on.

Despite a lifetime of her father's Christian teachings against such superstitious nonsense, midway through readying the children for the day Ana was ready to believe the nursery had been invaded by a host of mischievous gremlins. Furthermore, she was dangerously close to eschewing all her mother's teachings, stamping her feet, screaming, and perhaps even dashing something breakable upon the floor.

But she did not. Valeriana Grace MacPherson was a lady. A sensible Christian lady. Such behavior was beneath her. Or so she reminded herself repeatedly as she struggled getting four wiggling, boisterous children washed up and dressed.

It was at least thirty minutes past the breakfast hour she'd set when they finally trooped into the dining room. Brother Ian was already at the table. Clear-eyed and rosy-cheeked, he didn't show the slightest sign that he was the worse for a short night of sleep and a long session with a bottle.

Instead of the finely tailored coats and trousers he wore to his office each day, he had on a thick cream sweater that stretched snugly across his shoulders. A bright red scarf was tied nattily about his neck. Altogether, he looked far too bulky, utterly roguish—and too chipper for her peace of mind. *Thank goodness he would be leaving today.*

The broad smile he sent her as he rose from the table did nothing to brighten her day. "Sister," he said, tipping his head to her, and their eyes met for a moment before he lifted his to the cap that crowned her head. He frowned briefly, then turned his smile on his children. "Good morning, children."

Ian's clear-eyed cheerfulness grated on Ana's already frazzled nerves, and she barely mumbled, "Good morning, Brother Ian," before sitting down at the other end of the table. She braced herself for some comment about the lateness of their arrival but none came, by word or even the lifting of a brow. Undoubtedly she'd been saved by the children's chattering. Each of them was excitedly vying for his attention, and he was doing nothing at all to quiet them.

This sort of mayhem before their breakfast must not continue. In order that the body best digest the nourishment put into it, meals should be quiet times beginning with a prayer and proceeding with decorum and restraint.

"Joseph."

The three-year-old didn't hear her. She had to clear her throat twice and finally tap her cup with a spoon to gain his and the others' attention.

"Joseph, I believe it's your turn to say the morning prayer," she reminded when she could be heard.

His eyes tightly closed, the little boy began, "For . . . for . . ." A whispered prompt came from the eight-year-old seated beside him. "For what we . . . we are about to receive . . ."

More whispers from Maara.

"Let . . . us . . . be tru—grateful. Ahhhh-men! Can we eat now?"

How Papa would have disapproved of such irreverence, but it was difficult to maintain a severe pose against the child's charming exuberance. Ana pressed her lips together to keep from laughing. "Yes, Joseph, we may eat now."

She sent up a quick prayer of thankfulness for the joy Joseph and all the children brought to each of her days before leaving her chair to begin the next step in the morning ritual. While she tucked napkins under chins, she reminded Maara and Rob that they ought not dawdle, for they must be off to school soon.

"Mind your aunt Ana, Rob," Ian remarked when his seven-year-old seemed more interested in pulling his elder sister's hair ribbons than spooning his morning oatmeal into his mouth. Ian took out his pocket watch, noted the time, then pushed away from the table with a sigh. "I'm afraid I'm going to have to say good-bye to you all for a little while."

"You're going to captain the *Ulsterman*, aren't you, Da?"

In a stage whisper, the five-year-old, Jessica, informed Ana, "Papa's wearing the special sweater his grandmama made just for him when he went to sea the first time on his grandpapa's ship. He always wears it when he's going to be at the wheel of the *Ulsterman*. That's how Rob knew."

Ian grinned and ruffled his elder son's hair. "Yes, Rob, I'll captain the *Ulsterman* this trip."

Jessica tugged on her father's sweater. All seriousness, as was too much her way, she asked, "When will you come home, Papa?"

Ian scooped the little girl up in his arms and kissed her cheek. "I'm afraid it has to be two weeks this time, sweetheart. Now give your papa a hug that I can carry with me for the whole trip."

In the next several minutes, Ian was given so many hugs he was gasping for breath before the children were finished saying their good-byes. Crouched down at their level, he gathered them around him and said, "Now, I expect you all to mind Aunt Ana while I'm gone. Rob, behave yourself in school and tend to your lessons. I'll expect you to spend some time out in the carriage house with Mr. Ferguson each day. You know he's getting up in years and could use a strong lad like you to help him out.

"Maara, I know I can count on you to help your aunt Ana with the little ones and be a good girl in school as well. I'll be expecting to hear you play a new tune on the piano when I get back.

"Jessie, will you paint a picture for me for each day so I'll know what you've been doing while I've been gone?"

Jessica's giggles immediately stilled. She nodded solemnly as if she'd been given a holy quest. Ana marveled at her brother-in-law's knowledge of his children. Their whole lives it had seemed to her as if he'd been gone more than he'd been home. She never dreamed he'd spent enough time with them to know them so well. With the tasks he'd given them, he touched on the points where they took the most pride as well as the areas where they needed some work.

"And Joe—" Ian hadn't any idea what to suggest and cursed himself for not thinking this parting through more thoroughly. Just what could a little boy barely past his third birthday accomplish in a mere fourteen days?

He scratched his head and narrowed his eyes on the little boy, not having to feign deep thought. He had to think of some task that sounded terribly grown-up or important, lest Joseph feel left out, something he'd vowed would never happen.

The silence stretched out until Ana broke it. "I know Joseph can do it, Brother Ian."

Never had her voice been so welcome. "That's a pretty tall order; are you sure?" he asked, as if he knew what she was talking about, while the reality was he was stalling for time in case she needed it as badly as he did.

Ana came around the table and placed a hand on Joseph's shoulder. "A smart little boy like Joseph won't need two weeks to learn to count all the way to five; he'll be counting that far and further by the time you're back home again. And, with Jessica's help, he'll make sure Patience gets her carrot every day."

Ian stood, and over the children's heads mouthed "Thank you." How she was going to manage to get Joseph to keep his thumb out of his mouth long enough to count all the way to five he couldn't imagine, but he knew she'd certainly try. Ana surely did know how to handle children, and she clearly loved his . . . or, rather, her sister's children. He doubted she allowed herself ever to consider that they were also his. But it didn't really matter what she thought of him personally. He always hated leaving them; this parting so soon after their mother's death was even worse. But it was a comfort to know he was leaving them in capable, loving hands.

"I'll try to be back by supper time on the twentieth." Not trusting his emotions if he went through one more round of hugging, he hefted his sea bag onto one shoulder, touched the bill of his cap in a jaunty salute, and strode briskly out of the house.

Ned Ferguson was just bringing the pony cart up to the front door. Ian paused and talked with his stable master for several minutes. Then, waving again to his children, he turned and began the long trek to the waterfront. While the children shouted more good-byes, Ana remained silent as she watched his long-legged stride take him down the driveway and toward the street.

She gave herself a little shake when she realized just

how much she was admiring Brother Ian's jaunty step and the way he so easily carried his sea bag on his broad shoulder. The children were remarkably quiet now that their father had disappeared around the corner. A little too quiet, she realized as she noted some quivering lower lips and the glistening in their eyes. If she didn't do something to divert their attention, she'd have four weeping children on her hands. While their mother's passing deserved tears, there had been enough weeping in this house during the past several weeks.

"Well, Rob and Maara, you'd best be gathering up your books and slates. Mr. Ferguson and Patience are all ready to take you to school. You don't want to make your pony stand out there waiting very long, do you?" she asked, knowing an appeal for their beloved pony's well-being would set them into motion faster than anything else.

As soon as the older children were off to school, she turned her full attention on the younger ones. Joseph's counting lessons began with counting the steps as they went up them. Three sets of five with a few left over, and she quickly made up a little ditty to fill in the chant. While she gathered up their outer garments for a morning of errands, Jessica helped him count the number of items on the shopping list Ana had made. They counted the steps again on the way down.

The days took on the kind of regularity she thought best for the children. Most days they were able to stay on the schedule she'd set for them. Most days the children were, if not angels, well behaved and a joy.

And some days were so busy and the children so unruly or uncooperative that by the end of the day, she fell into bed completely exhausted. She marveled at the endurance of women who not only had their children to care for but had to do all the cooking, cleaning, washing, and myriad chores needed to maintain a family and home. She found herself thanking God that Brother Ian was so well situated he could afford servants.

With so much to do each day, May 20 arrived quickly. The children had worked hard on the tasks their father had set for them and were eager to share their accomplishments with him. Maara had practiced and practiced a simplified arrangement of a Mozart minuet until the piece surely played through the minds of every member of the household. Rob's school marks were improved, and he had a note from the schoolmaster complimenting his deportment. Jessica's paintings were arranged neatly into a little book held together with a ribbon. It remained to be seen whether Joseph could count to five without having to march up and down the stairs singing that silly song she'd composed for him. But he certainly would try. That is, if he could remember to take his thumb out of his mouth.

Fluffing the gray satin bow she'd just tied in Maara's shining locks, Ana urged her niece toward the cheval glass. "Look, Maara. See how pretty you are today?"

Sighing, the girl tugged at her gray dress. Shaking her head, Maara set her lower lip belligerently and stamped her foot. "I don't look pretty. This dress is ugly. Why can't I wear a pink dress with ruffles?"

"It wouldn't be proper, darling." How did one explain the mourning period to a child? "Simple dresses in dark colors are called mourning clothes, and we wear them because we're all still so very sad about losing your mama."

"But I don't feel sad today, Aunt Ana. I'm happy because Papa's coming home."

"Of course you're happy that your papa is coming

home today, but we must still wear our mourning clothes."

"Will I still have to be sad next week?"

"Yes, darling, I imagine you'll still be sad next week."

"I don't want to be sad after that."

Ana smiled gently and gave Maara's shoulder a little squeeze. "We'll all be a little bit less sad as each week goes by. It's not been quite two months since your mama died. Proper young ladies like you must wear mourning clothes for at least six. It's a way of showing respect for your mama and how much you miss her."

"Why? Mama never wore ugly dresses. She always said ladies should wear pretty clothes so they look pretty because people like pretty ladies best."

Her lower lip quivered when she announced, "Nobody'll ever like me because I don't look like Mama. I look like Papa. I'm just an ugly old red-haired beanpole."

Maara's self-disparaging remarks tore at Ana's heart. Crouching down beside her, she curled her arm around her niece's slender waist. "You're no such thing. Do you think your papa is an ugly ol' beanpole?"

"No . . . Papa's the handsomest man in Cleveland," Maara mumbled, her chin still resting on her chest.

"Well then, the handsomest man in Cleveland surely has a beautiful daughter if she looks like him, doesn't he?"

Maara shrugged. "Maybe . . . but I'm still a beanpole."

"No, darling, you are tall and slender," Ana corrected gently, remembering all too well the teasing she'd endured for her height when she'd been Maara's age. "One day you will be a lady of enviable stature and beauty. You have hair so thick and shiny it is as great a joy to behold as God's own sunsets. You have wondrous blue eyes, as bright and pretty as your mama's. And a perfect

rosebud of a mouth. That's why your mama named you
Maara Rose."

"Mama didn't name me," Maara corrected sulkily.
"She said Rob and I are Papa's children so she made him
name *us*."

Taken aback by the child's tone and the way she em-
phasized "us," Ana curled her arm tighter around her
niece and pulled her close. "You are all your mama's and
your papa's children, sweetheart," she said.

More than once she'd heard her sister remark that Jessica and Joseph were her children and Rob and Maara
were Ian's. Surely Lily hadn't meant anything by it other
than that two of the children had dark hair like hers and
the other two were redheads like their father.

"Parents have different ways of deciding how to name
their children. My mama and papa divided the privilege
of naming their children by Mama choosing our first
name and Papa choosing our middle name. That's why
your mama, Aunt Laurel, Aunt Primula, and I were each
named for a flower and a virtue. Your mama and papa
took turns naming their children for people who were
very special to them."

"Papa said he named me Maara for his grandmama.
She lived in Ireland, where Papa came from. He said he
loved her very much and she was a grand lady. Rose is
for Granna." She smiled, ever so small a smile, but still it
was a smile and Ana relaxed a bit.

"Yes, darling, he did name you for your grandmama
Rose because he likes her very much, too. And because
you are as pretty as the roses in her garden," Ana
declared, wondering about that other grandmother in
Ireland. In all the years Ian had been a part of the
MacPherson family, his grandmother had been the only
relative he'd ever mentioned. And even of her, he'd said

very little beyond what her namesake had just said, and
that she'd died shortly before he'd emigrated.

Seeing her niece's smile beginning to disappear, she
gave her another hug and said brightly, "God made all
the flowers beautiful, each in its own special way. And
He made all little girls beautiful, too. Each in her own
special way."

"Me, too?" Jessica asked, laying her dark head on
Ana's shoulder.

"Of course, you, too, darling." Ana swept her free
arm around her other niece. "Both of you are as pretty as
the prettiest rose in your grandmother's garden."

In a tiny voice, Jessica said, "Roses are mean flowers.
They hurt people. See my thumb? Granna's roses did it."

Ana dutifully kissed the long-healed spot where a rose
thorn had pierced Jessica's tender little thumb. The incident had occurred in early spring. The children had spent
the afternoon at the parsonage. Lily had been off to some
social engagement, or perhaps it had been one of the oc-
casions she'd entertained at home and hadn't wanted the
children underfoot. Ana couldn't remember the exact details, only that Jessica had injured her thumb while playing in the garden that day and that night Lily had died.

Having decided there had been more than enough
serious talk for one day, she swept both girls up in a
fierce hug, growling playfully until the two solemn little
faces cracked and, like a dam bursting, giggles followed.
Ana beckoned to Joseph to join them. To her disappointment, the little boy remained where he was. Today, of all
days, even little Joseph was determined to be stubborn
and uncooperative.

Remembering how her mother's bursts of original
song and the inevitable silliness that followed had been
the source of such fun when she and her sisters were
little, she pretended to fall. Landing with a crinkle and

crackle of heavily starched petticoats and two giggling little girls in her lap, she laughed and beckoned once more for Joseph to join them.

"Please join us, Joseph," she coaxed again. "We can make up songs for everyone's name."

The little boy remained steadfastly where he was, slowly shaking his head. He took his thumb out of his mouth long enough to say, "Gots to look like a proper gen . . . gen'lman for Papa. Can't get wrinkled and messy. You said so."

Ana sighed. As the saying went, she'd just been hoist with her own petard. She had lectured the children at great length about the importance of being tidy in both appearance and habits. And she'd spent endless hours teaching them manners and proper decorum.

"You are exactly right, Joseph. There is a time and a place for all good things. Proper ladies and gentlemen should not be rolling about upon the floor in their best clothes immediately before such an important occasion as their father's homecoming."

Reluctantly, she gently urged the girls to their feet. "Where do you suppose Rob has taken himself?" she asked as she tried to smooth the wrinkles in her apron.

"Here I am, Aunt Ana."

"Oh . . . oh, my." Shaking her head in utter dismay, Ana took in her nephew's appearance. "Oh, Rob, not today."

Mud covered the seven-year-old from the top of his coppery head to the tips of his best shoes. In between, his jacket, shirt, and knee pants were muddied and soaked through. His stockings, equally as disreputable, drooped to his ankles. A small puddle was forming upon the polished floor where he stood shifting his weight from one mud-clumped foot to the other. Muddy footprints and small puddles behind him gave evidence that a trail led all the way to the front door of his father's grand house.

"Robert Kendrick Patterson, you were supposed to stay inside, but you've been out sailing boats in the street again, haven't you?"

Taking in the bright patches on his cheeks and the bluish cast of his lips, she felt her irritation quickly turned to concern. "Whatever were you thinking, Rob Patterson? You'll be down with a fever if we don't get you warmed up."

Undaunted, Rob beamed as he held up the model sailboat his father had made for him. "My boat won! Wait till Da hears about it."

"I'm sure your father will be pleased his design won the day, but not so pleased if he returns to find you sick abed." Her tone was sharper than it probably should have been given Rob's delight in his win. Papa would not have been swayed by a bright smile and such a show of pride. He would have cut a fresh switch from one of the trees and firmly applied it to Rob's backside for such a breach in conduct.

"Spare the rod and spoil the child" and "We are all born from sin" and " 'Tis a parent's duty to drive the evil out of his children" were his mottoes when it came to child rearing. But Rob's pride in his boat's achievement was so great and such a joyous thing to behold, she couldn't think there was any evil in anything he'd done. None of Lily's children were bad children, just full of energy and bright intelligence that wanted only firm direction.

"I'm sure your boat is quite the most wonderful in all of Cleveland. And you, Rob Patterson, are a fine sailor, but I do wish you'd not ventured out in the midst of a storm to sail your boat."

More to herself than to Rob, she muttered as she started divesting Rob of his wet, sopping clothing. "Something absolutely must be done about Euclid Street. It's a disgrace that the street running in front of the town's finest residences is turned into a river every time it rains."

"Wouldn't be as much fun, though," Rob managed between chattering teeth. The mischief twinkling in his eyes was reminiscent of the light that so often shone from his father's. Ana could only pray he didn't inherit any of the man's faults as well.

Adding another muddied garment to the pile building on the floor, she glanced worriedly at the clock on the nursery mantel. It was already five o'clock. Supper would have to be set back.

"Maara, go ask Gerta if she would hold supper until six and if she could send up plenty of hot water. Also, ask her to have one of the Marys see to the trail your brother has left behind him. Mind you, be careful you don't slip as you go down the stairs."

All of the thirty minutes and then some were spent ridding Rob of the mud. Finally, when he was once again clean, warm, and dressed respectably, Ana lined the children up for a last inspection and nodded her approval.

"Good, good, you look very fine," she said, giving Jessica's sash one slight adjustment.

Maara tugged again at her dress. "Mama wore extra-special pretty dresses when Papa came home from his trips. Please, can't we dress up today? You, too."

"My dress will be just fine," Ana said firmly. She began shedding her soiled apron. "A fresh apron is all that's needed to set me to rights."

Her features clearly reflecting her stubborn streak, Maara shook her head. Grabbing a handful of the black linen that was the mainstay of her aunt's wardrobe, she started tugging her toward the doorway. "Come on, we'll find you a pretty dress. There's lots of them in Mama's room."

"No . . . no. I couldn't wear your mama's dresses. They're much too small for me."

It was a sound argument, for Lily had been such a dainty little woman and Ana was taller and more full-figured. But even had she and Lily been the same size, she could not have blithely helped herself to her dead sister's wardrobe. Bright-colored silk gowns with fancy trims had been right for someone like Lily, and perhaps they could be made over for her daughters someday. Simply designed gowns of dark, practical fabrics were quite sufficient and just right for someone like herself, even when she wasn't in mourning.

She glanced at the little porcelain clock on the nursery's mantel again. Since Brother Ian was not yet home, perhaps they should push supper back another thirty minutes or more. Then she'd have time to reattach a bow or ruffled trim to the girls' dresses. Lily had so loved pretty things. Even in mourning, her daughters could dress more prettily, and their papa coming home was cause for celebration.

"Come, children," she said, briskly leading them toward her small room adjoining the nursery. Not for anything was she going to let a single one of them out of her sight.

"Jessica, would you bring my sewing basket? Maara, can you find the box of trims we took off your dresses? I think it would be all right to pretty up your dresses just a little bit."

"And you, too, Aunt Ana."

Chapter Five

With nervous fingers, Ana plucked at the lace bertha the children had coaxed her to wear over her dress. It was Lily's, of course, one of the many furbelows stuffed in a box on a high shelf, purchased during one of Lily's many shopping sprees but never worn. Accompanying it was a pair of lace cuffs. They were simple accoutrements by Lily's standards but exquisitely made. Ana could only imagine the cost of the set, knowing it was more expensive than anything she had ever owned.

They'd even coaxed her to leave off her cap and wear a pair of their mother's decorative combs. She'd chosen the simplest in the collection, ivory with fluted edges. The small cameo she wore at her throat was her own. But it, too, had been purchased with Ian Patterson's money, for it had been a gift from Lily.

Glancing at herself in the cheval mirror, she was sure Ian would take one look at her and brand her as an opportunist for making so free with his wife's things. Ana would have removed it all would such an action not have disappointed the children. The girls had so enjoyed prettying up their dresses and hers. Their excitement had even infected the boys, and dinner had taken on a party atmosphere. Or would have had their father arrived in time to join them.

Now and again she glanced at the bank of Palladian

windows that filled the large dormer dominating the end of the nursery. The wind rushed against the house, setting shutters and windowpanes rattling. The rain was so heavy, visibility couldn't be more than a few feet. She didn't need to see it to know that the lake was a frothing mass of high waves.

"Don't worry, Aunt Ana. Da's a good sailor, and the *Ulsterman*'s the steadiest sloop ever made. That storm out there won't bother him a bit. He'll be home tonight," Rob announced, with all the certainty only a seven-year-old would muster under the circumstances.

"Yes, he is, Rob, but good sailors know when to seek harbor. That storm has worsened considerably since afternoon. Your papa may have put in at Sandusky, or even Toledo."

"I stay awake till Papa comes home," Joseph announced before shoving his thumb back in his mouth. Obviously struggling to keep his eyes open, he nestled his dark head more comfortably against Ana's bosom.

"Me, too," Jessica said, as droopy-eyed as her brother.

Resigned that the children would not be persuaded their father was not going to be home anytime soon, and most probably not even tonight, Ana sighed. "I think perhaps you all would be more comfortable waiting for your papa in your beds."

Before there were any more protests, she set aside the storybook she'd been reading to them. Jessica was already asleep by the time Ana carried her across the room and tucked her into her bed. She'd just slipped Joseph into his bed and tucked his rag doll into his arms when the nursery door swung open and clattered against the wall.

As if blown in by the winds battering the house, Ian Patterson rushed into the room. Without warning, he caught her at her waist and danced her around the room, then planted a kiss squarely on her lips. "I'm that glad to be home and out of that storm," he declared, then set her aside and opened his arms to his children. "Anyone in here happy to see their old da?"

With squeals of delight, Rob and Maara raced across the room and into their father's arms. The commotion aroused the little ones. Mere seconds later all four of her charges were tumbling all over their father.

Stumbling to the edge of the room, Ana strove to overcome the shock of Ian's lips pressed upon hers. No man had ever dared so much. The kiss had been brief, assuredly, no more than a fraternal buss, borne of nothing more than his gladness at being home safe and sound. That was all. But the taste lingered—rain and something else she couldn't begin to name, only that it was sweet and fresh and stirred a yearning for more.

Setting aside her shock from his kiss, she let herself share in the children's joy in their father's return. She actually started toward the squirming mass of arms and legs rolling about on the floor before pulling herself up short. Giving herself a mental shake, she reminded herself that this exuberant behavior was entirely inappropriate at this late hour.

Papa had never allowed—

A lump formed in her throat before she could finish her thought. Papa would never have allowed such a show of unrestrained joy and affection at any hour. She couldn't remember a time when when her father had actually played with her and her sisters. Certainly never like Brother Ian played with his children.

Watching the joyous reunion the children were having with their father, she found herself wishing she could join in. Wishing that the brief kiss had been something other than a spontaneous aberration. How wonderful to be held close, safe and protected within strong, masculine arms. Looked upon as Ian looked upon his children . . . with genuine happiness for just being.

Not by Brother Ian, of course. Save for that night before he'd left, she couldn't remember a time when he'd ever really looked at her. She certainly didn't want him looking at her again that way. Or, *heaven forbid*, to kiss her again.

It would be far safer for her peace of mind if he returned to looking at her with disdain or challenge, or if he just plain looked past her, as if she were invisible. The way he'd done since that first moment he'd clapped eyes on Lily.

Vicariously, she enjoyed the happy frolicking a bit longer before her responsible side won out over the whimsical. She'd caught barely a glimpse of Ian before the children had covered him. But it had been enough to discern that his clothing was plastered wetly to his body.

Clearly he was soaked to the skin. The children's nightshirts were sopping up the moisture like sponges. She'd be lucky if they weren't all down with the ague come morning.

"Come . . . come . . . stop this. You'll catch your deaths." When her cry went unheeded, she started lifting her nieces and nephews away from their father. "Brother Ian, have a care! You're getting them all wet."

Her words evidently permeated the merriment, for he had the good grace to sober his behavior considerably. "Go sit upon the hearth, children. While you warm yourselves before the fire, I'll tell you about my surprise."

The promise of a surprise worked like magic. The children raced across the room and lined themselves up on the raised hearth.

Rolling lithely to his feet, Ian plucked at his soggy sweater. He sent her a look that upon anyone else might have been one of chagrin and sincere apology; but his eyes still sparkled, and his mouth looked too ready to break into a careless grin. "I should have changed before I charged up here, but I was already so late, and frankly I didn't realize how very wet I was."

"Humph." Turning on her heel, she marched across the room and started extracting clean, dry nightshirts, socks, and quilts. On her way to the children, she flung one of the quilts at him with more force than she'd intended.

The quilt would have hit him in the face had he not caught it midair. "Thank you, Sister." The way he crooked one brow and grinned at her set off a fluttering deep in her belly that was most disturbing. "By the way, I like what you've done with your hair. Always thought it a shame to hide such pretty hair beneath a cap." His gaze swept her from head to toe. "You look . . . different. Very nice. Very nice, indeed."

For a moment, she felt like a dreamy-eyed young girl must feel after being paid a compliment by an equally dreamy-eyed beau. But she was no dreamy-eyed girl, and he was most certainly not her beau, dreamy-eyed or anything else. Collecting her wits, she turned her back on him and busied herself distributing dry things to the children.

"We're ready, Da!" Rob exclaimed as he pulled on the pair of warm socks Ana handed him. "What's the surprise?"

"Hmmm, did I say I had a surprise?"

Four little heads bobbed in unison.

"Then I'd best go fetch it."

The quilt wrapped about his shoulders, he disappeared into the hallway and returned again dragging his sea bag behind him. A mischievous grin on his face, he pulled the bag slowly across the floor, making an exaggerated show of strain. "It's such a very, very, very large surprise, your Papa can't even lift it."

The children were wide-eyed and giggling at their father's clownish behavior. It was a relief that his full attention was upon them, but much more of this and she'd never get them settled down for the night. Braving his attention, she said, "Brother Ian, I really do think tomorrow would be a better time for presents. The children—"

"Tomorrow!"

"Aunt Ana!"

"Want it now!"

These and other protests chorused from the children and their father. Ana knew she was defeated. "Oh, all right, tonight it is." Her acquiescence raised a round of cheers and applause. She included her brother-in-law when she shook a stern finger at the lot of them. "But only if you quiet down. Surprise or not, this is not the time of day to be dancing about and making so much noise."

"Your aunt is right, children," Ian said as he dragged a chair near the hearth. "Rest is very important so that you stay well and grow strong."

"I'm strong already," Rob chirped.

"Me, too," Jessica echoed.

"Ladies are delicate, not strong, Jessie," Maara informed her little sister with all the superiority three scant years of seniority afforded her.

In reaction to the rebuke, Jessica pushed out her lower lip and ducked her head. Ian patted his knee to coax his five-year-old daughter to his lap. "Ladies are strong in different ways than men." Once the little girl was settled on his lap, he tipped her little chin up and smoothed her lip back in place with a brush of his thumb. "They may not be able to carry as heavy a weight in pounds, but they are just as strong as men in their will and determination. Some women are even more strong-willed than men. Is that not so, Sister?"

Disarmed by his sensitive handling of Jessica, Ana was unprepared for his query and the challenging grin that accompanied it. As rattled by his direct gaze as she'd been by his kiss, she was saved from stammering a response when he turned his attention to rooting around in the bag until he'd extracted a small, flat parcel wrapped in oilskin.

"What kind of surprise is that?" Rob asked in a voice heavy with disappointment. The other children's expressions reflected the same.

"Now, children, you will be grateful for whatever it is and thank your papa properly," Ana prompted softly.

Ian could not fault them; the pieces of heavy parchment he unfolded were not the usual sort of presents he brought home from his travels. "What I have here, children, are two sketches of our new house. The first I did myself. It's how it looked yesterday when I was on the island. The other is by the architect, and it's how it will look by the end of the summer when it's all finished and ready for us to live in."

A gasp from Ana was the first response to his announcement. He'd expected that. Lily had hated the idea of purchasing the island, let alone living on it. And with someone like Lily, it had been a hopeless cause to attempt to explain why it would be best for the children and, most of all, for her.

Of course, the preacher hadn't liked the idea either. MacPherson positively could not sanction being parted by any distance greater than a city block from his darling Lily. And since he was certain Valeriana never entertained a thought that wasn't her father's, it stood to reason she'd be opposed, too.

Well, Ana wasn't his wife, and she wouldn't have to move there with the family. He really didn't care what she or any of the MacPhersons thought.

But the children's wide-eyed silence bothered him. A lot. "Come now, children, we talked about this before, and you were all very excited about it."

Hoping to jog their memories and renew their enthusiasm, he said, "Remember how I told you I was going to look for someone to run the shipping line for me, so I wouldn't have to travel hardly ever? Well, I've found someone. Captain Krupp, you all remember him, don't you? He captains one of my big ships and sometimes serves as my first mate on the *Ulsterman*. We talked about it during this trip, and I've persuaded him to take over the running of Patterson Shipping by the end of the summer. Once we've moved to the island, I can focus all my attention on the logging and mining operations and—"

This was all going right over their heads, Ian realized as he looked from one little face to another. "Why the sad faces?"

"Will Patience move with us?" Jessica asked.

"Of course your pony will move with us. You will take all your things with you. All your toys and your clothes."

"Will we get there on the *Ulsterman*?" Rob asked, clearly warming to the idea.

"Yes, and we'll use the *Ulsterman* to go back and forth to the mainland whenever we need to," Ian told him, relieved to be able to expound upon something he hoped would pump some enthusiasm about the move. "There's a nice natural harbor on the southeastern corner of the island where we'll keep her and any other boats we might acquire. I was thinking that we ought to get a smaller sailboat we could use for fishing and little trips around the edge of the island, perhaps over to some of the other islands nearby. When you're big enough, all of you can learn to sail."

Encouraged by the gradual brightening of the children's expressions, he expounded further. "You'll learn to swim, too. There are lots of things you can do on the island. Part of it is thick forest, and there are some very interesting rock formations on it. Some of them have pictures drawn on them by the Indians who lived there a long time ago."

Her eyes wide, Maara shivered. "They aren't like the Indians in Iowa, are they?"

"No, darlin'. Very different, and besides, no Indians have lived on the island for a very long time." Ian reached toward her to give her a reassuring pat, sorry now that he'd encouraged her to read the newspaper. The coverage of the Black Hawk Indian wars had been far too sensational for someone of her tender years. "If there were Indians still living on the island, your papa would not have bought it."

"If Indians were over there, you and me would get our guns and protect our womenfolk, wouldn't we, Da?"

"We Patterson men will always protect our womenfolk, Rob, but I don't expect anyone's going to declare war on us, so we'll have no need for guns. We aren't the sort of men who put people off their lands.

"You know, children, I think you should have more than Patience as a pet once we get to the island. What would you think about a dog, maybe two?"

"You mean it, Da?" Rob's smile glowed as brightly as his hair. "A dog? A big one? Big enough to keep away any ol' Indians that think to come back to our island."

"The dog might be a big one if you like, but it won't need to protect us from Indians."

"The only wild Indian on Patterson Island will be you,

Rob Patterson," Maara inserted with a glare at her brother. Smiling sweetly at her father, she asked, "Can we all have our own pet?"

"You can have as many pets as you can take care of," Ian assured her. "It's a wonderful life we'll all have on that island," he added, ruffling Rob's and Joseph's hair and winking at his daughters.

A sideways glance at Valeriana revealed she'd tightened her lips to such a thin line that they'd all but disappeared. It was really too bad; she'd looked quite attractive earlier when she'd been standing off to one side as the children had greeted him. There had been a sparkle of something that he'd interpreted as actual gladness to see him. A softness in her eyes as she'd watched his reunion with the children. Almost a look of yearning, as if she'd wanted to join in, and during those moments, he'd actually wished she had. A woman greeting him with real gladness for his return would have completed the circle.

Perhaps he was more exhausted than he thought and was seeing things that weren't really there. Whatever he'd seen had vanished as soon as he'd mentioned the island. Her expression had grown steadily stiffer ever since.

The chime of the clock on the mantel undoubtedly explained her displeasure. He didn't have to feign his large yawn. "Ten bells, mates. Long past time good sailors were in bed."

"I'll take the first watch." Rob would have set up a march around the perimeter of the room had Ian not grabbed a handful of his nightshirt and brought him up short.

"Grown-ups take the night watch, young man." Ian included all his children when he added, "Sailors your age are only on day watch. To your bunks, all of you."

Though the children scampered to their beds, they

were far too excited for sleep. Clearing her throat, Ana stepped forward. "Brother Ian, the children are understandably excited that you're home. I think they'll settle down more easily if you say your good nights quickly and take yourself off."

As if he were a naughty child, he was being dismissed. Ian was surprised she hadn't added "to your room," or sent him to a chair facing a corner. "Until tomorrow, children. Your aunt is right; you should be asleep."

Her attention anywhere but on him, Ana busied herself turning down the lamps as Ian moved from bed to bed, murmuring a few words to each child before brushing their brows with a kiss.

That island! Lily was hardly cold in her grave and he was making plans to move the children to that isolated, godforsaken island!

By the look of the building's progress already, it must have been started long before Lily's death. Lily had said nothing about a house. He must have had it started behind her back. With Lily gone, there was no one to stop him from moving the children away and never allowing them to return for even a visit with their mother's family. Or for Lily's family to visit them in return.

Squeezing her eyes shut, she tried not to reveal her distress at the very idea that in a few short weeks, she might never see her nieces and nephews again. *Oh, how could he do such a thing?* He was heartless, cruel and—and a host of other things that by tomorrow, perhaps, her brain would be better able to call up.

To think she'd actually been glad to see him. She'd been so relieved he'd made it through the storm safely, she might very well have flung herself at him if he hadn't snatched her up first.

That thought made her press her hands to her suddenly burning cheeks. *Oh, my stars, what has come over me?* The storm had obviously rattled more than the windowpanes.

By morning, the storm outside had long since quieted. Not so Ana's emotions. She'd spent another restless night, and all because of the man sitting at the opposite end of the table. Mercifully, the children were as excited this morning to see their father as they'd been last night. For once, she didn't try to quiet them. Their laughter and happiness were infectious, and as the meal progressed, the oppression she'd awakened with lifted, and she was even able to set aside any thoughts about the island.

That is, until Rob asked, "Are there wild animals on the island, Da?"

"I'm told there are a few wild hogs still roaming about."

"Wild hogs!" Ana gasped. Never in all her worrying about that island had she thought it might be home to dangerous animals.

"Only a few hogs, and they pretty much stay to themselves in the woods at the far end of the island," Ian supplied, and reached for the pot of preserves. As if dangerous beasts roaming the island were of no more consequence than a flock of doves, he calmly spread his toast with the preserves and answered Rob's questions about the size and all manner of habits of wild hogs.

Ana could not believe he could be so callous as to consider moving his children to such a dangerous place. Her mind began racing with images of terrible scenarios. Her stomach clenched, and bile rose in her throat. She reached for her cup of morning tea and managed to get it to her lips without spilling it.

Semirestored, she managed, "Ah . . . Rob, perhaps your questions could wait until this evening. I believe I heard Mr. Ferguson drive the cart to the door. You mustn't make Patience wait long for you."

What followed was a flurry of farewell hugs and then several hectic moments of gathering up books and coats before Maara and Rob were out the door. Determined that they must give their pony a morning pat, their little brother and sister were right on their heels. The pony cart was just heading down the driveway when Ana saw her sisters turning in. She'd never been so happy to see them in her life. With the little ones out of the house for a while, this morning was the perfect time to have a talk with Brother Ian. *Wild hogs, indeed!* What was he thinking?

"Jessica. Joseph. Go fetch your coats, hats, and mittens. Aunt Primmy and Aunt Laurel have come to take you to visit Grandpapa and Granna."

Closing the door to keep out the cold, she thought to wait there for her sisters until she saw one of the Marys hovering nearby. "My sisters are coming up the drive, Mary. Will you let them in while I make sure the children gather up their things?"

"Of course, miss."

Halting at the dining room doorway before she followed the little ones upstairs, she saw that Ian had resumed reading his newspaper. "Might I have a word with you, Brother Ian?" She checked the watch pinned to her bodice. "In the parlor at the top of the hour?"

Chapter Six

Reaching for the parlor's brass doorknob, Ana hesitated and stepped backward, taking an even breath. "Be calm and rational," she reminded herself. If there was any hope at all that she'd get that man to see reason, it would be best to remain calm and rational.

"Are you daft, Brother Ian?" The accusation popped out without any direction from her brain the minute she pushed open the door. So much for calm and rational.

Not showing the slightest hint of surprise, Ian took a sip of coffee. Setting down the fragile china cup without so much as a rattle, he quietly answered, "I don't believe so, Sister."

His calm made her want to scream at him. Tamping down the scream, she paced the width of the room and then back again.

"If moving your children to an island inhabited by man-killing beasts isn't daft, I surely cannot imagine what is. Lily hated the very idea of moving to that island. Lord only knows what she would have thought had she known about the feral beasts populating it. In her absence, I simply cannot stand by quietly and allow you to put her children in harm's way."

Ian raised a brow, restraining himself, just, from reminding her in the clearest of terms that she was in no position to allow or disallow any decision he made about his family. Hiding behind his newspaper, he reminded himself that her remarks were motivated strictly by concern for the children's safety, and he did appreciate that. It had been foolish even to mention the hogs. No need to provide even more ammunition for the war the MacPhersons had been waging against this move ever since he'd bought the island.

"The children will be less in harm's way because of the hogs."

"You are surely daft if you think feral hogs are some sort of watchdogs warding off even more dangerous creatures from the island. Are you suggesting they are keeping wolves away from the island?"

"I don't believe wolves have ever been a problem on the island, but rattlesnakes were a serious infestation at one time," Ian told her.

"Rattlesnakes!" Valeriana gasped, spread her hand across her heart, and stumbled backward. "Oh, dear God, it's worse than any of us thought. The island is infested with poisonous snakes, too?"

"Not now, thanks to the hogs purposely placed there several years ago. Helpful animals are hogs. They've eradicated the snakes from the island. They're no longer a problem, and I've already made arrangements to hunt down the remaining hogs."

Ian resettled himself upon the divan and hoped she was appeased by that answer. His newspaper before him once more, he tried to lose himself in an article on the second page. For a change, the details of the Compromise Tariff Act recently adopted by Congress could not hold his attention. Instead, he saw an image of Valeriana's eyes floating across the page.

Usually they were quite a lovely shade of blue, almost lavender. Just now they'd put him in mind of the deep gray-blue sky over Lake Erie yesterday, just before thunder had begun to rumble and black clouds had rolled in. Any sailor with good sense headed for safe harbor when he saw a sky turn that particular shade of dark gray-blue.

The swish and crackle of her starchy petticoats warned him she'd turned away from the window and had taken to pacing again. He was in for some stormy weather, all right. By now those eyes must be flashing lightning.

"How can you remove your children from everything familiar so soon after they've lost their mother?"

Holding his own temper in check, Ian barricaded himself behind the fragile safety of his newspaper. "I think new surroundings, away from this house and reminders of their mother, would be better for them."

Ana gasped. "You would have them forget her?"

Dangerously close to giving her an earful of just why that would be a good idea, Ian reminded himself that Ana was exceedingly loyal to her family. And particularly protective of Lily.

"Not forget her, but forget the details surrounding her death." Setting aside his newspaper, he gestured around him. "This room, for example. Have you noticed that none of the children have stepped foot in it since Lily died?"

Rising, he began to pace about, as agitated as Ana had been. "They used to come in here often. I sat upon the divan over there and read to them. We played checkers on the floor in front of the fireplace. I daresay Maara wouldn't have ever touched the spinet again if it weren't still in the dining room where it was moved to make space for Lily's bier."

His words hung in the room, and in the silence that followed, Ian was swept back to that time so long ago when he'd been barely Rob's age. A long and steady line of people had streamed in and out of that house, too, just as they had here. But there had been no one comforting and caring for a little boy who'd not understood why his beautiful mother was lying so still and pale on a bier surrounded by candles.

He shook away the memory and the emotions that always accompanied it. At least his children had a father who loved them and an aunt who'd totally astonished him with the kind of care she gave them.

Though she was sometimes stern, and was usually stiff and downright prickly around him, he'd seen the easy way she had of curling an arm around a child, sweeping him or her into a hug, and—*Lord Almighty!*—she actually laughed and sang with them. Not when she knew he was around, but during those times when she thought herself alone with them.

It was a shame she hid that side of herself so much. He quite liked it. Perhaps that was why he'd kissed her last night—wanting to share for just a moment in some of the warmth she showered on his children.

Oh, for God's sake. He wasn't that desperate for affection. He'd just been so drunk with relief to have made it through that storm and so glad to be home, he'd felt like kissing a woman, and she'd been the first one at hand. It hadn't had a thing to do with having been haunted every night of the damned trip with images of her standing in her nightgown, all her glorious, sweet-smelling hair hanging loose down her back.

The woman in question broke the silence and—blessedly—his ruminations. "Perhaps the room could be redecorated and refurnished," she offered. "Families don't move every time they've suffered a death."

"No, they don't," he allowed, gentling his tone markedly in the light of her reasonable suggestion. "But I can afford to move and had planned to do so anyway.

The house was well under construction by the time Lily died. I shall always believe that your sister would have been quite happy there once we were settled in."

Ana let out a great gusting sigh. He hoped it was a sign of resignation and correspondingly released some of the tension he was feeling. But she began to pace again, worrying her handkerchief as she walked. His hopes fled that the matter was solved and they might spend the rest of this day well beyond each other's company.

"You cannot mean to remove young, motherless children from kith and kin and set them down in a wilderness. Papa will simply not allow his grandchildren to be subjected to such deprivations."

"Frankly I don't give one iota what your fa—" He didn't finish the statement but let his own exasperation show with a long gusting breath. "They'll hardly be deprived. It's a beautiful island, and I will provide well for them there."

"You provide well enough for them right here," Ana said, knowing well enough it was an understatement. The truth was Ian Patterson provided extremely well. This was possibly the finest house in all of Cleveland, and the children wanted for absolutely nothing, save their mother.

Seemingly oblivious to her remark, he began to expound upon the island's merits. "Beyond its beauty, the island has acres and acres of hardwood forest for lumbering. Of course, lumbering can't go on indefinitely, but the limestone is virtually limitless and just waiting to be quarried. Lumber and limestone are valuable materials on today's market, Sister, and I stand to make a considerable profit."

His enthusiasm for the island's potential was infectious but not enough to sway her. "Your children don't have to live there for you to turn a profit."

Straightening, Ian fixed his gaze so directly upon her she was hard put to keep from cringing. "But *I* want to live there, and the children will live there with me. They are *my* children."

Ana opened her mouth to speak and then thought better of it. The man was right. The children were his, not hers. That simple truth took the wind from her sails, and she sank onto the nearest chair. Still, she hoped for a little bit more time, time in which some miracle would change his mind. "But Brother Ian, only two months ago, the children lost their mother. Must they be uprooted from the only home they've ever known so soon?"

"I think they'll adjust quite fine, Sister. They've known about the island for close to a year, and it'll be another two, maybe three months before the house is ready to live in."

Two months. If he'd said a year, five years, even ten, it would never be the right time to move the children to that horrid island. They belonged where they were. In Cleveland where she and the rest of their mother's family could see to their upbringing. She supposed that would not be reason enough to sway him, and instead tried, "They have such a wonderful life here."

"They'll have an even better life on the island."

"Running wild? No friends? No school?" She was horrified anew at the images that sprang to her mind of her beloved nieces and nephews running barefoot and ragtag on a remote island. "Oh, dear Lord, would you have them turn heathen and forget everything they know?"

"A site has already been chosen for a school. And one for a church as well. Even such as I will not have my children grow up ignorant or heathen."

Ana winced at the sarcasm in his words. Her accusation had been uncalled for. She knew how important the children's education was to Ian. And he'd made sure the children were in church every Sunday and said their prayers at meals and bedtime.

Fighting the lump forming in her throat, she said, "An island school, even if it has a good schoolmaster, will still mean the children will be wrenched away from the only life they've ever known." *And from me.*

Who would look after them? Make sure they learned their manners? Nurse them if they were ill, or hold them when they were hurt in body or soul? Whoever it was wouldn't be her, that was certain. Even for the children's sakes, it just wouldn't do for her, an unmarried woman, to move to the wilds with her brother-in-law.

Though her living under Ian Patterson's roof these past weeks had stretched propriety, the city's gossips hadn't voiced a word of censure. And there had never been the slightest indication on her brother-in-law's part that he harbored any licentious thoughts toward her. Oh, there had been the way he had looked at her hair and then that kiss last night when he returned. But they didn't mean anything, and she was sure nothing even close would ever happen again. Not here.

But . . . away from the close proximity of her parents? Civilization? On a godforsaken island out in the middle of Lake Erie? Born with the century, Ian Patterson was a man in his prime. His carnal desires would not have died with his wife.

She pressed her crumpled handkerchief to her lips. No, she wouldn't be going to the island with the children, and the thought made her heart ache and her arms feel already empty of the only children she thought ever to rear.

The tears that had been steadily gathering in Ana's eyes spilled over her lids. Not a mere trickling but a veritable flood ran down her cheeks. Her body shook with the force of her sobs, which were nearly as loud as her ranting had been.

Involuntarily, Ian reached a hand toward her shoulder and gave her an awkward pat. "Now, now, Sister, don't take on so."

"I—I am not ta-taking on. I—I do not ta-take on."

"Of course you don't. I'm sorry you are so distressed by this move." Disconcerted by her tears, he continued to pat her shoulder.

Shrugging away from his touch, she managed, "You—need not c-c-concern yourself," and fled across the room. "How could you possibly understand how I feel?"

"How indeed?" Ian asked of the room's ceiling, his hand still hanging in midair. Save for her fire-and-brimstone–preaching father, she didn't credit any male over the age of fourteen with having any merit, let alone any sensitivity. Considering the looks she had given him throughout each of Lily's pregnancies, Valeriana judged him a rutting beast of the field.

Well, this beast would be wise to leave "her holiness" alone and untouched with her misery. Intent on doing just that, he started toward the door. He made the mistake of looking back at her just when the sun decided to peek from behind the clouds.

Filtered through the mullioned panes, the light glanced off her silly little white cap, highlighting the nimbus of wispy curls that had loosened around her face. Instead of the almost blue-black that had been Lily's hair color, Ana's was a deep rich brown with touches of gold and deep red. The colors glistened in the sun's light, as if a fire smoldered somewhere deep within, waiting only for the right moment to burst forth in—

Good Lord! Ian shook his head to rid it of the direction his thoughts were roaming. Next he'd be imagining that the highlights in her hair indicated the existence of fiery passions deep within her soul. The only fiery passions that burned within Valeriana Grace MacPherson were for the temperance movement and for the dogmatic fire spouted at every opportunity by her father.

She sighed softly and turned ever so slightly when she lifted her hand to the fringed edge of the silk drape. The adjustment in her position gave Ian a view of her profile.

As if they were iron filings pulled by a lodestone, his eyes were drawn to her bosom, still rising and falling overrapidly beneath the fluttering lawn fichu caped about her shoulders, crossing her chest, and trailing a few inches beyond her waist.

Viewed from the side, the fullness of her breasts was not camouflaged by the yards of flowing lace-edged lawn. Unbidden, images of how her breasts might look unconfined and resting in his hands came to his mind, causing warmth to pool in his loins.

Damn! He really was a beast if he was ogling Valeriana MacPherson's breasts and getting hard while doing it. He'd been too long without a woman; that was for certain. Maybe he ought to pay Susan Donavan a visit, after all. An audible catch of Ana's breath brought his gaze quickly back to the safer territory of her head.

"Have you considered how lonely the children will be without their friends?"

So relieved was he to see that she was still looking out the window and unaware of his lascivious perusal, Ian didn't register her softly worded query. Her head was no more neutral territory than was her spectacular bosom.

Before he could direct his thoughts toward safer waters, he found himself marveling at the smooth lines of her cheek and the apparent soft dewiness of her skin. Her ears were delicate shells that enticed no less tantalizingly than the full curve of her breasts.

She turned abruptly, and he found himself staring

directly into her tear-drenched eyes. Her lips were slightly puffy and beckoned for more than the too brief sampling he'd had last night. Involuntarily, he took a step toward her.

"Brother Ian! Have you gone deaf as well as daft? I asked if you'd considered how lonely your children will be without their friends?"

Brought up short, he willingly agreed that he'd gone daft. A thorough kissing of the most prim, most pious, and most stern of the women in Cleveland, possibly of the entire Northwest Territory? The woman's presence in his household had turned him into a madman. "The children will make new friends."

"Hmmph! And what playmates would they be? Spawn of the wild hogs?"

He welcomed the return of her anger, as it brought him back to his senses. Tamping down a resurgence of his own anger, he responded, "There'll be plenty of children on the island."

"And just where will these children come from? Do they just spring from the trees and rocks on that island?"

Carefully keeping his tone steady, he explained, "Most of the men I've hired to work the quarry and forest are married. They'll be bringing their wives and children to the island as soon as houses are built for them. There should be enough children to fill a school."

Ana pulled her handkerchief from her sleeve and dabbed at her eyes. "Whole families? I can't imagine any family wanting to live in the middle of a lake so very far away from civilization."

"Well, a family has, and for several years. The Bercots, and they're as fine a group of gentlemen as you could find anywhere."

"Bercot?" Ana turned abruptly, a look of unadulterated horror on her face. "Frenchmen?"

"I suppose they're of French descent, but they're from Canada. There are three of them. Henri is the eldest. A man perhaps ten years older than myself." He settled himself once again upon the divan and reached for the newspaper, glad for something other than Ana's magnificent bosom and hair to hold his gaze.

"Then Eduard, only a year or two younger than Henri," he said absently as he scanned the headlines. Distracted by a headline, he took a moment or two before he continued. "And, oh, yes, Henri's son, Jaie. Around twenty is my guess."

"Is there a Mrs. Bercot?"

Engrossed in the news, Ian was barely aware that Ana had asked him a question until she forced his attention. "Brother Ian! I asked if these Bercot men have wives?"

Looking over the top of the paper briefly, Ian replied simply, "No."

"Papists *and* bachelors!" She was across the room in a flash.

Snatching the newspaper away, she tossed it aside. "You get them off that island, Ian Patterson. If my sister's children must go live in the wilderness, they'll not share it with papists! Indecent ones at that!"

Before he could offer a word of contradiction, she launched into such a tirade, Ian shut her out as he retrieved the newspaper and put it back in order. He'd heard this diatribe before, and though it was Ana delivering the drivel, it was as if his father-in-law were right here in the parlor. While he'd not had a lifetime of indoctrination the way Ana had, nine years as John MacPherson's son-in-law were more than enough for him to be able to recite the litany as easily as his daughter.

According to MacPherson, the Reformed Church founded by John Calvin was the only true church. The members of the other Protestant sects were to be thought of as errant children who would someday see the light. But those poor souls who worshiped in the old faith of the pre-Reformation days were beyond redemption. Worse even than a heathen, for the heathens could be excused for being ignorant.

On the subject of marriage, MacPherson was just as dogmatic. Unmarried men beyond the age of thirty were suspect of all manner of debauchery because they lacked the civilizing influence of a woman. And an unmarried Roman Catholic? Well, it didn't bear thinking what terrible mischief colored their lives.

Finally Ian had had enough. "Hogwash!"

"Wh-what did you say?"

"Hogwash," Ian repeated. "There is absolutely nothing indecent about the Bercots."

"But— But they're squatters. You do mean to run them off, don't you?"

"I'm sure a solution can be reached."

"Humph. Squatters *and* papists, what—"

Closing what little space there was between them, Ian gave voice to a rage he hadn't known was building. "You'll not use that word—*papists*—in this house or anywhere else within my children's hearing. God is God, and no matter what you've been taught by that narrow-minded father of yours, the Almighty doesn't give a rat's ass whether prayers come to Him from a Protestant or a Catholic."

Ana gasped. "Brother Ian! You dare utter such blasphemy!"

Her eyes wide with shock, she would have dashed across the room if he hadn't grasped her upper arms and forced her to look at him. "I'd dare the devil himself if I thought it would help shake all your father's prejudices out of you. You've got a good mind for absorbing, but how good is it for reasoning? For once, just think about what a moment ago spewed from your mouth. I can't accept that you honestly believe all of that . . . that hogwash!"

If she uttered the slightest retraction or anything to her defense, Ian was beyond listening. Years of keeping his mouth shut while John MacPherson spewed his litany of intolerance from the pulpit and even in this very room drove him on. "This is America, Ana. A land of religious and personal freedom. You were born here and have no idea how precious that is. Well, let me tell you, I do.

"The country I came from has been torn apart for centuries by religious differences. Irish Catholics are denied the privilege of practicing their faith. Men are hunted down and killed if they're even suspected of being a priest and conducting masses or any other sacrament integral to their faith. Irish Catholic children are denied an education. Families are turned out of the homes they've occupied for generations, cut down on the spot if they voice so much as a protest."

Unaware that he was doing so, he gave her a shake. "Blast it, woman! Is your head so filled by your father's dogma, there's no room for a thought of your own? Don't you realize that the sword of religious intolerance can cut any way it wishes? Or are you so blinded with prejudice that you don't care as long as it's Protestants wielding that sword?"

"Please . . . I didn't mean—" She winced and began to tremble. It was then he realized that not only was he shouting at her, he'd been gripping her so tightly he was causing her pain. And he'd actually shaken her.

Sickened by his loss of control, he jerked his hands from her. "I'm sorry, Ana. I didn't mean—" He had a glimpse of large lavender eyes wide with terror and cheeks drained of color before she fled to the other side of the room. Her back to him, she rubbed at her arms.

Ian felt ill. She'd have bruises by nightfall. He was guilty of much, but harming a woman had never before been one of his sins.

"Ana. I—" He sighed heavily. What could he possibly say? He was a beast *and* a brute.

He started for the door and would have left for certain this time, had he not seen the way her body bowed to stem the deep sobs racking her body and had he not caught another glimpse of her face and seen the tears once more streaming down her cheeks.

Ana felt as if the sword Ian had described had just cleaved her in two, her father's teachings in one half and her own conscience in the other. For too many years, she'd let the threat of violence crush her own thoughts. Papa was basically a good man. It was just that he believed himself so right in all things that any other position was wrong, and he simply could not fathom any of his family taking a "wrong" position on anything.

In most instances, Papa was right, but sometimes his judgment was clouded by a zeal bordering on the fanatic. At an early age, she'd learned not to argue with him. Later she'd learned to separate the wheat from the chaff in his philosophies and teachings. And yet, a little while ago, she had delivered a stream of the worst of them as fervently as her father might have. No wonder Ian assumed she had not a thought that was not her father's, and questioned whether she was even capable of forming one. That he should have such a low opinion of her hurt far more deeply than any physical blow could have.

"Ana." Her name softly spoken was her only warning before Ian gently turned her and wrapped his arms around her. Stunned by his embrace, Ana froze. Even breathing was nearly impossible.

"Please don't cry. Forgive me," he murmured softly

against the top of her head. Gently, he rocked her and brushed circles over her back, comforting her in the same manner she used to comfort the children.

Inexplicably, being completely surrounded by this man, Ian Patterson, whom she'd always thought too big and too male, made her feel she was in the safest spot on the earth. "I didn't mean to hurt you. I've never hurt a woman and never will again," he murmured.

With a shuddering sigh, she relaxed and rested her head on his chest. "You didn't hurt me. Not really. It was my fault. I shouldn't have said those things," she said, and as if it were a dam bursting, she rushed on. "They were hateful and unchristian and I didn't mean half of them. I'm not a religious fanatic. Or a bigot. I know you don't believe that, but I'm not. It's just that—"

"Shh, shh," he interrupted. "You've had that nonsense beaten into you, haven't you?"

She shook her head violently. "No," she answered too quickly and too vehemently to be believed. "I was reared gently. Papa merely corrected me. He didn't beat me." She was babbling hysterically, but she couldn't let him or anyone think ill of her father. "My father is a good man. He's never abused me or . . . or any of his children."

Ian's rocking rhythm and soothing touch halted for a long moment. She heard and felt the deep breath he took before saying, "All right. Just know that you are safe in this house and safe from me." He returned to the rocking and comforting stroking.

"You're merely overwrought. And tired." Ian tipped her head up and brushed his thumb on the tears still on her cheeks. "By the circles under those lovely eyes, you didn't get much sleep last night. Fatigue and strong emotions are a combination sure to make the sanest of us say and do things we don't mean."

Mesmerized by the warmth in his eyes and the low

rustle of his voice, Ana didn't even notice when she wrapped her arms around his waist. In a breathless voice she hardly recognized as her own, she asked, "You think my eyes are lovely?" and instantly flushed with embarrassment at such foolishness falling from her mouth.

"Very," he said with such conviction, it erased her embarrassment. He drew one finger lightly, slowly, down her cheek, setting off a melting warmth deep in her belly and beyond. Gently, he framed her face with his palm. "Your skin is so ... so smooth ... and so is your mouth." His eyes darkened, and he lowered his head. "And maybe neither of us is quite sane today," he muttered, just before he covered her mouth with his.

Her senses, already taut with a myriad of emotions, literally quaked. She edged closer until her breasts crushed against his chest and her hips met his thighs. *This is wrong.* The voice of her conscience repeated the admonition over and over. Ana couldn't have heeded it right then any more than she could stop her hands from clutching at his coat to hold herself upright. Or stop the sigh of pleasure when he traced his tongue along the soft fullness of her lips.

No man had ever held her or kissed her, and Ana wasn't prepared for the flush of heat that rushed through her body when his tongue tangled with hers. She heard the warning again—*This is wrong*—and again she ignored it and let herself explore and enjoy the dark mystery of Ian's mouth.

While a part of her was all woman responding to a man at the most basic of levels, another part, the avid scholar in her, was intrigued. Kissing and being kissed by Ian was a little bit frightening—but it made her slowly curl her toes and want to purr like a contented kitten being stroked on a warm lap.

His lips were firm and masterful. With each sensual

slide of his tongue, he led her farther into a world she'd never imagined. A world of sensual pleasure between a man and a woman that sent her fears up into a puff of smoke. He wasn't dominating or taking, but encouraging her to meet him, to take pleasure and give it.

Arching into him, she heard a moan. It was hers, and it turned into a whimper when he lifted his head.

She blinked. Overcome by the experience, she would have collapsed to the floor had he not still held her. Patently flustered, she blurted, "Oh. Oh, my."

"Oh, my, indeed," he said, and slowly loosened his hold on her until she could stand on her own. "That was . . . unexpected and . . . ah . . . enlightening, to say the least. I'm not certain exactly what came over me, but I'll take responsibility. I'll not apologize. You were—"

"No!" Awash with guilt, she couldn't bear to hear him condemn her. She didn't need to hear it to know that she was a wanton, a jezebel. Feeling a rush of heat to her cheeks, Ana couldn't get away from him fast enough. Slamming the door in her wake, she was halfway up the stairs to the second floor before the door stopped vibrating in its frame.

Once she reached the privacy of her room, she sagged against the closed door. "What have I done?" she whispered to the walls. Her sister was barely cold in her grave and she was in her brother-in-law's arms being kissed and kissing him back. At the memory of how it had felt to be held and kissed like that, a shiver raced down her spine and her mouth grew dry. She made the mistake of licking her lips and tasted him anew. She could smell him on her hands.

She began to pace the tiny room, muttering, "Oh, my. Oh, my," over and over as she paced. Her mind was muddled, and her skin felt as if it was too tight. She wasn't a bad woman. She hadn't meant to entice him.

Ian was right. Neither one of them was particularly sane this day. That was the only explanation for it. This was simply an aberration and should not have happened. It would never happen again.

If it weren't for the children, she'd pack her bags and be out of this house before the floor clock down in the foyer struck the next hour. The very thought of the children renewed the tears in her eyes. She couldn't abandon them, nor could she let him take those dear sweet ones away! She just couldn't. Somehow she'd have to find a way to change his mind about moving them to that horrid, horrid island. And while she was doing that, never, never, never be alone with him again.

Chapter Seven

My God, what in hell just happened? Ian ran a shaking hand through his hair, then took several deep breaths to calm himself. And did a little pacing himself to work off the adrenaline that had been pumping.

He'd intended only to console her a bit, just pat her shoulder as he'd done before. Why he'd turned her into his arms was beyond him, except it had just seemed the natural thing to do. She'd felt right there, and it hadn't even seemed strange that she didn't try to pull away.

Once he was holding her, breathing in the scent of her hair and feeling the press of her breasts against his chest, kissing her had just happened. Trying to convince himself that the kiss had been anything remotely close to brotherly was pure rubbish.

Damnation! He'd just kissed Valeriana MacPherson! Worse—once he'd gotten a taste of her, he'd wanted to strip off her clothes and find out if the rest of her was as sweet and responsive as her lips. Thank God he'd had at least a shred of sanity left, and they weren't now rolling around on the floor in a mad jumble of naked limbs and heaving, sweat-slicked flesh.

Mad. That was exactly what kissing her was.

Insane.

Daft.

Living with her for two months had obviously sent

him over the edge to lunacy. For a moment there he'd been thinking with his cock—just like he had all those years ago when he'd first met Lily.

What in God's name was it about MacPherson women? Whatever it was, once was enough. He sure as hell wasn't going to get entangled with another one. Most particularly not this one, even if she was as different from her sister as the sun from the moon. The sooner he got his family moved to the island and away from all the MacPhersons, the better.

"If it weren't for the children, I'd send that woman back to the parsonage this very day." Now that he'd had a taste of her, how he was going to keep his hands off of her in the weeks ahead, he surely didn't know. For the sake of the children, he'd find a way. A scandal of his own making right here in this house was the last thing he wanted. And a scandal there might well be if he ever kissed her again. If there were a next time, he doubted he would have the strength to stop with just a kiss.

Intent on putting as much distance between himself and Valeriana as possible—and quickly—he'd let his long legs take him out of the house and halfway down the driveway before he remembered he had a number of things to talk over with Ned. Besides, he always found the older man's company relaxing. God knew he could use some relaxing company.

As he expected, he found Ned in one of the boxes running a brush over an already well-groomed horse. "You wantin' the carriage hitched up, boss?" the older man asked when he spied Ian. "Won't take but a minute or two to get Pauley here harnessed up with Tillie over there."

Ian hitched a boot on the bottom rail and folded his arms across the top. "No, I'll be walking to the office, as usual."

Ned lifted his cap and scratched his head, which set his gray hair to standing on end, before smashing his cap back on. He resumed brushing. "Don't know why you keep such a full stable when you almost never use 'em. You're the walkingest man I ever did see."

Feeling better already, Ian chuckled. "Actually, this morning I was wondering how many of these beasts are saddle broken, and if we even own a saddle."

The rhythm of Ned's strokes didn't change a whit at that query. "Well, Pauley here is, and Tillie, too. And I've got a saddle in the tack room. And I know where I can get one for little ol' Patience. Say the word, and I'll start teaching the younguns to ride. Or you thinkin' of taking up riding yourself?"

"I wasn't always a sailor and a city dweller. I'll have you know I learned to ride not long after I learned to walk." Idly, he patted the big bay gelding's neck as he looked beyond to the little dapple gray pony his children so adored.

"You've brought up a good point. My children's education has been sadly lacking. They all should be taught to ride. Where I come from, being able to sit a horse well is a sign of a true gentleman and a true lady, too. See if you can find a sidesaddle for the girls while you're procuring a saddle for Patience," he added, warming to the idea and sorry he hadn't thought of it before.

"We'll get started right away on this," he told Ned, before returning to one of the main reasons he'd stopped by. "That is, if it doesn't interfere with your lining up all the draft horses and mules we talked about."

"I've just about got all we figured on. The owners are just waiting for the word to deliver 'em. If they've already fenced off some paddocks and built some shelter for 'em, we can start sending a batch on over there each time you got a ship with room going that way."

"And hostlers to handle them?" Ian asked, and was more than pleased when Ned revealed that he already had enough men lined up to handle and care for them. "You know, with the move coming up soon, I've been thinking it might be wise to get used to riding again."

That comment did alter Ned's stroking. Straightening, he looked over the horse's back with a questioning expression. " 'Bout time you started seeing it my way," Ned said with a twinkling grin. "You'd be wearing out a lot of shoe leather if you was to be trying to walk all over that there island seeing to everything."

Ned patted the gelding's neck, then moved around him to start on his other side. "Pauley'd get you around the island right fine. He's steady and has endurance. Won't give you no trouble."

Ian grinned. "No confidence in my horsemanship, Ned?"

The older man just shrugged and set to brushing again. "Well, I ain't never seen you on a horse, boss. Course, you handle the ribbons pretty fine those rare times you take out a carriage. But if you say you been riding most of your life, then I can take a look-see for a saddle horse with a bit of spirit, if that's what you want."

"I think I'd like that, Ned. The island's big enough and has enough open spaces that a horse could get a good run over there. Be a change to feel the wind in my face while riding a horse rather than standing behind the wheel of a ship."

Ned made a mock shudder. "I'd as soon feel the breeze from atop a horse, myself. Don't feel comfortable on boats. But I s'pect they's a necessary evil I'll just have to get used to ever so often if I'm going to be living on that island."

"You know, Ned, there's still time to change your mind about that. As much as I'd be glad for your coming with us, I'll think none the less of you if you should change your mind between now and moving day."

"If you're taking the pony and these horses, I'm coming, too. We're used to each other. Kind of like a family, I s'pect, and families ought not to be split up." He winked and grinned again. "The Marys or Gerta ain't changed their minds about going along, have they?"

Ian noted the glint in the older man's eyes. "Not that any of them have told me."

Ned nodded in satisfaction. "Good, I'd miss that woman's cooking. I'm thinking that island'll be a good home for all of us. Now that's settled, I've a wee favor to ask of you."

"Surely," Ian said.

"Well, next time you see that architect fella, I'd like you to ask if it'd be all right if I take a look at what he's planning for the stable up at the big house. I might have some ideas he ain't thought of. Like to see just how big he's planning the paddocks, too."

Ian clapped the older man on the shoulder. "He'd be a fool not to take advantage of your expertise, Ned. I'll tell him you'll be dropping by."

Ian settled his hat upon his head and started for the door. There he hesitated and turned back. Removing his hat, he ran the brim around in his hands for a moment or two as he gathered his thoughts. "Speaking of favors, Ned. Remember that business I told you about a few weeks ago?"

At the serious tone in Ian's voice and expression, Ned knew immediately to what his employer was alluding. He spit on the floor of the stable. "Sure, and I ain't seen hide nor hair of him, boss."

Ian shrugged his shoulders negligently, belying the unease he felt. "I don't imagine he'll be coming back to these parts, and I'm sorry to have involved you at all in this, but I'd appreciate it if you'd still keep an eye out."

"You're not thinking that little weasel'd be fool enough to come back here and stir up any trouble, are you?"

"Not really. Just being overly cautious, I guess. If you ever spot him, I'd like to know about it as soon as possible. And of course, I don't want him to have any contact with my children."

Ned snorted and spit again. "You can count on me, boss. Iffen he's fool enough to ever come back around here, he'll not get within shoutin' distance of those little mites iffen I can help it."

"Thanks, Ned. I knew I could count on you. It'll only be for a few weeks. Once the children are living on the island, they'll be sa—"

Without concrete evidence in that direction, implying he felt his children might be in some danger from Phillips was more than he wanted to admit. "Phillips isn't likely to show up here and certainly not on the island."

Ned fixed him with a steady eye. "You're a good pa, Ian Patterson. To all four of 'em."

"There's nothing more important to me than the safety and happiness of my children," Ian replied as he replaced his hat upon his head. Brightening again, he admitted, "I almost forgot the main reason I stopped by. I promised the children they could have a dog. You don't happen to know if anybody around here has a litter of pups that would be ready to go before the end of summer, do you?"

Ned scratched his head, then answered, "I'm thinking Watson what has that pretty farm at the end of Euclid Street has a shepherd bitch he figured be whelping a litter sometime this spring. I don't know who the sire was, but the mam's a real smart dog, good with the livestock and the Watson children. S'pect her pups'll be the same if they're raised up right, no matter who the pa was."

"If you could check on them for me, I'd appreciate it. If they look good to you and aren't all spoken for, set a time one evening real soon, tonight even, for the children and me to go pick one out."

"I can mosey on up there later this very day and let you know by suppertime."

"That would be fine." Ian headed for the door again. "Oh, and one more thing. Don't say anything to the children, Ned. I'd like to surprise them."

Well satisfied with his talk with Ned, Ian had a spring in his step as he started off for town. He'd stop by the cobbler's on his way to the office to see about having riding boots made for the children and a pair for himself. That seamstress of Lily's ought to be able to make up riding habits for Maara and Jesse. He'd stop by there, too. Nothing fancy, just practical, but with some color. He was tired of seeing them dressed like drabs. He started making a mental list of the other gear needed. Gloves. They'd need gloves, too.

Of course, Ana would probably rain objections on him, point out every danger imaginable. But by damn, they were his children, and they ought to know how to ride. All of them, including Joseph. By the time he'd been Joe's age, he'd been sitting a pony for months. By Rob's age, he'd had his own horse. A horse would make a fine birthday present. Maara should have one, too. The thought of riding all over the island with his children put a smile on his face.

By the time Ian arrived at the shipping office, it was nearly noon. He'd lost a half day toward getting through the mountain of paperwork he knew was waiting for him on his desk. But he didn't mind. Matters of far more import than shipping contracts had occupied the morning, and it was his satisfaction with those that put the spring into his step and prompted the merry tune whistling from his lips. "Good day, Kenneth. Fine day today, wouldn't you say?"

"Uh, yes, sir. I believe it is."

The young clerk started to rise, but Ian raised his hand to stay him. "Relax, Kenneth, go on with what you were doing. I apologize for interrupting you. I'll just go on back to my desk."

He glanced at the clock on the wall and remarked, "As soon as you're finished there, why don't you run over to the Erie and pick up something for lunch for the both of us. Whatever sounds good to you. Put it on my tab. Can't have you working on an empty stomach, now, can I?"

"Uh, yes, sir. I mean, no, sir. I'll see to it right away, sir."

"Whenever it's convenient. Is there by chance a pot of coffee on the woodstove back there?"

"Yes, sir, I made a pot when I came in this morning."

"Good, good," Ian said with an approving smile, though inwardly he grimaced. Kenneth could add up a column of figures with unerring accuracy, but he'd yet to conquer measuring coffee grounds. He'd have to add a good measure of water to the pot before the brew would be drinkable.

At the doorway that separated the outer office from his own, he paused. "Kenneth, I'm sorry to bother you again, but I'd like to hear your thoughts on a matter."

"Mine, sir?" The young man's voice came out higher than normal, almost an adolescent squeak. By the way his Adam's apple was bobbing up and down, Ian could guess he was swallowing repeatedly in hopes of recovering his voice. Ian wished the lad weren't always so nervous around him.

Leaning his shoulder against the doorjamb, Ian asked, "Tell me, Kenneth, how do you feel about Captain Krupp overseeing Patterson Shipping once I'm settled on the island?"

If possible, McClurty's eyes grew wider, and his Adam's apple bobbed more frantically. "Well . . . er . . . sir. I shall miss you, of course, but I find Captain Krupp to be a very fine gentleman and think he'd do a good job."

"I'm glad to hear you have such respect for Captain Krupp. I believe the two of you will deal well with each other. I've no doubt Captain Krupp will rely on you just as I have, and Patterson Shipping will be in good hands."

McClurty's spine appeared to straighten, and he sat a bit taller. "You can count on me, sir."

Glad to see the lad showing some confidence, Ian asked him for recommendations for a clerk for the island's operations and then sent him back to his work. Moments later, a steaming mug of Kenneth's dubious coffee at his elbow, he settled himself at his desk and reached for the cigar tucked into his waistcoat's chest pocket. Striking a match to it, he sent a curl of fragrant smoke into the air and leaned back in his chair. A man ought to be able to light up a good smoke now and then. In his office *and* in his own house.

That thought brought to mind what he'd most been trying to forget—the morning's "interview" with Ana. What an imbroglio that had turned out to be. The best thing he could do about it was chalk it up to temporary insanity, pretend it never happened, and concentrate on other matters.

He'd run into his contractor, Roger Fruth, and been assured that, by the end of the week, he'd have a second crew on the island to speed up the work on the house. If

all went well, Fruth thought the house would be habitable by early August. He'd accompanied Fruth to the offices of Fruth and Fruth and let the other brother, Alan,
the architect, know to expect Ned to drop in soon.

It had been a most satisfying meeting with the Fruth
brothers. The stops at the cobbler's and the seamstress's
had been slightly less so. The boot maker promised the
children's riding boots in only two weeks. That is, two
weeks after someone brought the children in for sizing.
He could also make gloves for them, once he had pat-
terns of their hands. The story was much the same at the
seamstress's. Miss Nancy would start on the girls' habits
immediately after the proper measurements had been
taken and the fabrics chosen.

He could take them in himself, but there was no possible way he'd be able to keep Ana from getting wind of
what he was up to. And that meant there'd likely be another confrontation between them either later today or
tomorrow. If, in her mind, the idea of the children taking
riding lessons should seem so fraught with dangers that
she burst into tears again, he sure as hell wasn't going to
chance being alone with her. He'd bring up the matter at
supper tonight when they were safely surrounded by
four children.

Satisfied he'd be able to handle the situation, he returned to enjoying his cigar and picked up the newspaper
Kenneth had placed on his desk. It was the latest issue, a
week newer than the one he had at home. An article on
the second page immediately caught his eye and sent
concerns over Ana's possible tears from his head. A man
by the name of Longworth had planted acres and acres
of grapevines on the hillsides along the banks of the
Ohio River outside Cincinnati. It seemed his experiment
was doing very well, and he was establishing quite a

name for himself as a vintner. His wines had even won a silver medal at a judging in Paris.

Ian's entrepreneur's mind began to race. When last he'd visited with the Bercots, they'd offered him a glass of wine they'd made from the wild grapes that grew in abundance all over the island. If they could make satisfactory wine from wild berries, what might they do with domesticated grapes? Might this fellow Longworth be persuaded to part with few dozen vines?

Despite the efforts of people like his father-in-law and the Sons of Temperance, wines and spirits were consumed in hearty amounts by the general populace of these United States and other countries. There was a market for good wines, just as there was a market for stone and timber. The cedar and hardwoods couldn't be harvested indefinitely. As each acre of timber was cleared, instead of replanting trees, why not plant those acres with grapevines, assuming the soil and climate proved at all hospitable?

He'd investigate the accessibility of grapevines. The hospitality the Bercots had extended to him every time he visited the island deserved a gift. Supplying them with the root stock for a small vineyard would be just the thing.

Any guilt toward betraying his in-laws' temperance and Presbyterian beliefs, he shrugged off. The occasional glass of good wine was a nectar from the gods, to be savored and enjoyed. And furthermore, wine production was legal and just might prove extremely profitable.

Despite his avoiding attending services whenever possible, Ian had more than a passing acquaintance with the Bible. Wasn't it the Apostle Paul who wrote: "Drink no longer water, but use a little wine for thy stomach's sake"?

Even the inestimable Valeriana MacPherson wouldn't argue with the teachings of the Apostle Paul.

"My riding habit can be any color I want?" Maara asked, her eyes wide with excitement.

"Any color you want it to be, darlin'," Ian assured her with an indulgent smile. "But do consider practicality when you make your choice. Riding can be a dirty business. Even a docile pony like Patience can kick up all sorts of dust and debris with her hooves, and it's more than likely you'll take a tumble from time to time. A big mud puddle makes for a soft landing but can wreak havoc on pretty riding habits."

Ian risked a glance at Ana. It wasn't difficult to discern where her thoughts were leading her. The color in her cheeks had disappeared at the first mention of riding lessons. The woman was absolutely terrified that the children were going to break their necks. There was nothing he could say to allay her fears, he was sure. Only time would prove her terrors unjustified.

"You're a sailor, Da. You don't ever ride a horse. How are you going to teach us something you don't know nothing about?"

Having his horsemanship called into question for the second time in the space of a day was galling. Hearing it from his eldest son and so bluntly struck a vein of conceit he'd forgotten he had.

"I'll have you know, young man, I was once considered one of the best riders in my home country," he began, and related what he'd said to Ned that morning. He expanded a bit on his country upbringing, ending with, "So you see, your old papa hasn't always been a sailor. But for sailing a small boat on a quiet river that meandered through the estate, I wasn't much of a seaman until I was around sixteen and my grandfather arranged for me to sail on one of his ships."

"Why not before then, Da?" Rob asked.

"There were a variety of reasons, son, the main one being England was at war with France and America for a number of years and much of it was fought on the seas. Even commercial ships were at risk, and my grandmother insisted I remain on land until all the hostilities were settled."

"That was Grandmama Maara, wasn't it," Maara stated more than asked.

"Yes, it was, and when Maara Fraser put her foot down, no one with any sense argued," Ian admitted with a twinkling grin. "My brother and I thought she would've made such a fine general, we were sure Napoleon would have been defeated far sooner if she'd been in command instead of Wellington."

"I didn't know you had a brother, Papa. What was his name?"

The merriment in Ian's eyes disappeared. "His name is Randall."

Chapter Eight

Despite Ana's attempts to direct her eyes anywhere but on the man at the opposite end of the table, she was aware of every word, movement, and nuance Ian made during the entire meal. The mention of a brother had drawn her full attention.

When he'd pronounced his brother's name, his tone had matched his expression—flat. Something else had flickered in his eyes, but it was gone before she'd been able to identify it.

A smile masked whatever emotion had been churning inside him, and a mischievous glint gleamed in his eyes when he said, "If you're all finished with supper, I've another surprise for you, but it'll require a short outing to acquire it."

Ana frowned, not that she disapproved of another surprise for the children, though God knew he'd given them enough surprises already with all the talk of riding lessons and the gear they'd be getting. But rather that he'd not said any more about this mysterious brother who, to her knowledge, no one had known existed. Those rare times he mentioned his family at all, he spoke of them in the past tense. Her curiosity was piqued about this brother. Randall. Was he older, younger? And most of all, why did stating his name cause such a shift in his mood and tone?

"That is, if you're interested, and your aunt has no objections to my taking you out at this hour," Ian said, favoring her with the full force of one of his warm, amber-eyed looks that invariably sent a wash of heat through her body, even when it fell elsewhere. Directed squarely upon her, it rendered her nearly breathless. Her heart pounding an erratic rhythm, Ana managed, "No, of course not," and a weak smile.

The words were barely out of her mouth before the children were scrambling off their chairs. But it was Ian who had the wherewithal to bellow, "Halt!" With an economy of motion and grace for such a large man, he was out of his chair and catching Rob by the collar before his order stopped echoing against the dining room walls.

"We will exit at a reasonable and safe pace. Eh, Rob?" As she would have done had she been able to gather her wits and set her body in motion just then, he kept a firm hand on the leader, Rob.

As usual, the boy danced impatiently from one foot to the other. "But somebody's got to tell Ned, so's the horses can be hitched to the carriage. We'll take the landau, won't we?"

"Yes, Rob, we'll take the landau. And we *shall* proceed slowly toward that goal, lest someone trip down the steps and break a leg or their head. If that should happen, the rest of us would just have to sit around waiting for Dr. Cooke, and the surprise would just have to wait until another time."

His face reflecting pure disgust, the boy begrudgingly allowed, "Oh, all right."

Not releasing his hold on him, Ian disappeared through the doorway, the other children in his wake. Ana was left marveling at Ian's firm and most effective handling of Rob's impatience.

The sound of rapid footsteps drew her out of her thoughts. Maara had returned, a puzzled look on her face. "Aunt Ana, aren't you coming?"

"I don't think so, sweetheart." Forcing a smile, Ana suggested, "You can tell me all about it when you get home."

"I don't know why you can't come, too."

Because I am trying my best to avoid spending any more time than is necessary with your father. "It will be nice for your papa to have you all to himself for a change." Turning her niece back toward the others, she accompanied her into the back hallway. "Now go on with you, and give your poor old auntie a few minutes of peace and quiet."

Never a child easily put off when she had that telltale gleam of determination in her eyes, Maara argued, "But Papa said the surprise is for all of us. All of us means you must come, too, Aunt Ana." She rose on her tiptoes and tugged a woolen shawl off its peg. "You should put this on and come with us."

Though she had no intention of obeying her niece's order, Ana's eyes followed Maara's hand. "But I am not—" All the children's hats and coats were still hanging on their pegs. Though the day had been pleasantly warm, evenings were usually quite chilly this time of year. Far too chilly for the children to be riding about in an open carriage without their wraps.

"I'll go out with you and see you off, how's that?" she asked as she draped her shawl about her shoulders and handed Maara her spencer and bonnet. Scooping up the other children's garments, she followed her niece out the door. On impulse, she snatched up Ian's hat and overcoat.

When she and Maara entered the side door of the stable, Mr. Ferguson was just finishing harnessing Tillie and Pauley to the landau. Each time the horses shifted a head or a foot, the harnesses jingled softly. It was a pleasant sound, one that called up many happy memories when she was a child and had visited her grandparents' farm.

She wasn't frightened of horses, never had been. And as a child, she'd even ridden a little and loved it. Why on earth had she felt cold, dark terror when Ian brought up the subject of riding lessons for the children? *Because you won't be there to watch them and share in their triumphs.* It wasn't terror she'd felt, but desolation.

Shaking the feeling off, she pasted a smile on her face and started handing the children their coats and hats. "Fasten all the buttons, Rob," she warned, knowing the boy wouldn't bother unless she insisted. "And wear your cap."

As she helped Jessica into her tiny spencer, she looked for Joseph and saw that Ian was just lifting the little boy into the open carriage. Involuntarily, her eyes were drawn to the movement of thick muscles visible beneath Ian's frock coat. Her palms tingled in memory of running over those corded muscles and feeling them ripple beneath her touch.

Scandalous. Just thinking about this morning was almost as scandalous as what had happened. She needed to put that moment and any thoughts about it out of her mind. With Ian's coat draped over her arm, that was something far easier said than done, she soon realized. His scent rose from it and reminded her too well of being pressed against his hard chest, his lips all but devouring hers, setting her body on fire.

She was glad for her chilled hands. She pressed them briefly against her cheeks in hopes of stemming the blush she felt rising in them.

If he weren't taking the children with him, she'd be thanking God that he'd bought that island and would be living too far away for any repetitions of the events of this morning. She had only a couple more months to guard against being alone with him. God will see you through this, she chanted within her head as she forced her feet to move forward.

"Ah," Ian exclaimed when he saw what she was carrying. "You've saved me a trip back inside for those. I hadn't realized how much the temperature had dropped since the sun went down. And you even brought my coat and hat, too. Thank you."

"You're welcome." Careful to avoid even the merest brushing of hands, she handed the garments and headgear to him.

"The children tell me you're not coming with us," he remarked as he helped Joseph on with his jacket and cap. "I hope you didn't think you were excluded from this little outing."

Sure he was inviting her only out of politeness, she shook her head. "No, I merely thought you would enjoy having them all to yourself. And . . . and I have things to do."

Out of the corner of her eye, she saw him touch the brim of his hat and dip his head slightly in her direction. "As you wish."

Was that relief she heard in his voice? And was it relief she was feeling that he'd not tried to persuade her to go along? Or disappointment?

Disappointment? What a ridiculous idea! She was relieved and would be even more relieved when he was out of sight for the next hour or so. Any exposure to that man seemed to drive her reason somewhere else.

And it certainly didn't matter to her whether he was relieved or disappointed that she wasn't going, she told herself, even as she peered at him in an attempt to discern exactly that. One glance and she quickly turned her head, hoping the dimness in the stable hid her perusal of him, blessedly short as it had been.

Valeriana MacPherson, you really are a ninny! If he'd felt either of those emotions, it had been short-lived, for he was already grinning up at the children. "Everyone in and ready to go?" he asked.

A chorus of "I'm ready," "Yes," "Me, too," "Let's go, Da!" answered him.

Giving last-minute orders to the children that they all remain seated, Ana followed the smartly designed carriage outside. The sharp contrast between the warmth of the stable and the chill air outside prompted her to pull her shawl more tightly around her.

Just before he cracked the ribbons across the horses' backs, Ian looked over his shoulder. There was a smile on his lips, but it wasn't reflected in his eyes. "Last chance, Sister. Are you sure you don't want to come along? We aren't going very far, and we won't be gone very long."

Still sure he was merely being polite for the children's sakes, she shook her head. "Thank you, Brother Ian, but no."

Gallantly, Rob stretched out his hand and invited, "Come on, Aunt Ana. You like surprises, don't you?"

"Of course, darling, but this is your surprise," she insisted. "Yours and Jessica's, Maara's, and Joseph's. You can tell me all about it when you get back."

"But—"

"I believe your aunt's mind is made up, Rob," Ian inserted. "Since we'll be bringing the surprise back with us, she'll get to enjoy it, too." He cracked the reins, and the horses stepped out smartly.

"Ain't no need for us to stand out here in the cold any longer," Ned remarked as soon as the carriage turned out of the driveway. "You go on into the house, Miss

Ana. Watching 'em ain't going to hurry 'em back no sooner."

Feeling a bit foolish, huddled into her shawl and staring up the street where the landau had disappeared, Ana nodded and turned toward the carriage house. Unable to stop herself, she looked back over her shoulder toward the driveway.

"Now don't you go worrying about the younguns," the older man called as he swung the stable doors closed. "They're not going far, and there's a couple of lap robes tucked beneath the seats in case it's colder on the way back."

"You know where they're going and all about whatever the surprise is, don't you?"

Turning his collar up, Ned shoved his hands in his pockets and said nothing for a few steps. "Reckon I do, but I'm not telling."

"The children aren't around to hear. You can tell me without ruining the surprise."

Ferguson chuckled. "Sorry, ma'am, but I ain't going to tell you no matter how much you beg. That'd spoil the children surprising you, and I s'pect they're going to enjoy that almost as much as when they was surprised themselves."

Her curiosity now thoroughly aroused, Ana paused and glared at him. "I was not begging, Mr. Ferguson. I was simply curious."

His grin was all too knowing, which made her wish she was Jessica's age so she could stamp her feet and threaten a tantrum if he didn't reveal the surprise. It wasn't one of Jessica's more attractive personality traits, even if it was effective.

Shrugging off the impulse, she picked up her pace. What on earth had come over her? Never in her lifetime had she raised her voice in anger and even contemplated throwing a tantrum. In the span of one short day, she was guilty of actually doing so and contemplating doing it again.

Whatever amount of time Ian and the children were out of the house, it would be best spent praying and reading the Bible. She'd had little time for either of late. Surely that was the reason she felt so out of balance and succumbed to such weaknesses of character. Reading the holy scriptures and drinking a good cup of tea would certainly restore her mental balance.

Stopping only long enough to pick up a cup of tea, Ana headed straightaway for the quiet of her little room. As she passed through the nursery, she noticed the Marys had lit several lamps and seen to the fire in the grate. The room was warm and far more inviting. She settled herself in the wide cushioned chair nearest the hearth and turned up the lamp on the mantel.

Clasping her hands over the worn leather of her Bible, she prayed fervently that God grant her His grace and forgiveness for her weaknesses and the many sins she'd committed this day. Her quiet meditations and communion with God settled her mind considerably.

Sipping her tea, she riffled through her Bible for the passages she sought. Finding the Psalms not as soothing to her soul as she'd expected, she turned to Corinthians and began to read. But her mind wandered, and she could not lose herself in the passages that had been her salvation other times when she'd felt troubled.

Closing her Bible, she set it aside and picked up her cup and saucer. Sipping at the tea, she stared at the fire. The heat against her face and the hypnotic flickering of the flames soon sent her eyelids drooping. She soon decided a short nap would certainly be restorative; perhaps it was just her body's fatigue that was causing her to act and feel so peculiar.

She hadn't been sleeping at all well of late. As tired as she was when she fell into her bed each night, her slumber was interrupted by a restlessness in her limbs, dreams whose details she could not remember upon awakening but left her on edge nonetheless, and sometimes worse. Too many nights, she awakened shaking, covered with perspiration and fearing she was coming down with some sort of fever.

She simply must talk to Mama or Laurel about a spring tonic. She had no signs of illness during the day—only at night. A mild case of the ague, no doubt. And best dealt with in its early stages before it became serious. The children needed her. She could not afford to be abed with some illness.

"Must shake this off," she mumbled as she slipped her shoes off and tucked her feet up on the chair. Settling her head against the winged corner of the chair, she gave herself up to a short nap. "Rest. All I need is rest."

"Aunt Ana. Aunt Ana. You have to come now. Hurry!"

Rob's cries brought Ana awake with a start. Alarmed by what sounded to her like panic in the boy's voice, she raced across the nursery in her stockinged feet. Her heart in her mouth, she was down the hall and to the top of the stairs before Rob had made it halfway up them.

"You've got to see her, Aunt Ana. Hurry!"

"Who? Maara? Jessica? What's happened?" Slowing only enough to grab Rob's arm, she continued down the steps with him in tow. At the base of the stairs, she caught her breath and tried to slow her heart and keep her voice remotely calm sounding. "Has someone gone for Dr. Cooke?"

"Dr. Cooke? You sick, Aunt Ana?"

"No, dear. But if someone's hurt, we'll have need of—"

The sound of children laughing and squealing with delight could be heard coming from the kitchen. "Robert, is or is not someone hurt?"

He drew his brows drew together in puzzlement. "No, ma'am, nobody's hurt."

"Then what is all this shouting about? You frightened me half to death, Rob Patterson." Her steps were still brisk as she moved through the dining room.

"I'm sorry, but it's the surprise. Just wait till you see her."

Having no idea who the mysterious female visitor could be, Ana paused a moment to smooth her hair and assure herself her cap was straight. Impatient to return to the surprise, Rob scooted around her and through the door.

Ana followed at a slower pace. Two steps into the room, she came to a halt. There before the wide kitchen hearth were Jessica, Maara, and Joseph, sitting cross-legged upon the floor. In the middle of their little circle frolicked a roly-poly ball of black, gray, and white fur. Ana gasped. "Why . . . that's a puppy!"

Jessica scooped up the little animal, laughing when it lapped at her chin with a moist pink tongue. "Isn't she wonderful, Aunt Ana? Papa took us to Mr. Watson's and—"

"We picked her out ourselves," Maara interrupted.

"She's the pick of the litter, Aunt Ana," Robert informed her. "Mr. Watson said so. The only blue merle in the bunch, and they're rare, he said. So she's real special. Let Aunt Ana hold her, Jess."

"Oh . . . I . . . ah . . . don't . . ." Ana backed up a step, but the wiggling little animal was thrust into her arms. Involuntarily, her arms closed around it. Too tightly, apparently, as it immediately gave a little yip and tried to scramble out of her grasp.

Ian came to the rescue. Whether hers or the pup's wasn't

clear, but as he lifted the puppy away, the animal managed to sink its teeth into the edge of Ana's cap. Pinned to the top of her hair, the scrap of lace and ribbons didn't come easily. She wasn't fast enough to save her cap or several strands of her hair from escaping the top of her head.

"Ouch!" Hairpins showered to the floor, and she felt the heavy coil at her nape begin to slip.

"Oh, I am sorry, and I apologize on behalf of the pup. I'm afraid she hasn't yet learned any manners." Ian grinned sheepishly as he tucked the animal firmly under one arm and tried to work the cap from her teeth.

Pushing her hair away from her face, Ana was torn between attempting to pin her hair back up and retrieving her cap. Deciding that getting her hair secured was hopeless under the circumstances, she tried for the cap. "Much more of that gnawing, and there won't be anything left," she said, and made a grab for it. The pup growled and clamped her teeth more tightly into the treasure, pulling in the opposite direction with surprising strength. Just as determined, Ana caught hold of a dangling ribbon and gave a sharp pull.

The sound of rending fabric preceded her little squeal of dismay as she stumbled backward, a frayed ribbon dangling from her fingers. Her stockinged feet slipped on the polished floor and flew out from under her. With an abruptness that would have been bruising had she not been wearing so many petticoats, her bottom hit the floor.

"Oh!" The jarring fall didn't knock the air from her lungs, but it was certainly startling, and enough to completely dislodge the heavy coil of hair she'd struggled that morning to secure at her nape.

Deep, decidedly adult male laughter sounded above her. It struck her as most ungallant and deserving of a set-down. She tried for haughtiness when she announced from behind the locks of hair veiling her face, "I don't believe there is anything humorous about what just happened," but the words came out between chortles of her own.

Her legs straight out in front of her, her gown rucked up, and her petticoats on full display—as well as her ankles and stockinged feet—she made a ludicrous picture, to be sure. And most improper. Pushing her hair out of her face, she yanked her skirts into a more modest position.

"No . . . no, there is not, and I beg your forgiveness for being so cavalier," Ian said in an oddly strained tone at odds with the laughter that had come from him but a moment before. "Are you hurt?"

Choking down more laughter, she wiggled her toes and took inventory of her body. "Just my dignity, I think," she admitted, and tried to get up, but her petticoats were tangled around her legs. Layers of heavily starched muslin rendered her as helpless as a turtle on its back.

"Here, take my hand."

It was a simple, courteous statement, nothing at all extraordinary about it, save for the look she saw in Ian's eyes when she reached for him. So dark and intense was his gaze, she hesitated. Putting her hand in his seemed something altogether different from mere assistance to her feet.

Before she could puzzle any further over it, he grasped her hand and pulled her upward so swiftly, she landed snugly against him. Thighs to thighs, breasts to chest, she was as aware of the sharp intake of his breath as she was of her own—and every hard line of his body. Heat flooded her, as hot and intense as when he'd kissed her that morning.

She gasped and started to shove herself free of him, but

her gaze fell upon the pup tucked under his other arm. Everything else was immediately forgotten. Her cap dangled so ludicrously from its mouth, Ana started to laugh, but the little creature's eyes completely captured her. They were large, liquid, and—

"Blue. She has blue eyes." Surprised by the animal's eye color and the emotion she saw in them, Ana wasn't even aware she still stood within the curve of Ian's free arm. She couldn't resist cradling the little white-streaked muzzle in one hand. Her blue gaze steady upon Ana, the pup pricked her ears and tilted her head to one side in such an endearing fashion, Ana knew her heart had been forever captured.

"Hello, little one. How strange we must all seem to you. Is it your supper time? You don't really want this cap. It's sure to give you a bellyache." Cooing a steady stream of nonsense to hold the dog's attention, she swept a finger inside the animal's mouth and carefully freed her cap from her teeth. Quickly, she stuffed what was left of it into a pocket, then slipped her hands under the puppy's chest and belly and lifted her into her arms.

"Has anyone thought about feeding this little dog?" she asked. "And just where is she to sleep? Perhaps Mr. Ferguson could find an appropriate box and some rags to pad it."

Nonplussed, Ian stood frozen where he was as she walked away. Dragging one of the kitchen chairs toward the hearth, she sat down with the puppy on her lap and instructed the children to settle themselves more quietly. "Your puppy is still a baby; we must treat her very gently and not frighten her," she told them.

The acceptance of the dog couldn't have been more surprising than if she'd hauled off and sunk her fist in his stomach. But that wasn't all that startled him. Not by a long shot.

Damnation! This shouldn't be happening. Not again. Not the difficulty he was having breathing. Not his skin feeling too hot and too tight and his blood rushing to his groin. And she had felt it, too. The way her eyes had widened and her breathing had turned erratic after he'd pulled her to her feet couldn't have meant anything else.

At least one of them had better gather up some sense before there was a repeat of that short scene in the parlor this morning and a whole lot more. The way the softness of her smile as she cooed to the puppy was affecting him, he feared it wasn't going to be him.

His resistance to her was only getting weaker with each passing tick of the clock. Her hair was still in such glorious disarray, he was having to fist his hands behind his back to keep them from plunging into the rich brown mass.

Hell! He'd counted on that dog to further distance her from himself and thus put a stop to his agonies. Memories of how she'd felt in his arms, the way her lips had melted beneath his, and the scent of her hair had superseded all else at odd and inopportune moments throughout the day. Many more days like this and he'd be a madman for certain.

Long before five o'clock, he'd made up his mind that it was imperative that there be no delay in the acquisition of the dog. If Ned hadn't met him when he'd arrived home this evening with the news that the Watson bitch had indeed whelped a healthy litter and that the pups were weaned and ready to leave her, he might have gone out after supper and brought home the first stray dog he encountered.

Throughout supper and during the drive to the Watsons', he'd imagined silencing the objections he was certain she'd voice by firmly stating that his children were going to have a dog, and if she didn't like it, she could just pack up her things and move back with her parents. In what he now recognized as total delirium, he'd struck upon "Salvation" as the perfect name for the animal.

When the little blue merle female had immediately separated herself from her littermates and practically leapt into Maara's arms, John Watson had remarked, "Nothing shy about that one, Patterson. Smartest one of the bunch. See how she sallies forward like that? She's a friendly one, like her dam."

Sallies. Salvation. Watson's word choice was surely providential. Consequently, on the way home he had shamelessly petitioned for "Salvation," or "Sally" for short, since the pup was a girl.

Watching a gentle-faced Madonna sitting in his children's midst, her hand moving in a slow, steady caress over the puppy she held like a baby, her head on Ana's shoulder, her body pillowed against Ana's breasts, was more than he could stand.

"That pup needs a trip outside." Ian strode briskly across the kitchen and scooped the pup up from Ana's lap. "Go ahead and start getting ready for bed, children. It's getting late, and this may take a while," he said over his shoulder as he and the puppy made a rapid exit.

"Why's Papa staying out so long with Sally?" Jessie asked as Ana dropped a nightgown over the little girl's head.

Ana had been wondering the same thing herself ever since Ian had dashed out the back door like the demons of hell were snapping at his heels. "He's probably having trouble setting up a box for her to sleep in," Rob supplied. "I'll go help."

"Not so fast, young man." Ana caught him at the nursery doorway and guided him back to the little table he'd just left. "I believe you have a few more arithmetic problems to finish."

"But Da needs my help with Patch."

"Her name's not Patch, it's Sally," Jessie insisted.

"Is not!"

"Is too!"

"That will be enough." Ana saw Rob start to open his mouth. Before the shouting match could begin anew, she said, "Naming a puppy is a serious decision. Patch is certainly a good name for a dog with a coat made up of such a mixture of colors. Gray, white, black, even some patches of brown. Her coloring reminds me of a kitten your aunt Laurel nursed back to health once. She called her Callie, short for calico."

Out of the corner of her eye, she saw the glint of battle in Jessie's eyes. "But Sally is a nice name, too. What made you think of it?"

"I didn't. Papa did. He says it's short for . . . for . . . what did he say, Maara?"

Her older sister carefully enunciated, "Sal-va-tion. Grandpa uses that word in his sermons almost every Sunday. That's probably why Papa thought of it. What does 'salvation' mean, Aunt Ana?"

Having recited the definition so many times as a child learning the catechism of the Presbyterian Church, Ana responded almost without thought. "Deliverance from the power or penalty of sin," she said, then instantly frowned. Ian Patterson suggesting a theological term as a dog's name was about as likely as his signing the pledge. He had to have said some other word or—

"I believe salvation is commonly used to describe deliverance from danger. Perhaps that is why your Papa used the word 'salvation,' " she said with some certainty. "Now that would be a good name for a dog if she should turn out to be a good watchdog and protector. Don't you think so, Rob?"

"Well . . . maybe, but she'll have to grow some before she can protect anybody from anything."

"She will, she will," Jessica insisted. "Her mama is a big, big dog. Sally will grow up to be just like her. Mr. Watson said so. And then when she's a big dog, she'll sal . . . sal-va-tion us from wolves and bears and anything that might try to bite us."

Ana pressed her lips together to still her laughter. "Well . . . ah . . . Jessica, I'm sure she would, but let us hope that Sally doesn't ever have to save you from wolves or bears."

Oh, please, Lord, let that be true. Ian said there were no wolves on the island, and she doubted there were any bears. But there were those feral hogs to contend with. Better he had given them a pup of a larger, fiercer breed than Mr. Watson's gentle shepherd. Or perhaps a second pup would be a good idea. Two shepherds against one wild hog might offer better protection.

Swallowing the lump that formed in her throat at the reminder of the short time left before the children were taken from her, Ana tried for a smile. "Rob, maybe those arithmetic problems could wait until later. If you'd all like to say good night to her, perhaps we'd better go now. She's such a ba—"

Four eager young bodies started scrambling for the doorway. Grateful she'd been standing so near, she could beat them to it, Ana quickly barred the way. "Shoes, everyone," she directed. "And we will proceed slowly and carefully. You will follow me," she ordered, fearing still that they'd all run pell-mell down the steps and into the night. After all, it wasn't every day that a new puppy entered a household.

"Coats, too," she told them in the hallway. Once

everyone, including herself, was properly garbed for the cold, she led them to the carriage house.

"Now go in slowly and quietly," she cautioned when they reached the smaller side door. "Remember, she's still a baby. You don't want to rush in there and frighten her or excite the horses."

The children rushed past her. By the time Ana entered and secured the door behind her, they'd disappeared into the dark gloom of the carriage house. Spying a lantern hanging in the far stall and hearing childish voices there, she imagined them all sitting in the straw with their new puppy—and their father.

With each step, her pace slowed. Whenever he was with the children, whether it was reading a story to them, playing a game, or just telling them a silly story, there would be that soft light in his eyes that was utterly devastating to her equilibrium.

With each step that drew her closer to the stall, she tried to dredge up anger or at least disapproval of the man, on general undefined principles, as a means of protecting herself. Braced to resist her brother-in-law's charm, Ana was completely taken aback when she looked over the door. "Where is Mr. Patterson?" she asked, her eyes scanning the stall and beyond.

Hunkered down between Joseph and Rob, his back to the stall's door, Ned Ferguson looked over his shoulder. "The boss, he lit out for town not long after he brought the pup out here. Said . . . ah . . . to tell you and the younguns . . . ah . . . that he needed to do something he didn't get done earlier, and he'd probably be late. Told me to say his good nights for him."

Ana felt her own eyebrows rise during Ferguson's explanation of her brother-in-law's whereabouts. Anger, resentment, and disapproval weren't difficult to conjure; she could well imagine what it was that needed to be

done at this hour! The way poor Mr. Ferguson was stammering, he was most definitely uncomfortable. How like
that man to have "lit out for town," leaving Mr. Ferguson to concoct a Banbury tale to cover his employer's
carousing at one of those horrid saloons down by the
waterfront.

"I see. Well, that is disappointing." For the children it
was disappointing. It was most assuredly not disappointment she was feeling! Not seeing him inside the stall with
the children had been a surprise, that was all. Surprise
made a person feel like their stomach had clenched like
a fist, their lungs had lost a good bit of air, and their
blood had briefly stopped moving through their body.
Didn't it?

"Damned woman, how was I to know she liked
dogs?" Ian ran the plane to the end of the board and sent
another shower of curling wood shavings to the floor.
"Her sister hated them," he muttered as he ran the plane
over the board again. "Not having a dog in the house
was about the only thing that woman ever felt strongly
about."

A sound from the outer office interrupted his one-
sided conversation. Ignoring it, he finished another run
of the plane and started again. "Probably just the wind,"
he muttered, as he sent a shower of shavings to the
floor. Knocking. Someone was knocking on the door, and
growing impatient by the sound of it, he decided as he set
the tool aside.

As he left the workshop and moved through the darkened offices between the workshop and reception area,
the knocking turned to heavy pounding. Growing alarm
quickened his step. Seen through the door's window, the
shadowy figure on the other side was clearly a man
wearing a tall brimmed hat. Certainly not Ned Ferguson.

Ian felt a wave of relief that there was no emergency at home. Unlocking the door, he swung it open and recognized his visitor. "Little late for you to be out and about, isn't it, Alan?"

The young architect shrugged. "I was on my way home and saw the light at the back of the building. I hoped it might be you. Have you a bit of time to spare me?"

Stepping aside, Ian waved the man in. "Questions about the house or the other buildings?"

"No, nothing like that." Sweeping off his hat, he shifted nervously from one foot to the other. "It's of a more personal nature."

Ian's brows rose. "Sounds serious. Come with me. I've a pot of coffee back in the workshop, or perhaps you'd care for something stronger."

"I'd be honored to lift a small glass of whiskey with you, sir, if you've got it." Fruth followed Ian through the rooms and mumbled, "Might as well, I'm already condemned."

Ian wasn't sure whether a laugh would be welcome, so he managed to stem the chuckle that rose in his throat. "I understand you've been walking out with my sister-in-law, Laurel," he remarked as he opened a cupboard and extracted a bottle and two glasses. "Problems?"

Fruth ran a nervous hand through his sandy hair and took the proffered glass. "Not with Miss Laurel. She's an angel, the most wonderful young woman I have ever had the good fortune to meet."

"Laurel is indeed quite a special young woman. Very pretty, too," Ian said, and motioned the younger man toward a stool. "But I sense you didn't stop by to expound upon my sister-in-law's many virtues and attributes."

Fruth took a long swallow of the whiskey, then sighed. "It's her father." He took another swallow, then raised a puzzled face to Ian. "I've not known you long, sir, but long enough that I believe I know the kind of man you really are. What I cannot comprehend is how you have endured the reverend's continual condemnations all these years."

Ian chuckled and shook his head. "It's been a challenge, my friend. Am I to deduct from this that you are quite serious about Laurel? And you're wondering whether you, too, will become the target of condemnations from the pulpit?"

Fruth visibly shuddered and gulped the rest of his whiskey. "God help me, yes on both counts. I'm not a saint, sir, but I do consider myself a man of honor, morals, and strong faith. But—" He rolled the empty glass between his palms. "I'm not much of a drinker, really, but I'm not about to sign that damnable temperance pledge."

"He's brought it up already, has he?"

"No, but Laurel's warned me, and I am a member of Grace Church's congregation," Fruth admitted with a wry grin.

"Then the question becomes, Is a life with Laurel MacPherson worth the torment of having the reverend as your father-in-law?"

"I can't imagine my life without her," Fruth admitted, sounding dangerously like a condemned man.

Ian refilled both their glasses. Raising his own in a salute, he said, "To the MacPherson women, then. And to salvation. Don't expect to find it from a dog."

Chapter Nine

June

"Lord, we ask Thee to keep our little loved ones forever safe in your palm. Though they may one day soon be cruelly wrenched from the bosom of their loving family, we are secure in our faith that You, their *Heavenly Father*—" MacPherson sent a narrow-eyed glare at the tall, auburn-haired man in the family pew before bowing his head once more. "—will not only watch over them but guide them along the paths of true righteousness."

A collective sigh and the rustling of clothing rippled through the congregation as it prepared itself for a lengthy benediction at the end of what had already been a lengthy sermon. Those who dared risk the reverend's censorious scowl for a breach in pious decorum during this the final prayer lifted their heads ever so slightly to cast an eye toward the front of the church.

While MacPherson rattled on and on, Ian Patterson faced his accuser straight-on and clear-eyed. No bowed head. No show of submission. No show of guilt. Not a hint of reaction save a slight tightening of his jaw.

Grace Church was filled to overflowing and not one soul regretted the discomfort. They'd come—the faithful, the not-so-faithful, and a sizable number of not-at-all-faithful—this Sunday and every Sunday since the word had spread that Ian Patterson was moving his family away from Cleveland later in the summer. Any suffering they might have to endure was a small price to pay to be a firsthand witness to the ever-intensifying battle of wills between the preacher and his son-in-law.

They had not been disappointed.

From the opening hymn onward, each word sung, spoken, or prayed that morning had been chosen specifically to condemn every sin the preacher thought his son-in-law ever might have committed or might commit in the future. Though his words were carefully chosen to expound upon the evils of certain activities in a general sense, his gaze rarely strayed from the tall man seated below him in the first pew, the family pew. Those few times it did, more often than not, it roved to the other end of the family pew where a lanky, sandy-haired young man sat next to the reverend's daughter, Laurel. Though he gave the young man a less censorious glare than those he sent Ian Patterson's way, the congregation was well satisfied that even after Patterson's defection to his island, the reverend's sermons were likely to be almost as entertaining as they'd been for the past nine years.

"Keep us safe in Thy Grace, most especially the little ones soon to be torn from the bosom of those who love them most. Now and forevermore. Amen."

The amens were loud and hearty as the congregation rose to its feet for the final hymn. If the words were sung more briskly and joyfully than was the usual tempo for the somber hymn that begged God's mercy for the sins of lowly man, it was because the singers were heartily rejoicing that they were nearing the time when they would be able to quit the now-stifling confines of the church.

As it had during the singing of every one of the hymns, Ian Patterson's voice rang strong and true above the others. Standing with little Joseph between herself and

Ian, Ana could barely get the words past her throat. Papa had given the congregation exactly what they'd come for this morning. She'd heard the twitters that had rippled through the church. The reason the church was so often filled beyond its capacity had not been lost on her this morning or any other morning Brother Ian attended.

Papa was a fanatic, and here in a frontier town that rarely saw any theatrical companies, people came for the entertainment of watching him work himself up into a frenzy. For years, she'd rationalized that whatever extremes her father went to in order to entice people to Sunday services were acceptable. The important thing was that people came together in Christian fellowship to worship and hear the gospel. For all the chaff Papa might toss into the mix, there was always a bountiful harvest of truth.

But not this morning. His condemnations were totally unwarranted. Countless times, she'd seen with her own eyes just how deeply Brother Ian cared for his children. Even if she still thought him misguided about moving them to the island, she could not think him guilty of ever endangering their well-being, consciously or even unconsciously.

Papa had gone much too far. He'd accomplished nothing with his sermon today but making a spectacle of himself and the entire family, even going so far as to glare at Laurel's beau.

His choice of language had been far too fearsome and delivered too thunderously for the children in the congregation, most especially his own grandchildren. It would be a miracle, indeed, if they hadn't realized he'd directed nearly every word toward their father.

Ashamed to be John MacPherson's daughter, she could hardly bear to look Ian or anyone else in the eyes when the service ended. Barely nodding to her mother, sisters, and Mr. Fruth, she quickly scooped a squirming Joseph up and headed for the door behind the pulpit. Beneath his protests that he wasn't a baby and didn't need to be carried, Ana muttered an excuse to those she encountered that the little boy's patience had been stretched beyond endurance.

"Wait, Ana."

Bracing herself, she turned and met Ian's gaze. Instead of the amusement that usually colored his features after one of her father's fiery diatribes, Ian's eyes held something else, something that in another man she would have interpreted as a silent plea for help. "Yes?"

"Perhaps they should all slip out the back door with you and Joe," he suggested as he gently directed Maara, Rob, and Jessica along the pew. "I'd prefer the children not run that gauntlet waiting out front on the church lawn. They've had quite enough for one morning."

"As have we all," Ana said beneath her breath before forcing a smile and reaching a hand toward Jessica.

With a glower and the stubborn push of her lower lip, the little girl pulled back. "I want to hold Papa's hand."

"Enough with your stubbornness, Jessie, darlin'. Be off with your Aunt Ana."

Ana heard more of Ireland reflected in his speech than was usual. A sign there was a chink in the armor he had encased himself in during Papa's sermon?

Jessica still refused to budge from her father's side. "Come, Jessie, dear. Come with me," Ana coaxed.

Shaking her head, the little girl wrapped an arm around one of her father's legs. "No. I want to stay with Papa!"

Gently Ian pried her loose and nudged her toward Ana. He raised a rare stern brow when his younger daughter turned and stamped her foot. "None of that this morning, Miss Jessica. I need for you to go with your aunt."

"Come on, Jessie." Rob caught her hand and pulled her along in his wake. "You can walk with me."

Jessie dragged her feet and sent a pleading look over her shoulder. Ian kept his expression stern. "Go with your big brother," he said, then turned toward the middle aisle.

Ana could scarcely credit that he should want to subject himself to the snickers, questions, and comments awaiting him on the church lawn. "Brother Ian? You don't have to go out there. You can slip out the back way with us."

"Thank you for the offer, but I thought to lend my . . . ah . . . comrade-in-arms, as it were, some support." Amusement finally glimmered in the green-gold eyes that looked back at her. "Alan Fruth's new to this."

"But—"

"Don't worry about me. I have a tough hide." He grinned, and her stomach did a flip-flop. A blush quickly followed.

Dipping her head, she hoped the brim of her bonnet hid her face. "I . . . I wasn't worried about you. I just thought this morning you might find it preferable to retreat."

"I'll not give him the satisfaction." He gave her and the children a jaunty salute and another grin. "And I need to set an example for my successor," he added before starting up the center aisle.

Ana watched his broad back disappear into the crowded center aisle. To think that for a moment, she'd actually felt protective of him.

Men! It was a game between Papa and Ian. A contest of wills played with as much alacrity and vigor as two teams pulling on the ends of a rope stretched across a muddy pit. The question was, Which one had more mud on his face this day?

"Humph." Ian's defiance was almost as bad as Papa's uncalled-for condemnations. And just as satisfying to the throngs who'd come to witness this Sunday's contest. How he could sit calmly and unflinchingly through Papa's lecturing when any fool knew it was directed specifically at him was beyond her. And to make matters worse, he'd had the audacity to stare straight up at Papa even during the prayers, when everyone else was dutifully bowing their heads.

Dutifully bowing their heads in prayer. Ha! But for a handful of the truly faithful, everyone had taken the opportunity of the prayers to hide their smirks. And now apparently Laurel's young man was being pulled into the contest. She sent a quick prayer heavenward that, if there were a contest building between her father and Alan Fruth, one of them would have the good grace to concede before it, too, got out of hand.

"Aunt Ana? Want down. You're smashing me!"

"Oh, Joseph. I am sorry." Realizing they were already halfway across the square, Ana set the little boy down and gently rubbed his arms.

"I just didn't want to drop something so precious as you, so I held you real tight." Forcing a smile to her face, she chucked him lightly under his chin. "All better now?" He nodded and looked up at her with one of his sweet smiles.

Careful to keep her touch light, she caught his hand and started across Euclid Street, making sure the rest of her little band was close behind. The street was nearly empty, she noted, but didn't spare a glance toward the churchyard. She didn't have to see them to know the congregation was lingering there. "Humph."

Hoping for a final act to today's little performance, no

doubt. "Humph." And if that grin and the jaunty step of his was any indication, Ian had marched right out to center stage and performed for them. "Humph."

"Why you keep making that noise?"

"What noise, Joseph?"

"That '*pfumff*' noise. Did a bug crawl in your nose?"

"Don't you know anything, Joedie? Bugs can't crawl up a lady's nose," Maara informed her little brother.

"Can too. Bugs go anywhere they want to."

"Not up a lady's nose," Maara stated emphatically. "Do they, Aunt Ana?"

Before Ana could form a suitable reply, Rob supplied, "Joe's right, Maarie. Bugs crawl anywhere they want to, looking for food or just for a nice warm place to crawl into. Sometimes gnats just don't pay no 'tention to where they're flying and they just get sucked into a person's nose. It's happened to me plenty of times when I've been running somewheres. Especially in the summer when there's lots of skeeters flying around at nighttime."

Letting go of his little sister's hand, Rob walked backward in front of them. "Did ya ever see maggots crawling all over a dead animal, in and out of their nose and mouth and anywhere they can get to? Maggots turn into flies, and I s'pect they just think a body's nose is like goin' back to where they was borned."

Not surprisingly, Jessica squealed. No less surprising was Maara's admonishment, "Stop it, Rob Patterson! Bugs and maggots are not appropriate topics to discuss in the presence of ladies. Isn't that right, Aunt Ana?"

As disgusting as the images Rob had painted were, Ana pressed her lips together to refrain from laughing at the relish Rob took in the telling. *Trust the children to lighten a soured atmosphere.* "You're quite right, Maara. Ladies don't usually enjoy those kinds of topics. Perhaps you boys could discuss bugs and dead creatures in the carriage house or somewhere away from us ladies."

"Boys should live in the stable," Jessica muttered, giving Joseph a shove toward Rob. Ana reached out a steadying hand to keep the little boy upright before his brother took over his care.

"Maybe at the new house, their rooms can be over the stable," Maara suggested.

"Far away from you prissy girls," Rob stated with glee. He clapped an arm around his little brother's shoulders. "What do you say, Joe? You think you and me could build our own house, maybe in the island's woods, and live all by ourselves? We could keep my collection right there with us and add more to it."

"I want a co-co-lec-tion, too, Rob."

"Then you shall have one, Joe. Come on, let's go look at mine before dinner." Dragging his little brother behind him, Rob started off at a brisk clip up the driveway. "I've got some extra things I can spare to get your collection started."

Ana smiled at the camaraderie between the two brothers even as she felt Maara's shudder. "Are you going to let him take all that old smelly junk to the new house, Aunt Ana?"

The new house. Ana's chest tightened, and she drew a shaky breath. "Those things are Rob's special treasures, sweetheart," she managed as evenly as she could. "I should think he'd want to take them, just as you'll want to take all the things that are special to you."

"I'm taking Mary Linda, 'cause she'll cry if I don't," Jessica said solemnly.

"Of course you'll take Mary Linda, and your other dolls, too," Ana said over the tears clogging her throat. "And your paints and books."

"And Sally, 'cause she's family, too. Isn't she, Aunt Ana?"

"Yes, darling. Sally is a member of your family."

"And Gerta and the Marys?"

"I think they have all decided to move to the island with you. And Mr. Ferguson, of course."

"Our house will be all empty, won't it, Aunt Ana?"

"Yes, Jessica, I suppose it will."

"Will it feel sad when we're all gone?"

"Houses don't feel sad, silly," Maara inserted.

"Ah, but perhaps they do, Maara, dear, for when their very heart has been taken from them, they are but an empty shell." *Just as I will be when you are taken from me.* Fearing she would fall to weeping if she said any more, Ana pressed her lips together.

A series of sharp yips signaled that the boys had freed Sally from her Sunday-morning confinement in the stable. Within seconds, the children's puppy was dashing about in happy circles as fast as her little legs could carry her still roly-poly body. Her show of uninhibited joy in being united with her loved ones was infectious. Despite her unshed tears, Ana was soon laughing along with the children. Was there anything quite so delightful as a puppy and a clutch of children frolicking together?

"Oh, to be that young and carefree."

"Oh!"

Assuming he was still in the churchyard, Ana was surprised by the sound of Ian's voice. That the low rumble had been so close to her ear set off a reverberation along her neck that continued across her shoulder, down her arm, and to the tips of her fingers. She managed not to jump or squirm but had to place her hand across her bosom to still the fluttering in her heart.

"Brother Ian. I didn't expect you so soon." Spying her sister and her beau right behind him, she set aside her discomfiture, broke into a warm smile, and opened her arms. "Laurel!"

After embracing her sister, she acknowledged Alan. "Mr. Fruth, how good it is to see you," she said as she extended her hand.

"The pleasure is surely all mine, Miss MacPherson."

Pressing her hand lightly, the young man tipped his hat and bent slightly at the waist. Charmed by his display of such refined manners, Ana graced him with a broad smile. "Do tell me that Brother Ian has invited you and Laurel for Sunday dinner."

"Only if it is not an inconvenience to you, ma'am."

"Of course not. Gerta always prepares more than enough. Simply a matter of setting two more places at the table," she said, feeling genuine gladness that there would be guests for Sunday dinner. Her joy had as much to do with the identity of the guests themselves as that they would add even more assurance she and Ian were not alone. And dispel the lingering discomfort of Papa's sermon.

Linking her arm in her sister's, she started walking toward the house. Looking over her shoulder, she saw that the men weren't yet following. Having circled the newcomer several times, Sally had evidently decided Mr. Fruth was no threat and was making his acquaintance. Ian stood nearby looking toward her with a most curious expression on his face.

"I'm sure you gentlemen have things to talk about, but do not tarry overlong. Gerta will have dinner on the table shortly." Turning her attention back to her sister, she remarked, "It's good to have you here today, Laurel. And your nice Mr. Fruth, of course."

"She's a great deal like their mother, isn't she?" Alan remarked as he knelt on one knee and scratched behind Sally's ears.

"Yes, she's very good with the children. Gentle, friendly,

and quite smart." Flicking only the barest glance toward his friend, Ian returned his full attention to the retreating backs of the two MacPherson sisters, Ana's in particular. Her back had such a graceful line, and her waist was so small. His hands tingled with the need to find out just how small it was without a tightly laced corset.

"Gentle, friendly, and quite smart?" Alan's chuckle drew Ian's attention away from the enticing sway of Ana's skirts. "Interesting way to describe a woman. The ladies must swoon at your feet with sweet talk like that," Fruth teased.

The way he was grinning at him made Ian decidedly uncomfortable. "Ah . . . I'm afraid I had not realized our conversation had shifted from the dog."

Fruth laughed. "I guessed that." He joined Ian in watching the MacPherson sisters retreat. "You know, I always thought Valeriana more like their father. I confess that, until today, I would not have thought there was much of their mother's warmth and laughter in her at all. Of course, I don't know the family as intimately as you do. I'm sure I have much to learn about them."

Once again Ian pulled his gaze away from the enticing sway of Ana's skirts. "Oh, the MacPhersons are full of hidden depths and surprises. Even after nine years of association with the family, I am continually learning new things about them." *And about myself.*

He shook his head, wondering if he could survive any more surprises when it came to Ana and the gut-wrenching, wake-up-in-a-cold-sweat nights he was experiencing because of her. "Come, we'd best not tarry. Valeriana likes to keep a strict schedule. By the way she greeted you, it's clear you've won her approval. Best not risk losing it by being late to dinner. You might need her to champion your cause with John."

Fruth visibly shuddered, and Ian laughed. "Only you can know if a life with the enchanting Laurel is worth being the reverend's son-in-law."

"I believe I'd brave almost anything if Laurel would agree to be my wife," Fruth solemnly vowed.

"You may have to, my friend. God only knows what motivates John MacPherson."

Chapter Ten

Laboring over the following Sunday's sermon, John MacPherson turned for inspiration to the painting Lily had made of Grace Church. She'd done a respectable job of portraying the church, including the spire he envisioned one day soaring from the belfry.

"My Lily's head was always in the clouds," he said to the empty room as he leaned back in his chair. A spire dedicated to her memory seemed only fitting.

Tipping his chair farther, he dropped his gaze to a portrait Anson Phillips had done of Lily. His chair legs immediately hit the floor with a crash. That painter had no sense at all, making such a fool of himself at Lily's grave.

MacPherson shuddered and shook his head. Not for the first time, he wondered if Lily had been an angel of patience and Christian charity, or just plain dull-witted to have spent so much time with such a miserable excuse for a man. "Forgive me, Lord, You know I did love her, but for all the beauty You blessed her with, You did short her on common sense."

With a sigh, he turned to the task at hand, primarily how best to wring donations from his congregation for the Lileas MacPherson Patterson Memorial Spire. Without Valeriana there to help him, he wrestled with the words, spending more time gazing around the room than moving his pen across the paper.

A spot near the ceiling drew his eye. A spider had spun quite an intricate web there, so long ago now the once silvery threads were blackened and heavy with dust. Looking about, he noted that a layer of dust had collected on nearly every surface in the room. Papers and books were scattered about in no order. Everywhere were signs of neglect. Rose was possessed of many gifts, but alas, housekeeping was not among them.

He'd speak to Ana about it. She'd not be pleased that the housemaid had let his study come to such a sorry pass. He reached for the handbell he kept at the corner of his desk, then replaced it with but a faint tinkle. Ana was no longer in residence at the parsonage. That he had two other daughters he could have called upon to take up Ana's supervisional tasks did not enter his head.

He forced his attention back to the sermon. After perusing what he'd already written, he crumpled the parchment and tossed it to join the other attempts he'd discarded. Ana. Her special gifts and contributions to the family extended far beyond keeping the household running smoothly.

"Gave her a logical mind, You did, Lord," MacPherson muttered. "Most logical mind in any woman yet created," he remarked, remembering how early Ana had shown a knack for learning.

Whereas her sisters had barely absorbed the lessons he'd given them in reading, ciphering, and a smattering of history, Ana had approached learning eagerly, and he'd been inspired to continue instructing her. As the years went on, he'd imparted to her just about everything he'd ever learned during his years at Princeton and the seminary.

Espying the framed diploma he was so proud of, he thought for a moment that it was a pity Ana would never have one. But it was the way of things. Women naturally just didn't have the strength of mind for much education. Even one as strong and logical as Ana's might not have withstood the strain of attending a university. He'd saved her from that ordeal. "And a good, God-fearing woman she is, too. She knows her duty to You, Lord, and to her family."

Rising, he moved to the windows overlooking the square. A haze of dust rising from the road that circled the patch of carefully clipped grass caught the sun, glittering almost as if it were gold dust. A fitting description, MacPherson mused, for marching away from the square's perimeter were the homes of Cleveland's wealthy. His son-in-law's home was by far one of the grandest of them.

The reverend felt a stab of sinful envy of the man, prompted most of all by the fact that his efficient daughter, Ana, was now overseeing his house, while her very own father had to suffer living in filth and disorder. His stomach growled, reminding him that the midday meal had been scanty, ill-prepared, and late—as all the meals had been since he'd packed Ana off to Euclid Street.

"Enough! If a man knows not how to rule his own house, how shall he take care of the house of God?"

If he was interpreting the scripture rather loosely in order to rationalize storming across the square and dragging his daughter back to his house, the reverend had not the slightest qualm. Surely the Lord would agree that the needs of his most devout of servants, John MacPherson, took precedence over those of that sinner Ian Patterson.

"Lord, it is time I look to what's best for the rest of the flock You've placed in my care. I simply cannot administer to them at all properly when I must suffer such rude conditions." Grabbing his top hat from the row of pegs just inside the front door, he set off down the steps of his house and across the square, muttering as he went.

Those few people he passed as he advanced toward the Patterson house hid their knowing smiles as best they could. The Reverend John MacPherson's habit of carrying on one-sided conversations was well known to the residents of Cleveland and was a source of entertainment to most. He'd had that tendency ever since he'd come to Cleveland. Since his collapse after Lily's funeral, it had become more pronounced. Strangers, however, assumed the tall, lanky man striding along the street, talking to apparently no one and occasionally gesturing wildly, was the local loony and best given a wide berth.

The shortness of the distance and the briskness of his long-legged stride brought MacPherson to the Patterson doorstep in good time. His vigorous use of the weighty brass door knocker centered upon the heavy carved door brought one of the maids to the door quickly. And his daughter did not make him wait long in the parlor before attending him.

"Papa . . . ?" Ana, still flushed from her hurried flight down the stairs, rose on her tiptoes to brush a kiss in the vicinity of her father's reddened cheek. "How good to see you," she said, as she tried to calm her fluttering nerves. Her father's flushed complexion and the way a muscle in his jaw flexed were proof that this was not a social call.

"Daughter, you must leave this house immediately," were MacPherson's first words. "Now. This very day. This very hour, if at all possible!"

Taken aback by the vehemence of his pronouncement, Ana could only surmise that he believed Brother Ian had committed some action so grievously sinful that he could no longer countenance his daughter residing under the same roof with the man. Knowing from long experience that when her father had worked himself into such a state, it was best to acquiesce and sort things out later, she said, "Of course, Papa, but it will take a few hours for me to pack up the children's things."

Her father's shaggy brows rose almost to his hairline. "The children? No ... no, they must stay here where they belong. That house up the way is in ruin enough without adding four youngsters running and screaming about it."

"But, Papa, surely you can't mean to leave the children behind. It was for their sakes that you sent me here in the first place," she reminded in as gentle tones as she could manage.

"A child's proper place is with his parent! Besides, Patterson has a houseful of servants to run the place and oversee his children. Your place is at home with your father!"

"But, Papa, I cannot leave the children with just servants."

MacPherson leaned toward her so that his face was nearly at a level with hers. "I'll not stand for any arguments from the likes of you. I set you to a task that was obviously not part of God's plan, and I've suffered for it. 'Tis clear that your calling is by my side as you were before. You will come home and see to your duties there. The house has fallen to sloth, and the meals are barely palatable. 'Tis a sign that I've erred in God's work."

Oblivious to his daughter's stunned reaction, MacPherson rambled on in his usual style—more thinking aloud than actually conversing with another mortal. "Now that Lily's gone, I shall have to look elsewhere for a wealthy patron. Once he's moved over to that godforsaken island, I can't expect much more from Patterson."

He paused, and a strange light came into his eyes that was even more frightening. When he spoke again, his voice had lost its anger and taken on a speculative tone.

"Perhaps there's still time. I shouldn't have sent you. Should've sent Laurel. She'd have done all right by the children and caught his eye, too. She's almost as pretty as Lily was. Dreamy, too, in her own way, and certainly a softer kind of female than yourself. And I can spare her. But I can't spare you, so come along now."

"But, Papa, Laurel has a beau. She and Mr. Fruth are—"

"Yes, that's it," he exclaimed as if he hadn't heard her. He tipped his head heavenward. "Lord, forgive me. I was too confused and distraught in my grief at the time. I was not thinking of the awesome burden that is Brother Ian's fortune. 'Tis Your work my Laurel will be doing in relieving him of it. She'll not fail you, Lord."

The implication of her father's words struck deeply and painfully. A heaviness settled so quickly in her chest, Ana could scarcely breathe. Staggering backward a step or two, she grabbed for the back of a chair to keep from collapsing to the floor. Swaying, her knuckles white as she clung to the support of the chair, she groped for words. None came to her mind.

"Don't stand there as if you were a fish tossed upon the beach," MacPherson commanded sharply. "Go pack your things."

Ana had spent her life obeying her father unquestioningly. God's commandments had been burned into her very soul. The fifth, "Honor thy father and thy mother," had been her father's most effective tool against any rebellion from his offspring.

Her mind numb, Ana staggered toward the parlor door. But when her shaking hand closed around the doorknob, it was as if the cold brass against her heated palm were a bucket of cold water emptied over her head.

Slowly, she turned around and faced her sire. Her chin up, though her insides were a quaking mass, she said softly, "No, Papa. I will not go pack my things."

So caught up was he in his own thoughts, MacPherson merely remarked, "Fine . . . fine. Call one of the maids to do it. More fitting, I suppose. After all, you are a woman of some importance."

Despite the sting of tears in her eyes, Ana's gaze was steady. Her voice more firm this time, she said, "Thank you, Papa, for at least that much. But I'll not call a maid to pack my things. I'm not leaving."

This time it was MacPherson who was so taken aback he could not speak. But not for long. Fixing her with a look his congregation knew to be the signal that they were in for a long sermon full of righteous anger, he advanced upon her. "Daughter! You will do as I say, and do it now!"

Swallowing hard against the lump in her throat, Ana moved a fraction closer to the door. Still, she did not turn and flee through the portal as survival instincts might best have served her. "No, Papa," she said again, hating the quaver she heard in her voice. The heaviness that had been in her chest making her breathing so difficult was replaced by a roiling in her stomach. She swallowed the bitter bile rising in her throat and turned slowly to face her father once again.

Nearly purple with rage, MacPherson took a threatening step toward her. "I've given you a direct order, Valeriana Grace. You will honor your father. 'Tis God's own commandment."

Shaking her head slowly, Ana said, "No, Papa. I shall risk breaking that commandment, for I cannot honor your order. I shall not leave the children. Nor will you send Laurel here with such a despicable task."

She took a deep breath, stiffened her spine, and declared, "I shall stay, for surely it is God's will that I do."

Unused to his authority being either questioned or

thwarted, MacPherson felt his rage explode. "Daughter! You dare to assume you know God's will better than I?"

"Forgive me, Papa, but in this I believe I do."

"Blasphemer!" he roared as he swung his palm to her cheek.

The force of the blow knocked Ana to the floor. And it was at that moment that the door opened.

"What the—"

Ian's blood chilled at the sight that greeted him in the parlor. Ana lay crumpled in a heap on the floor, a bright red imprint on her cheek the only color on her face. If it had been anyone but her father who'd delivered that blow, he would have leveled him with a fist to the chin. As it was he was hard put to keep his hands at his sides.

Shaking with rage, he shoved MacPherson out of his way and was at Ana's side in two more strides. Kneeling beside her, he gathered her into his arms. Like a frightened child, she huddled into the protection his body offered.

"I . . . I'll be all right," she said, even though her tears were already soaking his shirt and she was shaking violently.

"Shh, shh, you're safe now," he told her, gently pushing the hair from her face with one hand and running the other gently up and down her back. "John, I must ask you to leave this house and leave it immediately."

"Get out of my way, Patterson. My daughter is coming with me." He made a grab for Ana's arm, but Ian locked his hand around MacPherson's first. Keeping an iron hold on him, Ian rose and pulled the older man away from Ana.

"How dare you. Take your hands off me," MacPherson cried, and attempted to free himself.

Ian tightened his hold on the man. "Leave off, John, or

I shall forget who you are and give you the throttling you deserve."

"Valeriana!" MacPherson's eyes were wild with fury. "Come with me now!"

"Ana, stay where you are!" Ian's order was just as strong.

Staggering to her feet, Ana clutched at the back of a chair for support. Unable to look at her father, she said to Ian, "Please be . . . be gentle with him. He . . . he . . . is not himself today."

"No doubt," Ian remarked dryly, but didn't loosen his hold. "Will you be all right?" At her nod, he started through the doorway. "I'll see that he gets home."

Far from defeat, MacPherson still had guns to fire. "Valeriana. Leave this house with me, or I shall denounce you from the pulpit for the jezebel you are!"

"Papa!"

"There's no basis for that, MacPherson," Ian said, but pulled the man back into the parlor. Shoving him down into the nearest chair, he stood over him lest he attempt to make another move toward Ana. "Before we entertain the servants with any more of this nonsense, Ana, close that door."

Much as on the night of Lily's funeral, MacPherson began muttering almost incoherently. "Can't stay here. Got to get her home. Put Laurel here. Better. She'll do her duty."

Frowning, Ian looked to Ana. "What is he talking about?"

Mortified by what her father was saying, Ana shook her head. "Please. Pay him no mind, Brother Ian. He is not well." She knelt down beside her father and placed her hand on his arm. "Papa, Brother Ian will take you home now in his carriage."

The man worked his mouth nervously for a moment,

then looked first to her and then to Ian. "No sense in leaving you here." Catching her arm, he made to stand. "Come, we will both go in the carriage. Patterson, Laurel will be here shortly. She'll see to her sister's things," he said, his voice and even his expression sounding more rational.

"Perhaps that would be best," she said, thinking humoring him still the wiser course. Once he was back at the parsonage, Ana was sure her father would come to his senses. "Brother Ian, could you have the carriage sent around?"

"Of course, if that's what you want."

"Yes, I'll see to him. Joseph and Jessica are upstairs. Perhaps you should go to them. Assure them I'll be back soon."

The last statement was a mistake. She knew it the moment it passed her lips, for her father stiffened and wrapped his hand around her wrist. "No, you will not!" Pushing Ian aside, he started toward the door with her in tow. "No use having you here another minute. Home is where you belong!"

"But Papa, the children—"

"I'll hear no more disrespect from you, daughter."

Arm raised, MacPherson whirled about and might have struck her again if Ian hadn't caught his arm. Sweeping Ana behind him, Ian said, "She is staying here with me, John."

MacPherson narrowed his eyes on them. "So that is the way things are, are they?" Extending his arm, he pointed his finger at her and thundered, "Jezebel! Thy name will be struck from the church rolls this Sunday, and all will know you for what you are."

Ana gasped. "Papa. No!"

"Your daughter is no jezebel, John MacPherson."

"And what would you call an unmarried woman co-habiting with a man like yourself?"

"I'd call her a fine, upstanding woman who is of such good heart, she set aside her own life to care for her dead sister's children when they most needed her."

"Her sister Laurel can do that from this day forward. Valeriana belongs with me, and . . . and her mother, of course."

"No, Valeriana belongs with me," Ian stated firmly. "Here and on the island later this summer."

"She's not moving anywhere with you. Her place is with me, I tell you."

"Her place is with me," Ian announced firmly, and after the space of only a breath, added, "The man she's agreed to marry."

The room that had rung with voices now stood as silent as a tomb. Not even the breathing of the three persons occupying it could be heard in the stunned silence. MacPherson was the first to recover. "No. You lie. She'd not do such a thing, and if she had, she certainly would have told me."

Before Ana could say anything, she felt Ian's arm around her waist. "From what I could hear of your conversation when I arrived, I doubt you gave her the chance. Or perhaps she simply has not grown used to the idea, being as how it was so recently that I proposed to her."

"Brother Ian, I cannot—" Ian's hold about Ana's waist tightened slightly, warning her to keep silent. "Now, Ana, do you not think it is time you stopped calling me Brother Ian? Just Ian will do, or perhaps an endearment like darling or sweetheart."

Stunned by the extent of his spurious fabricating, Ana had no trouble keeping silent. Looking to Ian and then to her father, she was not sure which of them was "not himself" this day. Both, she was sure, for her father was looking close to an explosion from which he might never recover. And Ian was wearing such an odd smile she wanted to wipe it from his face by throwing something at him. Before she could say or do anything, he leaned close and whispered, *"Say absolutely nothing,"* and brushed his lips against her cheek.

The caress was soft and brief, but Ana felt its imprint long after he'd straightened. From what seemed a great distance away, she heard him say, "Now, John, if you're concerned about propriety, I'd be happy for Laurel or Primmy to move in with us between now and the ceremony. I assure you there is no need, as I give you my word nothing untoward has occurred nor will it before the wedding. But Ana would enjoy their company and could certainly use their help with the packing."

"There'll be no wedding," MacPherson began, not as explosively as Ana expected but with a calm certainty that was even more powerful. "Not between you and my Ana. It isn't God's plan for her, I tell you. I'll have no part of it."

"And I tell you, it is," Ian returned, his eyes never wavering as he stared down his father-in-law. "If you'll not perform the ceremony, I'm sure Pastor Harnish at First Methodist will be only too happy to do so."

MacPherson opened his mouth, then shut it tightly. His nostrils flared, and his face reddened. "Not while there's a breath in my body. I *am* that woman's father, and if there's any marrying to do, I'll do it." He glared malevolently at both of them and growled, "By the looks of things, it can't take place any too soon."

"This Sunday right after services would suit us just fine," Ian supplied smoothly. Ana's gasp earned her another silencing squeeze. "I'd thought to surprise Ana at supper with my news, but I suppose there's no time like the present."

Turning to her, he smiled and announced, "My dear, a house is ready for us. We'll be able to move to the island this Sunday."

Already dazed by the lies tripping from his tongue, Ana was benumbed by the announcement that the day she had been dreading for months was upon her. The children were to be wrenched from her only four days hence. If Ian had not been holding her up, she feared she would have crumpled again to the floor. "This Sunday? You . . . the children. This Sunday?"

"Yes, dearest. All of us, which means you, too," he said with a smile that seemed to spread from ear to ear. But absent was the mischievous glow that sparkled in those hazel orbs when he was truly happy.

"But—"

He silenced her with a finger across her lips. "I know you have many concerns about the move and the house, but we'll talk of them later, after your father leaves. I'm sure he'll want to tell your mother and sisters the happy news immediately." Gently but firmly, he guided her to a chair. "Wait for me here while I walk your father out."

After seeing MacPherson out the front door, Ian didn't much care whether the preacher found his way back to the parsonage or stumbled into the lake. He would have gladly helped him take a plunge in the cold waters if he hadn't known that would upset Ana even further. Attempting to rein in his rage, he stood in the foyer taking several deep breaths.

My God, if ever a man needed a drink. He considered, then quickly rejected the idea of retrieving one of the bottles hidden in the stable. He couldn't leave Ana alone in that room much longer, and she was distressed enough already. Smelling liquor on his breath would throw her into apoplexy and wouldn't help his cause any.

He ran a shaking hand down his face. He'd actually announced they were to marry and immediately. This coming Sunday. A mere four days hence he would be married again, and to a MacPherson . . . *again*! Most surprising of all was that down deep inside him, he was actually glad about it.

He didn't fool himself that he'd fallen madly in love with her. But he did have a high regard for her and actually liked quite a lot about her. She was a woman of uncommon intelligence and good sense. Loving, gentle, loyal.

Good God, he was again describing her as if she were a dog. A good dog was all those things, but a woman like Ana was a helluva lot more. No dog could smile the way Ana did, or laugh in a way that made the whole room feel warmer. Ana was all woman with a beauty all her own, part Madonna and a lot Eve.

She loved his children, and they loved her. He liked her, and he desired her. It was plenty to base a sound marriage on. And marriage would put an end to all the dancing around each other they'd been doing for the past few weeks, a vain attempt to deny the attraction between them. No more restless nights waking up in a cold sweat.

That is, all would be well if he could convince Ana to go through with the ceremony.

Deciding he'd already left her alone to think longer than was prudent, he reached for the doorknob. But instead of grasping it, he pulled his hand back, turned on his heel, and headed in the opposite direction. Tea. Women like Ana turned to steaming cups of tea when they were distressed.

Moments later, a small tray balanced in one hand, he let himself into the parlor. She wasn't sitting on the chair where he'd left her but standing at the far side of the room. What was left of a lace-edged handkerchief dangled from one shaking hand. Nothing was amiss in the room, but she'd been pacing ever since he'd left her. The way her fingers tugged at the shreds of lace and linen, he was sure of it. If there was one thing he knew about Ana MacPherson, it was that she paced when she was agitated about something.

The eyes she turned on him were red-rimmed and puffy from tears. The mark on her cheek was no longer as vivid, but her skin was so pale and delicate, she'd wear her father's mark for days. His outrage returned full force. He had to take several deep breaths before he could trust that his voice wouldn't reflect what he was feeling.

Pasting a smile on his face, he said at last, "I apologize for taking so long, but I thought you might like some tea to calm your nerves."

Sniffing, she dabbed at her eyes. "That was very kind of you."

There was still a slight quaver in her voice, and he could hear the shaking catches in her breathing. "I sent the Marys up to Joe and Jessie," he began, trying for as pleasant and temperate a tone as he could manage. "Since it's such a fine day, they thought to take them outside to play for a bit."

He set the tray down on the table before the divan. "Come, sit down," he invited, surprised that his own voice was so smooth. His hands, too, had stopped shaking, he noted, when he poured a cup of tea for her. "Gerta is going to keep an eye out for Maara and Rob. Once they're home from school, I imagine she'll gather them all into the kitchen and keep them busy for a bit."

The teacup halfway to her lips, Ana turned worried eyes to him. "The staff, did they hear? Do they know?"

"No, I'm sure not," he lied. When he'd entered the kitchen, one look at Gerta's face and he'd known she'd heard MacPherson's shouting. He'd taken a moment to assure the woman that the reverend had just "not been himself" for a little while but that all was well now. How the mark on Ana's face would be explained, he'd worry about later. "I didn't tell anyone yet about our marriage. I thought perhaps you'd prefer we did that together."

Abruptly, Ana set her cup and saucer back on the table. "There isn't going to be any marriage."

He'd anticipated her statement and was ready. "You have no choice, unless you want to desert the children just when their lives are about to be disrupted once again."

"But ... but you ... I assumed—" She gasped a breath and let it out quickly. "You have said nothing about my remaining with the children. Indeed, I have had the impression you hoped to see the last of me when you moved to the island."

Ian rose, shoved a hand in his pocket, and decided Ana's habit of pacing was perhaps a good course when confronted with a difficult situation. "Once that was true," he admitted, pausing before a small console where someone, probably Ana, had placed a vase of fresh flowers. "But I've changed my mind about that."

He ran the tip of his finger along a rose petal. The ivory tone of the blossom was very much like Ana's skin. And as velvety soft. Before his imagination sent him down a trail that would make it impossible for him to face her without embarrassing them both, he lifted his hand from the flower and pressed it hard against the cold, hard marble surface of the console. "We need you, the children and I, to come to the island with us."

She was shaking her head. Before she could say anything to the contrary, he presented what he thought was his most convincing argument for their marrying. "If there is one thing I'm certain of, it's that you love my children as much as I do and would do anything necessary to protect them. While it may be correct that your father was not quite himself today, do either of us really doubt that he would make good on his threats if you move to the island and remain under my roof without the sanction of marriage?"

The sharp intake of her breath and the way her eyes dulled was all the answer he needed. "It's immaterial what he might say of me. There's little he hasn't already accused me of over the years. But you? Could you bear for him to disown you? And denounce you from the pulpit?"

"Papa would not—" She paused, squeezed her eyes shut, and her shoulders sagged in defeat. But for the bruise on her left cheek, her face was blanched of color. He hated himself for adding to the ordeals she'd suffered this day, but he saw no way out of it. Assuming there was even a chance of succeeding, he did not have the luxury of time to woo her gently into accepting his proposal.

"Even if we kept the children away from him so that they never hear his denouncements of you and me firsthand, someone is bound to tell them of it. Given their ages, they might not understand what he is accusing you and me of. But in time they would, and in time they would be deeply hurt by it. No matter how honorably you and I might conduct ourselves, and no matter how honorably they conduct themselves throughout the long life ahead of each of them, there would always be whispers behind their backs and certain doors closed to them."

If possible, she grew even whiter, making the bruise on her left cheek stand out even more obscenely. Crouching down in front of her, he took her cold hands in his.

"Valeriana, would you please do me the honor of becoming my wife and, in truth, the mother of my children?"

With a shuddering breath, she closed her eyes. Finally, when he was beginning to fear she'd succumbed to an understandable swoon given all she'd endured this afternoon, she opened her eyes. Her gaze and her voice steady, she said, "I will marry you, Ian Patterson."

It wasn't until that moment that he realized he'd been holding his breath. Letting it out as unobtrusively as he could, he raised her hands to his lips and brushed a kiss across their tops. Before he could say anything, she added, "But on one condition," and pulled her hands from his grasp. "Our marriage will be in name only."

Chapter Eleven

Startled, Ian rocked back on his heels. "In name only!" Frowning, he shook his head. "No!" The denial came from the depths of his soul. And far too loudly, judging by the way her eyes widened and she shrank away from him.

Thinking quickly, he realized that for a woman as new to desire as Ana most probably was, it was natural that she would need some time to adjust to a change so dramatic as living as man and wife. Recapturing her hands, he said, "Ana, I realize you've suffered a great shock today. It's been a shock to me, too. I never expected to walk into my house this afternoon or any other time and find you lying on the floor in a crumpled heap."

She winced, and he realized he was gripping her hands too tightly. He loosened his grasp and drew in his breath to still the demons that raged within him. *Good God, what if I hadn't come home just then?* The possibilities were chilling. Never had he come as close to pounding someone to a bloody pulp as when he'd seen John's hand imprint on Ana's cheek.

Another deep breath and he was able to proceed calmly. "Certainly I didn't expect to be discussing marriage with you this afternoon, either. But we are, and it's only reasonable that it will take time for both of us to get used to the idea. Sunday is but four days hence. Not even by then would I expect either of us to be ready for the physical intimacies of the marriage bed."

That was perhaps the biggest lie of his life. But he sure as hell couldn't admit he'd been lusting for her body for weeks and that even Sunday night seemed a long way off. She'd likely dash him over the head with the first thing she could wrap her hands around, then pack herself and the children off to the parsonage while he still lay unconscious on the floor.

He knew she desired him. She couldn't respond to his kisses and not be feeling the same hot need that he felt. But it would be a mistake to force her to acknowledge that Valeriana Grace MacPherson felt anything so primal as lust. Especially not today, when her emotions were so raw.

"I'm a patient man, and I promise you all the time you need to become accustomed to your new status as my wife. You're a virtuous woman and gently reared. It's only logical that you should have some fears of the marriage bed. But when you're ready, I shall be as careful and gentle with you as is possible. You'll have no cause to regret becoming my wife in deed as well as name."

Ana yanked her hands free and jumped to her feet. The tea table would have toppled over during her flight if he had not made a mad grab for it. From the safety of several feet away, she began to pace. "Time won't make a difference. I'm just not the sort of woman a man like you wants for a wife, so there's no reason we should try to make this marriage into something it's not."

His brows shot up. "And just what is this marriage?"

"It's a practical arrangement, of course."

"Practical. I daresay most marriages are," he said. "But enlighten me as to why this practical arrangement of ours should be in name only."

"Don't be obtuse." She made an impatient sound and quickened her pace. "After your being married to someone like Lily, I have no delusions that you proposed marriage for any reason other than the children. And it is for their sakes that I have agreed to go through with the ceremony.

"I will be a good mother to them and run your household, but I assure you, that is all I have agreed to. At no time in the future do I anticipate any change in our relationship except that I shall carry your name."

"And am I to assume you will remain chaste for the rest of your life, madam?"

"Of course."

"Good, then I won't have married someone like Lily," he said, and started for the door. "But if someday you should find yourself experiencing something so mortal as desire, I expect you to come to me for satisfaction. No one else. Is that understood?"

Out of the corner of his eye, he saw her pick up the figurine and managed to sidestep in time. "Marriage to you, madam, will indeed be interesting," he said, eyeing the shards of scattered porcelain across the floor. "Not necessarily practical, though." Carefully stepping around the debris, he reached for the doorknob.

"Don't you dare leave yet. I'm not finished."

"Indeed," he said, actually glad to see her at her formidable Valeriana MacPherson best. It wasn't his favorite side of her, but it was definitely preferable to the downtrodden woman she'd been at the start of this discussion.

Her hands on her hips, her magnificent bosom heaved with every breath she took. There was such fire in her, and it was going to be his pleasure to direct it to more satisfying avenues. Not today. Not tomorrow. But one day. He could wait until she was ready. Days, weeks maybe. But not months. The way she heated his blood, he'd be dead if he had to wait too long.

Not his sort of woman? He would've laughed had she

not been standing so close to Lily's collection of porcelain figures. He didn't care if Ana broke them all, but she'd be mortified. After all, a "good Christian woman" like Valeriana MacPherson wasn't supposed to throw things.

"You have something more to discuss, my dear?" he asked as he wandered about the room. "Details of the wedding? More demands?"

As he expected, Ana counterpointed his movements, and he was able to guide her away from her source of ammunition. "I'm not going to sign that damned pledge, if that's what you're expecting."

"No, I didn't suppose you would," she admitted with a sigh of resignation. "The pledge is the farthest thing from my mind right now. However, now that you've brought it up, I want it understood that I will not countenance spirits in my house."

"I believe you've already made that perfectly clear. In turn, I shall confine my occasional indulgence in a glass of whiskey, brandy, or fine wine to other locations."

Pursing her lips, Ana dipped her head in acknowledgment. She walked several feet in a path paralleling the windows, turned, and retraced her steps. Whatever she was about to announce was troubling her a great deal, as her stride was brisk and she was further destroying the lace on her handkerchief.

Folding his arms across his chest, Ian leaned against the opposite wall, prepared to wait however long it took until she was ready to voice her concerns. When her pacing slowed and he saw renewed tears in her eyes, he frowned. She was more than troubled; she was suffering. Heaving away from the wall, he crossed the room and put his arm around her shoulders. "What is it, Ana? Is it marriage or marriage to me specifically that's so frightening?"

She swayed, and he caught her in his arms. Whatever hold she'd had on her emotions shattered. She buried her face against his chest and began to weep. "Shh . . . shh . . ." he said against her head. "You've had a bad time today. You deserve a good, long cry."

"It . . . it's not marriage . . . or you," she managed. "It's Paaapa." The last came out in a long, mournful cry, as if torn from the depths of her heart. "I won't have him perform the ceremony."

He'd have preferred anyone else, too, but there was more at stake than Ana's or his feelings. "You don't mean that. How would that look?"

Holding her carefully, he rocked her, thinking what a habit it was becoming. Only a few weeks ago, it had been he who'd caused her tears. Today, her father had broken her heart. In the span of a month, she'd probably cried more tears than she had in a year, maybe ten years.

"Everyone in Cleveland knows how devoted you've always been to your father."

"Not anymore," she wailed, and her tears fell more earnestly.

"Shh . . . shh. You said it yourself. John wasn't himself today. He hasn't been since Lily died. Else he wouldn't have said all that he did, or struck you," Ian added, though he wasn't so sure about the slap. From what she'd said that afternoon when he'd held her thus, he had the distinct impression John MacPherson had used physical means not only to discipline his children but to bend them to his will.

"He was himself," she stated coldly. "I've been a . . . a fool."

"No one would ever think you a fool, Ana," he assured her.

"Everyone must, just as they think Papa's a fool."

"Pious and zealous, but not a fool," Ian corrected,

thinking he was consoling her. Instead, his words set off another flood of weeping.

"Don't . . . be . . . so kind. He . . . he doesn't . . . care . . . about anyone or anything except . . . his ch-church." What followed was a halting summary of the argument she'd had with her father, finishing with her father's threat to dangle Laurel in front of Ian so that she could relieve him of the "awesome burden" of his fortune.

"There, there, put it all behind you. I'm marrying you, not Laurel. Your father means well. His zeal just overshadows all else sometimes. In time, I'm sure you'll find a way to forgive him."

"He—he doesn't deserve forgiveness for using people to accomplish his own ends. You have . . . have given and given and he . . . he has done nothing but revile you from the pul-pulpit. You . . . you're not guilty of even ha-half of what he accuses you of, are you?"

Sighing, he rested his chin on her head and ran soothing circles over her back as he'd done before. "I'm not as bad as John likes to paint me, but I'm hardly a saint. Don't feel sorry for me; I could have stayed away from his church, just as I could have tightened the purse strings years ago."

She sniffed and sounded a bit calmer when she asked, "Why didn't you?"

"I've done well in this country, better than I ever dreamed when I arrived here. But all I've achieved was not solely from the sweat of my own brow. Perhaps I've put up with your father's condemnations and even what some might think was extortion as a way of atoning for the means that provided the lifestyle I was born into and indirectly the one I have now."

Frowning, she lifted her head from his chest and asked, "And what kind of life was that? What was your family like?"

"Another time," he said evasively. "You've had enough to digest for one day." He smiled. "Feeling better?"

"Yes and no." She took a deep, hiccuping breath and explained, "I can't forgive Papa. I don't want him to perform the ceremony. I don't ever want to see him again."

"You don't have to," he told her. "But before I go make arrangements with Harnish or whatever other pastor in town you'd prefer, I want you to think about it just a bit longer.

"I know it would be difficult for you to face him again, but tongues will wag for certain if we have a clandestine ceremony somewhere else. And there'll be a breach between you and the rest of your family, and quite possibly the children and all the MacPhersons."

He shrugged. "In the long run, you would suffer far more than whatever discomfort or even anguish you'll feel this Sunday standing before him for a short time as he reads the marriage vows. It's no easy thing to be estranged from one's family."

His understanding and caring only added to her shame. "But he . . . I trapped you," she said, dropping her cheek to his thoroughly tear-drenched shirtfront.

"Trapped, my dear?" he drawled. Cradling her face between his hands, he smiled down at her, a soft amber-eyed smile that turned her bones to jelly. "I'm not so easily manipulated, I assure you. As I recall, it was I who said that we were going to marry. Your father was and probably still is quite opposed to it."

"But—"

He silenced her with a kiss. But what started as a whisper-soft brushing of his lips against hers quickly escalated to a full possession. "And I'm not letting you renege on your acceptance either," he growled against her lips before taking them again.

Large hands that had been cradling her face plunged

into her hair, sending her cap and hairpins flying as he freed the heavy coil at her nape. With the caress of his tongue against her lips growing ever bolder and more brazen, she sank more deeply into the kiss and his embrace.

Ana didn't even think to resist going where he led but opened willingly and welcomed each thrust and caress. Being kissed by Ian Patterson was a heady experience, to say the least. Each brush of his lips and caress of his tongue made her eager to learn more. Inexperienced as she was, she was certain that kissing was an art in which Ian was most definitely a master.

And he was indeed teaching her. Each time he sent his tongue sweeping through her mouth, he returned to guide and tease hers to do the same to him. Her head spun as she tried to analyze each facet and nuance, catalog each action of his lips, tongue, and hands. The way he sifted his fingers through her hair, loosening the braid until her hair fell completely loose and free about her shoulders and down her back.

If she hadn't given a tiny sigh and shifted closer when his hands drifted below her waist and across her bottom, or, when he lifted his head, if she hadn't lifted her hands to either side of his face and pulled him back down, he might have eased her away from him and ended the embrace.

Her kiss was instant proof she was a quick learner—hot, boldly exploratory, and incredibly exciting. Ian's senses reeled, and his blood surged to his groin. She was emotionally fragile right now, his conscience reminded him even as he cupped his hands over her bottom, lifted her, and pressed her against his aching erection.

Too many layers separated them. Driven by an over-powering need to sink into the sweet oblivion he'd find in her body, he clutched handfuls of linen and stiff muslin and started to ruck her skirts up.

A marriage in name only. That was what she thought she wanted.

Ian opened his hands and let her skirts fall back in place. Only a beast would take advantage of her fragile emotions today and rush the fences like this. And taking a virgin right here and under these circumstances was the act of a beast for certain. But the last thing she needed was a sudden rejection.

Slowly he set about calming himself and her. Carefully and expertly, he tamed the wildness of their kiss and gradually eased their lips and bodies apart. "You're a warm and beautiful woman, Ana." He kissed the tip of her nose and gently set her away. "We will deal well together. Very well, indeed."

Chapter Twelve

Sunday, June 22, 1834
Grace Church, Cleveland

"Dearly beloved, we are gathered here today in the sight of God and these witnesses to unite this man and this woman in holy matrimony. . . ."

Every pew in Grace Church was packed tight, and some parishioners stood along the back wall. By the time the bride's father finally got around to the opening lines of the marriage ceremony, it was no wonder the attention of some wandered afield. He'd already put them through a Sunday-morning service consisting of a two-hour sermon based on the Fifth Commandment. After a brief break to allow anyone to leave who cared to—nobody did—he'd started in for at least another hour on just about every passage in the Holy Bible that referred even remotely to the holy estate of matrimony.

"You could've knocked me over with a feather when the preacher said Ian Patterson and Valeriana MacPherson would be marrying up after services today."

"Seems like only yesterday we were burying Lily."

"It's been almost three months."

"Humph. Hardly cold in her grave, I say."

166

"I'd have thought Rose would have said something at Circle on Tuesday."

"Well, they're not the first couple and surely won't be the last to need a wedding in a hurry."

"Oh, you don't think—"

"Shh."

The whispers, along with a fair number of raised brows, had been rippling through the church ever since MacPherson had made the announcement of the wedding just before the final prayer. The gossips would be speculating about the timing of this wedding for the better part of the coming year. And there would be plenty of speculating over why the preacher had looked so angry as he conducted the ceremony.

Those of a more charitable mind thought it a sensible match. Ian Patterson needed a mother for his children, and who better than Valeriana, who'd been caring for them as if they were her very own. And Patterson was a man in his prime. He needed a wife, and no young flibbertigibbet would be right for him and those children. Valeriana was a good, sensible woman, and right pretty in her own way. It was a shame she hadn't done something more with herself for her wedding, though.

Nobody doubted how much she mourned her sister's passing, but many thought she could've set aside her dreary duds for today. At least she was wearing gray for a change, instead of black. Of course, there were a few who weren't sure they'd ever seen Valeriana MacPherson in anything but gray, black, or brown, even before her sister had died.

She was carrying a bouquet of pink and ivory roses from her mama's garden, so there was a spot of color fitting for a bride. And that little square of lace held on her head by a ring of rosebuds was a nice touch.

Ian Patterson surely did look fine, though. Very dashing

indeed in his charcoal cutaway coat. Matching trousers with straps fastening beneath shining black ankle boots were set off by a shawl-collared waistcoat of light gray and a sparkling white shirt and cravat. He was a fine figure of a man, and there were several weeping maidens and their anxious mamas who were going to be kicking themselves all the way to the lakeshore and back for letting Valeriana MacPherson beat them to the prize. A couple of them had to reach for a second hanky when nobody stood up to object to the union.

"And forsaking all others, keep thee only unto her, so long as ye both shall live?"

His gaze steady upon her, Ian placed his hand over his bride's where it rested limply on his arm. In a clear voice that even those whispering among themselves at the back of the church could hear, he vowed, "I will."

"Valeriana, wilt thou have this man . . ."

Ana swallowed hard and drew a shaking breath. Her hand was slippery with sweat as she clutched her bouquet. She felt trapped, as much by the firm hand detaining hers as by the unfathomable light smoldering in the gold-flecked eyes gazing so steadily into hers.

". . . only unto him, so long as ye both shall live?" sounded from somewhere seemingly far above her. It was a moment before she realized it was time for her to respond. Her hesitation was long enough that the rustling and whispers behind her ceased.

A flush of heat rose on her cheeks. "I will," she managed barely loudly enough for those straining forward in the first pews to hear.

Ian's voice rang clearly through the church as he repeated the words that would bind them together for a lifetime. When it was her turn to declare before God and all that were gathered that she, Valeriana Grace MacPherson, would take Ian Kendrick Patterson as her wedded husband, and promise to love and obey him until death parted them, she hesitated again.

Throughout the ceremony, she'd tried not to look at her father. But the anger resonating in his voice as he read the vows brought her head up. A cold tremor ran down her back at what she saw in his face. Deep lines grooved his brow and jaw. And his eyes were boring into her as if willing her to refute this marriage here and now. She stood frozen for a long moment until a gentle squeeze on her hand drew her attention to her groom.

His smile and the soft light in his eyes beckoned and reassured. Swallowing hard, she forced a tremulous smile and heard the marriage lines fall softly from her own lips: ". . . and thereto I plight thee my troth."

She had done it, pledged her life and body to the man now sliding a simple band of gold on her third finger. Ian's gaze still held hers; his smile, warm and intimate, wrapped protectively around her so that she barely heard her father declaring, "They are husband and wife together. Let us pray."

Ana bowed her head, grateful for the respite from being torn between the two men's wills. While her father recited a prayer, she gathered her wits and reminded herself why she had just pledged herself to the man whose strong, warm hand still held hers. *The children.* It was for them that she had made these vows, and it was by them she would stand in good times and bad—and love and cherish until the day she died. And no matter how kind and comforting Ian had been during the ceremony and throughout these past few days—or how thrilling his kisses were—she was sure Ian had recited his vows for the same reason she had—the children.

"You may kiss the bride."

Ana blushed to the roots of her hair and gasped when Ian lifted his hands to cradle her face gently between his palms. "Relax, it's only going to be a simple kiss," he whispered.

At the first touch of his mouth, she squeezed her eyes shut and pressed her lips together. There was the faintest sound of a deep male chuckle, then he moved his mouth so seductively over hers that she heard nothing but the hammering of her own heart against her ribs. And then it was over; he was tucking her arm into his, and Laurel was pushing her bouquet back into her hand.

What followed was a dizzying hour of receiving best wishes and fielding the inevitable questions from the congregation, followed by a hurried luncheon at the parsonage. Her father neither wished them happiness nor joined the family for luncheon. Ana did not seek him out.

"He'll come around, darling," her mother assured her. "Be happy, Ana. I shall miss you, but this marriage is right, and I'm happy for both of you." Sweeping her into her arms, Rose gave Ana one last hug before Ian whisked her and the children out of the parsonage.

They made quite a parade as they moved along Water Street and toward the docks. Primmy and Laurel had insisted on accompanying them. Never far from Laurel's side these days and having stood up for Ian, Alan Fruth came to see them off. Four children and their dog dashed about in circles as if to keep them all herded in a tight cluster, and of course Ian and Ana completed the company.

"Oh, Ana, living on an island will be such an adventure," Primmy gushed, looping her arm through Ana's when Ian excused himself to go on ahead and check on some things on the *Ulsterman*.

"I suppose it does sound quite an adventure," she admitted, forcing some enthusiasm into her voice. Seeing Papa again had caused a strain that was only minimally relieved by her mother's encouragement and all the other good wishes they'd received this day. All her life she'd sought her father's approval. She'd thought they were close but realized now she'd been more his puppet than his student and assistant—or even his daughter. And now that she'd cut those strings, he wanted nothing at all to do with her.

Listening only absently to her little sister's chatter, flitting from one topic to another, she wondered if she'd ever been like Primmy. Was there ever a time she'd had nothing more serious on her mind than finding the perfect hair ribbon or a pretty new bonnet? Been as carefree as Primmy had been, seemingly since her very birth?

The answer to both questions was no, never. She was Valeriana Grace, the responsible MacPherson daughter. Always doing her duty. *Her duty.*

Despite the pleasant weather and the sunshine warming her shoulders, Ana shuddered. Each day had been such a whirl of activity from dawn till dusk that she could hardly believe it had been but four days since she had stood up to Papa and then allowed Ian to talk her into marrying him.

Just what he meant by "dealing well" had troubled her ever since he'd said it. Lily had not spared her the details when she'd confided how much she loathed performing her "marital duty" and regretted having married such a lusty man.

Ian had agreed to Ana's demand that theirs be an "in name only" marriage, and he hadn't touched her again after kissing her nearly senseless Wednesday afternoon. But how long before he demanded his marital rights?

"Why, Ana, you're shivering!" Primmy's exclamation brought Ana's attention to the present. "You're as white as a sheet and your hands are like ice. Are you feeling unwell?"

"I'm fine, really," she lied, for she was feeling decidedly unwell. Every time Ian touched her or she even

thought of his touching her, she felt unwell. Perhaps unwell was not quite it. Feverish and terribly unsettled.
And confused as she found herself increasingly yearning
for him to sweep her into his arms and kiss her again.
Perhaps she could learn to endure the rest of what went
on in the marriage bed as payment for the moments of
pleasure and security she found in his arms.

Primmy was still looking concerned about her, so she
added, "I'm just a bit tired. It's been a busy four days getting ready for the move and all."

"And terribly exciting, too," Primmy said, seemingly
satisfied by Ana's answer. "I wouldn't have been able to
sleep a wink. I'm sure you can't wait to begin your life as
Brother Ian's wife. It's all so romantic the way he's
whisking you and the children onto his lovely boat to sail
away to your very own island. *Parras*, he said he's named
it. And that it means paradise. Oh, Ana, aren't you just
thrilled?"

"It does sound like a lovely place," Ana said, though
she wanted to shout: It's not a paradise, Primmy. There
are wild hogs, maybe rattlesnakes, too. And Lord only
knows what other terrors are waiting there. And what's
between Ian and me is far from romantic.

If Ana's comment was less than enthusiastic, Primmy
didn't notice. "And I'm terribly glad he's still my brother-
in-law. I wasn't sure exactly what he was to us after Lily
died. We called him Brother Ian, but you know he really
wasn't exactly our brother-in-law anymore, was he?"

Her query needed no answer, nor did she wait for one,
but went right on with her chattering about the joys of
retaining Ian Patterson as her brother by marriage. "He's
always been so kind to all of us and so gracious in
sharing his blessings. Didn't you think it very sweet of
him to donate all the money for the spire Papa's always
wanted for the church?"

"Ian gave Papa money for the spire?" Ana felt ill for certain.

"Yes, I thought you knew. It's to be a memorial to Lily. But he didn't want it announced today because of the wedding. He told Mama that he thought a wedding should be a day of happiness with no sad feelings, like there probably would be if Lily's name were mentioned.

"I was right there when he gave Mama an envelope with the bank draft in it yesterday, or maybe it was the day before. It was one of those times when we were over helping you pack and get ready for the wedding and all."

The dull ache Ana had been suffering since awakening early that morning turned into a pounding headache. "I'm sure Papa is very pleased." *But not pleased enough to give my marriage his personal blessing.*

"I know we're all supposed to be in mourning for Lily still, but I do wish you'd had a special dress for your wedding. You've had that gray silk for years. You married the richest man in Cleveland. You should have had a new dress made for the occasion. In lavender. To match your eyes. Yes, that would have been perfect. It's a semi-mourning color, so none of the old biddies in town would have raised a brow. Perhaps with a flounce at the hem, and a little lower neckline, some beading—"

"There wasn't time, Primmy," Ana interrupted. Unconsciously, she smoothed her hand over her skirts, then fussed with the dress's only adornment, a tiny lace collar. "There were only four days to prepare for the move and so many things to do."

"Miss Van Valkenburgh could have created something spectacular for you in that amount of time. Remember all the gowns and things Lily was forever having her make for her?"

Lily's things! No arrangements had been made for the contents of Lily's bedroom. Save for that time she and the children raided the closet for some furbelows to fancy her up for Ian's return, the door had been kept closed ever since Lily's death. No one went in there except to dust and air the room. She was so used to ignoring its existence, she'd paid it not a moment's notice during the packing.

Heedless that she had only a fraction of her sister's attention, Primmy went into a discourse of all the lovely things that Lily had worn and how clever and skilled the stylish seamstress was in creating all of them. "What was done with all her things?" she asked, putting voice almost verbatim to Ana's thoughts.

"Nothing as yet," Ana admitted as they reached the *Ulsterman*'s berth. "Something should be done and soon. I must talk to Ian about it."

"What is it that must be done soon, my dear?"

"Oh, Brother Ian, where did you come from? We thought you were already on the boat," Primmy answered quickly.

"I've been on and back again so I could assist my wife on board." Smiling, he tipped his head toward where the children were motioning excitedly from the base of the gangplank. "As you can see, our family is eager to be off. I've been charged with hurrying you along."

Bowing at the waist, he crooked his arm and invited, "Mrs. Patterson, are you ready to embark?"

Before she could answer, Primmy hugged her and promised, "No matter what Papa says, I'm going to come visit and stay just as long as I please."

"And we'll be happy to have you, little sister," Ian said.

"Oh, Brother Ian, I do hope you won't think I'm taking advantage," Primmy cooed.

"Of course not, and I'm sure Ana will be happy to have her family visit. Is that not so, my dear?" he asked, appropriating her arm in his and moving her along toward the boat.

"Of course, and soon," she said, wishing Primmy were going with them now. Pulling away from Ian, she wrapped Laurel in another hug. "And you, too. Please come visit."

Laurel assured her she would and promised, "I'll see that Mama comes, too."

"Aunt Primmy, Aunt Laurel," Rob's excited call interrupted anything else her sister might have said. "Da's having a sailboat made just for me. I'll take you for a ride if you come visit us."

"It's not just for you, Rob Patterson," Maara told him primly. "Papa said it's for all of us, and you can't ever take it out on the lake unless he or Mr. Ferguson is with you. Isn't that so, Papa?"

"That's right, Maara," Ian agreed. "Now kiss your aunts good-bye; we need to get moving."

A last flurry of tearful farewells and promises of letters and visits followed. All too soon the *Ulsterman* was pulling away from the dock, and her sisters were barely discernible from where they stood waving from the shore.

They'd barely gotten under way when Ian left her at the rail with the children while he took the wheel of the ship. Ana kept a firm grip on Jessica and Joseph as they continued waving toward the receding coastline. Once they'd cleared the harbor and were out on the lake, the way the wind tugged at her skirts, she was sure it could pluck up a small child and toss him or her overboard. That is, if that child didn't throw himself overboard first. She wished she had all four children on leading strings.

Maara, with Sally at her heels, was scampering about the deck busily exploring. And Rob was—*Oh, dear God!* "Robert Patterson, get down from there," she cried as she saw Rob scampering up the rope ladder attached to the mainmast.

She was sure her heart stopped beating when, already halfway up, the boy loosed his hold with one hand and turned to shout, "But I could see our house from up there," and pointed to the very top of the mainmast.

"Rob, no farther." Ian's firm order stayed Rob's ascent. "Get both hands firmly on the ropes and wait for me," he said as he shed his jacket, waistcoat, and boots. Careful not to joggle the flimsy ladder, Ian let mere seconds pass before he had overtaken Rob and curled his body protectively over his son's. Whatever he said to the boy was carried away by the wind, but Rob's head bobbed enthusiastically just before the two of them began to move in unison.

Ana released her breath, but her relief was short-lived. Instead of moving downward, they were slowly moving upward. She didn't think she could bear to watch, but neither could she tear her eyes away. "Da and Rob go up, up, up," Joseph said from beside her. "Me, too," he added with some glee, and tried to tug away from her.

"No!" She tightened her grip on both little ones. Ian Patterson was going to get such a tongue-lashing from her when he and Rob had both feet planted firmly on the deck once again, he'd think twice before taking a child all the way to the top of a mast.

Her heart was in her throat as she watched Ian and Rob climb. Then the deck tilted and she and the children slid against the rail. Enfolding the two little ones within her arms, she looked for Maara and saw that one of the crewmen had her safely in tow.

Fearing the worst, she looked upward to see the mast leaning as well. The rope ladder had swung away from the mast, and Ian and Rob hung suspended in the open. Ana couldn't breathe and was sure her heart stopped.

One moment stretched into many before the ship righted itself. The rope ladder swung back against the mast, and father and son continued their ascent.

"The lad'll be all right, missus," said the crewman, a pleasant man named Tom. " 'Tis a mild wind today, and the boss knows what he's about up in the rigging."

Only partially appeased by the crewman's words, Ana sent him an arched glare. "I would feel better if the children and I could go inside now."

"Aye, just follow me and Miss Maara, here, ma'am," the sailor said; he led them down a short companionway to a lower deck and opened the first door. "This is the captain's cabin. You'll be comfortable in here. If you need anything, ring that bell just outside the door here and someone's sure to come running. I'll tell the captain where you are when he and the lad come down from their look-see."

He was at the door when he turned back and pulled a spyglass from his back pocket. "Almost forgot, thought you and the children might like looking through this during the trip. You'll be able to spy your new home through that porthole yonder." He motioned to one of the round windows at one end of the cabin.

Ana managed to thank him. The children were immediately busy exploring the cabin, which didn't take long. She supposed it was quite grand for a schooner the *Ulsterman*'s size, yet its dimensions weren't much more than the tiny room she'd occupied next to the nursery. But eminently more efficient. Almost all the furnishings, cupboards, drawers, cushioned window seats, and even the bed were built into the walls, which left much of the floor free and gave the cabin an almost spacious feel. A table was anchored to the floor in the middle, its two chairs latched securely to one of the walls. Ana decided it was safest to leave them where they were.

Still worried about Rob, she tried to keep the other three occupied taking turns with the spyglass. Sally promptly made herself at home on the wide bunk built into a cabinet along one wall. It wasn't long before Joseph started yawning and Ana tucked him in between the outer wall and Sally.

Resisting the temptation to start pacing, lest her worry about Rob convey itself to the girls, she took off her bonnet and sat on the edge of the bed. Absently, she pushed her fingers back and forth through the dog's thick coat. With her nerves already on edge with worry about Rob, the slow to-and-fro sway of the boat was wrecking havoc with her stomach.

"There's an island," Jessica cried. "Is that our island?"

Oh, please, let that be so. Gulping air, she swallowed hard in a vain hope that her stomach would settle back down.

Maara took the spyglass from her little sister and peered through it. "No, it's too small and it's too soon to see our island. It'll be another hour, maybe two, probably before we get to our island."

An hour, maybe two before they reached solid land?

"Keep an eye on Joseph," Ana managed as she bolted toward the upper deck and fresh air.

Standing with Rob at the wheel in the pilothouse, Ian saw Ana dash across the deck and lean over the railing. "Keep her steady, Rob," he said, and signaled to the crewman standing by to take his place. Moving swiftly down the steps to the main deck, he got to Ana and put his arm around her waist to steady her.

"Oh, leave me be," she moaned, mortified that anyone should see her in such a state.

"A gentleman would never leave a lady in such distress to fend for herself. Especially when that lady is his wife," he told her, tightening his arm around her waist. "After all, I vowed to care for you in sickness and in health."

Ana moaned again. If there had been even a hint of teasing in his voice, she wasn't sure what she would have done. Nothing, she admitted to herself; she had not the strength even to stand up alone. Feeling as if she could barely hold her head up, she sagged against him, eternally grateful for his size and for his broad, firm shoulder to rest her aching head upon.

Beneath her cheek, she felt smooth, warm cotton, not the rougher wool of the jacket she'd expected. She opened her eyes just a bare slit, then closed them again. She'd barely glimpsed him but saw enough to know that he hadn't put his jacket or waistcoat back on; he had even removed his cravat and opened the top buttons of his shirt. With his sun-burnished skin and the way the wind was rippling through his hair, he looked like she had imagined Mr. Defoe's Robinson Crusoe, or even like a pirate in a book she'd read recently to the children. Her stomach made one of its strange flip-flop motions that had nothing at all to do with the swaying of the ship as it cut through the waves.

"You'll feel better in a little while. Take some deep breaths," he said, both arms around her now as he held her steady.

She did and breathed in the mingled scents of sunshine, the lake, and Ian Patterson. It was both pleasant and disturbing at the same time. As disturbing as the knowledge that only a thin layer of cotton separated her cheek from his bare flesh. If she moved her cheek just a little, it would be pressed to that warm, bare flesh.

Abruptly, she lifted her head and was immediately sorry, for the movement set her head to pounding. She didn't know if she moaned again, but Ian pushed her head back against his shoulder and gently rubbed her back. "Deep breaths," he reminded her again. Carefully, he set her away from him but kept one arm around her waist and guided her to one of the smaller barrels lashed to the bulwark.

Kneeling beside her, he pointed toward the horizon where a faint shadow broke the sharp line between the lake and the sky. "Try to focus on that spot. It's land and will hold steady. If you can't find that spot, then just focus on the horizon itself." He signaled to a crewman and within minutes a cup of water appeared before her. Holding it to her lips he ordered, "Drink."

Recoiling at the idea of putting anything in her stomach, she shook her head, but the motion made her feel worse. She moaned and tried to push the cup away, wishing with all her heart that he'd stop torturing her. "Rob?"

"He's fine. Right now he's at the wheel under the close supervision of one of my crew."

"Good. Promise me you'll not let him go up that ladder again," she managed, and then pressed her lips tightly and clutched at her stomach as another wave of nausea began.

"Don't worry about Rob. He's given his word he'll not go up any ladders again by himself. Now stop worrying about others and care for yourself. Keep taking deep breaths. It'll pass." Again, he pushed the cup to her lips and didn't relent until this time she swallowed some. "Keep looking at the spot I pointed out and take some more deep breaths. Feeling better?"

"I . . . I think so," she admitted, surprised that it was true. "How much longer before we reach land?"

He moistened a handkerchief and wiped her brow. "Not too long. That's our island you're focusing on. It might be best if you stayed above decks for the rest of the trip. It's really quite nice out here on the water today."

She didn't think there was anything at all nice about being "on the water" today or any other day. She would've liked to have crawled into the bunk beside Joseph. The only thing that kept her from doing just that was the strong suspicion that she'd be back up on deck within minutes, embarrassing herself once again at the rail. "But the children. They're alone in the cabin."

"I'll send Tom down to stay with them. He has children of his own. Dealing with ours won't be any trouble for him." He lifted the cup to her lips again, and this time she discovered she was eager for the water. "The girls, Joe, and Sally?" he asked with a lift of his brow and a small smile. "How are they taking to being on board?"

Suddenly feeling considerably better, Ana took a deep breath, filling her lungs with the fresh air. Self-conscious now of their closeness, she straightened her spine and was relieved when Ian dropped his arm from around her waist.

"I seem to be the only one affected by the motion of the boat. When I left the cabin, the girls were keeping vigil for the island with a spyglass, and Sally was napping with Joseph on the bunk. I think that puppy would be contented anywhere as long as she was with one or all of the children."

Ian grinned at her. "Or you. She's quite devoted to you, you know."

She shrugged and returned his smile. "She'd be loyal to anyone who saw to her needs and stroked her now and then."

The eyes that had been glowing with humor turned serious and curiously intense. "Not unlike a man," he said in a strange tone before rising to his feet.

"I think you'll be all right now, but I'd suggest you stay where you are. I'll go check on the children, then relieve

Rob at the wheel so he can come keep you company. Remember, if you start feeling ill again, look out toward the island or the horizon."

Feeling strangely bereft when he'd gone, she wished she could call him back. With so much to do to get ready for the trip, they'd had little time to talk since Wednesday. Since she'd spent most of her time sorting through the children's things and packing them while he'd directed the packing of furniture and household goods, they'd barely seen each other.

She had so many questions, beginning with the house. All she knew was that it was located atop a hill that overlooked the harbor. Gerta, the Marys, and Mr. Ferguson had been sent yesterday with a load of household goods. Ian had spared her a moment before he left with them to assure her that all would be made as comfortable and ready as possible for the family. But he'd also said that the house wasn't finished and that some adjustments would have to be made until it was.

She hadn't seen him again until this morning at the church. He'd spent last night at the island on board the boat and had set sail at dawn to be back in time for their wedding.

Her elbow on her knee, she rested her chin in her hand and kept her focus on the shadowy scrap of land that was growing gradually larger. Somewhere on the speck were the beginnings of a new village, planned and created by her husband, and where she would live out her life—for better or worse.

Chapter Thirteen

As soon as he'd settled the *Ulsterman* into her berth, Ian's eyes swept the harbor front and the hill beyond. Though he'd left it only that morning at dawn, he still marveled at how much had been accomplished in less than a year. A broad smile spread across his face as he took in the nascent settlement.

A freshly graveled road bordered the harbor, with several neatly laid out streets leading inland. Modest houses of varying designs and sizes would one day dot those streets. To date, a dozen were in varying stages of completion, and another half dozen were finished enough for occupancy. Smoke rose from those chimneys, and children could be seen playing on the front steps of two of them. Unfortunately, the large house rising from the top of the hill that would be his family's home was not one of those even under roof as yet.

The time to reveal that detail to Ana was at hand. The only question was whether to do so before or after she saw his "solution" for the "squatters."

Nearest the wharves was the commercial strip, or what he expected would one day be an area populated by commercial establishments. Except for the long, low barn that stabled the draft animals, the only other buildings were a warehouse and the combination dormitory, dining room, and tavern he'd had built to house the workers. A hand-painted sign hung over its doorway grandly declaring: MAISON BERCOT: CLEAN BEDS, FINE FOOD AND DRINK. It was a sign he hoped Ana didn't see today. She'd find out soon enough that "drink" included spirits.

"Paa-pa!" The impassioned wail was punctuated by the distinct slap of a hard leather sole against the wooden deck.

"Don't stomp a hole in the deck, Jessie, girl." Hurrying down the steps from the pilothouse, Ian chuckled when he saw that Sally was slowly circling his children and new wife. With each revolution she brushed against them, and the members of her "flock" obediently edged toward the center. He doubted any of them had even noticed what the young shepherd was doing.

Good girl, Sal. Perhaps you'll live up to your name for at least a little while today. The clever animal had Ana facing away from the tavern. Today might not have been a wedding day filled with joy and celebration, as were most, but something deep within him wanted to make it as pleasant a day as possible.

Espying the carriage drawing up to the dock, he waved at Ned, then offered his arm to his wife. "Ready, Mrs. Patterson?"

Before they had taken more than two steps toward the gangplank, Maara tugged on his coattail. "That's not our house up on the hill, is it, Papa?"

A sidelong glance at Ana warned him she was just as curious as his eldest child. "Yes, it is, Maara. We'll—"

"But you can see right through the walls, and there's no roof!"

"There will be a roof and solid walls soon." He snapped his fingers to get Sally's attention and waved her toward the gangplank. "Follow Sally, children," he called out with forced gaiety. "Ned's waiting for us."

Ana abruptly planted her feet. "But you said the house was ready for us."

"No, my dear, I said *a* house was ready for us. We'll be living in one of the houses closer to the harbor for a while."

Unwilling to meet her eyes, he kept his face averted. Grasping her elbow, he guided her toward the gang-plank. "You know, you're still looking a bit peaked. Best we not tarry. You'll feel much better once your feet are planted on solid ground. Perhaps a cup of hot tea will set you to rights. If I know Gerta, she's got a kettle on the hob keeping water hot for exactly that."

Just then the boat dutifully shuddered and rolled slightly to one side. Ana's stomach rolled with it and continued to roll even after the boat had settled itself again. Swallowing hard, she was grateful for his escort to the dock.

Infinitely relieved to have her own feet safely on the unmoving earth, she gestured toward the six houses scattered along the graveled roads. "And just which one of those cottages are the children and I to occupy?"

He pointed to a story-and-a-half dwelling made of stone at the end of the farthest street. "*We* will be living there."

"*We? All* of us?"

"Only the six of us and Sally, of course. Ned will be staying at Maiso—the workers' dormitory until the space over the carriage house is finished. Gerta and the Marys will be returning to Cleveland as soon as the crew has the *Ulsterman* ready to sail again. I'd rather the Euclid Street house not be empty too long before a new owner is found. And there are things for them to do there, still. Some things left to pack and—"

Aghast, Ana interrupted. "But . . . but there can't be more than two bedrooms in that house."

"Actually, there are three bedrooms," he supplied

smoothly, seemingly unaware of her distress. So much so, she was giving serious consideration to kicking him in the shins to call his attention to the problems inherent in their living in a house of even three bedrooms. "Two on the second floor and one on the first. Most families with four children or more live in houses that size or even smaller. Yours has, hasn't it?"

"Why, yes, but—"

"And you all survived quite nicely," he interrupted with a calm that infuriated her further. Cupping her elbow once again, he started moving her toward the waiting carriage. "Come along, my dear. I, for one, am eager to see what the ladies have accomplished with the place. I've only been inside the house once—yesterday when I deposited Gerta and the Marys there."

Yanking her arm from his grasp again, Ana tried for her most imperious pose. "Ian Patterson! You will cease bullying me about and answer my questions immediately."

"I beg your pardon, my dear. It was certainly not my intent to bully you. I was thinking only of your comfort, sure that you'd be happy to get off the boat and onto land as quickly as possible."

He both looked and sounded so genuinely sincere, she was for a moment swayed. But only for a moment. "Why must we be crammed into a small cottage when we could just as well have remained in Cleveland until your house was finished?"

"*Our* house, my dear," he corrected with a solicitous smile. Moving closer, he bent his head near hers so that only she could hear. "Given the depth of your distress on Wednesday, I thought you would be happier if we left Cleveland as soon as possible. Or was I wrong in thinking you're not ready to forgive your father?"

Feeling quite churlish in the light of his concern for her feelings, she sighed. "No, you were not wrong. I don't know that I'll ever forgive him." Tears stung the backs of her eyes, and she looked away.

The touch of his fingers at her chin forced her face back to his. "No tears, it's our wedding day. We've a new life to begin." He grinned and tipped his head toward the road behind him. "And there are four restless children bouncing around in that carriage over there. Ned's liable to leave us here at the dock if we don't get over there and rescue him."

"Oh, dear, I quite forgot them." She started around Ian, then stopped when she saw a cluster of people, including a trio of women and several children, gathered near the carriage. Her cheeks reddened, and she would have gladly allowed the earth to swallow her up. "Oh, my, I must look a mess. What must they think of me?"

Chuckling, Ian wound his arm around her waist and started them toward the carriage. "They're thinking you're a lovely bride and that I'm a lucky man to have won you, especially if we give them a little demonstration of what a happy bride and groom we are."

The glint in his eyes and the devilish grin on his face made his intent obvious. Ana gasped. "We will do no such thing," she declared, sotto voce. "Kissing in public would be most improper."

Before she could rush away, he caught her up against him again and murmured against her brow, "Afraid you might change your mind about this 'in name only' business, Mrs. Patterson?"

Stiffening, she reminded him, "You agreed to the arrangement."

"Yes, but there's nothing in our agreement against my trying to change your mind," he said, and promptly kissed her. And not just a brushing of the lips as he'd done at the end of the wedding ceremony, but a full possession that left her gasping for air when he finally relinquished her mouth. "Not a thing improper about a man kissing his bride in public on their wedding day."

"You—you are insufferable," she said, but the words came out too weak and breathless to be the set-down statement she'd intended.

His low chuckle followed her all the way to the carriage. Throughout the blessedly brief introductions to the people gathered and the short ride to the cottage, she didn't need to look at her husband to know his grin never diminished for a second. Nor did the heat beating in her cheeks.

Ana smoothed and tucked the bedclothes around Joseph, then pressed a light kiss to his brow. The little boy had long ago fallen asleep, as had his brother in the bed on the other side of the room. And his sisters in the other bedroom on the second floor.

Not yet ready to go downstairs, she went to the open window and rested her head against the frame. It was a clear night with a light breeze soughing through the leafy branches of the large elm that stood at the corner of the house. The window afforded a clear view of the harbor.

Overhead, the stars were bright in the darkened sky, the constellations easily distinguished from one another. A full moon hung low over the lake, sending a pale path of light across the rippling surface and limning silver the handful of boats moored in the harbor. The *Ulsterman* was not among them. Hours ago, it had left for Cleveland with Gerta and the Marys on board.

How ever was she going to manage without them? It wasn't that she didn't know how to cook; she'd just never done it alone. Housekeeping chores weren't beyond her, either. She'd been in charge of running a household almost as long as she could remember. Until her family had come to Cleveland, there had never been a maid to help. But she'd always had her sisters or her mother. And never four young children to watch over at the same time.

The house was small compared to the Euclid Street house but certainly no smaller than the house her family had occupied back in Connecticut. Besides, it was only temporary. Once the big house was ready, Gerta and the Marys would be back. Until then, she would persevere.

She went back to studying the view from the window. But within minutes it wasn't the view, the fresh scents borne on the breeze, or the sound of the waves gently lapping against the shore in the distance that captured her senses. It was the occasional sound from below stairs—the rustle of a page turning, the scuff of a booted foot as it shifted position upon the floor, the light chink of a cup against a saucer—that set her every sense on full alert.

And the memory of his rustling challenge: *Afraid you might change your mind about this "in name only" business, Mrs. Patterson?*

Absolutely not!

Yes!

The two opposing answers to his audacious query screamed simultaneously within her. She rubbed at the ache above her brows. Her head felt as if it were a battleground, and she longed to rest it on a pillow. Or better yet on Ian's broad shoulder, with his strong arms sheltering her.

She squeezed her eyes shut. It was fatigue, nothing more, that was making her mind play such tricks on her. She didn't dare risk being in Ian's arms again for fear of where it might lead. To a bed. Too clearly, Lily's warnings rang in her head.

When they hold you and kiss you, it's quite wonderful, Ana. But men are not content with that, and no matter what any of them say, it's always the same. Their hairy, sweating bodies lying on top of you and pounding into you with that horrid thing.

Ana shuddered just as she had the day Lily enlightened her. But Mama had described the marriage act quite differently. Not in the kind of detail Lily had, of course. Using unspecific terms, she explained it as an act of love. And further, she'd told her that desire between a man and a woman was natural and part of God's plan; from the union of a man and a woman would come children.

She didn't know whether to believe her mother or her sister. Mama had never lied to her. And Lily? She'd had no reason to lie about something like this. It was all so confusing. The only thing she knew for certain was that she and Ian did not love each other. And without love, the marriage act would surely be as sinful as fornication.

"Children all asleep?" Ian asked when Ana finally came downstairs.

"Oh . . . yes," she answered, seemingly startled by his question. "It took a while for them to settle down, what with new surroundings and all, but I think they'll sleep quite soundly now."

"Well, it's been quite a day." Ian folded his newspaper and laid it across his lap. Sally awoke from the spot where she'd curled up next to his feet. Her tail wagging, the dog deserted him for the side of the woman she so adored.

"Yes, it has," she remarked absently as she trailed a hand across the back of a chair and then bent to pat Sally's head. Without another word or so much as another glance in his direction, she moved to the far end of the great room that comprised the majority of the first floor.

Only the rustle of her skirts, the occasional opening and closing of a cupboard, and the click of Sally's nails upon the floor as she followed Ana about the cottage broke the silence.

It was an awkward silence. For the life of him, Ian wasn't sure how to put her at ease. He couldn't very well blurt out: I'm sorry, Ana. I'm a complete dolt and should have my tongue cut out for issuing that challenge about our arrangement. I don't know why I said it and—

Hell, he knew exactly why he'd said it. He enjoyed seeing her blush, and that wasn't all he enjoyed about her. He'd liked her in his arms, kissing him back and melting into his body.

Not tonight, though. Unless he was very mistaken, she was as skittish as a doe in an open meadow on a sunny day. If he made the slightest overture toward her, she'd likely run out the door, hop in the first boat she found, and row it all the way to Cleveland herself if necessary.

"Gerta and the Marys did a fine job with the house in such a short time, don't you think?" he said, as much to redirect his thoughts as to break the silence. "But it is your house, Ana. You are free to make any changes or re-arrangements you wish."

She had her back to him and was doing something at the table. A cup clattering against a saucer signaled he'd been correct in assessing how nervous she was.

"They've arranged everything quite satisfactorily," she said with a slight quaver in her voice. "The larder is well stocked. But I was wondering how to replenish the supplies. Is there or will there be a market here? Or is everything ordered specifically from the mainland?"

"There isn't a market or store as yet. We've just been sending for supplies to the mainland when needed," he explained, hoping a discussion of the mundane would prove to her he wasn't about to leap upon her. "We should set up something so at least a supply of staples might be available. I think a store could be created in a corner of the warehouse. If you'd care to draw up a list of foodstuffs you think should be kept in stock, I'll see that they're delivered on the next trip of the *Ulsterman*."

She swept her gaze around the cottage before suggesting, "And perhaps a few bolts of muslin and calico. I should think the ladies would like to make curtains for the windows."

Ian looked around the cabin, seeing it through her eyes. "It does look a bit bare, doesn't it?" He smiled and asked, "Have you something in mind for these windows?"

A thoughtful look on her face, she picked up her teacup and walked about the room. He thought he saw a gleam there, but it disappeared just before she spoke. "It would be impractical to make curtains for this house since we'll be here only temporarily. Whoever lives here next will probably want to decorate it themselves, and there are bound to be a lot of expenses with the big house."

"If you'd like curtains for this house, then you shall have curtains, Mrs. Patterson," he announced, pleased with her practical streak, and even more pleased that she was more comfortable now. "I can afford a bolt of calico or whatever you want to use. Temporary as this place may be for us, make it a home. That is, if it's not too much work for you."

"Making curtains is hardly difficult work, though with everything else there'll be for me to do each day, it may be a while before I have them all finished."

"Everything you have to do," he repeated, then let out a gust of air. Tossing his newspaper aside, he stood. Shoving his hands in his trouser pockets, he took a few paces and then stilled. "Ana, I apologize."

"Whatever for?" she asked, a frown of confusion marring her brow.

"I don't doubt you could think of a long list of things if

you put your mind to it," he remarked dryly. "But I'm apologizing for heaping so much responsibility and work upon you. I should have made arrangements for at least one of the Marys to stay. I'll think of someplace for whichever of them you'd prefer to have return, and send the boat back for her, or both of them if you wish, the minute the *Ulsterman* docks tomorrow."

Clearly taken aback, Ana set her cup back down. "And just where are you going to house a maid or two? There's no space in this house, and I'll not have virtuous young women like Mary Flick and Mary Cunningham living all alone with a bunch of single men in that . . . that barracks by the waterfront."

Now this was an Ana he knew all too well. Relieved to see fire rather than wariness in her eyes, he was even more relieved that she'd missed seeing the sign that hung over the door of "that barracks," as she called it.

Nervously, he cleared his throat. "I'll give it a bit more thought, but I think there may be a solution," he said. "I promise I'll have one or both of them back over here by the end of the week at the latest."

Clearly unappeased by what he'd thought was a thoughtful proposal, she accused, "You think me so weak and inept I cannot take care of four children and a household by myself?"

She didn't wait for his answer but blurted, "I'll have you know, Ian Patterson, that I'm no stranger to cooking and performing household chores. Besides, most women don't have help with their children and houses this size. Why should you think I would?"

"Why, indeed," Ian murmured under his breath. "I apologize for underestimating you, my dear. I was only thinking of making your days a bit easier between now and when the big house is finished and is functioning much as did the household in Cleveland."

"Hmmph, you might have thought of that before moving us all over here before it was finished."

She turned her back on him, and he decided it was best to leave alone any further discussion of the timing of the move. Retrieving his newspaper, he settled himself again in the comfortable wing-back chair from his study, one of the few pieces he'd had moved from the Euclid Street house.

Ian had barely opened the newspaper again when she asked, "Just when do you expect the big house to be finished?"

He glanced up, then quickly returned his eyes to the newspaper. She had her back to him again, her head bent slightly as she adjusted a stack of napkins on the table. He absorbed nothing from the words, but the printed letters kept his gaze from straying to the enticing loose curls that lay on his wife's nape.

Damnation! One wisp of her hair escaped confinement, and all he could think of was how all of it would look trailing across a pillow and his lips brushing it away from her naked breasts.

Clearing his throat again, he admitted, "I'm afraid it'll take most of the summer to get the outer walls and roof on the big house. Finishing the interior could take as much as a year, perhaps more."

"A year!" She whirled around then, almost as if she'd been felled by a powerful blow, and dropped to one of the kitchen chairs. Shaking her head, she muttered, "No . . . no . . . no. This will never do."

As if she were confronted by a specter that was truly horrifying, her eyes were wide and fixed unblinkingly on a spot beyond him. A glance over his shoulder revealed what was terrifying her. The open door to the bedroom—their bedroom, or what would be if theirs were a normal marriage.

Closing his eyes, he let his head drop to the back of the chair and sighed in resignation. She enjoyed his kisses, but clearly the idea of sharing a bed with him absolutely horrified her. How in hell he was going to get her past whatever fears or overblown sense of propriety she had, he didn't know, but he wasn't going to spend the rest of his life in an "in name only" marriage. That was for damned sure.

"Of course, even though the interior won't be completed, it doesn't mean the house can't be occupied," he said in a carefully schooled nonchalant tone, and tossed the newspaper aside. "Once the outside walls and roof are completed, we can move in, if you'd like."

"Yes, I think that would be best," she said, and he could hear the relief in her voice. But he also saw the way she tightened her mouth and her chin came up. Definite signs that an edict regarding their sleeping arrangements was about to come down.

Before she could open her mouth, he added, "About all the big house will offer at first is more space. But I should imagine living in it will be an asset when making your choices on the decor and furnishings."

Her brows rose in surprise. "*My* choices?"

"I don't know who else's they'd be. You will be the lady of that house, and I confess I'm not particularly good at choosing colors, draperies, and all those little details that make a house a home. I'd like to be consulted about the furnishings but ultimately, the decisions will be yours."

He tossed his newspaper aside, stood, and stretched. "I've already instructed Kenneth to obtain a number of catalogs from furniture and textile manufacturers. He should be sending them over to you shortly. Just let him know what you've decided upon, and he'll place the orders. Alan is making a copy of the floor plan for you. It should be in your hands sometime next week, but in the meantime you can look over the plans the construction foreman is using. Will you be needing anything else?"

"But—but what of all the furniture from the Euclid Street house? You can't mean I'm to order all new. There are some very expensive pieces there that—"

"Were purchased for that house," he finished for her as he headed toward the door. "If you noticed when you left the house this morning, except for the nursery and my study, most of the rooms are still full of furniture. Those were Lily's choices, and they're staying in that house until whoever buys it decides whether they want them. I'd as soon never see them again."

One hand on the door latch, he paused to say, "It's been quite a day for all of us. I'm still a bit too keyed up for sleep and thought a walk would settle me down." *And thanks to that damned loose curl on your nape, a dip in the lake.* "You're welcome to come along. I'm sure the children will be fine here alone for a little while."

"No, I'd rather not leave them alone." She gave him a clearly forced smile. "Perhaps another time."

"Perhaps," he repeated, his mind racing with images of a walk with Ana along a moonlit beach, the breeze off the lake loosening more and more of her hair. "Well, I'll be on my way. I'll take Sally with me, unless you'd feel safer having her stay with you."

"No, I'm sure I'll be fine, and she could use the exercise."

"Well, then, we'll be off." He snapped his fingers, and the dog started toward him, then hesitated and looked back at Ana.

"Go, Sally," she urged. "Go with Ian."

Patting the dog's head, he said, "When I get back, I'll bed down on the couch. It's quite comfortable." He tipped his head toward the bedroom. "I can vouch for the bed in there as well. It's from my bedroom. I'm sure you'll spend a good night there."

Sometime, he would have liked to have added to his statement. But his idea of what a good night in that bed meant made him hurry from the house and put some distance between himself and the enticing woman who'd kept him from restful sleep for weeks.

His long strides made short work of the distance between the house and the shoreline. A few minutes more and he arrived at a secluded cove. Ordering Sally to stay on the beach, he made short work of stripping off his clothes and wading into the water.

Once he was out of the shallows, he dove and swam beneath the surface until his lungs demanded air. Breaking the surface, he grinned. His body was cooled enough that he could let his imagination play with the thought of *perhaps* strolling along the shoreline with her some night and *perhaps* enticing her to join him in the water.

Valeriana MacPherson skinny-dipping in a moonlit lake? Improper. Scandalous.

His laughter rang across the lake's surface, startling the flock of gulls bedded down on the two promontories that sheltered the cove and causing Sally to let out a sharp bark and start toward the water. After ordering the dog to stay where she was, he went back to thinking about sharing a midnight swim in this cove. *Someday.*

As he began a pattern of long strokes that took him from one side of the cove to the other, he took some heart from those moments that she'd seemed actually to welcome his arms around her. *Someday* damned well better happen, and soon. This water was damned cold. He'd never survive much more of this.

Chapter Fourteen

"Shh . . . Papa said not to wake Aunt Ana." The sound of small feet walking away was joined by the clatter of china and the murmur of voices at a greater distance. Fearing what could happen if the children were attempting to prepare their own breakfast, Ana leapt out of bed, ripped her nightgown over her head, yanked open the top drawer of the dresser, and started groping for fresh underwear.

It was then she realized that she was standing as naked as the day she'd been born before a pair of uncurtained first-floor windows not ten feet from the street. With a gasp, she dropped to the floor.

Getting dressed while crouching on the floor was no easy task. Pantalettes, chemise, and petticoats posed minor problems, but a corset proved utterly impossible. She was just reaching for the first gown she could lay her hands on when a crash and a loud "Damnation!" sounded from beyond the door. Ana was through the bedroom door and halfway across the sitting area before coming to a skidding stop.

The children were safely seated at the table. But Ian was standing next to the iron cookstove, an expression of consternation on his face as he looked from the down-turned pan on the floor to the porridge splattered on his trouser legs. "Children, it appears breakfast will be delayed."

"Not Sally's," Maara chirped as the dog began lapping at the bounty pooled upon the floor.

"Stand still, Da. Sally'll clean you up in no time," Rob suggested, then burst into laughter when the pup dutifully started licking the splatters from his father's trousers.

"Now, children, show your old da some respect. This is not a laughing matter," Ian stated with exaggerated loftiness, which increased the children's giggles and set off Ana's.

Ian turned at the first sound of a woman's laughter, and the laugh that had been rising from his chest came out sounding like a strangled wheeze. Helpless to do otherwise, he let his gaze rush from the top of Ana's head to the tips of her bare toes with the desperate eagerness of a thirsty man racing toward an oasis in the desert, fearing that if he so much as blinked, the image might disappear.

Her face was flushed and unguarded, and laughter sparkled in her eyes and added a wide lushness to her lips. Her hair tumbled in a riotous mass of curls about her face and over her shoulders—her very bare shoulders. Sunlight from the window behind her lent a warm glow to her hair and skin and outlined the lush curves of her breasts beneath her surprisingly delicate chemise.

Slowly, Ana became aware of Ian staring at her so strangely, and her laughter stilled. Before she realized just what was causing the wide-eyed, gape-mouthed expression on his face, Maara cried, "Aunt Ana! You forgot to put on your dress."

Flushing hotly, Ana stared in horror at the gown clutched in her hand and then glanced down her body. "Oh!" Holding the dress against her bosom, she backed away slowly. "I . . . ah . . . didn't think—I mean, I heard the crash and—"

More mortified than she'd ever been before in her life-time, she spun and fled to the bedroom. Slamming the door behind her, she leaned against it and took several deep breaths to compose herself. Then, remembering the two bare windows in the room, she couldn't get her gown over her head and fastened quickly enough.

Hurrying about, trying to find her shoes and stock-ings, she caught a glimpse of herself in the mirror. A new horror swept over her. She'd had a splitting headache by the time she sought the bed last night, so she'd taken the pins from her hair and left it loose. A night of restless tossing and turning had resulted in a wild, tangled mass.

Oh, my God, what must he think of me! She'd not only raced into the living area in nothing but her under-clothing, but her hair had been loose and wild about her like a woman of easy virtue.

He probably liked it! Beast that he is, it probably re-minded him of the kind of women with whom he consorts, she told herself as she began wielding her comb and brush with all the vigor of a knight of old attacking an enemy with his sword. The knowledge that he wasn't anything like the degenerate sinner she'd thought him for years niggled around the edges of her conscience as she battled the tangles. He was no gentleman, though. A gentleman would have quickly averted his gaze, turned his back . . . anything but stand there gaping at her near-nakedness.

Groomed and attired more properly, she practiced a no-nonsense expression in the mirror until she felt ready to face her husband and the children. No one made a re-mark about her earlier state of undress as she hustled about the cookstove preparing a new batch of porridge and setting out jam, butter, and a plate of Gerta's scones. She might have relaxed and stopped blushing had she not felt Ian's gaze upon her every time her back was turned.

"Your aunt makes a far better breakfast than your papa does, children," Ian said, tossing his napkin upon the table when the meal was finished. "What say we thank her by clearing up this table and doing the dishes for her?"

"Oh, but that isn't necessary." Still unable to face him fully, Ana rose and started clearing the table. "I'm sure you have things to do."

Coming up behind her, Ian gently guided her back to her chair. "Top of my list for today is giving you and the children a tour of the island and introducing some of the folks living here. Why don't you just relax for a bit while we clear up, or perhaps you'd like to start that list we were talking about last night. There should be paper, pens, and pencils in the little desk by the door."

Picking up a bucket, he gave her a wry smile. "We're a bit low on water, what with having to mop the floor already this morning. Until we dig some more wells and set up cisterns, we'll have to use the community well at the end of this street."

He beckoned to the boys. "Bring the other bucket from under the worktable, Rob. Joe, pick up that little pail by the back door. You may as well become acquainted with the pump this morning. Toting water to the house will be one of your jobs. It'll build your muscles."

Once the water expedition was gone, Ana ignored Ian's directive. Setting the girls to work clearing the table, she began what she'd already decided was the first order of business for this day—tacking a sheet or blanket over the windows in the bedroom.

Assured of some privacy at last, she stripped off her dress, put on her corset, and donned a gown more appropriate for a day of touring and visiting. Surprised Ian and the boys hadn't yet returned, she sent the girls upstairs to make beds and then bring down their hairbrushes and ribbons. While they were gone, she discovered there was enough water in the stove's reservoir to start the dishes. By the time the Patterson males and their dog returned with buckets of water, Ana was just finishing plaiting Maara's hair.

Seeing the kitchen and dining area set to rights once more, Ian gave her a rueful smile. "I'm afraid the community pump is a busy place this time of day, and, well—"

He ducked his head and shuffled his feet. "We got to talking to some folks, and before we knew it we'd been there a lot longer than we'd planned."

If he weren't so tall, she'd have sworn it was Rob trying to think of an alibi or apology for some misdeed. She was as charmed by his contrite pose as she always was by his son's. And was having just as much trouble keeping a serious expression.

Lifting his head, he grinned. "We won't dawdle next time, will we, boys?" Sauntering toward the kitchen with his bucket, he tousled Rob's hair as he passed. "Tell your aunt and sisters about your new friend while I fill the water crock and clean up a bit."

"His name's Joseph, like me," Joseph said, tugging on her sleeve. "But he's big like Rob. Sally liked him."

"His whole name is Joseph Michael Francis O'Houlihan, but we can just call him Joe," Rob supplied. "He's got two brothers and a baby sister, and he likes dogs, ships, and wants to see my collection."

"It certainly sounds as if you've found a kindred spirit, Rob. It'll be nice to have such a friend. Are either of his brothers our Joseph's age?"

"I think so, but neither of 'em were with him. His da wasn't either because he already showed him how to use the pump. And he had a wagon to carry the buckets of water so he didn't need his da. Da says Mr. Ferguson can make us one so we can fetch the water by ourselves."

Rob was fairly bubbling over with the details of the great adventure of the water pump. "There were some men there, and Da talked with them. And they talked to Joe and me, too. They were real nice but talked kind of funny. But we didn't have no trouble understanding them 'cause one of 'em talked like Gerta and the others like Da when he gets excited or he's real tired. I s'pect they're from Germany and Ireland, don't you?"

"Yes, I *s'pect* they are, Rob." Ana made the mistake of looking over the children and toward the kitchen. Ian had stripped to the waist and was lathering his face. One glimpse of his bare back, muscles rippling with the slightest movement of his arms, was enough to set goose-flesh rising from her toes to her crown and to have her unpredictable stomach turning a somersault.

She quickly turned her back and led the children toward the stairs. "Why don't you tell me all about the people you met while we unpack some more of your things.

"This simply won't do," she muttered under her breath as she hurried up the stairs. *Has the man no modesty?* He simply could not just strip down to the waist in front of her or his daughters. They'd have to set up some sort of schedule so he could perform his morning ablutions in the privacy of the bedroom—after she'd vacated it. She'd speak to him about it at the earliest opportunity.

"This will be the dining room." Ian walked ahead of her, pointing out various features that would one day exist. They'd left the children with Ned in the almost completed carriage house and stable. The children were delighted to be reunited with their pony and were happily taking their first riding lesson while Ian gave her a tour of the house—what there was of it.

Right now it was little more than a cellar beneath a

framework of vertical posts placed every two feet. But some of the future rooms already had the beginnings of stone fireplaces rising from their floors. A small army of carpenters were busy everywhere, and it was difficult to hear Ian above the racket of hammering and sawing.

"And back here is what Alan calls the morning room, though I think of it as more of an informal parlor, a place for the family to gather comfortably. But it will catch the morning light and be quite a cheerful place early in the day."

Trying to take it all in, she was still standing in the area he said was the foyer of the new house. Ana felt her dismay increase as she looked around. There was so much to be done, she had little faith the house would be habitable before winter.

"So what do you think of the floor plan, Ana?"

"I think it will be very nice," she managed over the lump in her throat. Thankful for the wide-brimmed bonnet she'd worn for the excursion, she ducked her head so he couldn't see the tears seeping from the corners of her eyes.

He was so proud of the house and the progress that he'd insisted it be their first spot on the tour of the island. She could no more dampen his spirits about it than she would have Rob showing off a model boat.

She walked toward the space that would be his study. "You certainly will have a lovely view of the harbor from here." With her back to him, she tried to fish a handkerchief from her reticule as surreptitiously as possible.

She was wiping her nose and dabbing at her eyes when she heard his footsteps behind her. "You're not at all impressed with the house, are you," he said, his disappointment clear in the rough edge of his voice.

"No, no. I mean, yes, I am impressed with it." It wasn't a lie. The house would be impressive and quite a wonderful home for the family. Months and months from now.

Before she could slip away, he placed his hands over her shoulders and turned her to face him. It was no use ducking her head as he caught her chin between his fingers and turned her face up to him. "Tears, Ana? Do you hate it that much?"

Torn between wanting to shrink out of his grasp and to melt into his arms and dampen his shirtfront with her tears, as she'd done so frequently of late, she merely stood where she was and shook her head. "I don't hate it."

He bent his knees so that his face was nearly level with hers. "But? Come now, Ana, we must be honest with each other. I insist on it."

Pulling out of his grasp, she moved away from the temptation of his strong arms. "You must think me a regular watering pot. I cannot think why I am so given to tears of late."

"I should think it quite normal for any woman who's been subjected to the emotional upsets you've suffered these past several days," he offered.

His kindness only made it more difficult to stem her tears. She took a shaky breath. "Be that as it may, these fits of weeping really serve no purpose other than making my head ache and my eyes all red and swollen. I am quite determined that they shall cease."

Even to her own ears, her statement sounded spin-sterish and comically haughty. A glance over her shoulder proved Ian must have thought so, too, for he was having trouble stifling a grin.

With a narrow-eyed glare, she warned him against laughing. "I assure you that they have nothing to do with the design of the house. I am not at all disappointed with it. It will be really quite perfect. It's just that . . ."

She swallowed and decided now was as good a time as

any to test just how well he responded to honesty. "It's just that," she repeated, "there's so much to do before the house is remotely habitable. As nice as the cottage is, it's going to be quite impossible for us to live there so long."

"Impossible? I thought we'd all survived a night and part of a day quite successfully. How can you say it's impossible?"

It seemed the "earliest opportunity" that she had wanted for discussing their living arrangements had arrived. "We simply cannot live in such intimate surroundings unless we make some sort of considerations for the sensibilities of others."

"Sensibilities of others? Whatever do you mean, madam?" he asked, though he suspected he knew exactly what she meant.

"Perhaps *sensibilities* isn't quite the right word," she began, her discomfort apparent by the way her fingers were plucking the edges of her handkerchief. "What I mean is, I believe we will all get on together far more comfortably if we are modest in our . . . ah . . . behavior and mode of dress."

"You needn't worry yourself about this morning. I quite understand why you came bolting out of the bedroom in a state of dishabille. Put it out of your mind, my dear. I think none the less of you for it."

Ana gasped. "*My* state of dishabille. At least *I* had an excuse. I heard a crash, and all I could think of was that one of the children might be hurt."

Her arm fully extended, she waved her finger at him. "But you . . . you have no such excuse. Stripping down like that right there in front of your children and me is . . . is . . . Well, it's simply not done. I insist you keep yourself properly clothed at all times."

"And what would you have me do? Remain unshaven and unbathed?"

"Well, no. Of course not. But you must find a more private place to perform your morning ablutions. I will not have you shocking your daughters with such displays of immodesty."

"I rather doubt the sight of their father's bare chest and back is going to cause them any emotional damage, but I shall bow to your greater knowledge of child rearing," he said, deliberately coloring the statement with sarcasm. "Now in regards to this privacy issue, I would point out that if we shared the first-floor bedroom, there would be no problem."

"Exactly!"

Nonplussed, Ian stared at her. She'd chosen a helluva time and way to inform him she was ready to expand their marital relationship beyond that "in name only" silliness, but who was he to gainsay her? No wonder she'd been stumbling around over her words.

Lest he frighten her with his eagerness, he chose his words carefully. "That would seem the most practical arrangement. I'll do my best to assure that you'll not be sorry you've come to this decision so quickly."

A slight frown and a look he couldn't quite identify was her first response. Then she shrugged and said, "Well, something had to be done. We certainly could not go on as we are any longer. Now as to the details, I believe we can work out a reasonable schedule that will prove satisfactory to us both."

"Schedule!" Ian was incredulous. "Good God, woman! Do you mean for me to perform only on a given hour on a given day? Now that, madam, is something that is *simply not done*!"

Clearly taken aback by his vehement outburst, Ana

stared wide-eyed at him for a long moment. "Well, I don't see why not. Normally—"

"*Normally!* There's nothing *normal* about your proposal."

"Mr. Patterson!" Casting a worried glance in the direction of the workman laying stone at another corner, she moved several steps closer to Ian. Lowering her voice, she said, "I would prefer we not make all the carpenters privy to every detail of this conversation."

Looking about, Ian noted that they were attracting an audience. "I quite agree, madam." The last thing he wanted was for it to get all around the island that he had to schedule making love to his wife. He'd be the laughingstock of not only the island but perhaps the continent.

Frowning, she studied him. "Perhaps you should have worn a hat today to protect your head from the sun. It is quite bright, and you're looking quite flushed."

"I assure you I'm quite fine," he said as he took her arm and guided her toward a spot well away from the hearing of others. That it happened to be in the shade of a towering cedar pleased Ana immensely.

"I'm sure you'll feel better soon. Obviously the sun has affected your thinking, for I cannot think why you should find scheduling our times in the bedroom so peculiar."

"No, I don't suppose someone like you would," he muttered under his breath.

"Well, I do believe any household runs best if it is run in an orderly fashion. Schedules maintain that order, and order is conducive to both physical and mental well-being. Now let me explain what I have in mind."

Ian crossed his arms across his chest, closed his eyes, and shook his head. *This kind of schedule cannot be good for my physical or mental well-being.* "Please, madam, proceed. I don't know that I've ever been so eager to hear the details of a schedule."

Frowning at his sarcasm, she began. "This morning was an exception; I'm normally an early riser. Beginning tomorrow, I shall endeavor to ready myself for the day as early as possible. You will then be able to avail yourself of the bedroom long before the children arise and thus have complete privacy to perform your morning ablu—"

Ian's laughter, as hearty and deep as she'd ever heard it, interrupted her. It was not infectious.

Stamping her foot, she placed her hands on her hips and glared at him. "How dare you laugh at me."

It was another moment before Ian could contain his laughter enough to say, "Forgive me, my dear, but I'm not laughing at you. I am the unfortunate who is the brunt of the joke."

"You? I don't understand."

Continuing to chuckle, Ian remarked, "I'm sure you don't, which is my misfortune. I'll try to abide by your schedule as long as it proves necessary." He took her arm and started toward the front steps of the house. "Come, let's gather the children and finish the tour."

At the stable, the children insisted they each demonstrate how well they sat their pony. While Ana applauded them, Ian took over the leading strings, and Ned readied the landau for their tour. After promises that a second lesson would occur later in the day, they were able to settle the children and Sally into the carriage and be on their way. "This road will eventually encircle the island," Ian explained as they headed north. "I'd like to show you where all the operations are, but I'm afraid they're not yet accessible by carriage," he told them. "But we'll be able to get to several points of interest that I think you and the children will enjoy seeing."

What followed was a pleasant drive along the island's shoreline. Cedars, maples, and pin oaks made up the stands of forest, growing almost to the shoreline in some spots. Even though they could travel barely half the perimeter of the island, it was enough for Ana to appreciate how beautiful it was.

Most notable of the sights he showed them was at the cove where they stopped for lunch. A large, flat slab of limestone covered with drawings etched into the surface lay near the water's edge. "We believe these were drawn by Indians many centuries ago," Ian explained, and the children—and Ana—were suitably impressed.

Knowing the children were getting hungry, she left them there speculating about the meaning of the figures and the people who'd created them while she went to retrieve the basket Ned had loaded into the carriage. It wasn't until she opened it and started laying out its contents on a blanket spread upon that ground that she began to wonder who had prepared the food.

Cold poached chicken, crusty fresh bread, delicately herbed vegetables, and for dessert a fruit and custard tart that melted in one's mouth. A most unusual meal to have been prepared by someone hired to feed men living in the barracks. Ian hadn't hired a cook; he'd hired a master chef. If she was any judge at all of the cuisine, that chef was French.

She kept her curiosity tamped until the children had finished eating and gone off to play before asking, "Who is the cook at the dining hall?"

Chapter Fifteen

Reclining on the blanket, one arm resting on his bent knee, Ian sounded as casual as his pose when he replied, "Actually there are two chefs. Henri and Eduard Bercot. They manage the dormitory and dining hall."

Having anticipated the answer, she was nonetheless disconcerted to hear him confirm her suspicions. Unable even to look at Ian without wanting to bash him over the head with whatever was near, she swept her gaze around the cove. At the horses grazing near the edge of the woods. The narrow strip of sand that made up the beach. The gulls perched on a rocky spit stretching into the lake.

The idyllic setting did nothing to stem the flow of disappointment that washed over her. "Ian Patterson, you are the most deceitful, glib-tongued—" She took a deep breath to compose herself. "Not more than an hour ago, you insisted that we be honest with each other. Yet you've been lying for days, maybe weeks," she accused, keeping her voice down as best she could.

"I have never lied to you, Ana."

"First the house and now the Bercots? Every time I asked about those squa—" She took another deep, calming breath. "—those people," she corrected, "you said you'd do something about them."

"I did. I sold them a piece of land and then I talked

211

them into staying year-round and managing the rooming house."

"A perfectly acceptable solution, so why didn't you tell me?"

Too surprised that it was his failing to tell her rather than that the Bercots were still residing on the island that was upsetting her, Ian couldn't even begin to formulate an excuse. Fortunately, he didn't need to, for she paused only long enough to catch her breath before asking, "There are three of them, aren't there? What is it that you have the third one doing, or is that to remain a secret until I stumble over him?"

"Jaie is about to graduate university in Montreal. He's expected home soon."

Ana's brows shot upward. "Well, it would . . . ah . . . seem the Bercots are a family of . . . of some means. What is it that they do beyond managing the dining hall and dormitory? Or is that to remain a secret until I find out myself?"

"It's no secret, or I should say it's not my secret." He shrugged and revealed, "The source of their income is none of my business. I have never asked, and they've not volunteered beyond that they've taught at the university in Montreal for several years."

"How could you let me continue believing they were squatters?"

Ian's brows rose. "My dear, as I recall you didn't give me a chance to explain anything about them the day their names came up in our . . . conversation about the island."

Heat immediately rose to Ana's cheeks. She could almost hear herself ranting and raving about squatters and papists, and Lord only knew what else had spilled from her mouth. Uncomfortable with remembering anything about that day, she concentrated on the issue at hand—

Ian's habitual deceit. "You had to know I would assume you'd forced them off the island. How could you be so deceitful about something that, as it turns out, was perfectly acceptable?"

"I wouldn't call it exactly deceitful. You didn't ask how I solved the problem. Therefore, I didn't supply the details."

She sent him a narrow-eyed glare. "Omission can be the same as deceit. But I'm asking now. Is there more beyond hiring them to cook and take care of that barracks?"

"Yes, considerably more, actually," he returned as pleasantly as if he were describing the puffy clouds in the sky overhead. Propping himself on his elbows, he stretched out his legs and crossed his ankles. His gaze directed to where his children played around the inscription stone, he was the very picture of a man without a care in the world.

"I sold them several acres of land, and we have formed a business partnership on a venture or two."

"And what kind of business ventures would these be?"

"An inn. What you call a barracks today will one day be a fine inn," he told her. "Currently the second floor is an open dormitory, but we'll partition it off and create separate and more luxurious guest accommodations when there's no longer a need for the dormitory.

"The first floor, where the Bercots prepare and serve the meals, is rather open right now also. But gradually, it will be divided into several spaces, a more refined dining area, perhaps a small private dining room, and a . . . ah . . . public room."

Ian inwardly cringed and nearly tugged at his cravat to ease his discomfort. He was evading the truth again and eventually he would pay for the deception. The "public room" already existed. The dining hall was a place where the men gathered for more than just meals. They played cards, checkers, and darts. And they could enjoy a glass of whiskey or mug of beer while they were doing it. In short, it served as a pub.

If he told her the full truth, she'd see the place as no different from the worst of the waterfront taverns in Cleveland. *Demon rum. Ladies of easy virtue. Gambling.* Her imagination would run the gamut and include them all and probably more.

That there weren't now and never would be any working girls plying their trade at Maison Bercot would be beside the point. He rationalized the deception with the firm belief that once she met Henri and Eduard Bercot, she'd realize that never would men of their ilk run anything but a respectable establishment.

"That's one venture," she began, apparently innocent of exactly what a "public room" meant. "You said 'venture or two.' What else are you and the Bercots involved in developing?"

"Vineyards." Before she could ponder the ultimate product of a vineyard, he hastened to explain, "Wild grapes abound on the island, and as more acres are cleared by the lumbering, we thought to plant several of them with domesticated varieties of grapes. Sort of an experiment to see how well they do in this soil and climate."

A raised brow and gimlet eyes preceded her question, "And if they thrive, what will you do with the crop harvested from acres and acres of grapevines?"

"They can be eaten fresh, and the juice made into jelly, of course." It was another evasion. As surely as he knew the sun was shining from the sky above them, he knew she knew it. Like an expert angler, she'd thrown it out as bait and was just waiting to see what he was going to do with it. By God, she'd already secured the hook. There was no use running anywhere but to the truth.

"Once the vines mature and we have a facility built, we'll press the grapes and make wine from the juice."

She was up from the blanket faster than Ian thought humanly possible. Her hands on her hips, she was the epitome of righteous indignation as she accused, "How could you! My own husband, a partner in the creation *and* selling of spirits? You know how I feel about alcohol of any kind. Spirits are an abomination, a . . . a poison that leads to ruination."

"Now, Ana," he began, keeping his voice conciliatory. "It's only wine. A glass of good wine never led anyone to ruination or perdition either. Even the Apostle Paul advised, '. . . use a little wine for thy stomach's sake.' "

"Oh." She stood sputtering for a moment. "Leave it to you, Ian Patterson, to have memorized that singular passage from the Bible."

"I had to memorize quite a few in my youth," he told her. "Shall I recite more?"

"No. I'm sure you've memorized only those lines and verses you can misconstrue to your own ends."

"Not a franchise held exclusively by us sinners," he muttered beneath his breath as he rose to his feet. Grinning, he recited more loudly, " 'Be not righteous over much.' "

It was the wrong thing to do. In the face of her darkening regard, he sobered. "My dear, calm yourself," he began, reaching for her shoulder. She shrugged off his touch and sent him a withering glare.

"Whether it's wine, whiskey, beer, or lemonade that anyone's drinking at Maison Bercot, neither Eduard nor Henri are going to allow anyone to overimbibe. They're not the sort, and furthermore, we have a rather select clientele here on the island. Almost every man here is a family man. They're all, including the few single men, hardworking and responsible. There is absolutely nothing wrong with a man having a glass or two of something stronger than water at the end of the day while enjoying the fellowship of friends."

Judging by the rise of her brow and the tightening of her lips, Ian could see Ana wasn't at all mollified. "Humph." She took a few brisk steps, turned, and marched back. Her hands on her hips, she declared, "If you ever stumble home drunk from that place, the children and I will be on the first boat headed toward Cleveland. Is that understood?"

"Yes, ma'am," he said quickly, struggling to keep from grinning.

She nodded, seemingly content with that, but a slight frown furrowed her brow.

"Something else?" he queried.

She sighed. "What about the other men? How can you be so sure of their character? Do you interview each and every person hired to work here?"

"Not everyone. Kenneth McClurty did some of the hiring of the men who'll be lumbering and quarrying. Ned hired the hostlers. The Fruths hired all the construction workers. I trust their judgment. They know the kind of community I intend to build. No drunkards or ne'er-do-wells of any kind will slip through."

She worried her lower lip for a moment. "Slip through," she repeated. "You make Parras sound like a fortified castle." She shook her head, then boldly demanded, "Are you building your own private kingdom?"

Was he? It had not been his intent. Not consciously anyway. But perhaps unconsciously it had. That was an idea that didn't sit well at all. "Of course not," he said, but the denial didn't convince himself or Ana. Skepticism was practically stamped all over her face.

"It won't work, you know," she stated. "As you once

reminded me, this is a free country. Do you honestly think you can bar anyone who doesn't meet your approval from stepping foot on this island?"

"I have to try," escaped from his lips before he had a chance to think about it. From a throat and mouth suddenly gone dry, the words had come out in a quiet rasp, but Ana's, "Why?" banished his hope she hadn't heard him.

Forcing a grin, he replied blithely, "Why, to make the island live up to its name, of course," and he tried his best not to squirm beneath her searching gaze.

Sally's sharp barking and a scream from one of the children drew his and Ana's attention. Every fiber in his body chilled before he saw there was no cause for alarm. The children were playing tag. The cry had been one of delight, nothing more, except it provided him the diversionary tactic he needed. "There are four children over there who aren't going to be content much longer. I think we'd better pack up and get on with the tour."

He started to move past her, but she laid her hand on his arm and stopped him. "This conversation is not finished."

He started to argue that it was, but the look on her face told him she was through with his evasions and omissions. Well, he'd demanded honesty, and he couldn't very well expect it to come only from her. "We'll take it up again tonight. After the children are asleep, we could take a walk along the beach. A nice setting, I think, for a good, long talk."

"We can't leave the children alone."

"I'm sure Ned would be happy to stay with them for a while."

Still Ana hesitated, and Ian would've bet the *Ulsterman* that her curiosity was warring with her fear of being alone with him. There was certainly a war going on within him. Consequently, he wasn't sure whether he was glad or sorry when she finally said, "Ask him to come at half-past eight."

He nodded, wondering how many truths she'd pry out of him and if there was a chance any of his fantasies of last night might be fulfilled.

As the carriage bowled along the road that followed the coastline, the children chattered and Sally barked at any gull she thought swooped too close to her charges. Seated close to Ian on the narrow driver's seat, Ana felt every shift of his arms and legs as he managed the team. Though the scent and heat from his body surrounded her, it was his voice as he explained the points of interest they passed that held her in thrall. There was such a depth of love in the way he dealt with the children, patiently answering their questions as he carefully guided them about the quarry, making the trip meaningful as well as fun for them.

Sorting through the chips at the base of a large pile of newly quarried stone, Ian had carefully chosen one for each of the children and for her. "Look carefully," he instructed. "You'll see what looks like a picture on each of these. It may be what looks like a shell or the imprint of a leaf. They're called fossils. They're not pictures but a remnant of a shellfish or plant that lived thousands of years ago."

When Ian explained how the fossils came to be created in the stone, Ana had been impressed with the extent of his geological knowledge, a subject in which she was not at all conversant, but she knew enough to recognize his authority in the area. She'd known Ian Patterson for more than nine years, and yet she didn't know him at all. He was a man of great talent, knowledge, and depth. Like the rock she held in her hand, locked deep within him were secrets of another life. And like the men digging for the limestone hidden beneath the earth's surface, she would have to delve just as industriously to unearth those secrets that drove him and made him the man he was today. The clues he dropped from time to time had her curiosity thoroughly piqued, and she was eager to begin her own brand of quarrying.

The process of quarrying limestone could have been dull indeed if described by anyone else. But Ian had a way of making it exciting, as if each slab of the dull gray rock were a priceless treasure about to be set upon a journey of high adventure. And his description of the process of grinding some of it into powder for cement and how that cement would be used was positively thrilling. Or so it might have been to Ana had she not been more excited by the anticipation of what she would find out about the man himself later tonight, and in the weeks ahead.

"The limestone from Parras Island will find its way all over Ohio and beyond," Ian explained as they drew away from the pit, a hole in the ground that he'd told them would grow steadily wider and deeper in the years to come as the limestone was extracted.

"Just think of it, children," he said, slowing the horses and looking back over the new quarry and the piles of stone waiting to be carried down to the dock for shipping. "Roads, homes, churches, and all sorts of buildings will be created by the limestone and cement we ship from here. Imagine the people who'll be sheltered by our stone. It's a grand thing to know you've contributed to something that'll be here long after you, your children, and even your children's children are gone."

"Will our house be limestone, too?" Maara asked.

"Aye."

"And will my children and their children live there someday?"

"If God is willing, Maara, darlin', there'll be Pattersons living in that house and on this island forever. No one will ever take it from us or ours." Ian spoke so fiercely that Ana knew it was another clue to the man.

Had his family been one of those he'd described being thrown off their lands in Ireland? Weeks ago when he'd said he had a brother named Randall, she'd wanted to ask about him, but there had not been the opportunity. Tonight, when they took that walk along the beach, she'd ask him about Randall and Ireland.

Once back on the shoreline road, they'd not gone too far before it became a narrow footpath, which Ana surmised continued on to the northern point of the island. To the right was the lake, and to their left was a track that led into a dense forest.

Reining in the team, Ian explained, "We can turn around and go back the way we came or cut across here and hook up with the road along the opposite shore. The track through the woods isn't as smooth as the road, but I think the scenery's worth any discomfort in the ride."

The children were, of course, all for cutting across, but Ana wasn't so sure. The woods appeared to cover the whole upper half of the island. Dense with trees and heavy thickets, it looked dark and menacing. She shivered.

"But what about the—" She clamped her lips together. There was no need to frighten the children unnecessarily.

Ian patted her knee and said, "Wild boar was a featured dish at the dormitory for a while this spring. I believe there might still be a ham or two hanging in the smokehouse that Henri's saving for a special occasion. I don't expect there's anything bigger than a rabbit or maybe a groundhog in those woods now."

Tamping down her fears, she gave him a tremulous smile. "If you say it's safe, I'm sure it is," she said, and was rewarded with one of the smiles he usually bestowed on the children.

Shifting the ribbons, Ian enveloped Ana's hand in his free one. "I appreciate your trust, Ana, and hope I never give you cause to question it."

Warmed by his smile and the glow in his eyes, Ana nodded. "There's much I don't know about you, Ian Patterson, but I do know you'd never knowingly endanger your children."

"Or my wife," he added, and gave one more squeeze to her hand before he released it. Clicking to the well-trained team, he tugged on the reins and guided them on the track toward the forest.

"The Bercot brothers tell me there are plenty of wild blackberries in these woods. How are you at baking, Mrs. Patterson? I have a particular liking for blackberry pie and blackberry cobbler."

Her fears of the woods and what might be lurking there were pushed to the back of her thoughts and she struggled to suppress an answering grin. Her tongue in her cheek, she pulled herself up in mock hauteur. "Well, Mr. Patterson, if someone were to present me with a bucket of berries and provide enough wood for the stove, I believe I could manage at least a cobbler and even a pie."

Ian chuckled. "Mrs. Patterson, I'm getting the distinct impression that you are a woman of many talents and—" He grinned, waggled his brows, and leaned closer so that his voice was a deep rumble in her ears when he finished the statement. "—hidden depths."

And if that weren't enough to set every inch of her skin to tingling, he added in a low, husky tone, "I'm looking forward to our walk in the moonlight tonight."

Glad they'd entered the heavy shade of the woods so that the heat beating in her cheeks wasn't as obvious,

Ana swallowed hard. In a voice she hardly recognized as her own, she said, "You, too, have many depths, Mr. Patterson. And I intend to explore them tonight."

"My dear, I can't imagine anything more pleasurable."

Ana's breath caught in her throat. "We are talking about a continuance of our earlier conversation, are we not?" she managed. "You did promise answers—"

Any further reminder of the purpose of their walk was interrupted by a low growl from Sally. It was a sound like no other the young dog had ever made. Glancing over her shoulder, Ana noted that Sally was on her feet and peering steadily into the dark thicket they were passing. The fur on her back bristling, her muscles quivering, she looked ready to leap from the carriage at any second.

Either picking up on the dog's unease or something else, the horses began tossing their heads and straining at their bits. The carriage began to sway and bounce dangerously on the rough track as the horses quickened their pace. Having all he could do to keep the horses from bolting completely, Ian ordered, "Rob. Grab Sally and hold on. Don't let her leave the carriage."

The urgency in Ian's voice was alarming, and Ana turned to help Rob. She was not a second too soon, for the dog was determined to free herself, and Rob was hard put to keep his hold on her. Heedless of the danger to herself, Ana scrambled to her knees on the seat and faced the back of the carriage. She made a dive and was able to grab the dog's collar just in time. Giving her a sharp jerk, she commanded, "Sally! Sit."

The dog promptly sat down on the carriage seat between Rob and Joseph but continued to tremble and whine. Fearing that at any minute she'd go tumbling head over heels from her own precarious position, Ana was grateful when she felt Ian grab hold of her skirts where they covered her backside. As inelegant as her po-

sition was, at least she was no longer in danger of following her bonnet to the floor of the carriage or flying
into the thickets.

She didn't relax her hold on Sally, nor did Ian relax his
on her, until they were some distance beyond the woods
and he'd slowed the horses to a more reasonable pace.
Once again in a broad, open space with a wide stretch of
beach on one side and a freshly plowed field on the other,
Ian pulled the horses to a stop.

"Remind me either to leave that dog at home or bring
a leash next time," Ian muttered as he helped Ana right
herself. "Are you all right?"

"Yes, I think so." She smoothed some of her hair from
her face and tried to still her racing pulse. "Oh, my, I
must look a fright."

"No, you look like a woman who's just had one." He
smiled and looped a strand of her hair behind her ear. "A
pretty one who gave me quite a scare, I might add. I
feared you were going to fly off the seat and break your
neck when you made that dive for Sally."

"I nearly did. Thank you for grabbing me when you
did," she said, then blushed as she remembered where
he'd had to grab. He'd dug his fingers into her clothing
so deeply, she was sure he'd caught the seat of her
drawers. "Whatever was bothering Sally?"

Ian let out a gust of air. "I'm not exactly sure, but
I have my suspicions." He gathered up the ribbons,
clicked to the horses, and started them moving again.
"Rob, everybody all right back there?"

"We're fine. Sally, too. She's never acted like that before. What'd ya think got into her, Da?"

Ian sent Ana a sidelong glance before he answered his
son. The look of horror growing on her face told him she
anticipated his answer. There was no use shielding her or
the children from the truth. "It might have been a wild

hog, son." Ana gasped and he reached across the seat and gave her hands a reassuring squeeze. Finding them as cold as ice, he left his hand over them.

Tamping down his own agitation, he kept his tone calm but serious. "Until I tell you otherwise, don't do any exploring in that region or anywhere near it. I want your word on that, Rob."

"Yes, Da."

"I'll warn everyone about the incident and send some men through there to investigate. A wild hog can be a very dangerous animal. We'll get rid of it." He turned to Ana and added, "I thought we'd gotten rid of them, I swear it."

Ana nodded and offered, "Perhaps it was only a groundhog."

"Perhaps, but I'm not taking any chances." Looking over his shoulder, he saw that all the children were wide-eyed and sober. Good. They needed to be. Ian let silence stress the seriousness of the situation until they neared the edge of the village. "Next stop, the O'Houlihans's," he announced with forced gaiety.

"Oh . . . oh, I can't call on anyone looking like this," Ana protested, and started smoothing her hair back. "Couldn't we meet everyone tomorrow?"

He shook his head. "After what happened back there, the reason for the visits will be twofold. Don't worry, you look lovely," he told her and meant it. Her hair was the way he liked it, loose and framing her face with curls.

To his disappointment, she began smoothing the wayward tresses and repinning them in place. "Jessica, could you hand me my bonnet?" The bonnet appeared over the back of the seat and she quickly plopped it atop her head, tucked errant curls up in it as best she could, and tied the ribbons snugly beneath her chin.

She was still fussing nervously with her appearance when he pulled up in front of the tidy stone house located on the far edge of the village. "You look fine," he told her again as he helped her from the carriage.

She shook out her skirts and straightened her bodice. "I still think it would have been better if you'd taken us home and then made the rounds to warn people."

"And leave you and the children cowering in the house, thinking any minute a wild boar was going to come charging into the yard? Making plans to pack up and board the next boat to the mainland?"

"That's not what—" She looked away. Now that her feet were on the ground, her legs were trembling so much she could hardly stand. She swayed and was glad for Ian's strong arm at her waist.

"It's exactly what would have happened," he told her. "Don't you think it better for the children if this outing ends on a happy note?"

She gave a sigh of resignation. The face she turned toward him was still pale, but he knew exactly how to put the color back in her cheeks. Bending low, he said into her ear, "The O'Houlihans happen to practice the Roman Catholic faith, as do many you'll meet today. Kate O'Houlihan could be a good friend if you'd allow yourself to see her as the very fine woman she is."

Her chin came up, and color was already rising in her cheeks. "That was unnecessary and ill-timed," she said through gritted teeth. "After all Rob said about her sons this morning, I'm very much looking forward to meeting Mrs. O'Houlihan. And I'll have you know, I need no coaching in civility or courtesy from the likes of *you*, Mr. Patterson." To prove her point, she flashed a warm smile that would have rivaled her mother at her most welcoming.

Dipping his head to hide his grin, he murmured, "Touché, Mrs. Patterson. I am suitably chastened."

He was rewarded by a silvery glimmer in her eyes that in someone else he would have thought a spark of mischief.

Her warm smile remained as she gathered the children around her and started up the graveled walkway to the house. It stayed there when the front door of the little house opened and out tumbled a trio of towheaded boys, followed by a pretty blond woman with a plump baby in her arms.

Introductions were made all around, and Ana found herself quite charmed by the entire family. If it were not for the fright they'd just had that still had her trembling at times, she would have thoroughly enjoyed the visit.

Save for the warning of the possibility of a wild boar in the vicinity, Ian appeared completely relaxed and was as pleasant and charming as ever she'd seen him. He stayed close by her side, and she was always aware when his gaze was upon her.

Knowing they'd been married only the day before, Kate O'Houlihan mistook his attentiveness. At the end of their visit, as she walked them to the carriage, she gave a dreamy sigh. "Ah 'tis sure you're like my Kevin and me when first we married. Hardly did we take our eyes off each other."

Ana was grateful for the wide brim of her bonnet and that only Ian could see the glare she sent him. She wanted him to know that he might have fooled Kate O'Houlihan, but she knew better. He wasn't looking upon her with the eyes of a loving husband or even for signs she was still suffering from the scare they'd had. He was being watchful and ready to intercede if she should say anything that would upset their hostess. Throughout the visit, she'd been torn between wanting to conk him on the head or burst into tears that he should think so ill of her.

"These days when your love is so new, 'tis a sweet time and one you'll be treasuring all your years together," Kate added once they were all in the carriage. " 'Tis certain just looking at you that you'll not be needing my good wishes for your happiness, but I'll give them to you just the same. And though you won't be needing them, I'll be remembering you and these sweet children in my prayers."

Ian slid his arm around Ana's waist and pulled her snugly to his side. "Ana and I thank you, Katie O'Houlihan." The lilt of Ireland was nearly as thick in his speech as it was in Katie's. "For sure if we find half the joy in our union as you and Kevin have in yours, we shall be blessed indeed."

Ana could hardly wait until the carriage had pulled away from the O'Houlihans's to give him a sharp elbow in the ribs. Her anger had won out over her pain. Just loud enough for him to hear, she hissed, "Ian Patterson, you are a silver-tongued scoundrel for misleading that woman like that."

"And what would you have me do, my dear?" he asked in a drawling whisper. "Tell her this is merely an arrangement, not a true marriage at all? Katie O'Houlihan is a sweet woman, so happy in her own loving marriage, I doubt she'd comprehend such a thing. The knowledge would only sadden her. I'd not like to ever dim the light in her pretty eyes, would you?"

When he put it that way, Ana could not fault him for his behavior. Not too much, anyway. "Well, you needn't play the love-sick swain quite so heavily," she whispered back.

"That convincing, was I?"

His grin was so broad she was surprised his face didn't

crack in two. The arch glare she sent him was most satisfying. He sobered considerably.

There was no opportunity for any further private remarks between them as they made the rounds of the other families and stopped to chat with some of the men whose families had not yet joined them. By the time they'd finished working their way through the village, Ana was thoroughly exhausted and her head was spinning as she tried to remember all the names and connect them to faces.

Flaherty, O'Connor, Muhlenhaupt, Keegan, Sheets, Knez, and so many others, she could not have listed them all had her life depended upon it. How Ian kept them all straight and could even remember their children's names was a miracle.

Ian didn't ask her to get down from the carriage when he pulled up in front of the large building next to the warehouse. "I'll not be long," he promised as he lifted the basket from the carriage. "Just need to return this. Next stop, home, I promise."

He gave the children a mild admonishment to behave for their aunt Ana and disappeared through the door beneath the sign that read: MAISON BERCOT: CLEAN BEDS, FINE FOOD AND DRINK. The carefully scripted gold letters blazed against a bright red background.

It was the final word on the sign that made Ana's blood chill. Though Ian had assured her overimbibing would not be tolerated, it still rankled that her own husband was a partner in an establishment that sold liquor. After sending up a prayer that his claim would not prove false, she vowed that she'd never step foot in the establishment.

Studying the stone and timber building, she was surprised to see flower boxes attached beneath the windows flanking the doorway, an incongruous touch to a building she knew housed only men. Violets and a white-blossomed vining plant she couldn't identify were thriving in them. She had not long to ponder who had planted them before Ian emerged, two distinguished-looking men following in his wake.

"Ana, children, let me present Messieurs Henri and Eduard Bercot."

Chapter Sixteen

"Madame Patterson, it is a pleasure to meet you," the taller of the two gentlemen said, a friendly smile upon his patrician face. "Ian tells us your name is Valeriana. Such a beautiful name you have. Just right for such a beautiful lady. Ah, and your eyes are the very color of the valerian blossom, *n'est-ce pas*? Are you familiar with that plant, madame?"

Unused to such gallantry, Ana hardly knew how to respond. "Thank you, sir. And yes, I am familiar with the plant. My mother grows them and named me after it."

"A wise *maman*. She is a gardener? I should enjoy meeting her someday. Perhaps we could share our knowledge and some cuttings."

"I'm sure she would enjoy that, Mr. Bercot."

"Henri, madame, please," he invited.

"Henri," Ana repeated, warming to the man despite herself. "And thank you for the picnic luncheon you provided for us."

"My brother and I are pleased you enjoyed the simple repast we prepared for you."

"It was most delicious." She managed the best smile she could, but she was exhausted, and a sharp pain knifed between her brows. *Could Ian not have saved these introductions for another day?* "You are a master chef, Henri."

"You are too kind, madame. Eduard and I have always enjoyed cooking, and now, thanks to your kind husband, we have at last our own tavern."

Tavern? Ana's eyes swung to Ian and saw the same intense watchfulness in his eyes that she'd suffered most of the afternoon. He could watch her all he liked, but he wasn't going to find a single fault in her words or demeanor.

"It is a rustic tavern now but one day, we hope it will be a fine inn serving our very own wine. The climate and soil here should produce an excellent grape. We have high hopes that your husband's investment in the vines will turn a profit eventually."

Unaware of the turmoil his every word was causing, Bercot positively glowed with pride. He gestured toward the building behind him. "This building is crude, *oui*, but its patrons are not. You have the word of Henri Bercot that a lady such as yourself would be comfortable in our establishment.

"It would be our joy to serve you, Madame Patterson, the wife of our dearest friend. You must tell us when you are coming, and Eduard and I will prepare our best dishes just for you."

I will never step foot in that . . . that saloon! The words screamed inside her head, but she was determined to exercise tolerance if it killed her. At the moment it had merely struck her dumb.

"When we are settled," Ian said, and Ana prayed fervently he would somehow explain to Mr. Bercot that his wife would never, ever step inside an establishment that served alcohol. But he brazenly suggested, "Perhaps my wife *and* the children might come for one of your special Sunday dinners."

"Of course, the children must come!" Bercot moved toward the back of the carriage where the children were.

"Such fine, beautiful children you have. Perhaps we shall make Sunday dinners special for families. What say you, Eduard?"

Silent until now, Eduard stepped forward. "Madame." Bowing elegantly, he spoke as charmingly as his brother. "Family dinners would be a fine tradition. As the wife of the founder of our little village, would you be so kind as to serve as our guest of honor at the first one? This Sunday, we could arrange such a special banquet for all the families. It would be a fine way to celebrate the first mass to be said upon our island."

Ana gulped. "A mass? Here?"

"Ah, *oui*. With your husband's help, Mesdames O'Houlihan and Flaherty have arranged for a priest to come from the mainland," Eduard continued. "We have no church yet, of course, but your husband has donated a plot of land for one. If weather permits, the priest shall say the mass on the very spot where one day a small church shall rise."

"You did well, Ana," Ian said as he helped her down from the carriage. Once her feet were again upon the ground, he kept his hands on her waist so that she could not dash away. "I'm glad to see how much your mother's daughter you can be. And every bit as lovely."

He tugged playfully on one of several curls that had escaped her bonnet. "Especially so with these pretty curls framing your face."

She looked him fully in the face for any sign that he was mocking her, but she saw only approval in the warm glow in his eyes. Still, she wished he hadn't treated her like a naughty little girl who needed constant reminding of her manners.

She swatted his hand aside. "And you, sir, are the

most . . . most— Oh! There are not words to describe you!"

Turning on her heel, she stalked toward the house, keeping an iron control over her tears until she'd closed the bedroom door behind her.

There, alone, she crumpled to the bed and buried her face against a pillow. The tears fell as she loosed all the pain she'd suffered throughout the afternoon.

He didn't think her at all like her mother.

He thought her such a mean creature she needed to be told how to act, warned not to hurt anyone's feelings. Oh, she knew she had strong opinions, but was she really so offensive when she stated them that she had to be warned to be polite?

She'd hidden her pain from his rebuke under a mask of smiles and friendly chatter all afternoon. And then she'd discovered what a deceitful man he was. A tavern, wine manufacturing . . . and a Catholic church on the island?

She was expected to practice religious tolerance while only a Catholic priest had been sent for. Well, there'd be a Protestant minister here next Sunday or she and the children would be on the first boat off this island.

The heat of her growing fury stanched the flow of her tears. Shoving herself upright, she wiped at her dampened cheeks.

"You are who you are, Ana Patterson," she reminded herself as she yanked off her bonnet. Freed from its confinement, most of her hair tumbled loose.

She rifled her fingers through the mass. As she freed the rest, she felt almost as if she were freeing her own spirit. She was so tired of being ever dutiful, doing and saying what others expected of her.

Expected?

"More like dictated," she grumbled aloud. First Papa and now Ian Patterson. She wasn't sure which of them was worse. It didn't matter. She wasn't going to be bullied or treated like an errant child ever again.

Picking up her hairbrush, she began dragging it through her hair. But looking into the mirror, she saw that no amount of brushing could ever tame her curls into a curtain of silk like her sister's. Lily's hair had never fallen willy-nilly from her bonnet, like a wild thing with a mind of its own. She yanked the brush through her hair several more strokes and then began to fashion it into a snug plait.

Lily would have smiled and agreed with everything Ian said. She'd have done everything he told her to do, including totally ignoring spirits being made right in her backyard. And she wouldn't have needed to dash into a room and cry her eyes out after doing so.

He couldn't be thinking he could mold her into another Lily, could he?

That thought had her shaking her finger at the mirror as if the reflection there were Ian's. What she saw was a face that was anything but beautiful with its red-rimmed eyes and pale skin splotched from her tears. The mirror was large enough that she could see herself almost to the waist, revealing a woman with substantial bone structure and a too-big bosom beneath a simple gown of dark brown linen.

In lieu of Ian, she shook her finger at the mirror and declared, "I'm not *her*. There's nothing delicate or beautiful or fashionable about me. You said so yourself—*you're not Lily*. Remember that! For better or worse, you're stuck with Valeriana, the plain, outspoken sister."

"That was a fine meal, Ana."

Ian's compliment was ignored, just as had been every other statement he'd directed toward her since he'd walked into the house after returning the carriage.

Without so much as a flicker of an eyelash in Ian's direction, Ana gently wiped Joseph's face with a damp cloth. "All clean, sweetheart. You may get down now."

"Ned said he'd be happy to come by later," Ian remarked. Ana merely nodded.

"Why is Mr. Ferguson coming here?" Rob asked. "We just saw him this morning."

"Your aunt and I thought to take a walk later, Rob, but we didn't want you to be left alone." At least the children were talking to him.

"Didn't you get in enough walking today? I sure did. I'm tired."

"Sometimes grown-ups like to take walks by themselves, Rob."

"At night?" Rob's expression indicated he thought his father must have lost his sense. "Can't see much at night. Better not walk too far; you don't know this place very well yet. Things look different at night. You might get lost or something."

Ian chuckled. "We'll be careful, *Da*," he teased, then reached over and ruffled Rob's hair.

"Rob, if you're finished, would you take your little brother out to the necessary?" Ana's question effectively snuffed any further queries by Rob about grown-ups going off by themselves. "Maara, would you start clearing the table while I get the dishwater ready? Jessica, darling, do try to finish your milk. Then you can help your sister and me."

There was a scraping of chairs, and Ana and the children went about their tasks. Except Jessica, who was still dawdling over her milk. As soon as Ana's back was turned, the little girl leaned across the table and whispered, "Papa, why was Aunt Ana crying when we got home?"

Jessica's whispers weren't all that quiet. Ian was sure Ana had heard. Assuming she had, he merely lowered his voice when he said, "I think I said something mean to her."

"Then you should tell her you're sorry."

"I will when we take our walk."

"And give her a big, big hug, too. And a kiss. That'll make her feel better."

There was a crash from the worktable, followed by what almost sounded like a muffled "Damnation!" She'd heard Jessie's suggestion. He was sure of it. Her back was turned, but her ears looked a bit reddish. And he thought the back of her neck did, too, as she bent to pick up the pan she'd dropped.

"That might be a good idea," he said, and pushed away from the table. "Finish your milk, then help Aunt Ana clear the table. I'll go check on the boys and hurry them along."

The sky was clear and the moon was full. Ian and Ana had no trouble finding their way as they walked along the beach. It was an unusually still night, with only a faint breeze even this close to the water. The only sound this far away from the village was the gentle lapping of the lake against the shore.

Desperate to break the silence that had stretched between them now for hours, Ian discarded one opening remark after another. Finally he settled upon, "The children certainly fell asleep quickly."

Ana sighed. "Yes, they did. It was a long day for them."

It was Ian's turn to sigh. "Well, that's a relief."

"What? That the children fell asleep so easily?"

"No, that you're finally talking to me."

Halting abruptly, Ana placed her hands on her hips and demanded, "That is what this walk is all about, isn't it? That we talk? Or is it only for you to talk at me or give me lessons in decorum?"

Frowning, he repeated, "Lessons in decorum. When did I—"

"Don't be obtuse. You know perfectly well that you lectured me throughout the afternoon on how I was to behave." Shaking her finger, she advanced on him. "You will not ever do that again. I am not a little girl." She stabbed him in the chest with her forefinger and continued to do so as she stated, "I'm not Lily, and I'm not my mother. I'm Valeriana, and I do know how to behave in public."

"Yes, ma'am." He caught her finger and grinned. "You are most certainly a lady of refined manners, and I do apologize for my remarks."

Her "humph" let him know his apology had been sadly lacking. Before he could expand upon it, she wrenched her finger from his grasp and immediately started to lose her balance.

Ian reached to steady her, but she managed to right herself. "Perhaps it would be best if we sat down," he suggested, and would have helped her toward a fallen tree just beyond the edge of the beach had she allowed it.

They took a few more steps, but the smooth beach rocks shifted beneath her feet, and she would have fallen if Ian hadn't caught her around the waist. "I didn't realize how difficult the going would be along here," he said, and without any warning dipped down and wrapped his other arm behind her legs and lifted her up against his chest.

"Put me down," she cried, even as her arm went around his neck. "The footing is just as bad beneath your feet as mine."

"My feet are bigger. I can walk on this beach easier

than you," Ian said, but didn't make a move toward the fallen tree.

"Put me down," she repeated, but with less conviction than before. Even after having been angry and disappointed in him so much of this day, it felt surprisingly good to be in his arms. Briefly, she let herself enjoy the comfort of being held before she tried again. "Please. You'll hurt yourself carrying me."

"I believe I'll hurt myself if I let you go," was his enigmatic remark, its husky tone sending a tremor down her spine.

"I . . . I'm too heavy. I must feel—"

"More right than I could ever have imagined," he said, deftly turning her more snugly against his chest until she could feel his heart beating against her breasts. His face was so close, she felt his every breath against her skin.

Whether it was she or Ian who closed that tiny space, she didn't know or care. The first touch set her heart hammering against her ribs and increased the fluttering sensations deep in her belly. No gentle brushing of her lips as he had yesterday after their wedding ceremony, this. He settled his mouth over hers in a consuming possession that swept her away on a wave of mindless pleasure.

His tongue plunged inside her mouth, sweeping, plundering, and challenging her to follow where he led. From somewhere—far away or deep within herself—she heard a call that she end this. Kissing was not why they were out here alone on the beach. But she didn't want to heed the reminder, not yet, not until she'd practiced the lessons he'd taught her during those two long kisses before.

Cradling his face with one hand, she savored the taste of him, circled his tongue with hers, and then retreated. Emboldened by his moan of pleasure, she returned to reacquaint herself with the intriguing cavern of his mouth. When he broke off the kiss, her sigh of disappointment turned to a breathless "ah" as he spread kisses across her cheek and down her throat.

He lowered her feet to the ground beside the log and continued the delicious assault on her throat and to a spot just below her ear she'd not known was so sensitive. His mouth returned to hers, and she was only dimly aware that his hands had covered her breasts. Under his touch they swelled, and her nipples tightened to hard points that ached. Arching her back, she found some relief by inadvertently pressing her breasts more firmly against his palms.

Ian kneaded and caressed her through the layers of her gown and chemise, then fumbled for the hooks hidden beneath a pleat down the front of her dress. His lips followed the deeper and deeper opening of her bodice. At the first brush of his fingertips against the fullness of her breasts above her chemise, Lily's warning sprang to Ana's mind.

Being kissed and held was wonderful. And—oh, my— being caressed was even more wonderful. But Lily had set it in her mind too well where such intimate touches invariably led. Chilled at the images, she pushed against his chest.

"No. Please. We . . . we came here to . . . to talk," she managed. Turning her back, she frantically refastened her bodice and stumbled toward the log.

"I suppose you think I should beg your pardon again," Ian said. "But I'm not going to. You have irresistible lips and a body to match. I'm not made of stone, and you, Valeriana, are my wife."

Alarmed by the determination in his voice, Ana said, "But we agreed that ours would be a marriage in name only."

"I had no choice but to agree to your demand. But I

remind you again, my dear, that I did not agree never to try to change your mind. And you will, you know."

"I will do no such thing," Ana declared primly, though she was not at all sure he wasn't right. He consistently rendered her nearly mindless with his kisses and caresses. There had not been one moment in his arms that she hadn't enjoyed. Nor had she ever felt anything but regret when one of their embraces ended.

Shifting uncomfortably on the log and paying inordinate attention to smoothing her skirts, she cleared her throat. "We are here to continue an earlier conversation. I believe that would be a better use of our time alone, don't you?"

A low chuckle from Ian sent a shaft of heat through her body. "No, but I'll bow to your wishes." With a shrug, he closed the space between them and gestured to a spot next to her feet. "May I?" he asked.

She nodded, wishing he'd chosen someplace much farther away. The tree trunk had to be a good fifteen feet long. Why did he have to choose a spot right next to her?

As soon as he settled himself upon the ground, his back propped against the log, she considered requesting he move down a bit but rejected the idea. Admitting she was discomforted by the brush of his shoulder against her skirts or that his head was so close she had to clasp her hands together to refrain from running her fingers through his hair would be analogous to admitting how affected she was by his kisses. She wasn't about to hand him ammunition for his war on her senses.

Grateful that at least she couldn't see his face, she asked, "What is the real reason behind isolating your family on this island?"

Ian didn't answer immediately. The only indication that he'd heard her was the way he began thrumming his fingers on his bent knee. She heard him let out a long gust of air before saying, "When I first bought it, I thought it the perfect solution to some . . . ah . . . problems Lily and I were having."

Ana frowned. That Lily and Ian's marriage hadn't been perfect was not a surprise, but she didn't want to hear Ian describe the problems. Lily's discussion of how distasteful she found the marriage bed was quite enough. Isolating Lily on the island would certainly not have solved that problem.

She heard him mutter, ". . . how to explain this" before he sighed again. "Lily needed a husband who could pamper her and pay her constant attention. Unfortunately, my business required my being away from home a lot, sometimes for weeks on end. Because of her need for affection, she was easy prey for a certain kind of man. I don't think she meant to betray me and our marriage vows; it was just something that happened. I'm as much to blame as she was."

Lily? An adulteress? No, it wasn't possible. Lily was nothing but good and sweet and gentle. "You . . . you must be mistaken. It's not possible. Not Lily."

As if he hadn't even heard her, Ian went on, "I thought that if I could rearrange my businesses so I could cease traveling and get Lily away to a place where I could better control her contacts, everything would be all right. And the children would be safe."

"The children? What do they have to do with this?" she asked, though she had a sick feeling she knew the answer. *Rob and I are Papa's children. Joseph and Jessica are Mama's.* That, or words to that effect, was what Maara had said.

Ana shook her head, trying to rid it of the horrible truth those simple statements revealed. "Joseph and Jessica aren't yours, are they?"

Ian didn't say anything, but his silence was answer

enough. "Who?" she asked. "Who was Lily's—" She swallowed hard before she could say the word. "—lover?"

"Their identities are not important."

Their? She felt as if someone had just sunk a fist in her stomach. Shock, hurt, sick of heart, she could barely speak. "More than one? Oh, dear God, who else knows?" she whispered.

"Your mother. Jim Cooke. Neither of them will ever tell anyone."

"Papa?"

"No, Rose and I agreed it was best that he not know."

Ana squeezed her eyes shut. Fighting a wave of nausea, she took several deep gulps of air. "How could I have been so blind?" she breathed.

"She was your sister, and you loved her."

Unable to sit still any longer, Ana leapt to her feet. Careful to stay on the more even footing beyond the rocky beach, she took a few paces toward a nearby tree. Staring blindly into the darkness, she wished with all her heart that she could refute what Ian had just told her. "She bore two children by another . . . other men and . . ." She wiped at the tears flooding her eyes. "Yet you didn't denounce her. You must have loved her very much."

"Loved her?"

She jumped when Ian's voice came so close behind her.

"That was one of the vows I took. To love her. At first I was just plain besotted by her beauty and that helpless way she had that made me feel like a—" She turned in time to see Ian running a hand through his hair, as was his habit when he was perplexed or exasperated.

His single bark of laughter was low and self-deprecating. "Suffice it to say, it appealed to my male ego. And for a while, having Lily as my wife made me the envy of nearly every man in town, which stroked that ego as well. But love her? Not in the way a man ought to love the woman who is his wife.

"I doubt what she felt for me was love, either," he admitted with a surprising lack of bitterness.

"By the time Rob was born . . ." He sighed and shoved his hands in his pockets. "I knew I didn't have a wife, merely a beautiful child/woman who loved having the trinkets I could buy her, owning a closet full of pretty gowns, and living in a big, beautiful house. She was always pleasant and agreeable. An easy person to live with, actually. Hardly disrupted my life at all."

He moved closer to the water's edge. Watching him pick up a stone and send it skipping across the lake's surface, Ana waited in silence. Dear God, she didn't want to hear any more, but every instinct told her that Ian needed to tell it.

"She never turned me away from her bed," he began. "But it was never an enjoyable experience for either of us." He skipped stone after stone as he spoke, calmly and unemotionally, as he revealed the intimate details of his marriage to her sister.

"A man doesn't take much pleasure in the act when his partner just lies there. After a while, I ceased putting either of us through such an ordeal. Since she never did more than tolerate it, I certainly didn't expect her to give herself to anyone else."

He turned away from the lake. "I should have paid closer attention to her, protected her better. But for a long time, we essentially led separate lives. I didn't even know she was pregnant again. Or that she'd ever take something in an attempt to rid herself of a baby. She shouldn't have died the way she did. God, there was so much blood, and she was in such pain."

Sickened by the images he was painting, Ana heard a loud rushing sound, and then the world seemed to tilt.

The next thing she knew, she was in Ian's arms again. "Ana, I'm sorry. So sorry," he muttered against her forehead. "You didn't need to hear all of that. Forgive me."

"No, Ian, there's nothing to forgive," she declared, glad for the strong arms holding her up. "I demanded honesty, and you gave it. Deep in my heart, I knew Lily had her weaknesses. All of us—Mama, Papa, Laurel, and Primmy—knew. We just focused on her sweetness and her beauty, looking past the hard truth about Lily's character. We made excuses for her and doted on her, all the while deceiving ourselves as well as others."

She gave a short, humorless laugh. "'Oh, what a tangled web we weave, When first we practice to deceive!'" she quoted. "Was there ever a more tangled web than this?"

"This web should have been buried with Lily. You needn't have been hurt by it."

"You can't protect everyone, Ian."

"I have to try. As long as there's a breath in my body, no one will ever hurt my children or anyone I'm responsible for," he vowed, tightening his arms around her. "I've taken a lot of steps already to protect them, and I will do whatever's necessary in the future to keep them safe from gossip."

She was ashamed that she'd ever questioned Ian's devotion to the children or to Lily, or that she'd ever thought him a selfish man. Shamed anew by her father's continual attacks on his character, unable to look him in the face, she buried hers against his chest.

If anyone was at fault for the failure of his marriage or Lily's adulterous behavior, it was most certainly not Ian. "Mama and Papa shouldn't have allowed her to marry," she said bitterly. "It wasn't fair to you."

"Don't be too harsh on them, Ana," he said as he rubbed her back, easing the stiffness there. "I know what it is to love a child so much you'll do anything to protect her. And that's what they did. They wanted to make sure she was taken care of. Lily would never have been able to run a household and raise her children without servants. So they found someone who could afford to hire servants and cosset her."

"It still wasn't fair to you," she insisted. She knew so little about his family. And he'd left home so young. Had anyone ever loved him so much that they'd sacrifice anything and everything for him? "If the truth were known about Lily, there's not a person in all of Cleveland who would have condemned you for leaving her or sending her back to Mama and Papa."

Abruptly, he grasped her forearms and forced her to look at him. "Pray to God that the good people of Cleveland or anywhere else never learn the truth."

"But—"

"Lily can't be hurt by the truth, but her children would be. Give me your word, Ana, that this will go no further."

"Of course I won't tell anyone. When we married, in my heart I vowed to love, honor, and cherish the children. I will never break those vows."

She almost squirmed under his intense scrutiny. Finally, evidently convinced of her sincerity, he nodded and relaxed his hold on her. He might have stepped away from her entirely had she not reached for him.

Slipping her arms around his taut middle, she rested her head against his chest. Beneath her cheek she felt each strong beat of his heart, a heart with such a capacity for love and devotion. He deserved so much more than Lily had given him. And now he had a second wife who, like the first, gave him nothing.

Would it really be so awful to give her body to Ian? It was foolish to cling to fears based on what Lily had told her. Mama certainly described the marriage bed differently.

An act of love, she'd told her. At the time, Ana hadn't given any credence to the idea that love would ever be a part of her marriage to Ian. Theirs was to be a marriage of convenience. But Mama hadn't known that and had prattled on and on about how happy she was that she and Ian had found happiness in each other and how deserving of it they both were.

Perhaps they could find happiness. Even love. For the first time in far longer than she wanted to admit even to herself, Ana was glad she wasn't anything at all like Lily. And most definitely glad she'd married Ian.

"Ian?"

"Hmmm?" he murmured at the top of her head.

"I want to know— I mean, would you . . . ah . . . sleep with me tonight?"

Chapter Seventeen

Ian froze. Surely he'd misunderstood. "Ana, do you know what you're asking?"

"Not entirely," she admitted, keeping her head exactly where it was, plastered against his chest. Too embarrassed to face him, he was sure. "But I . . . I've changed my mind about a marriage in name only."

"So soon?" he asked, allowing his skepticism to color his voice.

"Well, yes. I've thought it over and realize it's not fair that you should suffer another marriage with no . . . ah . . . physical gratification."

Any pleasure he'd had when she'd put her arms around him and pressed her lush body against his fled. "Ah, so this offer is a noble sacrifice," he said, sarcasm dripping from every word. "Prompted not by anything so mortal as desire on your part but by some sort of obligation or guilt about your sister."

She pushed out of his arms, and he was glad to let her go.

"That's not—"

"Or is it pity?" he demanded, too incensed to feel any regret for putting that look of hurt in her eyes. "Pity for this poor beast of a man who must be suffering for having endured years of a marriage without sex. Is that

247

why you're suddenly offering to endure my lust for your precious body, Ana?"

As he hurled the words at her, her face drained of color. "No! It's not pity or obligation," she practically yelled at him. "I'm told that couples find a kind of comfort in the act and . . . and I thought you—and I—were in need of some after what you've just told me."

He had to give her credit for courage. And candor. But then those were traits he'd always thought she had in abundance. He'd just never thought they'd lead her to propose they share a bed. "Comfort, eh? That's what you're expecting?"

She didn't answer, but he hadn't really thought she would. Even Valeriana MacPherson had only so much courage, and she'd probably come damned near to using it up. Yet she was still standing her ground. He felt a mixture of admiration and surprise that she hadn't taken off for the cottage as fast as her legs could carry her.

He watched her bite her full lower lip and turn her gaze to some spot down the beach, all the while rubbing at one hand with the other. Her nervousness showed in her breathing, too. It was deep and rapid, and with each intake her breasts strained against her bodice. His palms tingled at the very idea of freeing those lush treasures and holding them in his hands.

Hell and damnation, he was suffering, all right. Just looking at her and imagining her naked and panting beneath him was making him hard.

Jesus, he wanted her, but not under these circumstances. He seriously doubted her denial that obligation played any part in her decision. She was one of the most responsible women he'd ever known. And loyal. Too loyal and too responsible for her own good.

Physical gratification, even comfort, he could get from any woman. They weren't what he wanted from his wife.

And he sure as hell didn't want her to give herself out of some misplaced sense of righting a wrong she thought he'd suffered from someone in her family.

His anger spent, he stretched a hand toward her. "Come, Ana. Let's go home." She stared at it for a long moment. He didn't realize he was holding his breath until she slipped her hand into his.

Lifting her hand to his lips, he brushed her knuckles with a kiss before setting a leisurely pace toward home. "I apologize for flying off at you like that, but I don't need anybody's pity. I heaped enough on myself when first I realized the way things were going to be between Lily and me. And for a while, I conducted myself in a way that I'm not proud of."

He sighed ruefully. "Suffice it to say, I haven't led the life of a monk for all of the past seven years, but—"

"I think that's perfectly understandable under the circumstances, Ian."

He stumbled. He couldn't have been more surprised if she'd suddenly sprouted wings and flown off across the lake. Her remark, delivered in a tone utterly devoid of censure, was enough to make him a believer that a full moon cast strange spells on some people.

"Well . . . ah . . ." He ran a hand nervously down his face and cleared his throat. "On the other hand, I'm a long way from being the depraved fornicator your father has made me out to be."

"I already know that," she said, with what sounded very much like a hint of laughter in her voice. "You told me so yourself, the day you proposed. And I believe you. . . . And, Ian? I apologize for ever having looked down my pious nose at you. You have never deserved censure from any quarter, least of all mine."

He looked quickly at the woman beside him to assure himself it was indeed Valeriana. "Pious nose?" *Who was this woman with the laughter in her voice?* Whoever she was, he hoped she never disappeared.

"Has living with me been so corrupting you are no longer as devout as you once were?" he teased.

She shrugged. "There is a difference between being devout and being pious to the point of being a . . . a . . . what do people call it?"

"Is 'prig' the word you're searching for?"

"Yes, prig. I'm sure that's the word I've heard whispered behind my back. More exactly, 'insufferable prig.' "

"Oh, Ana, I'm sure not," he rushed to assure her, though guilt spread a wave of heat up from his neck.

"It's true, Ian. That's what people in Cleveland think I am, especially the men. And they've been right, for I've been guilty of forgetting an important lesson."

"And that would be?" he asked.

" 'Forbear to judge, for we are sinners all.' "

"Shakespeare, my dear? You, Mrs. Patterson, are full of surprises. I'd not have expected you to have even read the Bard, let alone be able to quote him."

"Nor would I have thought you would recognize the author of that line," she replied with a matching measure of astonishment. "Or have a complete collection of Shakespeare's works in your library. You, Mr. Patterson, are full of surprises as well."

"I suspect we've a lot to discover about each other," he commented. Using the terrain as an excuse, he tucked her arm under his. "I'm quite looking forward to uncovering all you've been hiding."

"Humph. I fear you'll be quite disappointed, as I assure you there's nothing at all mysterious about me and very little you don't already know. You may probe all you like, sir, but there's naught about me that could possibly be very interesting."

Trying not to laugh at her innocent pun, Ian nearly

choked. If he hadn't indulged in a fit of noble pride, he'd be "probing" her "mysteries" right now. "Oh, I'm sure I'll find a lot to interest me," he said. "I already have."

The look she sent him was one he'd call puzzled skepticism.

"How old were you when you left Ireland, Ian? Eighteen? And before that, you'd gone to sea? For how many years?"

"Just short of three," he supplied, reining in his wayward thoughts.

"Fifteen. A rather young age to have acquired much of a taste for Shakespeare, I should think," she commented thoughtfully. "What kind of schools did you attend before you went to sea? You can't have come by all the knowledge you have by just reading books yourself. Someone must have guided you along the way."

"He who demands honesty should be damned by it," Ian muttered.

"I don't recognize that line. Is it Shakespeare?"

"No, it's Ian Patterson," he replied sardonically. He took a deep breath and considered where to begin. Having a wife as curious and as intelligent and educated as Ana was both a pleasure and a curse.

"You already know I grew up in the country in Northern Ireland. It was an estate called Fiegel, and the Pattersons have owned it for almost two hundred years. I had a private tutor at first. Then my mother died, and I was packed off to a boarding school."

"How old were you?" Ana asked softly.

"Eight."

He heard her suck in her breath. "So young."

"In England and parts of Ireland, too, the upper classes commonly send their boys off to boarding school at that age, even younger," he told her. "It was a good school, but I hated it and ran away every chance I could get. After the third time, the squire gave up on schooling me and a lot of other things. When my grandparents stepped forward and claimed me, he was more than relieved to turn me over to them."

"Claimed me" seemed an odd phrase to Ana. And who was the squire? His father? She was full of questions, but she held her tongue. This was as forthright as Ian had ever been about his past. She didn't dare interrupt as he described seeing Belfast for the first time, exploring the city with his new tutor, Colin Fraser, a distant cousin, and his fascination with the shipyard.

"Colin was wise enough to use my interest in ship design to teach me geometry, and the shores of Belfast Lough were an endless source of science lessons. But it was my grandfather who taught me to sail."

He chuckled wryly. "I don't think Grandmama ever forgave him for that, as it marked the beginning of my pleading to serve on one of the big ships. By the time the wars were over, I'd worn down even that formidable lady, and I was allowed to sign on to the crew of one of Grandfather's merchant ships. But they attached one condition—that I not forsake my studies. So poor Colin, who was not much of a sailor, and a crate of books went with me."

"Oh, Ian, what an adventure," Ana exclaimed. "The whole world was your classroom. Where did you go? Were you able to spend any time on shore?"

"England, France, the Mediterranean, the Canaries, and America," he told her as he guided her up the front walkway.

Envious and greedy for the details of his travels, Ana hoped he'd continue telling her about them once Ned left. But her hopes plummeted when he yawned as he reached for the doorknob.

"It's been quite a day," he said, holding the door for

her. "I'm sure you're looking forward to a good night's sleep as much as I am."

The children had been tucked in bed and were fast asleep. Ana had long ago finished her evening chores and bidden Ian good night. She'd washed up, donned her nightgown, let down her hair, and given it at least one hundred strokes, an activity that normally relaxed her. It had been another full day of cooking, cleaning, keeping track of four active children, and receiving visits from two of the women who lived nearby.

She should have been plain old bone-aching exhausted, with just enough strength left to climb into bed and pull the covers up. Instead, she was pacing from one side of the bedroom to the other, just as she'd been doing every night since they'd taken the walk on the beach. And as on every one of those nights, her mind was awhirl with the same questions.

For three days, the right moment had never presented itself to ask Ian why he had come to America and elected to build a life in this country and so far from the ocean. Nor had there been a right time to ask about Fiegel, the identity of "the squire," or anything else related to his family, his life, or his travels before coming here.

But overriding all were the far more haunting questions she had about intimacy. Those were the answers she wanted most, and she waited anxiously for the "right moment" to present itself. But Ian seemed most determined that such a moment not happen again.

For three days and three nights, he'd been unstintingly polite. And just as unstinting at keeping his distance. Unless one counted those quick pecks on the forehead he gave her each night before he sent her off to bed—and she didn't—he hadn't made even a single attempt to make their marriage more than "in name only." A man like Ian didn't abandon a challenge so quickly. Not after the way he'd so bluntly stated that it was his intent to do everything he could to change her mind.

Mulling over his abrupt turnaround, she'd taken several trips across the room and back again before she had an explanation that made any sense at all. She'd badly bungled the timing of her request that night on the beach. Ian had been right. Her sense of duty and responsibility for family *had* impelled her to blurt out that clumsy invitation. Hardly a flattering or romantic overture. No wonder he'd been so angry.

But Ian never stayed angry long, and surely after he'd calmed down and thought about it, he realized he'd misjudged her reasons for asking him to sleep with her. A man of his experience had to know how much she enjoyed his kisses and what effect they had on her. And that if he'd ignored her protest even one second longer, they'd have made love right there on the beach.

She stopped cold. *That devious, arrogant . . . reprobate!* He hadn't given up trying to change her mind at all. He'd just resorted to more subtle methods. He was purposely refraining from kissing or holding her to see just how long it took her to break down and extend that invitation again.

Humph! He was going to have a very long wait. She was not about to beg her husband to exercise his marital rights. She'd lived twenty-eight years without knowing physical intimacy with a man, and she could just live another twenty-eight without it.

Picking up her brush, she started dragging it through her hair again. Decent women didn't even think about matters of the flesh. A decent woman didn't yearn for her husband's mind-boggling kisses so much that she could think of little else every time she looked at the man.

In the mirror, she could see the bed that occupied most

of the room behind her. It was a very wide bed that would easily accommodate two people. She'd spent one night worrying that Ian would claim a place in it, and the next three nights worrying that he wouldn't. And she was likely to spend countless more with only her priggish sense of propriety keeping her company unless she did something to bring about an end to this impasse.

Hadn't Ian told her that if someday she should experience something so mortal as desire, he expected her to come to him for satisfaction? She wasn't totally sure what satisfaction meant, but she did know that she *desired* a lot more than a peck on the forehead from her husband. And if a real kiss led to something more, she'd find out for herself exactly how pleasurable or unpleasurable the marriage bed could be.

She started for the bedroom door, pausing briefly at the dresser to eye the bottle of toilet water her mother had made especially for her. Ian had remarked once about liking her scent; it couldn't hurt her purpose any to use a little now. She dabbed a drop behind each ear. Emboldened by the memory of Ian stringing kisses down her throat and across the upper fullness of her breasts, she opened the top three buttons of her nightgown and trailed a few drops of the light floral mixture in those places as well.

Taking a good look at herself in the mirror, she wasn't at all satisfied with what she saw. She was far too pale, for one thing. She needn't look as frightened as she was. A good pinch on each cheek added some color, color she didn't need when she realized her gown was gaping open, exposing the shadow between her breasts. Flushing, she quickly did the buttons back up. Then, in a moment of surprising boldness, she undid the top one again. She reached for her wrapper, then pulled her hand back. It was a warm night, and it wasn't as though her nightgown were made of some diaphanous silk that revealed more than it concealed. Yards and yards of good, sturdy—and opaque—linen covered her from neck to ankles and shoulders to wrists. It was what it was. Plain and practical, like the woman who wore it. And it was the only kind of nightgown she had.

Straightening her shoulders, she marched purposefully toward the door, and saw the front door quietly closing behind Ian just as she entered the main room.

Chapter Eighteen

"Something wrong?" Ian asked as he followed Sally through the front door.

"No." Ana closed the book she'd been attempting to read for the past hour. To his continued look of puzzlement at seeing her seated at one end of the couch in the living room at this hour, she remarked, "Everything and everyone is just fine. I . . . ah . . . just wasn't sleepy and thought perhaps I'd read for a while."

"Oh," he said with a slight rise of his brows and a short nod. Then he totally ignored her and went straight into the kitchen area. He busied himself doing she knew not what and didn't care. It gave her a few moments to collect herself.

Now that the moment was finally at hand, Ana hadn't the faintest idea what to say or do to bring her goal about. And the way Ian had looked just now wasn't helping her composure one little bit. Glad for the distraction of Sally, she stroked the silky head pressed on her lap.

His hair was decidedly damp and disordered, as if he'd taken a recent dunking and done little but shake his head to rid his hair of the water. Darkened to a deep auburn by the moisture, an errant lock or two fell across his wide forehead, making her yearn to reach up and push them back in place, the way she would if he were Rob or Joseph. But Ian was no little boy.

His full-sleeved white shirt was open halfway down his chest and clung damply in places. It was tucked into a pair of snug-fitting black trousers Overall, he seemed bigger, more male, and even more appealing than usual.

She'd likened him to a pirate the previous Sunday afternoon during their voyage to the island, and tonight she thought the comparison even more pronounced. She almost wished he were a real pirate. A lady wouldn't have to ask a pirate to take her to his bed. A pirate would just scoop up any woman he wanted and carry her off.

Damn him for being such a civilized man.

She just barely managed to catch a nervous giggle. During all the years she'd been his sister-in-law, she'd thought him a barbaric beast. Married to him for not even a week, and she was bemoaning his civility—and losing her own.

The woman she'd once been would have dashed back into her bedroom and probably spent the next hour or two on her knees begging God for forgiveness and guidance for cursing and being so occupied with prurient thoughts—she'd have spent yet another lonely night in that bed with her curiosity keeping her awake. But the woman she was tonight was determined to stay the course.

While her resolve might be steady, her nerves weren't. Her hands were cold and shaking. She occupied them by ruffling her fingers through Sally's warm, thick coat and scratching behind the dog's silky ears. But all the while she indulged Sally's pleas for attention, she was acutely aware of Ian's every movement.

Finally he sat down at the opposite end of the couch and asked, "What really brought you out here?"

At her continued silence, he commented, "If you'd wanted to read yourself to sleep, you'd have picked up a book and scurried back into the safe haven of that bedroom."

"What if I said I just didn't feel like being alone tonight?" she asked, having decided that the direct approach was the only one she had.

"Hmmm . . . then I'd have to ask exactly what you meant by that. Just wanting a little companionship, are you? Or is there something else you desire?"

Sally's short yelp warned Ana that her fingers had tightened in her fur. Uttering a string of apologies, Ana smoothed her hand over the spot she'd just abused. Loyal, forgiving animal that she was, Sally accepted the apology with good grace, then trotted off for her bed near the back door.

Left without the dog's presence as an excuse to focus her attention elsewhere, Ana gathered what little courage she had left and faced her husband. "Something else." Her heart fluttering madly, she took a deep breath. "I'd like you to kiss me. Really kiss me. On the mouth."

His brows nearly disappeared in the lock of hair that had fallen over his forehead. Ana wasn't sure whether it was a good sign that her request had startled him. Recovering his composure, he peered at her intently for a long moment before asking, "Why?"

"Why?" she squeaked. Honesty, she reminded herself. They'd agreed always to be honest with each other. But that didn't make it easy. Averting her face, she revealed in a rush, "Because . . . because I like your kisses very much and . . . and I'd like to experience *satisfaction*."

Out of the corner of her eye, she saw him shift his position and run a quick hand down his face. If he so much as grinned, laughed, or said anything remotely sarcastic, she was going to be across the room and slamming her bedroom door faster than he could blink an eye. Her cheeks burning, she geared for flight and edged forward on the couch.

"Stay, Ana." His softly worded request was followed by another. "Look at me, sweetheart."

Reluctantly, she did, and saw nothing but heartrending tenderness in his eyes. Mesmerized, she hadn't realized he'd captured her hands until he brought them to his lips. The caress of his mouth was no more than a whisper against her knuckles, but it sent a shivery tremor up her arms.

"A few nights ago, I told you that I wasn't made of stone. Be sure you're here for more than kisses," he warned with an unwavering gaze and a low-timbered voice that rustled down her spine and increased the fluttering in her belly. "I've already had one dip in the lake this evening; I don't fancy another."

"Why on earth would you bathe in the lake?"

"Bathing had nothing to do with it, my sweet innocent," he admitted with a light chuckle.

Ana's puzzled frown elicited another very male chuckle. "A long swim in cold water can have a considerably subduing effect on a man's . . . ah . . . ardor. It's made sleeping out here each night with you just on the other side of that wall considerably more comfortable."

Understanding dawned, and Ana's mouth formed an "O." It was heartening to know she hadn't been the only one suffering each night.

Sighing her disappointment, she prepared to go back to her bedroom, alone. "Then tonight wouldn't be a very good night to expect anything more than kisses."

Dropping his hands to cradle her face between his large palms, he said, "Don't underestimate yourself." Ana's pulse quickened and her heart lurched almost painfully in her breast as slowly and steadily Ian's face came closer. "Or me."

The first touch of his mouth on her lips was a mere whisper. Anticipating more, she whimpered when he lifted his lips away. But her disappointment was short-lived as he brushed his lips gently against her eyelids, her nose, and finally her mouth once more.

The return of his lips to hers set her heart hammering against her ribs and intensified the fluttering sensations deep in her belly. This time he did not stop after a gentle brushing of lips but settled his mouth over hers in a consuming possession that elicited such a wave of pleasure she could not squelch a moan.

Ian had wanted to go slowly, initiate her into sexual pleasure carefully and gently. He could only guess at how difficult it had been for her to come to him tonight. The last thing he wanted to do was frighten her in any way. But the way she returned his kiss with such eagerness nearly snapped the thin thread of his control. He'd been too long without a woman, and these last few nights of extreme frustration had built a need more overwhelming than he'd ever experienced.

Fearing he'd take her right here on the couch or the floor, he gathered her up in his arms and started for the bedroom while he still had a shred of sense left. He'd taken only the first of the few steps needed when she buried her face in the crook of his neck and breathed a kiss there. The soft caress was so sweetly given, it nearly brought him to his knees and dangerously threatened his resolve to get her to the bed.

Steeling himself, he made it into the bedroom and managed with the greatest of control not to leap immediately upon her when he laid her down. "I'll be right back," he told her, surprised he was able to talk. "I . . . I'd better blow out the lamps in the other room."

Once he'd escaped to the main room, he took several deep breaths before seeing about extinguishing the lamps scattered about. The task didn't take long, but it was enough to take the edge off his raging arousal.

Go slow, my boy. Go slow, was the mantra he chanted within his head as he picked up the one small lamp he'd left burning and headed back to the bedroom. What happened during the next half hour or more could well determine the character of his marriage for all the years to come.

Am I supposed to lie here and just wait? Ana wondered when Ian left her. Was his concern for the lamps merely an excuse to allow her time? For what? She hadn't any idea except that lying here on top of the bedcovers didn't seem right.

Guessing she had very little time, she sprang off the bed and pulled back the covers. She was about to slip between the sheets when she hesitated. Should she take off her nightgown? No, surely not. Mama hadn't said anything about having to be completely naked to make love. The sound of Ian's boots clicking nearer and nearer made the decision for her. She'd just gotten back into the bed and pulled the sheet up over her when he came through the doorway.

"Sorry for that interruption." He placed a small lamp on the dressing table and turned it down until it cast only a pale glow over the room. "No sense wasting good lamp oil when no one's in the room to need the light."

"Of course," she said, thinking his sudden concern for conserving lamp oil odd. But she was glad for the glow from the lamp when he slid his shirt over his head. Fascinated by her first view of his bare chest, she didn't look away as she had the first time he'd bared himself to the waist in her presence. The glimpse she'd had then of his well-muscled back didn't prepare her at all for the view of his naked chest.

If any man's body could be called beautiful, Ana was sure Ian was that man. His chest was broad, with a haze of curling hair spreading from one hillock of muscle to the other. His torso narrowed, and his belly, as uniformly ridged as a washboard, was bisected by a narrow line of hair that disappeared beneath the waistband of his trousers. At the suggestion of exactly where that line of hair ended, she grew warm all over and felt an embarrassing moisture gather in her most private place.

Seemingly unconscious of her perusal and the effect it was having on her, he sat down on the side of the bed and tugged off his boots. But when he stood and she saw his hands move to the buttons of his trousers, she squeezed her eyes shut. Even her abundant curiosity couldn't be sustained without an ounce or two of boldness. Unfortunately, she'd used the last of her allotment of that commodity when she'd asked Ian to kiss her.

"Ana, open your eyes."

Standing totally naked before her, Ian wanted to give her a chance to look at him, all of him. As desperately as he wanted her, he'd vowed to himself that he would not take her unless he knew for certain that she was as eager for him as he was for her. He'd not survive another martyr.

"I want you, Ana. I want to give you all the pleasure a man can give a woman with his body. And take pleasure from yours as well. But only if you're sure that's what you want."

He watched her eyes skim down his torso and saw them widen the moment she beheld his erection. He waited for a cry of shock or any other sign that she was revolted by the sight of his body and the blatant evidence of his desire for her. And he thought he might die if she rejected him.

He waited in near agony until she opened her arms and invited him with a single word. "Please."

Her whisper was like a caress to his soul.

Ana trembled a bit with fear, but a far more compelling sense of urgency rose from the deepest recesses of her body as Ian moved into her arms. He didn't cover her completely with his body as she'd expected, but lay beside her. Winnowing his fingers through her hair, he asked, "Do you have any idea how many times I've fantasized about seeing all this glorious hair spread across a pillow?"

Not waiting for any kind of answer, he leaned over her and buried his face in her hair. Breathing deeply, he admitted, "These wild and glorious curls and the scent you wear have been keeping me awake at night for weeks. It's been torture to keep from following you around sniffing at your wake."

Ana giggled. She couldn't help it. The image of Ian stalking behind her sniffing at the air was just too ludicrous.

"You laugh at my misery?"

His question was flavored with such obviously feigned affront, she giggled again. "There's only one way to stop this kind of insult," he murmured, and he gathered her into his arms and smothered her giggles with his mouth.

Ana sobered immediately. Sliding her hands up his bare chest, she held his head where it was, needing his mouth on hers as much as she needed her next breath. The hot, deep kisses that followed were a mutual feast of tasting, teasing, and conquering. When he finally released her mouth and she felt the warmth of his breath against her neck and the press of his lips against the tender flesh of her throat, she moaned a plea of need she didn't understand.

But Ian did and moved one hand between them to address the long line of buttons that closed her nightgown. With each button released, he spread the two sides of the gown open, following the deeper and deeper V with his lips. When he'd cleared the last barrier to the bounteous treasure that had haunted his dreams and waking moments for weeks, he rose above her. His breath caught in his throat.

"Beautiful ... so beautiful," he murmured before lowering his head and taking one of her nipples into his mouth. Gently at first, he laved it with his tongue, coaxing it erect. At the same time, he lifted her other breast with his hand and strummed his thumb across its nipple.

Ana writhed beneath the gentle assault of his tongue curling around her nipple. At the first hard tug upon it, a shaft of heat cut through her that made her tremble and moan.

"Ian." She urged him on unwittingly with her husky cry and the rhythmic clenching of her hands on his shoulders.

Shifting his position, he knelt between her thighs. "This is superfluous," he remarked as he lifted her and whisked her nightgown from her. Leaning back on his heels, he gazed at her full nakedness.

Self-conscious of her body and what she thought was an unattractive overabundance in her proportions, she automatically moved her hands to cover herself. Ian caught them and held them away from her. "Don't ever be ashamed of your body, Ana. It's beautiful and perfect in every way."

Laying his palms lightly on her breasts, he told her, "These are the stuff of a man's dreams," then moved forward and pressed his lips to each in turn. Not stopping with her breasts, he praised, kissed, and caressed every curve: her waist, her belly, her hips, her thighs, even her knees and calves.

By the time he'd finished his inventory and covered her with his body, she was writhing beneath him, brushing the very portal of her warm, woman's core against the tip of his manhood, inciting his urgency. Rearing above her, he would have plunged inside her but remembered her innocence at the last second.

Shifting slightly, he fitted his aching erection against the softness of her belly and took several deep, calming breaths. He kissed her, but gently this time, needing to settle himself as well as her. "You are exquisite," he declared in a throaty rasp, then lowered his head to her breasts once more.

Sliding his mouth between her breasts and down to her stomach, he swept his hands down her flanks and along her inner thighs. Ever mindful of her innocence, he stroked her gently but moved ever closer to the dark triangle between her legs. When at last he delved into her, he was gratified to find her wet and ready. Gently, he prepared her as best he could for the invasion that was to come. Only when he was sure her need was as great as his own did he rear above her again.

Slowly, he entered her, sliding carefully into her swollen folds. When he met the fragile barrier that marked her virginity, he nearly shouted with the joy of it. Until that moment, he'd not realized that deep within him, in a place he'd thought buried with Lily, he'd feared another deception.

But this was *Ana*, who came to him unsullied, honest, and as eager for him as he was for her. He could feel it in the way her body undulated and grasped his member as he retreated. And he knew from the way her arms were around him, holding him, welcoming him, that she would always be his, only his.

Battling baser instincts, he tried for enough control not to hurt her any more than was necessary. He entered

her again, stopping just before full possession, and retreated again, wanting to wait for her body to accommodate him. But she lifted her pelvis up from the mattress,
and he was lost. Ablaze with need, he took her mouth in
a voracious kiss as he thrust through the barrier, burying
himself deep within her.

Ana felt a sharp sting of pain and stiffened. Stretched
and filled more than she thought she could bear, she cried
out and tried to shove him away. But then the burning
melted away, and all she felt was an intense yearning that
made her begin to move in the erotic rhythm he was
rapidly escalating to an ever faster pace.

Torrents of heated pleasure like nothing she'd ever
known or even imagined raced through her as again and
again he plunged and retreated. And Ana met his every
thrust, their coupling melding them into one being, a
mutual possession that carried them to an explosive
climax.

Their damp bodies lay intertwined as harsh breathing
slowed toward a normal rhythm. Replete, Ian drifted
languidly down from the summit, humbled by the experience. He had been lost within her, more aroused than
ever before and finding a greater satisfaction than he'd
ever experienced. But still there was more. The first
feeling of complete peace he had known for years, perhaps his entire lifetime.

Carefully, he lifted his head from the lush pillow of her
breasts. Balanced on his forearms, he was almost afraid
to open his eyes. It had been too fast, too rough. Not at
all the extended and gentle taking he'd intended. He'd
given her pleasure, yes, but had it been enough?

Forestalling the moment of truth when he'd see either
a soft languor in her eyes or reproach for having hurt her,
he pressed his lips against her forehead. He'd intended to
stop with just that but couldn't resist trailing his lips

down her face and throat. With an extreme act of will, he resisted the temptation of her breasts, knowing he'd not be able to stop with just kisses if his mouth encountered those silken mounds that had more than fulfilled his expectations.

Reluctantly, he eased away enough to roll to his side and fit her against him. Groping for the sheet, he dragged it over them. In an effort to keep her warm, he curled his body around her, her bottom snuggled against his groin. Not a good idea, he realized with a wince as he felt his manhood stir with renewed life.

"Ana?" He wasn't sure whether he was asking if she was all right or if she would welcome him into her body again.

Still aglow with the aftermath of what had just happened, Ana didn't know how to answer him or what he expected of her. She had enjoyed every caress of Ian's mouth and hands and being filled by his hard maleness. Lying in his arms now, his big strong body curled so protectively around her, she wanted the night never to end.

But years of hearing her father expound upon the sinful weakness of the flesh intruded upon the pleasure she had drawn from his body and what they had done together. And that was all it had been—a base, wicked act of sinful pleasure. Not a word of love had he used before, during, or after.

Suddenly she felt chilled, and a shudder ran down her spine. She'd satisfied her curiosity about the act, but was she really satisfied? *No!* She wanted more from him. She needed him to love her.

He heard the catches in her breath and felt the shudder that had racked her body. "Ana?" Carefully, he turned her onto her back.

Tears.

Tears crept from the corners of her closed eyes. She

couldn't even bear to look at him. This was worse than all the times with Lily when she'd lain beneath him completely unresponsive, making it clear she was merely tolerating his bestial invasion. But this was Ana, not Lily. What could possibly have gone wrong? She'd welcomed and enjoyed his lovemaking. She'd been with him every step of the way. As aroused and eager as he.

"What is it, Ana?"

"Thank you for . . . for satisfying my curiosity. That was . . . was . . ." She wouldn't debase herself further by admitting how pleasurable the experience had been. "I won't trouble you again," she said, and curled herself into a tight, miserable ball.

Chapter Nineteen

"I've been in contact with a young Methodist minister. He's willing to come and conduct services once a month. I've arranged for him to start this Sunday."

"Thank you, that was very kind of you."

Polite. She was so *damned* polite. He couldn't stand it.

All day he'd watched her smile and even laugh with the children. And watched that smiling, animated visage turn bland and her mien turn stiff and uncertain the moment she was forced to endure his company. If only he could figure out what was going on inside that beautiful head of hers that had turned a glorious, incredible experience into something to cry bitterly over.

If only she'd talk to him, tell him what was bothering her. *Hell.* Much more of this silent treatment and looking right through him, and he'd be grateful if she yelled at him, almost happy if she threw something at him. Anything, if she'd only stop being so terribly civil and distant.

The children were asleep and the house was so quiet, he swore he could hear her needle pushing through the socks she was darning. Clearing his throat, he tried again to coax her into conversation. "I thought, if the weather is pleasant Sunday, we could hold the service outside on the land where the church will be."

"Where will the Protestant church be built?"

"Over on Second Street, the same place as the Catholic

church," he said, keeping his face directed toward the open ledger book he'd spread out on the dining table.

He heard a sharp intake of breath and sat perfectly still, almost afraid to breathe, lest any sound or movement keep her locked within that pleasant, polite shell she'd been wearing steadily since this morning.

"We cannot worship in the same building."

She still sounded courteous, but he thought he heard a little edge to her voice. He certainly hoped he hadn't imagined it. "With a population as small as we have here on the island, I see no reason why both faiths can't use the same building."

A rustle of starched petticoats brought his head up. He contained a whoop of joy when he saw her standing with her hands on her hips, her color high, and the light of battle shining brightly in those lovely lavender eyes.

"There's every reason! Their services are entirely different. Why—why the *papi*—" She stopped the word with the press of her fingers against her mouth. "The Catholics," she corrected, starting again, "don't even have their services in English. They burn incense and shake holy water all over the church."

"Bad as all that, is it?"

Ian leaned back in his chair, tamping down the laughter that would surely earn the water pitcher being dumped over his head. "I'm sure we can work something out. Perhaps the Catholics could throw open the windows to air out the incense and mop up the holy water before the Protestants arrive for their service."

"*Before* the Protestant service?" She moved around the table and stood over him, shaking her finger right in his face. "Now you listen to me, Ian Patterson. I'm trying to be tolerant of the Catholics on this island. I've met most of them, and I agree with you that they're very nice people.

And I agree that they have a right to worship any way they want. But I and all the rest of the Protestants do, too.

"And if you're so tightfisted you cannot see your way clear to donating a separate plot of land and materials for a second church, then I suppose we will all just have to make do. But if we're going to have to share the church, I insist that the Protestant service be held first."

Now this was his Ana! Ian wanted to grab her around the waist, pull her onto his lap, and kiss that sweet, animated mouth until they both fainted from lack of air. He didn't dare for fear she'd retreat again. "I suppose that would be all right. I'll talk to Katie O'Houlihan and some of the others. If there's no objection, then we'll set up the schedule your way."

"Hmmph. *I'm* your wife. I should think my preferences would take precedence in this."

"About time you remembered that."

"Remembered what?"

"That you are my wife. Completely. This is not an in-name-only marriage anymore, and I'm not spending tonight or any other night sleeping on that couch ever again."

The color drained from her face, and she started to retreat. But Ian snaked his arm around her waist and pulled her onto his lap. She tried to push away, but he wrapped both his arms around her and held her still.

"Please. Don't put me through that again. I'm ashamed enough as it is."

"Ashamed!" And then realization struck him. He dropped his head to the back of his chair and rocked it back and forth. "I should have known."

"How could you? I didn't know until we—" She hid her face in her hands.

"Ana, Ana, Ana," he repeated ruefully. Prying her

hands away from her face, he crooked his fingers beneath her chin.

"Look at me, Ana. What happened between us was not shameful or wicked or anything else you've gleaned from your father's sermons on the 'sins of the flesh.' It was absolutely beautiful and good. We are a married couple. Our union was blessed by God. We made love. We did not fornicate. There is a difference."

She looked at him through tear-drenched eyes. "But we don't— And I— Oh, what must you think of me! I behaved like a wanton. I wanted *it*. I enjoyed *it*."

"Praise be to God!" he declared.

At her look of surprise, he smiled. Pressing her head against his shoulder, he gathered her in more closely. "I suspect you've been told some nonsense that decent women don't enjoy the marriage act. That only men, loose women, and harlots enjoy sex."

He felt her nod and kissed the top of her head. "Nothing could be further from the truth. You, my darling wife, are a good and decent woman. There's nothing sinful about feeling pleasure. If that were true, then it would be sinful to enjoy another person's smile, enjoy sweets or the sound of a bird singing. All of those things bring pleasure to our senses."

"They're not the same," she said with a sniff. "Those are not sins of the flesh."

She started to get off his lap, but Ian refused to let her go. "God created our bodies, didn't He? And we are made of flesh?"

She nodded.

"And He gave us the gift of sight, hearing, smell, touch, taste. Do you really think He'd have given us such gifts had He not expected us to use them?"

"Well . . . they're for practical things," she maintained

stiffly. "Like gathering and preparing our food or avoiding danger. We feel heat so we can keep ourselves from burning. Feel the cold so we can clothe ourselves. Taste, so we don't eat something that would poison us."

"Foods that are good for us are pleasurable on our tongues, aren't they?"

"Well . . . er . . . yes," she said, uncomfortable with the direction he was turning the discussion.

"And when something brings pleasure to our tongues, we want more," he said, and flicked the tip of his tongue just behind her ear. "And more." He dragged his tongue along her jaw. "And more."

A tremor of pleasure rippled down her spine. Her resultant squirm brushed her breasts against his chest. "Touches warn us of danger but bring pleasure, too. Especially here." He placed a quick kiss to her lips. "And here." He covered her breast with his hand, flicking his thumb back and forth until her nipple sprang to life beneath the layers of dress and chemise that separated flesh from flesh.

She gasped and would have knocked his hand away, but he caught hers and pressed it against the hard length straining against the front of his trousers. "And most certainly here," he rasped.

Involuntarily, Ana's fingers curled over the hard length and she felt it surge against her palm. Startled into realization of what she was doing, she yanked her hand away and managed to scramble off his lap. "Some touches are dangerous, Ian Patterson."

His eyes glittered with mischief as he stood up from the chair. She jumped back from him and squealed, "You stay away from me."

Her cry aroused Sally, who began barking and dancing around them. "It's all right, Sally. Shh . . . shh." She made a grab for her collar, but the agitated animal evaded her.

"Sally. Down," Ian ordered, then sent Ana a triumphant grin when the animal obeyed. "There's lots more about our senses that I'd like to teach you. Perhaps we should take this . . . ah . . . experiment elsewhere. Up the beach a way, there's a perfect spot for experiencing the touch of the lake against your skin—all of your skin."

Ana gasped. "Naked? In the lake?"

He grinned wickedly. "It's a lot easier to swim without clothes. You'd enjoy it, I promise."

Ana gasped. "You're not luring me out to that beach for a swim or anything else your devious mind is thinking up."

"Coward," he quipped, a devilish gleam in his eyes.

He'd taken only the first step toward Ana when Sally insinuated herself between them. She didn't growl or threaten in any way, but Ian sat back down at the table. Sally immediately sat beside him. Her tail wagging, she placed a paw on his thigh as if seeking his approval. He dropped a hand to her silky head and remarked, "Yes, girl. You're a good protector."

Eyeing Ana, he growled, "You needn't look so smug. She wouldn't have attacked me. I just thought it was an opportunity to reinforce her natural instincts, just in case they're ever really needed."

Ana merely raised a superior brow, turned on her heel, and went back to the sitting area. Plopping back in her chair, she picked up her sewing basket and resumed darning socks.

Sally rose, stretched, and without so much as a backward glance at Ian joined Ana. "I'm going to have to get a dog of my own," Ian muttered to himself.

One elbow propped on the table, his chin resting in the heel of his hand, Ian went back to the ledger but quickly discovered it was a waste of time. Ana's chair was angled away from him; all he could see was the back of her head. And the back of her neck. That enticing ivory column with a row of wispy curls lying on it was far more interesting than columns of figures.

What would happen, he wondered, if he strolled over there and planted a kiss on her neck? He'd find out how convincing he'd been about the rightness of giving and taking pleasure. And whether Sally had any loyalty to him whatsoever. He closed the ledger book and blew out the lamps in the kitchen and dining area.

Ana's first warning that Ian was behind her chair was a prickling awareness and then his hands gently curling over her shoulders. Before she could fathom what he was about, she felt his lips nuzzling the back of her neck. Her startled "Oh" quickly turned to a soft, moaning "Mmmm" as a delicious shiver of want ran through her body.

"Like that?" he murmured against her neck, then gently blew against the surface he'd dampened with his tongue. He slid his hands down from her shoulders and covered her breasts. Her darning egg dropped from her hands and rolled to the floor.

"You are a wicked, lusty man, Ian Patterson," she said, but in such a soft, breathless tone, her statement didn't sound at all like a condemnation.

"Not wicked, just lusty," he said, his fingers making short work of the hooks down the front of her dress and the ribbon of her chemise.

When his big, warm hands cupped her bare breasts, she squeezed her eyes shut, gripped the chair arms, and sucked in her breath. "Oh, please . . . I haven't made the curtains yet."

"You weren't planning on making them tonight, were you?" he said as he swirled the tip of his tongue in the shell of her ear.

Sensing her wits scattering further with each brush of his tongue against her ear and her throat, she struggled to hold on to coherent thought before it was too late. "The windows are bare. Lamp . . . someone might pass . . . by and see in."

"Easily solved." Releasing her breasts, he picked up the only lamp still lit in the house, the one that sat on the table next to her chair. "Come, my love," he said as he pulled her from the chair and led her toward the one room that had coverings over the windows.

He set the lamp on the dresser, and as he'd done the night before, turned it down until the room was lit with the same soft glow. No surer what she should do than she'd been last night, Ana stood beside the bed, exactly where he'd left her. Her bodice hung agape. Her breasts freed of her chemise and corset were completely exposed, but she didn't move to cover them.

When he slipped off his shirt and tugged off his boots, she assumed she was to undress herself but couldn't seem to move to do so. He was such a magnificent-looking man was all she could think as steadily more and more of him was revealed. With the eager curiosity and thoroughness she'd once employed in attacking her lessons, she studied every part of him.

He was so tall and lean. His shoulders were so broad, their squareness softened by the heavy muscles wrapped over them. More muscles rose in a long, broad line on each side of his spine. His flanks were lean, and his thighs corded with the same kind of heavy musculature that dominated his torso.

Her new familiarity with his body didn't alter her fascination. *Magnificent. Magnificently male.* She almost said the words aloud.

Turning away or chastising herself for looking upon him was the farthest thing from her mind as she gazed upon his nude body. Her eyes followed the tantalizing line of hair down his rippling belly to the thick thatch where his manhood nestled, and she watched in silent awe as beneath her gaze, his erection stirred and lengthened.

A knowing smile on his lips, Ian reached for her, drawing her fully against him. As if of their own volition, her hands slid up his chest, over his shoulders, and settled into the thick hair at his nape. When his lips sealed over her mouth, she parted her lips instantly, hungry for the taste of him and the touch-and-parry game he'd taught her.

With a groan, Ian pulled back from their kiss. "No guilt this time. Not during and not after," he told her, his eyes warm with tenderness and something else. Doubt? Question?

She shook her head slowly. "No guilt," she repeated.

"Good. Tonight will be even better than last night," he promised as he pushed her dress off her shoulders.

He undressed her slowly, paying homage with his mouth and hands to every part of her as he bared it. By the time he knelt to remove her stockings, she was trembling with the strain of keeping herself upright. She was sure every bone in her body had liquefied.

He stood and began removing the pins in her hair. When he'd finished, he picked her up and placed her on the bed. Following her down, he settled himself between her thighs, his erection nestled against her soft belly.

She was too overcome with need to care whether wanting what they were about to do was wicked or good. Wrapping her arms around his back, she tried to shift her hips beneath him, impatient to draw him into her and end the emptiness.

He swept his hands to her hips and held her still. "Slow down, sweetheart. I want us to savor this."

Her disappointment must have communicated itself to him, for he rose above her and said, "If I'm going to last long enough to bring you the pleasure you deserve, I must beg you to lie still." He bent and kissed the tip of her nose. "But only for a little while longer. I want you wild and frenzied later."

Ignoring her shocked gasp, he began arranging her hair across the pillow. "I love your hair. You're so incredibly beautiful when it's falling all loose and wild around your face and over your shoulders."

A look of pure bliss on his face, he sifted his hands through the long strands. "Promise me you'll stop winding it so tightly each day and covering up all this glory with those silly little caps."

"But it's so stubborn and uncontrollable, without the braid and the cap it'll be flying wild all day long," she argued, only to see him pull an exaggerated frown.

"Not a good idea then," he said with a shrug. "If you went about the island with your hair falling down your back, my workers would be distracted, and there'd be little work done."

She rolled her eyes. "That is a bold-faced lie if I've ever heard one. Helen of Troy I am not."

Lifting a handful of her hair to his face, he breathed in the mingled blend of chamomile, rose, and lavender that always clung to her. "Mmmm, definitely not Helen of Troy. You're Aphrodite, and if you gainsay me on that, I'll know you're merely fishing for compliments."

She closed her mouth against the denial she'd been about to make.

Holding the handful of hair up so it could catch the light, he remarked, "That day we argued in the parlor, it was your hair and the way the curls seemed to want to escape that utterly intrigued me. When you stood by the window, the sun caught in those curls and nearly drove me to distraction."

She snatched her hair from his hand. "If you don't stop going on and on, *I'm* going to be driven to distraction."

Ian laughed, the sound filling the room and wrapping around her. "Would you prefer I tell you what I think of your ears?" he asked, as he swirled his tongue around the edge of first one and then the other until she was squirming.

"Or your throat?" He promptly slid his mouth down the column of her throat, which made her arch her back and moan.

"Or your breasts?" He closed his lips about one already tightly furled nipple and began suckling gently, then harder and harder until Ana was writhing beneath him. He lifted his mouth from her breast, and she clutched at his head to bring him back to that aching place. He chuckled. Resisting her demand, he shifted his attentions to the other breast. When he'd laved it to the same excruciating peak of feeling, he slowly soothed it and then did the same to its twin.

Shifting lower, he explored her navel and then placed a series of hot, openmouthed kisses across her quivering belly. And downward. Into the soft, dark curls. Her shocked cry of his name when he began the most intimate of kisses didn't faze his tender assault.

Her fingers clenched in his hair, her eyes squeezed shut, she surrendered to the spreading heat fueled by each stroke of his tongue across her throbbing flesh. He delved, teased, and tantalized until she was sobbing from the pleasure that was spinning her toward culmination. For one dazzling moment, she hovered in such glory she was sure she would die of it.

Ian slid up her body and caught her cry of exultation in his mouth. He swept his arms around her and rolled to his back, holding her snugly atop him when she shattered, and soothed her with tender brushing strokes down her back until her shudders subsided.

"Oh . . . oh, my," she said on a long, shuddering sigh. "I shall never be able to move again."

Smiling a bit grimly, Ian swept her hair away from her face and kissed her damp forehead. "Oh, my sweet, innocent love, I certainly do hope you can."

Confused, she managed to lift her head in time to see him grimace. "Are you in pain?"

He gave her a wry smile. "Yes, but it's a pain that's easily soothed."

Still disoriented, she muttered, "I'm too heavy for you. I'm sorry. I—I don't know how I got here."

She started to scurry off of him, but he clamped his arms around her. "You're staying right where I put you," he growled, and brought her head down to kiss her to silence. It was when he was kissing her that she felt the rampant hardness pressing against her belly. Fascination emboldened her and guided her to reach between their bodies to touch him.

Ian groaned and caught his breath when she curled her fingers around his shaft. Bringing her with him, he sat up, positioning her so she straddled him. He lifted her, and, murmuring darkly in her ear, he told her what to do.

Shivering with renewed desire, she guided the throbbing head of his sex to the heated flesh between her thighs. Slowly, she lowered herself over and around him, and Ian groaned again. He lifted her and thrust upward as she lowered herself to him again. Learning quickly, she set a slow, languid pace that soon had him gritting his teeth to keep from bucking wildly beneath her.

Fearing he would spend himself long before she was near her pleasure, he reached between them and slid his fingers into her damp curls. Finding the tiny nub, he caressed her. Within seconds, he felt her convulsing around him and let himself go. This time when she started to soar toward the glory of climax, he went with her. With a ragged cry, he gave himself over to her welcoming embrace. Surging deep within her, he let his seed pour into the fertile gate of her womb.

They clung to each other, savoring and sharing that magical instant together. And together they drifted slowly downward.

"That, my darling, was making love."

It wasn't quite the open declaration she wanted to hear, but it was close enough. Smiling, she succumbed to exhaustion and fell asleep in her husband's arms.

Dawn's early light had just begun to sift through the sheets she had hung over the windows when Ana awoke. It took a moment before she realized she was naked and not alone in the bed. Ian lay curled protectively around her. Her head was pillowed on his arm, and one of her breasts was cupped in his palm.

She blushed when she thought of all he had done to her throughout the night. Her blush grew hotter when she remembered all she had done to him. She shifted a little, but he mumbled something unintelligible and began moving his hands over her. His manhood stirred against her buttocks.

He was insatiable.

And so was she. She yearned to turn and fit her body to his, take him inside her and soar to that warm, magical place he'd shown her over and over again throughout the night. Her resistance to that temptation wavered when his fingers plucked lazily at her nipples and they instantly sprang to aching life. She pressed her lips together to keep from moaning.

"No," she whispered and tried to brush his hands away. "Ian, we must get up. The children will be awake soon. Sally's whining at the door. Go let her out."

"Uhmm, Sally, that traitorous bitch," he muttered

sleepily. "Thwarts me every chance she gets." After another growl condemning the dog for what he considered her uncanny knack for ill-timing, which set Ana to giggling, Ian rolled out of bed and padded toward the bedroom door.

"Ian."

He turned back, a hopeful expression on his face. She shook her head and said, "You're naked. One of the children could come down any minute."

He retrieved his trousers from the floor, pulled them on, then leaned over her. Grabbing her shoulders, he lifted her partway off the bed and kissed her soundly. "Good morning, wife," he said, then left her wanting more as he tended to the dog.

She lay in bed savoring that kiss until she heard the sounds of the children moving around in the rooms above. With a groan, she swung her legs off the bed and reached for her robe. A quick wash in cold water from her pitcher cleared some of the cobwebs from a night with little rest.

As she hurried about getting dressed, she noticed twinges and soreness in places that made her blush at the memory of what had caused them. Her hair was a mass of tangles that defied her brush and comb. Deciding she'd deal with it later, she secured it away from her face with a ribbon at her nape.

To assure herself she looked presentable, she took a last glance in the mirror. She barely recognized the woman reflected there. With her hair loosely arranged, she looked almost like a schoolgirl. Her eyes seemed brighter. Her lips were plumper and decidedly rosier than usual. Her cheeks had a warm glow, as did her neck.

She tugged at her collar, but it was no use. The children were bound to remark on the redness of her neck. She could hardly tell them it was from the scrape of their father's beard. And she couldn't very well hide the evidence of their passion with a scarf or kerchief. She'd look a fool and only draw more attention to her neck. She pulled some of her hair forward on each side of her neck. It was all she could do. Perhaps the marks would fade before the day grew too bright.

Ian Patterson, what have you done to me?

"You did what?"

"I invited the reverend to the family dinner at Maison Bercot."

Ian finished doing up the line of hooks at the back of Ana's new dress. Made of mauve sprigged muslin, trimmed with white lace, it had a matching parasol and bonnet. It was a gift from her husband, and she'd been overwhelmed when she saw it. "I thought you might like to wear something special tomorrow," he'd told her when he'd presented her with a large box.

"You look especially beautiful this morning," he murmured against the base of her neck.

Ana squirmed and shied away from him. "Now you stop that, Ian Patterson. I've so been looking forward to attending Sunday services this morning, and I can't very well attend if I have scratches and abrasions on my neck and cheeks. What would people think?"

Grinning mischievously, Ian pulled her back against his chest and wound his arms around her waist. "They'd think you're a lucky woman to have such an attentive husband," he declared, and ran his tongue down the side of her neck. "Don't worry, I've already shaved this morning. My jaw is as smooth as a baby's. You'll be able to 'keep up appearances.' Mmmm, you have such a delicious neck."

"*Ian,*" she protested, but let her head drop back against his shoulder. Two nights of sharing a bed with Ian and she was sure she was absolutely addicted to the press of his lips on her skin. There was very little of it that hadn't felt his mouth. And not a square inch of it didn't begin to tingle with anticipation whenever he so much as looked at her.

He covered her breasts with his palms. "These are delicious, too."

She sucked in her breath. "No," she wailed. "Services are scheduled at eight, and I've still to get the children up and dressed."

Ian dropped his hands to her hips, took a deep breath, and rested his forehead on the top of her head. "That's what I get for agreeing that the Protestant services be held before the Catholic mass."

Ana had to take several deep breaths to quiet her racing pulse. "You are insatiable," she muttered as she put several feet between them.

"Only for you, darlin', and aren't you glad?"

"I refuse to dignify that question with an answer," she told him primly, a blush rising prettily on her cheeks. "You're already cocky enough for three men."

He knew she'd not intended a pun, but he couldn't keep from laughing. She was far too prim and proper even to know the word, let alone to include a vulgarity in her vocabulary. That was one thing about her he didn't ever want to change.

"You're incorrigible," she said, not sure why he was laughing so uproariously over her previous remark, but very sure she'd be better off not knowing. "And you're very adept at changing the topic. Whatever was in your head when you invited the reverend to take his meal at Maison Bercot?"

Sobering, Ian sat down on the edge of the bed and began to pull on his socks and boots. "The man has to eat somewhere, Ana. Or would you have him just hop back on the boat and head back to the mainland the minute he finishes his sermon?"

"Of course not. But to suggest a Methodist minister take his midday meal at a tavern? The Methodists are even more opposed to strong drink than the Presbyterians. The poor man must have been appalled. What were you thinking?"

"It seemed only hospitable. Everyone on the island will be sharing the midday meal today at the Bercots."

"Not everyone, Mr. Patterson!" She jabbed the last pin into her braided coil. "I'm not stepping foot inside that saloon, and neither are the children."

"Yes, you are, and so are the children," he told her, his temper flaring only slightly less than hers. "Henri and Eduard have gone to a great deal of trouble to prepare for this event, and I'll not have you spoil it by not attending."

He stood and stomped his feet into his boots. "Maison Bercot is not a saloon! We've been over this before."

"I'm not going."

"Oh, yes, you are," he maintained. "For a woman who's so worried about what people might think if she should show a rosy face or neck in public, you'd be better served worrying about what people *will* think if you don't show up at this community dinner."

"You . . . you can tell them I've a terrible headache and send my regrets."

He raised a brow. "Lie for you? And on the sabbath? Valeriana Grace, I am shocked."

Tight-lipped, she stood tapping her foot and looking at the floor, the ceiling . . . anywhere but at her husband. "They won't be serving any strong drink, will they?"

"I don't believe anything stronger than lemonade or tea is on the day's menu."

"You're sure?"

"Henri is so concerned about pleasing everyone, you

in particular, he stopped me yesterday and insisted I go over the menu to ensure that all was acceptable."

Surprised and somewhat mollified, she asked, "And did you?"

"I did not." At her gasp, he explained, "I told him I wouldn't presume to do any such thing as he is the expert with food and I was fully confident that anything he and Eduard prepared would be not just acceptable, it would be superb. However, I did request that nothing stronger than lemonade be served, as there were several who are staunch temperance types. Satisfied?"

She bobbed her head. "Yes, thank you."

"Good. Now put an apron over that pretty dress and go start breakfast. I'll wake up the children."

"Valeriana Patterson, Reverend Mitchell," Ana said as she offered her hand to the young minister. "That was a fine sermon this morning. I do hope you will consider coming to our island on a regular basis."

"Mrs. Patterson, it would be my pleasure to include the island's church in my circuit," the tall young man said as he clasped her hand in both of his. "I must obtain approval from my bishop, of course, but I do not foresee any difficulty. The Methodist church is always happy to welcome a new congregation into the fold. It is surely God's plan that I had the third Sunday of every month free and was thus able to answer this congregation's call for a minister."

"Then we can expect you next month?" Ana asked.

"As long as the weather permits the crossing, I shall be here. Or perhaps I should say 'we,' for Father Quinn will be here, too. We traveled over from Sandusky together this morning.

"Over the course of the past year, Father Quinn and I have come to know each other quite well. He's a young priest who, like me, travels to small congregations scattered about northern Ohio. Often our schedules coincide and we travel together. Far more enjoyable to have a traveling companion, and I confess he's saved me many a time from wandering in the wrong direction. Thomas has a far better sense of direction and knowledge of the territory than I do."

Mitchell's attention was drawn by someone beyond her. "There's Thomas now. Let me introduce him to you and your family."

"Buck up, my girl. I'm sure Quinn is not the devil incarnate," Ian whispered in her ear.

"I was thinking no such thing," she whispered back.

Ian's response was a low chuckle that she prayed no one but she could hear. "Trust me, Ana. I've met a few priests in my day, and they're as human as you and I."

"Keep your voice down. He'll hear you."

"Oh, yes, must keep up appearances, mustn't we?"

Turning to greet the priest, Ana briskly swung her folded parasol behind her. It "accidentally" connected with a sharp thwack to Ian's shin. The smile she turned on the young priest was especially bright when she heard her husband's muffled "Ouch."

Hours later, she was still "keeping up appearances" as she presided over a table in the dining room at Maison Bercot. But she sincerely feared her expression was steadily becoming more grimace than smile.

It was only half-past one in the afternoon, and she was utterly exhausted. She simply had to start getting more sleep.

Chapter Twenty

"Ian, I've been thinking about the church."

Ian looked up from the pile of papers he'd spread out on the dining table. "Please tell me you're not thinking of changing the order of the services again. I seriously doubt it makes any difference to God which congregation's prayers reach Him first."

Ana laughed. Six weeks as Ian Patterson's wife had wrought many changes in her. Being able to laugh at herself was one of them. "No, nothing like that. I think having the Catholic service first is the better way. Father Quinn always keeps his service to only an hour, sometimes less. And . . . well . . . Reverend Mitchell does tend to be rather long-winded. It isn't fair for the Catholics to have to stand around outside waiting."

Ian smiled to himself. Sometimes the changes in her were truly astounding. Concern for the Catholics, never missing the family dinners at Maison Bercot—not only attending but enjoying them so much. It had been her idea that they become bimonthly instead of just once a month on "church Sunday." Next thing he knew, she might actually speak to the Bercots more than twice a month. She'd certainly made friends with just about everyone else.

289

"If it isn't the order of the services, what is it about the church you want changed? The name?" he asked almost absently, his thoughts more focused on how very pretty she looked this afternoon. Her face seemed a little fuller and her cheeks a bit rosier. And she smiled. A lot. And at him. That is, when she wasn't having a weeping attack, which she seemed to be doing quite a lot of lately as well.

"No, Ian. Second Street Church is just fine. It's the building itself. Not the building, per se, but its use."

"What else would you use it for?"

Ana picked up a pair of Rob's trousers from her mending basket and shook her head at the rent in the knee. Rooting through the basket, she found a scrap of fabric that would suit as backing for the mended spot. "Katie O'Houlihan, Joanne Knez, and I think it could be used for a school."

"A separate school building is already in the planning."

"I know, but the church is already finished enough to be usable, and we don't want a construction crew taken away from the house building. The first priority needs to be houses for the families waiting for them."

"We could hire another crew to build a school," he told her.

"But it isn't necessary. There's no reason whatsoever why the church couldn't be used as a school during the week. It's the right size, and all we'd have to do is add desks between the rows of benches we use for pews. Ouch."

She sucked on the needle prick in the tip of her finger for a moment. "And replace the altar table with a desk, and add some shelves along the sides for books, of course. Oh, my, that is a lot of things to do and purchase, but it would be far cheaper than building a separate school, especially since there aren't all that many students yet."

"It's a fine idea, Ana, and my bank account thanks you for your thriftiness. Have you and your ladies hired a schoolmaster, too?"

"Ah . . . no . . . We won't need to hire one; we have one right here on the island who's very well educated and quite qualified, I think."

The Lord be praised! She's finally recognizing what assets to this community the Bercots are. "And just who is this paragon of knowledge and ability?" he asked.

"Me."

"You?"

"You needn't look as if I've just sprouted a second head." The trousers could wait till another time. Setting them aside, she folded her hands in her lap and straightened her spine. "I'll have you know, Ian Patterson, that Papa tutored me and said he'd given me the equivalent of a college education. From Princeton, no less. I don't have a diploma from an institution, but I don't need one. All that's required is a passing grade on the state teachers' examination. I'll apply to sit for the examination when next it's given."

"And when is that and where?"

"It's being given in Cleveland the third Monday of this month. I should be able to sail over to the mainland early in the morning, take the exam, and be back home by nightfall."

"I see you've already researched this quite thoroughly." Recognizing the fire of determination in her eyes and the set of her chin, he tempered his voice carefully. "And who is to oversee our children while you're at the school teaching everyone else's all day?"

"Well, Rob and Maara will be in school with me, of course. Since their house is so close to the school, I mean the church, Katie O'Houlihan said she'd be happy to look after Jessica and Joseph during school hours."

Ian raised his brows. "Don't you think Katie O'Houlihan has enough children to watch with her own brood and a new one on the way?"

"Oh, you know Katie. She volunteered and says two more won't make much of a difference. Plus, it's only temporary. As soon as the big house is finished, Gerta and the Marys will be with us, and they can keep an eye on the little ones during the day."

Ian shook his head. "No."

"No?" she repeated. "Just like that? No?"

Sensing the coming storm, Ian began straightening his papers into a pile and looking for something to anchor them. "Not so long ago, you thought the children should only be in the care of a member of the family. Not servants."

"That situation was not the same." She rose from her chair and strode toward the bedroom door. "They'd just lost their mother." She turned on her heel and walked back to her chair. "And there was no one to read to them of an evening, tuck them in at night, get them up in the morning, and—" She turned and paced toward the bedroom door again.

Ian groaned inwardly and set one of her heavy irons on top of his papers. He was really in for it. He counted the seconds before she pulled a handkerchief from her sleeve or apron pocket and began shredding it.

Ana was making the turn at the bedroom when the scrap of lace-edged lawn came out of her pocket. Ian wisely hid his grin.

"I'll still be able to do those things. I'll only be gone during the day."

"The answer is still no." Before she could retort, he added, "It's just too much for you. You have the house to care for, the cooking, the laundering; you spend every evening mending, darning, or ironing. That's probably why you cry so easily these days. You're exhausted, sweetheart.

"You won't let me send for at least one of the Marys yet—though you clearly need help—and you want to take on another job?"

"I can do it," she maintained.

Ian saw the first glimmer of tears and wanted to scoop her into his arms, promise her anything, and coax her to smile. But he kept himself where he was. He felt guilty enough that she had so much to do. He couldn't let her take on more responsibility. He decided on a different tack.

"I know how much you like to read. When is the last time you read a book other than to the children?"

She paused at the fireplace and rearranged the items on the mantel. Once she had them in a neat, evenly spaced row, she said, "I read sometimes on Sundays. Once we move into the big house and Gerta and the Marys are here, I'll have more time."

"Just how much extra time did you have in Cleveland?"

Shrugging, she pushed away from the mantel and resumed her pacing. "I can do it, Ian. I—I'll just get up an hour earlier each morning and go to bed an hour later."

"No." Unable to resist any longer, Ian caught her around the waist on her next pass. "It's too much for you. I'll not have you working yourself to the bone each day when it's absolutely unnecessary." He kissed her on the forehead, then the nose, and murmured, "Speaking of bed," as he aimed for her mouth.

"It's the middle of the afternoon, Ian." She pushed out of his arms. "The children are right outside in the yard playing."

Ian captured her again. "No, they're not," he told her as he nuzzled her ear. "Ned drove a large wagon up just as I came home. Said he thought the team could use some exercise. He loaded up the children and Sally, and the last I saw of them, they were headed toward the Flahertys'. By now, I imagine Ned's got all the children on the island in that wagon. You know what a Pied Piper he is. I don't expect them back for an hour or so."

The color drained from her face, and her eyes widened with horror. "Oh, Ian, Mr. Ferguson won't take them anywhere near that . . . that *place* where we . . . we had the *incident*, will he?"

"No, dear. We killed two hogs after the incident and haven't seen a sign of any more. We think that was the lot of them."

She shuddered and curled her palms around her forearms. "But you only *think* you got them all."

Ian folded his arms around her. "Now, now. You know the children are as safe with Ned as they would be with us. I'm as sure as I can possibly be that there are no more wild hogs left on the island. Besides, a carriage full of children will be making so much noise, if there were any hogs left, they'd run the other way. They're not very sociable creatures, you know."

Keeping her head down, she toyed with the buttons on the front of his shirt. "I suppose they'll be all right. But I'm still not going in that bedroom with you this afternoon."

He kissed the crook of her neck and started making lazy circles with the tip of his tongue against her throat. She squirmed but stayed within his arms. "Well, at least . . . not . . . until we get the . . . matter of the school's teacher settled," she managed, having trouble holding on to the thought as he continued the tender assault on her throat.

"Then let's not waste any more time and settle it right now," he said as he started edging her toward the bedroom. "There are two imminently qualified schoolmasters already on this island, and another one about to arrive. Henri and Eduard Bercot taught at the university, and Jaie has just graduated. He's already passed his certification exams and wants to teach—"

"The Bercots!" She wrenched away from him. "I'll not have saloon keepers teaching young children," she declared, putting several feet between them. "The very idea." Her pacing resumed. "Lord only knows what kind of influence they'd be on impressionable young minds. Probably teach them how to build a still or make wine."

"They'd do no such thing, and you well know it. Don't be ridiculous."

"Ridiculous, am I?"

"No, sweetheart, *you're* not ridiculous," he said, having a difficult time holding on to his temper. "But accusing the Bercots of teaching the children to make whiskey or wine is. I would have thought by now that even you would recognize what educated gentlemen they are."

"They still peddle spirits."

"Technically, as part owner of the tavern, so do I. Shall I keep my distance from 'impressionable young minds' as well?"

"Don't make light of this, Ian."

"I assure you, I'm not. I merely pointed out that by your standards, I'm as unsuitable to be in close association with children as the Bercots."

"Now *you're* being ridiculous. No children could have a better father than you."

"Thank you, my dear, I do my best. Just as I know Henri, Eduard, or Jaie—if he'll agree to make his home here—will do their best for the island children."

She set her mouth in a tight line, sent him a withering glare, and stalked toward the kitchen. Ian sighed and ran a hand through his hair. "This matter is settled."

Ana stared sightlessly out the back window for a long

time, willing the tears stinging her eyes not to spill over her lids. She'd never taught all day in a classroom, only two hours a day during a handful of terms at Mrs. Parker's Seminary. She'd been so busy with the children, she hadn't thought she'd missed teaching, but when she, Katie, and Joanne had started discussing the school, she'd grown steadily more excited at the prospect of being its mistress. So excited, she'd dashed off a letter to Mrs. Parker asking about certification and had sent it to the mainland that very afternoon.

It wasn't that she didn't love what she was already doing. Being Ian's wife and mothering his children was the fulfillment of a dream she hadn't even realized she'd had until it was a reality. But the prospect of teaching was so very appealing. It wouldn't be just teaching Bible history and the geography of the Holy Land, as she'd done at Mrs. Parker's. The material covered in those lessons had been determined by Papa.

The island school would give her a chance to teach history, mathematics, science, and reading. The texts and other materials would be chosen by her, the lessons planned by her. Teaching here on the island was the first chance she'd ever had to do something by her own choice. She just couldn't let Ian or anyone else take that opportunity away from her.

Having lost the battle with her tears, she dabbed at them with her handkerchief, growing increasingly annoyed by each tear that dared spill down her cheek. What was the matter with her? For the past week or two she'd felt almost continually on the brink of tears, even though she'd never been happier in her life. Ian's stubborn refusal over the issue of her teaching was a disappointment, but it made her angry, not heartbroken. If she was going to win this battle, she needed to be firm. Tears wouldn't help her case.

Drying her eyes, she stiffened her spine once more and marched back to the dining table. "The matter of the school's teacher is not settled!" For emphasis, she smacked her hand down on the table. "I've given in on a lot of things this summer, Ian Patterson. But this is not going to be one of them. I will teach at the island school."

"Oh, leave off that course, Ana," Ian said with obvious impatience. "None of the Bercots would taint the children."

"Their suitability or lack of it is not the issue. I want to be the schoolmistress," she declared firmly.

"For once and for all, Ana, you will not. I'd already decided this anyway. One of the Bercots will be schoolmaster."

"*You* decided? Has no one else any say in this?"

"None whatsoever," he baldly admitted. "But I don't think anyone's going to complain about my choice."

"How do you know? Have you taken a vote or even a survey?" She didn't give him a chance to answer but recklessly declared, "Of course you haven't. *King Ian* makes all the decisions for Parras Island. After all, it is your island, and you decide who lives here and what each person's job is."

"Ana," he warned. "I think it would be best if we ceased this conversation right now before one or both of us says something we'll regret."

"Best for you, you mean," she said contentiously. "If we stop now, you'll just find a way to avoid the topic ever coming up again. That's how you handle everything you don't want to talk about."

"That's not true," he said, but Ana thought she saw a faint redness on his cheeks, and his gaze didn't quite meet hers.

"Shall I list the topics you so carefully avoid? Your brother, for example. It wasn't until recently I even knew you had a brother. You mentioned his name, quickly changed the subject, and I've been wondering ever since why you don't want to talk about him."

"If you want to know about him so badly, why haven't you ever asked?"

"It really wasn't my place to ask before we were married."

"And now? Have you the courage to ask today?"

"Will you give me the answers?" she countered.

"Ask away, my dear," he told her with forced airiness.

"All right, I'll take advantage of your sudden expansiveness. God only knows when such a moment might occur again, but I want your word that the issue of the school and who will be teaching in it has not been abandoned."

"You have my word. If you want to discuss it further, then we shall."

She raised a skeptical brow but proceeded. "Randall. Older? Younger? Where is he now, and what does he do?"

"Younger by two years. He was at university the last I had any communication from him. He always loved the land, and I assume he's at Fiegel now, champing at the bit waiting until he inherits the place, if he hasn't already."

Save for an air of annoyed impatience, the divulgence was supplied so unemotionally she thought Ian might as well have been summarizing a newspaper article covering a day's proceedings of the state legislature.

"If Randall is the second son, why would he inherit Fiegel?"

"Randall is the squire's first and only true son," he supplied. "My sire, Lieutenant Ian Fraser, third son of the honorable Robert Fraser and his wife, Maara, failed to marry my mother before he sailed off to Malta and promptly got himself killed. Whereupon my mother immediately accepted Squire Patterson's long-standing suit for her lovely hand on the condition that he give her child a name. Delighted to finally land the belle of the county, he agreed, but demanded a pound of flesh—a son of his blood."

Throughout this dissertation, Ian had worn a mask of indifference and continued in the same emotionless tone, but she'd come to know him too well these past weeks. Talking about the circumstances of his birth had re-opened a wound, one so deep it was hurtful for her even to witness it. "Ian, I—"

"As long as my mother was alive, Patterson lived up to their agreement and treated me no differently than he treated Randall. But my mother was barely cold when he told me the truth of my ancestry and that only a 'true Patterson' would inherit Fiegel," he continued, a touch of bitterness in his tone.

"I'll give the man credit; he didn't completely wash his hands of me and toss me out. He sent me to a good school, but when I kept running away from it, he decided it was high time my sire's family take responsibility for me."

"They didn't know about you until then?"

He shrugged, and his expression softened. "No, but evidently it took only one look at me for them to see the truth of the squire's claim. They spent the next ten years making up for the eight they'd lost with me.

"They died within a few months of each other, and I no longer had a reason to return to Belfast between voy-ages. Along with what would have been my father's por-tion, they left me wonderful memories I'll carry with me forever."

"No wonder you loved them so much you named your children for them," she said, tears streaking down her cheeks in earnest now. Not for herself, but for the lost little boy Ian had been.

"Two of my children," he corrected. "I have *four* children, and they *all* share equally in whatever I have now and whatever remains after I'm gone."

In the blink of an eye, his mood shifted, and he grinned mischievously. "Four now." He waggled his brows and started toward her. "Maybe five by this time next year."

"No." Holding her hands out in front of her to ward him off, she backed up. "You gave your word we'd settle the issue of the school."

"What else is there to discuss? The church will do double duty as the school. Ned's a good carpenter. As is Tom Knez. Between the two of them, they can get shelves, desks, and whatever else is needed built in plenty of time for a fall term to begin. I don't know how long it'll take to get the books and other materials, but I'm sure either Henri or Eduard will have some ideas on the sources and—"

"No, no, no!" she shouted, her disappointment and anger returning full force. "Neither of the Bercots nor anyone else is going to choose the materials. I will."

"All right, if you feel that strongly about it, you can choose the books and things," he said, clearly placating her with that allowance.

"Good, thank you. I'll order them when I'm in Cleveland taking the certification examination."

"You may take that test and you will no doubt pass it, but you are not going to teach—"

"Yes, I am. I'm not bending on this issue, Ian. It's too important to me. I've thought this through very carefully and made my decision. I will teach or . . . or—" The tears threatened again, and control snapped. "—I'll leave you. And . . . and take the children with me."

Her threat hung in a frigid silence. It had just popped out with no direction from her. She was about to take it back when Ian exploded. "You're not taking *my* children anywhere! They're staying right here, and they're going to go to the island school and be taught by Jaie Bercot. And you're not going anywhere, either. We made a bargain, and your place is here in this house, taking care of my children during the day and me every night."

Aghast that he would say such a thing, Ana's anger soared higher. "Is that all I am to you? A nanny and a . . . a whore?"

"You're not a whore, you're my wife. I wouldn't have to work so hard to get a whore into my bed."

"You . . . you insufferable—"

"Bastard? Is that the word you're searching for, my dear? I believe I just explained to you that that's exactly what I am."

Ana opened her mouth, shut it, then opened it again. "I'll not stand here and be insulted like this!"

"You don't have to stand," Ian roared back.

"No, I don't, and I won't!" She spun on her heel and walked straight out the front door.

"Stubborn, bigoted woman!"

It was a good hour before Ian had cooled down enough to go looking for his wife and beg her forgiveness. He wasn't about to back down on the teaching issue, but he had a lot of retracting to do for the insulting way he'd described their marriage. Unfortunately, by the time he'd checked all the houses to which he thought she might have gone for refuge, the boat with Ana on it was halfway to Cleveland.

He rejected going after her immediately, deciding a short separation might be a good idea. Besides, she wouldn't be gone very long. She wouldn't be able to stay away from the children. Or him . . . he hoped.

Chapter Twenty-one

Rose MacPherson picked up Lily's jewelry box, sighed, and set it carefully in a small trunk. "What are you going to do about this, Ana?"

"I'll have it shipped to the island, I suppose. Maara and Jessica should . . . should . . ." She wrapped her arms around her middle and turned to the window to hide her tears.

Rose packed a few more things from Lily's dressing table into the trunk, then with a sigh sat down on the corner of the bed. It was painful to be in this room. Months ago she'd buried the memories of Lily's suffering, but being here reopened the wounds left by that night.

Sighing again, she reminded herself that there was nothing she could do for that daughter save remember the good times and the joys during Lily's brief life. It was the living who were her first concern. The pain emanating from Ana made Rose want to weep right along with her. Ana stubbornly refused to talk about what had sent her fleeing her husband with only the clothes on her back. It was so unlike Ana to behave so impulsively. And knowing Ian as she did, she couldn't imagine what he could possibly have done that would upset Ana to such an extent.

"Ana, dear, you've been wandering about this house

for more than a week; it's time you decided what you're going to do. Soon, everything will be packed up here, the house closed, and even Gerta and the Marys will be on their way to Parras Island. What will *you* do then?"

Ana swallowed the painful lump in her throat that had been her constant companion ever since the boat had pulled away from the island's dock. Sniffing, she wiped her nose and patted at the tears in the corners of her eyes. But she didn't turn away from the window. It overlooked the front driveway, and she'd not been far from a view of it since her arrival.

"Ana?" her mother prompted.

The driveway was as empty today as it had been yesterday and the day before and all the days since she'd come back. He wasn't coming for her. "I shall await the results of the teaching examination and find a post somewhere. If not at a school for young children, perhaps there's a position at Oberlin College that I might fill."

"A teaching position? I don't think that would be wise, dear."

Ana stiffened. "Why, Mama? Don't you think I'm qualified to teach, either?" she asked bitterly.

"Any school, or even Oberlin College, would be fortunate to have you, but you wouldn't be happy there," Rose calmly replied. "I just don't believe it's the life for you, darling."

She turned her tear-streaked face to Rose. "And what kind of life is that, Mama? If anyone was prepared to be a minister's wife, it certainly was me. And that is the primary purpose of the curriculum for the women students at Oberlin, isn't it?"

"Yes, dear, but I really don't think you should—"

"I'm not moving into the parsonage. I'll not live out the rest of my days as the spinster daughter, helping her father with his sermons, the old maid aunt for all my sisters' children."

"You're not the spinster daughter, Ana. You're a married woman with a fine husband who needs you."

"No, he doesn't. If he did, he would have come after me. I'm sure by now he's found someone else to take over all my . . . so-called duties. Ian only offered for me in a moment of misguided gallantry. Then he was just too honorable to go back on his word. Or that's how it seemed at the time, but he's not honorable. He's not honorable at all. He's an insufferable bas— Oh, it doesn't matter what he is or what I am. We never got along; you know that."

"Yes, I recall that at times you and Ian had trouble being civil. I always wondered at that. Why do you suppose that was?"

"He thinks I'm bigoted, opinionated, and overly pious. And intolerant," she added with extra vehemence. "He can't abide any of those things. And I'm all of them. And I can't change. I tried but I . . . I failed. I'm too prideful. And he . . . he is, too, or he would have come for me by now."

Rose hid her smile. Now they were getting somewhere. Anger had added some starch to her daughter's backbone, dried her tears, and put some color back in her cheeks.

"There's no more ill-suited pair on God's earth than Ian Patterson and me." Ana began to pace. "We married only because of the children."

"*Only* the children?" Unless she was very mistaken— which Rose very much doubted—Ana was pregnant. She wasn't far enough along to notice the signs herself, but the more subtle ones were already there. That is, if Ana's pregnancies patterned at all after her own. The fullness in her face that softened her features so becomingly, the emotions right on the edge. But most telling of all, at this early stage for the women in her family, was a unique propensity for taking orderliness to the extreme. Rose hid another smile as she watched Ana push around the boxes they'd already filled until they were aligned in a perfectly straight row.

With an exaggerated sigh, Rose commented, "There are worse things to base a marriage upon."

"Yes, I suppose there are," Ana said, eyeing the boxes and giving one of them a little nudge until it was out of alignment by not so much as a half an inch.

"But there needs to be more, and we didn't have anything else." She refused to think of what more there had been between them. Lusting for each other's body wasn't enough, either. "Our marriage was doomed. Doomed from the beginning."

"And why was that, dear?"

"Isn't it obvious?"

"No, dear. I think you'll have to explain it to me."

Ana paced across the room and back again, pausing at one point or another to rearrange one of Lily's many collections of china figurines or a stack of hatboxes. Finally, she stopped and said, "I could take care of his children. I could run his house. I could even warm—"

She caught herself. That was something far too intimate to discuss with her mother. "I'm not the kind of woman who's content to just be pampered and taken care of. I'm not easy to live with, you know. I have opinions, and I'm not afraid to state them or take action on them, even if it does discompose my husband. I'm not at all like Lily."

"No, you're not. Thank goodness! I could not have borne the guilt for putting the dear boy through that sort of injustice again."

Seeing the torment lining her mother's face, Ana rushed to her and put her arm around her shoulder. "Oh, Mama, you could not have known that she would be unfaithful."

"Then he's told you about her. I'm glad. I was afraid he'd keep it all inside and let you go on thinking Lily was an angel." She patted the place beside her on the bed. Once Ana was settled, Rose took her hand and patted it. "Such very capable hands you have, Ana. Just like you. So capable of anything you set your mind to."

Though her eyes glistened with unshed tears, Rose smiled gently. "Lily was beautiful but had so few capabilities. Papa saw in Ian someone who could take care of her, give her all the things she craved." She shrugged. "And help him build his church, too. It was shameful the way he threw Lily at Ian. I should have stopped it, but I did not. I shall regret that to my grave."

"Oh, Mama, don't. Don't blame yourself like this," Ana said, though she had blamed her mother for this and more not many weeks ago. "Ian understands and doesn't blame you or Papa. And the rest?" She shook her head. "You couldn't have known."

"Oh, but I did. God forgive me, I did. And your father did, too."

Shocked by her mother's admission, Ana was at a loss to think of anything to say.

The tears spilled from the corners of her mother's eyes now. "Oh, my, I thought I had cried all my tears over Lily," she said as she wiped them away. "There is no easy way to tell you this, Ana. I regret that I must be so blunt." She took a shaky breath. "Ian was not the first man to . . . to have your sister. It is a miracle that she was not carrying another man's child when we left Connecticut."

Ana sucked in her breath. "No, that cannot be true. Not Lily. She was good and fine and—"

"Not very wise," Rose supplied. Squeezing her eyes shut for a moment, she took a deep breath and let it out in a long sigh. "Lily was not weak-minded like that poor soul Toby, back in Brookfield. I'm sure you remember him, dear."

Rose waited until Ana nodded in confirmation. "But she was not nearly as capable as you or Laurel or Primmy. Your father and I made allowances for her, thinking her beauty and sweet, gentle personality were blessings that made up for what she lacked. She was able to function quite well in most circumstances, but as she grew to womanhood, the traits we had thought were blessings proved to be a bane.

"As soon as she developed, the young men, and some not so young, were attracted to her and . . . well, she was very easily manipulated. When the opportunity to found a church here in Cleveland arose, your father and I saw it as a godsend. We could take Lily away from Brookfield before the tongues started wagging.

"Oh, my, Ana, your father and I did a lot of praying on that trip. That it was the right thing to do and that we would be better able to protect her. Ian seemed the very answer to our prayers. And he has been. No man could love those children more. All of them," Rose said, and Ana understood the reason why more than her mother did. She knew her mother would think none the less of Ian for the circumstances of his birth, but it had to be Ian's secret to tell.

"That man has gone to such lengths to protect Lily's reputation, Ana. For the children, of course, but for all of us. You, me, your sisters, and your father."

"And yet Papa has condemned him so pointedly from the pulpit all these years. If Papa's always known about Lily, why does he act as if Ian's the devil incarnate?"

Rose gave another long sigh. "I don't fully understand

it myself, but I suspect it has something to do with disappointment that Ian, too, hadn't really been able to protect Lily any better than he did. And perhaps, unable to bear his own guilt, he finds every possible way to throw guilt upon Ian."

"That's insane."

"Yes, at times I suppose he is. Your father has not been the man he once was for a long, long time," she said wistfully. "Not since— Not since we felt it best to leave Brookfield. He's a good man, but he does not deal with deep disappointments well. And Lily was a deep disappointment."

"You carry far too many burdens." Ana clasped her mother's hand and stroked it. "I don't know how you do it."

"We do what we must, darling. I have my gardening. A good, long session down on my knees with my hands in God's life-giving soil does lift my soul. And love gives us strength, dear. The love we receive and the love we give. I am blessed to have your father, you and your sisters, and four wonderful grandchildren to love and be loved by in return. And I have a son-in-law whom I love no less than if he were a son of my body. And I think he has fairly high regard for me, too," she added with a twinkling smile.

Picking up on her mother's lighter note, Ana allowed herself a small chuckle. "I believe Ian thinks you're just about the most perfect woman there is."

"I'm hardly that," Rose said with a self-deprecating laugh.

She cradled Ana's chin in her palm, forcing her daughter to look at her. "No matter what happened between the two of you, I believe it can be mended. Ian is a good, honorable man with so much love in his heart. The kind of man you deserve, Ana."

"Oh, Mama." Ana burst into tears, deep, heavy sobs that wrenched her mother's heart. "I *don't* deserve him."

"Yes, you do, Valeriana Grace. You are strong and good and honorable. You have a good heart, one as full of love to give as Ian's. I know you love those children as much as if they were your very own. Can't you love him, too? Love him for all that is good in him and even those faults he has? Be a wife to him in every way?"

"I—I—think I already do love him," she wailed. "But . . . he . . . he doesn't love me. He said such terrible things to me. And . . . and I said awful things to him."

Rose wrapped her arms around her daughter. "Words said in anger are usually the most foolish of all. Did you mean everything you said to him?"

"I . . . I thought I did when I said them."

"Do you now?"

Ana took a deep, shuddering breath. "No, but Ian doesn't know that. I'm sure he's glad I left him. He . . . never wanted another wife . . . certainly not the one he got stuck with."

Rose rocked her and smiled against the top of her head. "I don't believe for one minute that he allowed himself to be stuck with you. He's made of much stronger stuff than that. No matter how your father threatened you that day, Ian wouldn't have married you if he hadn't felt something very strong for you. He probably didn't recognize at the time that it was love, but I suspect he knows it now that you're gone."

"Then why hasn't he come after me?"

"Pride. Hurt. The same reasons you haven't gone back to him."

"Even if I should go back, things wouldn't be right between us," Ana stubbornly maintained. "He'll never relent about letting me teach."

"Is teaching so important to you that you'd leave a man and four children whom you love more than your own life? And raise another one all by yourself?"

Staring at herself in the mirror, Ana spread her hand across her stomach. A child. Hers and Ian's child. She'd had three days to get used to the idea, and she still couldn't believe that it was true. Such a silly thing, arranging items in perfectly straight lines. Whoever heard of that being a symptom of pregnancy? According to Mama, it was as sure a sign for the women in her family as missing one's monthlies—something she now recalled she hadn't had since shortly before her marriage to Ian.

Ian would welcome and love this child, of that she was certain. But would he welcome its mother and ever learn to love her? There was only one way to find out.

Lifting her hand from her still-flat stomach, she smoothed it nervously down the bodice of the fashionable amethyst traveling ensemble her mother had talked her into purchasing in Miss Van Valkenburgh's shop. "Perfect, she'll take it," her mother had announced when Ana had relented and tried it on. "Nancy, have you anything else that would suit my daughter's coloring and figure?" And then she'd embarrassed her thoroughly by insisting that the garments all have wide enough seams to be let out in the weeks ahead and exactly why that would be necessary.

What had followed was a spending spree the likes of which Ana had never seen her mother lead. Ana had stood wide-eyed with mouth agape as her mother selected a half dozen frocks, matching slippers, several nightgowns, and a collection of undergarments, as well as fabrics for the same number to be made up in designs suited for an expectant mother. Once she finished, she'd directed Miss Van Valkenburgh to send the bill to Ian's clerk at the shipping office on Water Street.

"Mr. McClurty will handle them; you need not worry about that," Rose had declared with a confidence that made even Ana believe her. "When you have finished the alterations, please pack them in the trunk we'll send over later today. You may deliver it to the same address as the bill. We'll take the traveling outfit, a change of the undergarments, and she'll wear that green gown she tried on first."

To soothe her daughter's concerns, Rose had said, "Trust me on this, Ana. Ian will not think you presumptuous for charging it all to him. You are his wife, and it's time you looked like his wife, not a governess, a housekeeper, or a spinster aunt. Heavens, dear, you had to have something to wear. You arrived here with only what was on your back. I'm amazed that dress has held together after so many washings these past two weeks."

Turning to the pretty seamstress, she'd instructed her to toss the dress Ana had worn to the shop in the closest dustbin. "It's not fit even for the church charity box," she declared.

And now, barely more than a day later, she stood in that travel ensemble, taking one last look at herself before setting off for the dock and the boat leaving for Parras Island in approximately one more hour. She smoothed her hair, praying the voyage across the lake wouldn't ruin the new style—another of Mama's innovations—a softer, looser coiffure Ana wasn't confident she'd ever be able to re-create by herself.

When she heard the crunch of carriage wheels on the drive, her heart took a sudden leap, only to plummet when she saw that it was Laurel and Alan. It was foolish to think Ian had come for her after all. Grabbing up her bonnet, a small valise, and her reticule, she started toward the stairs.

"Oh, Ana, you look absolutely lovely," Laurel complimented as Ana descended to the foyer. "Don't you think so, Alan?"

The young man blushed but smiled warmly. "I shall be the envy of every man in town to be seen riding with two pretty women this morning," he said as he reached for Ana's valise. "Is this it?"

"Yes, the rest of my things were sent ahead," Ana told him. "I'd like to say good-bye to Gerta and the Marys. Have we time?"

"Certainly, I'll just put your valise in the carriage and wait for you." Fruth started back through the door, then turned back. "Oh, I nearly forgot." He extracted an envelope from his jacket pocket and handed it to her. "This was about to be delivered when we were arriving."

It was from the state teachers' certification board. She'd passed the exam. Included in the letter of congratulations was a list of a half dozen schools that were searching for a teacher. Calmly, Ana folded the letter and tucked it in her reticule. "I won't be long, Laurel," she said, and started for the back of the house.

"Ana." Her sister's call halted her progress. "Aren't you going to say anything? That was from the state teaching board."

"Yes. I passed."

"Well, of course you passed. What are you going to do about it?"

"I honestly don't know, Laurel. It isn't important anymore." Seeing her sister's astonishment, she grinned. "You'll catch flies if you don't close that mouth."

With more spring in her step than there had been since her return, Ana headed for the kitchen to say her good-byes to Gerta and the Marys. What she'd just said about the certification was true. It was enough that she'd passed and could teach if she chose. Right now she chose *her* home and *her* family—*her* husband and *their* children. Those were the things she'd always wanted, and never so much as she did right then.

Chapter Twenty-two

Ana stood at the end of the short walk in front of the house. Never had the little house looked so beautiful to her. Her family was inside the house. The children and their father—the people she held most dear.

Straightening her bonnet, she hoped the trip hadn't done too much damage to her appearance. The lake had been smooth and the trip across it on the mail packet had been lengthy but quite uneventful. However, she hadn't taken any chances on another bout with mal de mer. Eschewing the captain's invitation to make the trip inside his cabin or the small salon used by the few passengers the ship occasionally carried, she'd remained on the open deck, keeping her focus on the horizon as Ian had instructed her the day of their wedding.

A flutter low in her belly drew her hand. Nerves, or was it the babe? Perhaps he or she was as anxious as she was. "We can't stand out here all day, can we?" she muttered. There was only one way she'd find out if Ian was glad for her return.

Tightening her grip on her valise, she marched the final few feet to the house and opened the front door. Stepping inside, she called, "Ian?"

There was no answer; not even Sally greeted her. She ran upstairs, calling the children's names. The house was empty. But only of people and the dog. The furnishings and everyone's possessions were still there, including her own. Exactly where she'd left them.

"But not in the state I left it." She ran a gloved finger over a table, drawing a line in the dust collected there. In the kitchen were piles of dirty dishes. Muddy footprints marred the floors. Later, after she'd found her family, she'd attack the house.

Disappointed but not daunted, she walked back outside and headed up the hill to the big house. "That's where they are, I'm sure of it." As she grew nearer, she was relieved to see how finished the house looked. Gerta and the Marys would have someplace to stay when they arrived tomorrow. And plenty to do, she was sure, just making their own quarters habitable. The rest of the house would wait until the new furnishings arrived. There was no hurry; her family had a snug little house down in the village to live in until then.

A familiar yip and a bark sounded from the stable. Sally. The children and Ian couldn't be far away.

"Missus! Don't you look fine. You sure are a sight for sore eyes," Ferguson told her when she stepped through the stable door. Sally leapt around her. "That dog sure is happy to see you."

Uncaring of the dusty footprints the dog was putting on her new gown, Ana bent and hugged the excited animal. "Is my family here?" she managed between dog kisses. *My family.* How good that sounded.

"No, you just missed 'em. The boss brought Sally up here, then loaded up the younguns on the *Ulsterman* and headed for Cleveland."

"For Cleveland!"

"Yep, said he was going after you and bringing you back where you belonged if he had to tie you up and throw you over his shoulder."

"He said all that?" Ana didn't know whether to laugh or cry.

"Yep. Only left maybe an hour ago. You must've passed 'em on the way over here."

"I didn't see the *Ulsterman*," she admitted. Only an hour and they would have met right on the dock. Even if Ian started right back from Cleveland once he discovered she was gone, it would be hours before he returned.

Ferguson lifted his cap, scratched his head, and replaced the cap. "Well it's a mighty big lake. How'd you get over here?"

"The mail packet, and it stopped off in Sandusky before it came here."

"Well, now, that explains it then. How you missed seein' the boss's boat." Ferguson pulled out a pocket watch and checked the time, then went to the stable door and peered up at the sky. "Them clouds is getting a bit dark and movin' a mite faster than they was earlier." He squinted toward the lake. "Looking a mite dark and choppy out there, too. The boss might have to wait till tomorrow to come back."

Now Ana was sure she was going to cry. She blinked and swallowed, but the tears slithered out of her eyes just the same. "Now, now, missus," Ferguson soothed and patted her shoulder. "The important thing is you came back and you'll be here when the boss and them younguns get home. They're going to be mighty glad to see you."

Ana wiped her cheeks. "You think so?"

"As sure as I know I'm standing here," he assured. "The boss said nothing was goin' right since you left." He chuckled. "That little Maara. What a caution that child is. Gave her pa a good set-to, she did. Told him he was a bad daddy for making her aunt Ana run away."

"Oh, but it wasn't Ian's fault. It was mine. I'm the—"

"You and the boss can decide whose fault it was when he gets back, missus," Ferguson said. "You and Sally go on back down to the little house and wait for him. And don't you get to worryin' none if he ain't home tonight. He'll be along soon's he can."

Ana took his advice and with Sally trotting happily at her heels retraced her route back to the house. Once inside, she looked about and saw that it was in a worse state than she'd first thought—and that had been bad enough.

"Well, Sally, we might as well get to work. It'll give us something to do while we're waiting." She looked down at herself. "First, I'd better change into something more serviceable." As soon as she'd changed, she took a good look at the bedroom and decided to start there first.

She ripped off sheets she was sure hadn't been changed since she'd left and made the bed with fresh linens. She'd finished with the bedroom and was just starting to straighten up the sitting room when Tom Knez arrived with her trunk. "Joanne's going to be mighty happy to see you back, ma'am," he remarked as he carried the trunk into the bedroom for her. "She and all the ladies have sure missed you. All of us have."

"And I've missed you all, too, Tom. Please tell Joanne I'll be over to see her as soon as I get, uh, settled." She sighed and swept her gaze around the great room.

Knez followed her gaze, then lifted his cap and ran his hand over his hair. Shaking his head, he said, "My missus would have my hide if I let the house go like this. Anything I can do for you, ma'am? Want me to send Joanne, maybe some of the other ladies, over to help you?"

"That's very kind of you, Tom. But I may have a lot of hours to kill. The work will make the time go faster. But if it's not too much trouble, could you bring me some water?"

"Right away, ma'am. Looks like you'll be needing plenty."

"Thank you, Tom. You're a good friend."

He gave her the twinkling-eyed smile and slow grin that was so much a part of him. "I'll be back as quick as I can, ma'am. How about the woodpile? Got plenty?"

"I think so, thank you. And Tom? Please call me Ana," she said. "This is a small island, we're all neighbors, and I do hope that you will be as much a friend to me as Joanne has been."

"You can count on it, ma— Ana."

Tom wasn't long in returning with a cart loaded with several buckets of water. He emptied them into the new spigoted water barrel that sat in the corner of the kitchen, and went back for more. She needed all he could bring her.

She was down on her hands and knees scrubbing the kitchen floor when she heard Sally make a series of short yipping sounds and start scratching at the front door. Her tail was wagging so wildly, it had to be someone she knew approaching the house.

"Not now," she wailed as she tossed the scrub brush back in the bucket. "They would come home now when I'm a bedraggled mess."

Drying her hands on her apron, she whipped off the kerchief she'd tied on her head. She was almost to the door when she heard the sound of someone knocking. "Not Ian, he wouldn't knock at his own front door," she muttered with a mixture of relief and disappointment. "Probably Mr. Ferguson."

She flung the door open and found a handsome young man on her doorstep, a large basket dangling from one hand. "Jaie Bercot, Madame Patterson," he said with a slight bow as elegant as his father and uncle might have given.

"I'm pleased to meet you, Jaie," she said, and meant it. During her return trip, the animosity she'd been carrying toward the Bercot family was something she had figuratively tossed over the side of the boat. The Bercots had never been anything but gracious and kind to her. She still didn't like it that they sold spirits at their establishment, but her own husband was in partnership with them, and she knew him to be as good and fine a man as there was to be found anywhere. Surely it followed that the Bercots were of the same ilk.

"And I am most pleased to meet you, Madame. Papa and Uncle Eduard speak so highly of you and what a grand lady you are."

Ana's chagrin to hear they'd praised her so highly was compounded by the realization that this elegant young man should first meet her when she was looking her worst. "How kind of them, but I'm hardly a grand lady, especially not today."

"The mark of a grand lady is not silks and jewels, madame. It is in what lies in her heart and her ways."

Ana was at a loss how to respond but didn't need to. Indicating the basket, Jaie told her, "Papa and Uncle Eduard were worried you would have nothing to eat tonight and sent this for you. It is quite heavy; they packed enough for the family in case they returned tonight."

He bent and patted Sally on the head. "And something for Miss Sally, too," he said, obviously familiar with the dog. "If you will permit me, I'll carry it to your table for you."

"Thank you, Jaie." Ana stepped aside. "This is very kind of your father and uncle. Please thank them for me," she said, sincerely touched. "But for their thought-fulness, I'm afraid I might have gone hungry tonight. There doesn't seem to be a scrap in the house."

He set the basket on the table. "Ah, well, Mr. Pat-terson and the children have been taking their meals in our dining room."

"I'm relieved that they have been eating well in my . . . ah . . . absence," she said with a twinge of discomfort that the children had been eating at the tavern.

"I see you are busy, and I must go. Papa and Uncle Ed-uard will be expecting me back to help. It is a busy time of day for them."

"Of course." She started to let Jaie out the door. "Jaie, I understand you have just graduated from university and want to teach. Have you a position yet?"

"No, madame, not yet."

"Good," she said with such enthusiasm Jaie sent her a startled look. "I mean, I'm glad you're still available. Would you consider teaching here on the island?"

"*Oui,* madame, so few students as there will be this first year would not occupy my time fully, and I would be able to help Papa and Uncle Eduard with the inn and the start of the winery. That would be my fondest wish to be able to do both. But I had understood that you would be the school's teacher."

In her surprise, it was all Ana could do to keep her mouth from falling agape. "Who told you that?"

"Why, Mr. Patterson, of course. Last night after he and the children took their supper, he mentioned that you are a highly educated woman who would be a fine teacher for the school. Did you not travel to Cleveland to take a certification examination?"

"Yes, I did," she said, relieved that Ian had given that excuse for her sudden leave-taking. "I lingered there to clear up some matters and visit a bit with my family, too." It was the truth. Stretched a bit and with details left out, but still the truth. And far less embarrassing than to admit that she'd left her husband in a fit of pique over the issue of teaching.

"I have my certification now but have given the matter some thought. With the children and the house to take care of, I don't believe I could do a proper job as school-mistress all by myself. I would love to teach, though."

A short time later, she leaned against the closed door, feeling quite proud of herself. The island had a school-master and an assistant schoolmistress who would sub-stitute for him whenever necessary and give a history lesson once a week. In addition, Jaie had graciously wel-comed her offer to assist him in deciding upon supplies and textbooks. If Ian was willing to let her teach full-time, she was more than willing to admit that he'd been right about it being too much. The arrangement she'd proposed to Jaie felt just right, and she was confident that Ian would agree. Perhaps sometime in the future she would teach full-time at the school. For now, she would be more than content to give her children the life lessons and the additional tutoring they needed from a mother and merely assist at the island school.

Glancing about the cottage, she realized she'd better light a few lamps if she was going to get any more clean-ing done. The sky had darkened considerably during the time she and Jaie had discussed the school. A storm was definitely moving across the lake. Ian and the children wouldn't be back tonight.

She and Sally spent an uneasy night in the house all alone. Ana wasn't frightened by the wind and lightning, but Sally was continually circling the house and occasion-ally scratching at the front or back doors. Once during the night, the dog's hackles were raised, and she began to growl. As agitated as she'd been the day something in the woods had alarmed her, she hurled herself at the back door, and it was all Ana could do to pull her back. Sure that it was only the loudness of the thunder rumbling overhead, Ana tried to calm the dog and herself.

"Nothing's out there, girl," she told Sally over and over, assuring herself as much as the dog. There were no more wild hogs to worry about. Ian had assured her of that, and she believed him. And there was no one on the island who would pose any kind of threat, either. Ian had made sure of that, as well.

"Your master has made this island a safe place, Sal. Nothing and no one can hurt us here," she told the dog, feeling infinitely better when Sally finally relaxed and settled down for the night.

However, the dog didn't take up her usual spot on a rug in the kitchen. Instead, she insisted upon following Ana into the bedroom and hopping up on the bed. No amount of telling her to get down or shoving her would convince the dog to get off the bed. Stubbornly, the animal stretched out beside her and placed one paw over one of Ana's legs. With her head high and her ears still pricked alertly, the expression on the animal's face clearly conveyed, I'm staying right here.

"All right, girl, but don't make this a habit," she told her, not sure whether the dog was protecting her or seeking protection from her mistress. Whichever it was, she had to admit it was comforting to have the dog next to her in what was a very lonely bed without Ian.

Despite what had been a very short night, Ana was up early the next day. With Sally still shadowing her every step, she finished what tasks remained to put the house back to rights, then readied herself for her family's return.

When they'd still not returned by noon, Ana couldn't bear to pace the cottage any longer. Dressed in one of her new frocks, her hair styled in a fair semblance of her new coif, she walked up the hill and took up a watch from the widow's walk atop the new house. Her heart leapt every time she saw a sail on the lake, only to be disappointed when it didn't turn into the harbor below.

After another hour passed, her nerves were more on edge than they'd been through the night. A walk would settle them. She'd stroll a little way into the woods behind the house and pick some of the blackberries growing wild there. They should be ripe by now, she decided, remembering Ian's stating a fondness for blackberry pie.

"Where's Aunt Ana?"

"I don't know, Maara." Ian put Joseph down and looked around the house. "But she's definitely been here." Seeing the house so sparkling clean made him realize what a disaster it had been when he and the children had left. By the looks of things, she must have worked all night. Some homecoming. He had a lot of making up to do.

"Maybe she's at the big house," Rob suggested.

Sure that they'd find her there, Ian and the children hiked up the hill. They stopped off at the stable first. She wasn't there, but she had been.

"Left Sally with me and went on up to the house," Ned told him. "She was going to watch for you from that widow's walk on top. Surprised she's not down here."

"Maybe she came down for a bit and didn't see us dock." She could have seen the harbor from any window at the front of the house. Ian felt a bit of unease but tamped it down. "We'll go look for her. And Ned. Gerta and the Marys should be arriving any minute. I left them down at the docks overseeing the transfer of a wagon load of crates. You might want to get on down there and lend them a hand."

Ana wasn't at the house. One of the workmen mentioned having seen her earlier and thought she'd gone out the back door and toward the woods. No one had seen her since. Ian went a little way into the woods and called and called for her but got no answer.

Trying to convince himself there was no need to panic, Ian left the children in Ned's care, saddled up the gelding, and began making the rounds of the houses in the village. No one had seen her. Ian's last hope was the Bercots. They knew the island better than anyone.

Henri was hanging up his apron before Ian finished explaining the situation. "I do not think there are any more wild hogs in the woods, but who can know for certain? We must find Madame Patterson quickly just in case.

"Eduard, Jaie, gather as many men as you can, armed if possible." With the efficiency of a general deploying his troops, Henri organized a search party.

Chapter Twenty-three

She was lost.

It didn't feel as if she'd gone very far, but she couldn't seem to find the way back. Sure that she must be wandering in circles, Ana stopped and tried to get her bearings. But the forest was so thick, she couldn't determine the direction of the sun.

"I should've brought Sally with me," she mumbled as she squinted through a break in the canopy of cedar bows and hardwoods. "She'd have led me back."

Looking around, she thought she could see a large patch of sunlight up ahead. "At least she'd have been company," she muttered as she struggled to free her skirt from a thorny vine.

It was then she heard a rustling in the underbrush behind her. Her heart in her throat, she turned very slowly, terrified that she'd see a bristle-backed boar with long, curled tusks like the sketch she'd seen in a book of Ian's. It wasn't a wild boar but a man who stepped out from the bushes.

"Good afternoon, Miss MacPherson."

Sagging against a broad oak tree, Ana caught her scream. "Mr. Phillips. Thank goodness it's you. I feared you were a wild boar," she admitted. As soon as her heart settled into a more normal pattern, she had the wit to realize how odd it was that the painter was anywhere on the island, especially here in the woods. "How did you— Whatever are you doing here, Mr. Phillips?"

"I came to paint, of course. I heard of the island's beauty and came over to apply my humble skills to capturing it," he said, gesturing to the pack he carried on his back. He looked about the little clearing, then back at Ana and smiled. "I must say it exceeds my expectations. What luck that I should . . . uh, stumble upon you, of all people, here in these woods . . . and all alone."

The small measure of relief that it was a human who'd stepped through the bushes a moment ago fled. To her knowledge, no one who didn't have specific business on the island ever visited it. Parras Isle, as lovely as it was, was not a scheduled stop by any of the touring ships plying the lake's waters.

"How did you get to the island?" she asked, not caring if her query was blunt. Nothing about Phillips was right. Not his presence here and certainly not how he looked, all disheveled, dirty, and worse. There was an odd look in his eyes, cold and wild, not at all the eyes of the sensitive artist she'd known.

"The same as you. On the mail packet yesterday," he told her glibly.

"Yesterday? The mail packet? I didn't see you on the boat."

"But I saw you, though at first I didn't recognize you. You've changed, Miss MacPherson. That was quite a fetching ensemble you were wearing yesterday. Very fashionable. Such a shame there was no one waiting for you at the dock. And no one to appreciate the pretty frock you're wearing today."

Alarmed by the way he was looking at her and even more by what he was saying, Ana's mind raced over the possibilities of how best to handle the situation. He'd been stalking her. Why? Had he been outside the cottage last night? Was he the reason Sally had been so upset? If only she'd fetched Sally from the stable when she'd left the house. The dog was barely half-grown, but she didn't think Phillips would chance doing anything that might inspire the animal to attack. Her barking must have scared him off last night. It might have done the same today.

"I—I returned unexpectedly yesterday, Mr. Phillips," she told him, deciding that talk was her best defense until she could think of something better. "The island's small. There was no need for anyone to meet me at the dock. Of course, Mr. Ferguson knows I'm here. You remember him, don't you? He was Mr. Patterson's stable man in Cleveland and moved here with the family. I left him just a little while ago. He'll be looking for me if I'm not back soon."

She was babbling but couldn't stop. She needed to make it very clear that she wasn't really alone but that scores of people knew where she was. And that the island was so heavily populated that at any moment dozens of people would come strolling through the woods. "So much going on here. All over the island. Have you seen the quarry? There are so many men working there. And crews of carpenters are just all over building houses and other buildings. It's as busy as an anthill. And people here are so very neighborly and caring, and they watch out for each—"

"You seem to know quite a lot about this place and its people. And you say your return was unexpected. You reside here now?"

"Yes, of course, I—"

"You live with Patterson and Lily's bra— Lily's children!"

The strange light in his eyes as he moved closer sent a frisson of fear snaking down her back, and a cold knot formed in her stomach. Involuntarily, she spread her hand protectively over her belly. Growing increasingly alarmed with the direction of the conversation and Phillips's manner, Ana began to wonder if confronting a wild boar might not have been preferable. She could have climbed a tree to escape a hog.

Furtively, she looked about, hoping for a solid branch or something that she might use as a weapon if necessary. The artist had always seemed such a gentle soul, a polite gentleman, and not at all threatening. But everything about his manner today made the hairs on the back of her neck stand up.

Feeling trapped with the tree at her back, she began to edge away from it. "You couldn't have known, since you left town a few weeks after my sister's funeral, but Mr. Patterson and I married a couple of months ago," she said, and heard him take in his breath in a sharp hiss. She'd managed to edge beyond the tree and take a step backward, though she hadn't put much distance between herself and Phillips. With each step she took, Phillips moved forward.

"I—I was berry picking," she said nervously. She lifted the pail, wondering if she could swing it fast enough to catch him off guard and hard enough to at least stun him. "I'm going to make a pie for supper, my husband's favorite. He should be back by now and must be wondering where I am." *Oh, God, please let that be true. And help me find my way out of these woods.*

She glanced over her shoulder, hoping to see some sort of path or trail. "I'm sure you'd like to get on with your work . . . and . . . and I should be getting started on that pie if it's going to be ready by supper time. It's . . . ah . . .

been nice seeing you again, Mr. Phillips, but I really must be going."

Gathering up her skirts, she whirled and started toward an opening in the thickets surrounding the little clearing. She'd gone only a few feet when she heard Phillips close behind her. Her heart pounding, she started to run, but Phillips grabbed her from behind, pinning her arms to her sides. She screamed and tried to wriggle out of his hold, but his wiry arms were surprisingly strong. "Shut up or I'll have to hurt you," he warned.

Tamping down her hysteria, she tried for the most imperious voice she had. "Let me go, Mr. Phillips, and I'll forget that you've overstepped yourself."

He laughed. "That bossy tone isn't going to help you here. You aren't who I came for, but you'll serve the purpose just as well," he said, and started dragging her back to the little clearing.

"Who . . . who did you come for?"

"My child, of course." He thrust her up against the oak tree, pinning her there by her arms.

"*Your* child. Here? You don't—" Feeling sick, she realized exactly what her sister's relationship had been with the artist. "You. You're one of Lily's lovers."

"There were no other lovers," he snarled. "Only me. I was the only one she ever wanted. The others were just beasts who used her, like that crude barbarian you married used her. She was disgusted by anyone else in her bed. I was the only one who could satisfy her."

Sickened by his declarations, Ana tried to shut them out. "Stop it!" She struggled to free her hands so she could cover her ears, but Phillips continued to spew filth, describing in lurid detail what he and Lily had done together and bragging about how much her sister had wanted him.

"It didn't take Patterson long to find a replacement for Lily, did it? My beautiful Lily was hardly cold in her grave when he married you.

"Lily was such a very fertile woman. A man hardly had to do more than breathe on her to get her pregnant. You're probably the same. How long were you spreading your legs for that bastard before Lily died? Has he planted a brat in you already? That why the two of you got married so quickly?"

"No," she said, fearing what he might do to her if she confessed her pregnancy. "It wasn't like that with us. He . . . we love each other."

"Love you? Animals like Patterson don't love women, just use their bodies." With insolent thoroughness, he ran his eyes down her torso and back up again, lingering on her bosom. "All the better if you are breeding. The way that fool loves children, I should be able to bargain for twice as much."

"Money? Do you want money? Let me go, and I'll get you however much you want."

He laughed. "You think I'm a fool? If I let you go, I'll have nothing to bargain with. Oh, yes, I want money. That bastard will pay dearly this time."

"Wh-what do you mean by this time?"

Phillips was more than happy to relate to her the details of how Ian had tracked him down after Lily's death and forced him out of town. God forgive me, Ana begged as she listened to the tale. She'd condemned Ian for carousing in saloons all those nights while in reality he'd been hunting for Phillips in order to protect her sister's reputation.

"Thinks he's a king, he does, but he'll soon find out different. Thought he'd gotten rid of me with a paltry hundred dollars and some threats. Maybe that worked with the others, but not with me."

"What are you going to do? You can't hold me here forever."

He grinned nastily. "I told you I'm no fool. There's a nice cave near here where you and I can while away the hours until your husband shows up with the money. If you're a good little girl and follow my orders, you won't get hurt. You might not like what I'd do to you if you misbehave."

To illustrate his threat, he pressed his body fully against her, sandwiching her between himself and the tree. "Then again, maybe you would like what I could do for you."

Swallowing bile, Ana shook her head. "No. Please. I— I'll do whatever you say."

"Good."

Slowly, he eased away from her and released her wrists. Knowing she'd have one chance and only one, Ana waited until he'd taken a step away. She still had the pail gripped in her right hand, hidden in the folds of her skirts. As he reached for something in his pocket, she swung the pail with all her might. It struck him in the head, and he went down.

Ana didn't wait to see if she'd knocked him unconscious or what he'd been reaching for. Screaming, "Help! Help me!" as loudly as she could, she went crashing through the woods, praying someone would hear her. Surely she wasn't far from the woods' edge. The quarry must be nearby. There were plenty of men there, men who were her friends. Good men who'd save her if they heard her—if they got to her before Phillips did.

"You bitch," she heard, and ran even faster, mindless of the briers tearing at her hair, dress, and flesh. Behind her, she could hear him crashing through the underbrush after her. The center of her back prickled and tensed in anticipation that at any second a pistol ball would slam into her or a knife would slash through her. Trying for a zigzag pattern as she ran, she bent over to make herself a smaller target.

Please, God, give me strength, she prayed as she ran. A stitch was developing in her side, and the muscles in her legs were burning. She ceased screaming, saving her waning strength. The island couldn't be more than three miles wide, and she must have started somewhere near the center. She had to reach the peripheral road soon.

Her heart was pounding so loudly and she was making so much noise herself crashing through the underbrush, she couldn't hear if Phillips was still following. All she could do was keep moving and pray that she found someone and soon. She began begging God's forgiveness for all her faults, mistakes, and misjudgments and making promises to correct them—if only He would grant her time on this earth to do so.

As she ran, she sensed that the ground was rising gradually. There was only one hill on the island that she knew of. The big house. It must be near. Just a little farther. She used some of her last strength to scream, "Ian!"

And then her foot caught on a root, and she hit the ground. Stunned by the impact, she tried to scramble to her feet, but Phillips landed on her. "Bitch. You're lucky I didn't shoot you," he said as he rolled her onto her back and pinned her arms above her head.

Bucking and writhing to get free, Ana screamed for Ian again and again. Phillips let go of her wrists and slapped her, but she didn't stop screaming. "Shut up! Shut up." He wrapped his hands around her throat and squeezed.

Ana clawed at the hands around her throat. She couldn't budge them. She bucked and tried to claw at the twisted, snarling face above her but couldn't reach, and her strength was ebbing. She couldn't breathe and was beginning to black out. *No, I can't die. My baby.*

Ana's were not the only prayers being offered. Ian was praying, too. And calling himself ten times the fool for ever insisting on moving to this island in the first place. If only he hadn't lost his temper that day and said such rotten things to her. If only he'd gone after her immediately.

He and more than two dozen men had fanned out across the island and moved steadily north. On foot now, Ian, flanked by Henri and Eduard, moved into the thick forest and kept moving farther and farther toward the northern-most tip of the island, where the land rose and there was nothing but cliffs separating the lake from the land.

He was numb with fear for Ana's life when Henri touched his arm and signaled that he'd heard something just ahead of them. A scream. A woman's scream. Ian would have rushed forward, but Henri stopped him. "No, *mon ami,* slowly and quietly," he cautioned. "We do not know what is up ahead."

His throat too dry to speak, Ian nodded his agreement, though his every instinct was to get to her as fast as he could. Their rifles already primed with powder and ball, they slowly cocked the hammers. Cautiously, they moved in the direction from which they'd heard the scream. Every sense attuned to any noise ahead of them, they moved as quietly as possible through the underbrush.

There were no more screams, but there was the sound of someone or something moving rapidly through the bushes. Closer and closer, and then there was another short scream followed by a long, wailing, "Ian!" And again, "Ian!" Long before the second cry, Ian was running.

He didn't have to go far. The scene he came upon was more horrific than anything he'd ever imagined. Phillips had just enough time to turn in Ian's direction before the butt of Ian's rifle crashed against the side of his skull. The force of the blow lifted the smaller man up and away from Ana.

Throwing his gun aside, Ian dropped to his knees beside his wife. Gently, he lifted her into his arms, praying he'd not been too late. "Ana . . . Ana . . . Ana." He cradled her limp body against his chest. "No . . . no . . . no. Please, God, no."

She shuddered and coughed. "Ian?" she rasped so softly he could barely hear her, but it was the most welcome sound of his life.

"Oh, my darling." He wanted to crush her against him, but he held her lightly, rubbing her back as she gasped for air.

"Phillips?" she managed.

Briefly, Ian glanced to where Phillips's body lay sprawled on the ground. "He can't hurt you now," he told her, unsure whether the man was unconscious or dead.

"He . . . he wanted Joseph . . . he wanted money."

"Shh . . . shh . . . it's all over now. Save your voice." Carefully, Ian lifted her into his arms and started in the direction from which he'd come, wanting to get Ana away and safe as quickly as possible.

"Madame? She is all right?" Henri asked as he, Eduard, and several of the others arrived.

"She will be, thank God." Ian nodded to the spot behind him. "Check on him."

"Who?"

As he turned, Ian's eyes widened when he saw that Phillips had disappeared. "There was a man. I bashed him with my rifle butt. He can't have gone far."

"We will find him," Henri assured him. "You take Madame Patterson home."

"Be . . . careful . . . armed . . . gun . . . or knife," Ana rasped.

"*Merci,* madame." Alerting the other men, Henri set off after Phillips.

Ana wrapped her arms around her husband's neck, clinging to his strength and the safety of his big, strong body. "Find him . . . the children?"

"They're safe with Ned at the big house, and by now Gerta and the Marys are probably fussing over them," Ian assured her as he steadily carried her out of the forest. "Phillips can't have crawled off too far. The men will find him quickly."

"What will you do—" She paused to swallow. "—with him?"

"Don't worry about it," he said between gritted teeth.

"Don't kill him."

"You'd protect him after what he did?"

Almost frightened by the rage she felt in him, Ana swallowed again and said, "No . . . protect you. You'd hang. He's not worth it."

The tension in the arms around her relaxed, but only slightly. "No, he's not." He filled his chest with air and let it out in a long, slow gust. "I honestly don't know what I'll do with him when they catch him. He should be turned over to the closest constable. That would be in Sandusky. Kidnapping and attempted murder should be enough to lock him away for a long time."

"Trial? What if he tells about Lily and that Joseph is his child?"

"First, I don't think Joseph is his child. He's too good and fine a little boy to have been sired by that miserable excuse for a man."

"If not Phillips, who?"

Ian named a man Ana didn't recall ever meeting. "I don't think he even knew he'd gotten Lily pregnant when I convinced him he should never do any kind of business in Cleveland again," Ian told her. "He wasn't the most honorable of men, obviously, but a far sight better than Phillips. He has a wife and family in Erie. He'll not risk the scandal by even inquiring about Joseph or letting anyone in Cleveland know about his little affair with Lily. None of Phillips's get survived to take their first breath. He saw to that."

"How? How do you know that?"

Ian didn't answer immediately. Finally he said, "I didn't know until the night Lily died. She . . . she . . . It was a long night, and the laudanum Jim Cooke tried to give her for the pain didn't stay down. She . . . she did a lot of talking and . . ." He took a deep, shaky breath. "She did a lot of talking."

Ana couldn't bear to ask any more. They'd reached the edge of the forest where he'd tied the gelding. From there it was a short ride home.

Despite her insistence that she could walk, Ian carried her into the house and laid her on the bed. After he'd gotten her to drink some water, he carefully cleaned her scratches. His lips tightened when he saw the bruises developing on her throat. "Damn my arrogance. I underestimated that bastard. I was so sure I'd gotten rid of him. Forgive me, Ana."

The defeat she heard in his voice was more painful than the worst that had been in her throat. "There's nothing to forgive, Ian. You couldn't have known he'd come here."

"But I—"

"Shhh." Ana placed her fingers across his lips. "I told you once before that you can't protect everyone from everything. It's my own fault that I was out in the woods all by myself."

Grasping her hand, he kissed her palm and placed it back across her chest. "What were you doing out there?"

Still shaking from her brush with death, Ana giggled, a

mad mixture of relief, fear, and joy that everything was going to be all right. She was safe. Safe in this snug little house with Ian. "I was picking blackberries for that pie I promised my husband weeks ago, and I got lost." She lifted her hand to curve it against his face, seeing then the scratches on her flesh and the rips in her sleeve. A lump formed in her throat that had nothing to do with her injuries. "I wanted to look pretty for you. Now I'm a mess. My dress . . ." She pushed a heavy lock of hair from her face. "My hair . . ."

"You're beautiful. You've never looked more beautiful. You're the most beautiful woman I've ever seen." He caught her hands, kissed them, and then leaned over her and kissed her softly on the mouth.

"But it was a new dress and I—"

He quieted her with another kiss. "I'll buy you another one. When we get back to Cleveland, you can have Miss Van Valkenburgh make you up a dozen, two dozen. We'll get the children and be on the first boat to Cleveland, as soon as you're feeling able to travel. I promise."

"Cleveland!" Ana stiffened in his arms and leaned back to get a better view of his face. "Why would we go back to Cleveland?"

"So something like this never happens again. Neither you nor the children can get lost in a woods there. If Phillips could get to the island, anyone could. And there could still be a wild hog or two out in those woods, or something else equally as dangerous. We don't know for sure. You never wanted to move here, and you were right. It isn't a safe place to raise children. I've been selfish, thoughtless, and so full of my own arrogance I was sure I'd created a perfect little world here."

Ana smacked him with an open palm against his chest to quiet him. "You listen to me, Ian Patterson. We're not moving back to Cleveland. How dare you consider such a thing. And we're not any less safe here than we would be in Cleveland. Maybe there aren't any wild hogs in Cleveland, but there could be other dangers. Anyone really bent on doing harm wouldn't find it any easier here than they would in Cleveland. It's not perfect. No place is perfect. But this island and the people on it make it as perfect as any place could possibly be to raise a family."

She considered telling him that there would soon be five children for them to raise here on the island but decided now was not quite the right time. She didn't want the horror of today marring such an important announcement. "I didn't come back here to pack up the children and take them to Cleveland. But if you really want to go back to Cleveland, then we'll go."

"Why did you come back?"

"Because I love you. Cigar-smoking, whiskey-swilling, arrogant bastard that you are."

Ian grinned. "As bad as that, huh?"

"That bad and probably worse," she teased with a giggle. Draping her arms around his neck, she pulled him closer. "As they say, 'hate the sin but love the sinner,' " she quoted. "Now you tell me exactly why you and the children went to Cleveland."

"You know damned well why. To bring you back. Nothing was right without you. We were all miserable, and the children were mad at me for being so mean to you that you ran away from us," Ian confessed. "Forgive me, sweetheart. I didn't mean any of what I said that day. I love you, you temperance-advocating, prudish saint. And I'll do anything to make you happy so you'll stay with me."

"Anything?"

"That's what I said. Anything. I'll even sign that damned pledge if that'll make you happy."

She couldn't help but laugh at the pained look on his face. "That desperate, are you?"

"Hell, yes, I'll do anything, agree to anything, as long as you promise never to leave me again. You can teach if you want to. I've already told everybody on the island that you'll be the new schoolmistress. Gerta and the Marys are here, and Jessie and Joe will be just fine in their care."

"I don't want to teach, not every day," she told him, and explained the arrangement she'd made with Jaie.

"You're sure that would make you happy?"

Ana nodded. "Very. But what would really make me happy right this minute is if you'd quit making wild promises and kiss me. Really kiss me."

Happy to comply with that request, Ian took her mouth with such a thoroughness, Ana's toes curled like they'd never curled before. His hands were everywhere, caressing her breasts, her hips, her legs, her back—every place he could reach, as if he had to keep assuring himself she was there in his arms and all in one piece. Ana's hands were far from idle. She ran them over him, loving the feel of his hard-muscled body beneath her palms, reveling in his utter maleness and size.

Finally, when they were both trembling with need for each other, he lifted his mouth from hers and with obvious reluctance lifted his hands from her. "I'd better get out of here and leave you alone. You've been through an ordeal. You need rest."

"No, I *need* my husband."

"Ana, are you sure? I want you so badly, I don't think I can be very gentle. I don't want to hurt you."

"I'm hurting now, and only you can heal me," she told him as she attacked the buttons at the front of his trousers.

"Good Lord, woman. It's the middle of the day," he teased.

"Don't be such a prude."

Ian's laugh quickly turned to a groan of pleasure and want.

It was a long time before either of them was capable of coherent speech. Lying completely exhausted and thoroughly sated in Ian's arms, Ana recovered enough to say, "Ian, is there a small bedroom next to ours at the big house?"

"Mmmm . . ." He nuzzled her temple and spread his hand over her belly. "Are you thinking we'll need to put a cradle in there in about nine months?"

"No. In about eight months."

"Eight? You mean you're already . . ." Shuddering, he gathered her into his arms. "Oh, my God. I could've lost you and another baby today. No more walks in the woods, young lady. You and the new little one are far too precious. You promise?"

"But how will I ever get blackberries for a pie?"

"I can live without blackberry pie, but I can't live without you. I will have your word that you'll never go into the woods alone ever again."

"All right, I'll take Sally with me."

"And Ned and me and at least six other big, strong men, armed to the teeth. Promise me, Ana."

He was so serious, Ana began to laugh. "I'm not making any such promise. That would be as ridiculous and unnecessary as you promising to sign the pledge."

"You don't think I was serious? I can live without whiskey, brandy and wine, too. Just not you. If it'll keep you from wandering around the woods with only a half-grown dog as a companion, I'll sign the pledge right now."

"I think we should compromise on this. You don't sign the pledge, and I don't go in the woods without Sally and one other human being."

"I suppose I can live with that." He raised a skeptical brow. "You will keep your word on this, won't you?"

"How could I not when I'm married to as good and kind and honorable a man as you?"

Epilogue

Anson Phillips was taken to the constable at Sandusky. But he did not stand trial for kidnapping, attempted murder, or any other charge. Just before sunset on the day Ian Patterson rescued his beloved wife Ana, Phillips's body was found on the sharp rocks along the island's northernmost shore. It was assumed that in his flight from his pursuers, or perhaps as a result of the blow to his head, he stumbled over the edge of the cliff. Loath to have his be the first body interred on Parras Isle, the residents of the new community agreed that the body should be transported to the mainland early the following morning.

In the years that followed, the island's population grew steadily. The vines Ian Patterson imported thrived under the expert care of the Bercots, and their winery produced a robust wine that established Bercot and Sons as one of the country's leading vintners. That wine, along with the fine cuisine and gracious accommodations to be had at Maison Bercot, drew so many visitors to Parras Isle that regularly scheduled trips from the mainland were established throughout the temperate months, and other establishments were created to provide accommodations for the tourists.

The quarry flourished, and Patterson Shipping kept busy transporting stone. Throughout the state, buildings, roadbeds, homes, and churches were created from Patterson limestone.

No wild boars were ever reported again on the island, nor any poisonous snakes. The forest was thinned some by the lumbering of the cedars, but when the underbrush was cleared, the workmen had strict orders not to disturb any of the blackberry bushes, as their fruit was highly prized by the islanders, most especially by its founder and his wife.

To accommodate the growing community, two new churches were built: Our Lady of the Angels Roman Catholic Church and Trinity Methodist. Second Street Church became the town hall, and a larger school was built and educated many fine scholars, including Ian and Ana's eight children: Maara, Robert, Jessica, Joseph, Fraser, Nathaniel, Elizabeth, and Randall, as well as their aunt Primmy and uncle Jaie's children: Annalisa, Lorraine, Henri, and Eduard Bercot.

Generation after generation were sheltered in the large stone house on the hill overlooking the harbor. In the summer months, Patterson House welcomed family and friends from all over Ohio and beyond, even as far away as Ireland and Scotland.

Author's Note

In the original 1796 survey of Cleveland, Euclid Avenue was not even charted. It was not until 1816 that Euclid Road was surveyed and platted on a map of what was then a rustic village of fewer than one thousand souls. As the village grew, Euclid Road became known as Euclid Street. By the mid-1830s, Euclid Street had replaced Ontario as the fashionable residential street. Gradually, as the growing community's population flourished, the leading lawyers and a handful of other prosperous factors and financiers began to settle on Euclid. But as impressive as the houses were, the condition of the street was the disgrace my Ana Patterson declared it. After a heavy rain, boys were not only sailing toy boats on it but floating rafts. As late as 1855, an anonymous letter of complaint was written to a local newspaper stating that: "In wet weather it is full of ditches and puddles and in dry weather it is an elaborate Sahara, the dried up mud becoming dust and sand." Others voiced even stronger complaints. "Euclid Street is worse than a mud hole—it's a lake—an inland sea." It was reported that several buggies and wagons were capsized when attempting to "cross the waters" on Euclid Street. And so my heroine indeed had just cause to fear for her nephew's safety when he played in the "waters" of early Euclid Street. When Ian Patterson leapt across the stream that was the street in this story, the reality of Euclid Street in 1834 was perhaps far more dramatic than fiction. Instead of walking home from the dock, Ian might have been wiser to have unlashed a dinghy from the *Ulsterman* and paddled it home that cold, rainy night.

Finally, in 1863, the city fathers did improve the street, first with wood-block paving, and later with Nicholson pavement—wooden blocks soaked in hot coal tar—which made for a smoother carriage ride and a more pleasing appearance. Considering the descriptions I have read of Euclid Street's early days, I surmise that prior to 1863, Cleveland's residents might have been wise to eschew carriages in favor of their feet or the back of a horse when traveling Euclid . . . that is, when it was dry.

Euclid's prominence rose and it was distinguished as an avenue in 1865. Starting in 1850 and continuing into the first decade of the twentieth century, Euclid Avenue was not only Cleveland's most elegant street but hailed as "Millionaires' Row," and "the finest avenue in the West." Sadly, Euclid Avenue's days of glory are long past, and what was once called "the most beautiful street in the world" has been swallowed up by progress. Little remains to bear witness to those days, as many of its loyal residents refused to sacrifice their beautiful homes to commercial development. Rather than have them subdivided into rooming houses or offices, several specified in their wills that their homes be demolished after their deaths.

To anyone interested in learning more about Euclid Avenue's glory days, I highly recommend *Showplace of America: Cleveland's Euclid Avenue, 1850–1910*, written by Jan Cigliano and published by Kent State University Press, Kent, Ohio, in 1991.

This story is not just about Cleveland but the islands scattered across the western basin of Lake Erie. Parras

Isle does not exist beyond my imagination. The story of Parras Isle and Ian and Ana Patterson was merely inspired by the history and geography of a handful of those islands and their early settlers. And by my own fantasies as I swam in the lake or sat upon the beaches of Catawba Island during the summers of my youth.